"I WOULD GRANT ALL YOUR WISHES,"
SPLENDOR VOWED SOFTLY.
" 'TWOULD MAKE MY HEART SING TO
SEE YOU HAPPY."

Her promise wrapped around him, and he felt as though he were being embraced by comforting arms that would hold him for as long as he cared to be held.

He leaned toward her, his gaze centered on her mouth.

She softened in his arms, and small sounds came from her throat, and although his eyes were closed, he could see the light of her shimmer. And when she curled her arms around his back and squeezed him, he moaned with hunger for her, with a need so fierce that it took control of his every thought and action.

He crushed her to him, his mouth, body, even his soul devouring her warmth and tenderness the way night swallows up day.

"Please," she whispered, "don't stop. Your kissing makes me feel so strong. 'Tis a strength I never knew before you shared it with me, and now that I have had a taste of it I don't think I can ever live without it."

God help him, he felt like pulling her into his arms and kissing her again. . . .

Also by Rebecca Paisley
*Heartstrings*

# Rebecca Paisley

# A Basket of Wishes

A Dell Book

Published by
Dell Publishing
a division of
Bantam Doubleday Dell Publishing Group, Inc.
1540 Broadway
New York, New York 10036

ISBN: 0-440-21651-6

Printed in the United States of America

Published simultaneously in Canada

August 1995

10  9  8  7  6  5  4  3  2  1

You'd sit at the head of Mama's dining-room table, and I remember thinking how that should have been my daddy's place. But, of course, he'd been in heaven for years by then, so you sat at his place. Yes, there you sat, playfully commenting on my pimples. Or my weight. I'd run up to my room and slam the door. Once I slammed it so hard it fell off its hinges and Mama liked to have never stopped being mad at me. And you always picked all the egg out of the salad. By the time the bowl got around to me the only egg I saw was the image of one I had in my mind.

I was convinced that I hated you during those Sunday afternoons around Mama's dining-room table.

You made me take those impossibly high jumps while we rode in the country, too. You knew I was scared to death, but you made me canter my horse toward those mile-high fences anyway. My mount would refuse the fence, and I'd be the one to jump the dang thing, flying straight over it and landing on the other side. And while lying in the leaf-strewn sand, I'd hear you chuckle softly. "Who does he think he is anyway?" I wondered. "My father? He's not my father, and I shouldn't have to do what he says." Then you'd make me take the fence again.

I was sure I double-hated you during those rides.

Years later came my wedding day. You walked me down the aisle, gave me away, and paid for my beautiful reception.

And I realized how much you cared about me. Pondered how many times you'd come to my rescue when I was in serious trouble. Remembered how you'd always been there for me.

I guess Daddy would have gotten a kick out of teasing me, too. And I know he would have made me tackle things I was afraid of. I don't think he'd have eaten all the egg out of the salad like you did, but I reckon I'll forgive you for that.

You were a father to me when I needed one most.

And I'm all-the-way positive, with nary a doubt certain that I love you, Uncle Van.

The power of Faerie glittered most brightly on All Hallows Eve, for it was a time of the year when mortal rules were suspended. The tiny inhabitants of the enchanted world were always capricious with their moods, but never more so than on this date. With a twinkle of their eyes they could grant a bounty of good fortune.

Or a lifetime of doom.

Out of fear and uncertainty, most people remained close to home on this magical night.

Virgil Trinity was not one of them . . .

# Prologue

**P**anting with exertion, Virgil stopped running and glanced over his shoulder. Across the moonlit meadow glowed the lights of his cottage, where his beloved wife lay dying. Virgil swore he could hear her cries of agony, and vowed to help her at any cost.

Fear fired his determination. He fled into the black woods ahead, instantly blinded by the darkness. Shivering with apprehension and cold, he eased his pace and forced to mind every notion he'd ever heard about the Wee Folk.

"Fairy ring," he whispered. "I must find a ring."

Eyes cast to the shadowed forest floor, he searched for evidence of a glowing circle. Long moments passed; his brow began to bead with the sweat of desperation, and a tinge of hopelessness slowed the frantic beat of his heart.

"Little People," he called, his voice barely louder than the drifting of a cloud. "I beg your help."

He saw nothing. Heard nothing.

Covering his face with his hands, he fell to his knees at the foot of an ancient oak. Stones and gnarled twigs cut into his legs, but he could feel only the painful knowledge that his sweet Pegeen was going to die.

And with her would die their unborn child.

He wept, his tears seeping through his chilled fingers and splashing to the ground. Finally, after what seemed like hours, he perceived eerie changes occurring all around him. The cool night breeze warmed as if heated by sunbeams of high noon. The rustling of the oak, birch, and elder branches became almost musical, a soft, stirring melody that sounded like hundreds of flutes playing in harmony. From between the narrow spaces of his fingers, Virgil saw lights. Among the mist-dampened leaves, the sparkles swirled in a small, perfect circle.

They were here. They'd come.

The fairies.

"Virgil," a small male voice sang out.

Virgil took great care to stay outside the edge of the circle, for he knew that if he stepped inside the dazzling ring he would be pulled into the world of Faerie with little chance of escaping. Crouching lower to the ground, he strained to see the fairies. He saw nothing but the leaping shimmers of light, but remembered suddenly that the Wee Folk could quickly turn themselves into human form.

He edged away.

"Speak now, Virgil," the voice demanded, "or the aid you seek will be swiftly denied you."

Virgil took note of the authority that laced every word the tiny voice spoke. "My wife," he blurted out, more tears slipping to the ground. "Pegeen. The babe—the babe won't come. It's been near two days, it has. Please . . ."

"What would you be willing to sacrifice to save the child and its mother?" the voice asked.

"Anything," Virgil answered impulsively, clasping his hands together as if in prayer. "Anything you ask."

He saw the sparkles come together on the dark ground to form one large ball of gleam, and he realized the Little People were discussing the bargain. Silence ensued, and then the lights separated once more.

"In return for the lives of your wife and child," the voice finally said, "I demand a betrothal. One of your descendants must wed one of mine. Do you agree to these terms, Virgil Trinity?"

Virgil took not a second to ponder the fairy's stipulations. "Yes! Oh, yes!"

The lights glowing among the leaves grew brighter, so

bright that Virgil could not bear to look at them any longer. He shut his eyes.

"Your plea is granted," the small voice announced. "Pegeen is delivered of a fine healthy girl."

Virgil shook with happiness, but he didn't respond. The Wee Folk shunned gratitude.

"Go now, Virgil Trinity, and raise your daughter, but speak of our bargain to no one," the fairy voice instructed. "Although you will have naught to do with its fulfillment, you may be sure that the promise you have made on this night shall come to pass."

His eyes still shut, Virgil rose from the ground, raced out of the woods, and bolted across the wide, grassy field. When he finally arrived in the front yard of his cottage, the proof of fairy magic lilted into his ears with the lusty wails of his healthy newborn and Pegeen's cries of joy.

Clapping his hands together, Virgil laughed and danced around the yard and saw that in the distant woods the fairy lights continued to shimmer faintly.

*In return for the lives of your wife and child, I demand a betrothal.*

Still dancing, Virgil nodded as he remembered the fairy's words.

*A betrothal.*

Suddenly, his dancing stopped, his laughter faded. Now that he was assured of Pegeen's and his daughter's well-being, the true significance of his agreement with the fairies came to him at last.

He groped for the fence and leaned against a wooden post, and his forehead beaded with sweat once more. Was it his infant daughter who would one day marry into the enchanted world? Would it be one of his grandchildren? Great-grandchildren? He could not begin to guess, for the fairy voice had given no hint whatsoever.

All he knew for certain was that the rash and desperate promise he'd given only a short while before had irrevocably doomed *someone* of Trinity descent to the powerful clutches of Faerie.

**J**ourdian Amberville, the twelfth duke of Heathcourte, had concluded that there wasn't a female in the world who met the requirements he'd set for the woman who would be his duchess.

"Bloody hell," he muttered. Swallowing his second glass of brandy, he reached out and stroked his pet cat, Pharaoh, a sleek Siamese who tolerated no one but Jourdian.

"What's on the boil?" Jourdian's cousin, Emil Tate, asked, confused by Jourdian's sudden curse. They'd been discussing Jourdian's recent purchase of a mine in Egypt, but obviously Jourdian's thoughts were elsewhere now.

Emil pondered the mine a moment longer. Jourdian had bought it for no reason other than a passing suspicion that the pits might yield treasure, purchasing it right beneath the nose of a second interested buyer. Not only had miners discovered emeralds within those dark, damp Egyptian caverns, but authorities claimed the mine to be one of the richest ever found. Practically overnight, the vast Amberville fortune had tripled.

Yes, in many ways Jourdian led a charmed life, even as a boy. Once, when he and Emil were running through a field of wildflowers, Jourdian had spotted a sprinkling of tiny diamonds within the mass of trodden blossoms. Only Jourdian Amberville could have found jewels scattered amidst a lot of broken weeds. Since then, everything he touched had turned to wealth.

Sipping his own brandy, Emil felt the familiar spark of envy flicker through him, but since he bore no ill will toward his cousin he didn't feel a jot of guilt over his bit of jealousy. He'd decided long ago that only a saint of the highest heavenly order could resist coveting the title, riches, and power of the illustrious duke of Heathcourte.

He leaned forward on the satin settee by the fire. "I've often thought you were born under a lucky star, Jourdian. You were never even stung by a wasp, do you remember? Whenever we came upon the vicious creatures, it was almost as if they were blown away from you. Why, even the snakes we found that day near the pavilion slithered out of your way!"

Jourdian turned a sideways glance toward his cousin, a devil-may-care chap whose thick sandy hair was forever tousled and whose burnished gold eyes were almost always filled with a mixture of mischief and merriment. A relative from Jourdian's mother's side, Emil didn't possess a drop of Amberville blood or any other rightful claim to a place among England's peerage, but the unshakable bond between them was something no member of the nobility ever dared to ignore.

Emil was the only family Jourdian had.

"Jourdian? Do you remember the snakes?"

"Snakes?" Jourdian frowned. "What the devil are you talking about?"

"I might ask the same of you," Emil answered, flashing a lopsided smile. "In fact, I think I did."

Jourdian reached for the bottle of brandy.

"Women," Emil guessed suddenly. "Your lack of a duchess always drives you to drink. One thought of the elusive lady turns you into a regular ale knight."

"Emil, I am in no mood for any of your cheek. Furthermore, the subject of my love life is not up for discussion."

"The deuce, you say!" Emil laughed. "Jourdian, your love life is *the* discussion, the most talked about subject in all of England. Why, I even heard it said that the queen herself once wondered why you could not seem to pick a bride from the masses of beauties the season produces year after year."

"Indeed."

"Niall Marston can barely wait for you to wed."

"Niall Marston," Jourdian said, pondering the disreputable womanizer. "So he desires the chance to seduce my wife, does he?"

"It's his hobby, as you well know. Just last month he succeeded in enticing Lord Villier's new bride into meeting him in the garden during a small gathering that the Dunmores gave. Harold Villier is still none the wiser. Neither is Thacker Ainsbury. Rumor has it that Cherise Ainsbury is still seeing Niall whenever possible."

"If Niall Marston dares to look at my wife—"

"Seducing a woman who doesn't exist would be quite a feat."

Jourdian poured more brandy. Liquor wouldn't get him a bride, but it for damn sure would help him forget he didn't have one.

Accustomed as he was to having everything he desired the moment it occurred to him to want it, he simply could not fathom why the trivial task of choosing a duchess proved so infuriating.

He'd been covertly watching society's marital offerings ever since his twenty-eighth birthday, when he'd first decided the time had come to marry and produce an heir. He was thirty-two now and had yet to encounter a single woman who suited him.

Damn it all, finding the perfect wife should have been as effortless a goal to accomplish as any and all he'd ever undertaken.

And yet . . .

He shook his head. "Finding a basket of wishes would be far easier," he murmured.

Running his fingers through his wavy hair, he glanced at his surroundings.

The green salon was a lofty room, its elaborately sculpted ceiling supported by pink marble columns. Four exquisite crystal chandeliers dripped from the ceiling, their sparkles of light dancing upon the silk draperies and magnificent gilt chairs, all of which were a warm shade of moss green.

This room had been his parents' favorite. A pity Their

Graces had rarely been home long enough to truly enjoy it, Jourdian thought.

"You know, Jourdian," Emil said, "you're getting quite the reputation for being a man utterly impossible to please. There are many who say that if the goddess of love and beauty herself appeared before you, you would spurn her." He rose from the settee and joined his cousin in front of the huge window. Careful not to stand too close to Pharaoh—who was watching him with glacial blue eyes full of a promise of violence—he helped himself to a glass of Jourdian's brandy. "People are trying to imagine the woman who will finally appear in your life and win you over. And it's not only your peers who wonder, but your tenants and servants as well."

Jourdian twirled the stem of his snifter, watching the brandy slosh around the sides of the delicate glass. "I'm glad to hear I've provided everyone with such entertainment."

"Entertainment?" Emil smiled wryly. "You don't know the meaning of the word. You have no interests other than those related to the Amberville estate."

"With the exception of my need for an heir, I am satisfied with my life exactly as it is."

"You have no life. And if you don't mind my saying—"

"Mind?" Jourdian set his glass down on a silver tray. "Since when have you cared whether or not I mind your perishing interference? It has become increasingly more apparent that you've damn all else to do. If I weren't so daft as to consider you a friend, I would have you barred from this house so I could enjoy a bit of peace."

Gleefully, Emil continued with the dressing-down, an admonishment he gave his cousin at least once a month.

For all the good it did him. "Jourdian, this place already resembles a mausoleum. If you were to obtain any more peace than you already have, you would be a corpse. And that is the top and bottom of it."

"But I've no doubt you will soon get to the middle."

"Spot on." Emil clasped his cousin's broad shoulder. "Dedicated cousin that I am, I have been doing a bit of research on your behalf. Some observing and interrogating, if you will, and I have decided that Edith Hinderwell and Caroline Pilcher would suit you admirably. Caroline stands to inherit her maternal grandmother's fortune, you know. No small sum if the hearsay is to be believed."

Jourdian feigned an expression of excitement. "You don't say? Well, pauper that I am, I imagine I should ask for the lady's hand straightaway."

"What? Oh. Yes, Caroline's inheritance would be but money for jam to you. But perhaps you could find it in your heart to marry her and give her grandmother's money to *me*? It's frightfully difficult living on the pittance I make as an investor."

Jourdian retrieved his brandy, took a sip, and looked at Emil over the rim of the glass. Most men could live quite comfortably on the money Emil made from his various investments, all of which Jourdian had advised him to make. Of course, most men did not possess the same passion for such an extravagant lifestyle.

But Jourdian understood that it wasn't greed that caused his cousin's relentless fascination with money and luxurious possessions. Rather, it was the unforgettable memory of a destitute childhood.

"Are you in need of funds, Emil?"

Emil felt poignant emotion well up within him. But for Jourdian, he'd still be in Mallencroft plowing the same fields his father had, living in the same crumbling cottage he'd been born in, and wondering day after day if there would be enough food on the table to assuage his hunger.

But Jourdian had intervened, and Emil loved his cousin like a brother. Indeed, there was nothing he wouldn't do or dare to help him find happiness, an emotion that became more alien to Jourdian with each passing year.

"What I need," Emil began softly, "is for you to find the true contentment you deserve, but so eludes you."

Shifting uneasily, Jourdian bowed his head and stared at the raspberry colored carpet. He never knew how to respond to Emil's affection.

Nor did he know how to express his own. "Might I remind you that you have yet to find wedded bliss, either?"

Emil shrugged. "I'm not in your position. I've no important title to bequeath to an heir."

"Borrow mine for a while."

"Would that I could."

Jourdian smiled. Emil had longed for a title for as long as he could remember. Alas, a title was the one thing Jourdian was unable to procure for him.

"We wandered from the subject, Jourdian. Where was I?"

Jourdian sighed. "Caroline's inheritance."

"Ah, yes. Very well, cousin, you don't need Caroline's inheritance. But what do you think of her personally?"

"She owns a python. Quite the most outlandish choice of pet I have ever heard of."

Emil glanced at Pharaoh. "A python is a much safer pet to own than that hairy ball of evil *you* have. I shall never forget that time he sprang off the mantel in your office, landed on my chest, and attempted to take a bite out of my Adam's apple. He would have ripped my throat out if I had not dumped that pitcher of water on him. The conceited beast cared more for his wet fur than eating my neck, thank God for that."

"Nevertheless, a cat is a *normal* pet."

"You once kept a lizard—"

"I did not have the lizard as a pet, but only because my schoolmaster was having me study the creature's eating habits and—"

"You loved that lizard."

"One cannot love a reptile."

"Why ever not?"

"And not only does Caroline own an absurd pet," Jourdian added, refusing to discuss the possibility of emotional bonding with a lizard, "but she also enjoys riding."

Emil clutched at his chest, as if shock had almost stopped his heart. "*Riding?* Dear God, she should be beheaded for committing such a heinous crime!"

"I do not object to her riding, but I once overheard her say that she has long wanted to know what it would be like to perform equestrian stunts in a circus. Such a longing is completely unorthodox."

"A fact I feel certain she understands. She merely *wonders* about riding in the circus, can't you understand that? I've always wanted to wrestle a crocodile, but that does not mean I'd jump into a swamp to satisfy my desire."

"Wrestle a crocodile, Emil? Why in God's name—"

"To see if I'm strong enough to win the match, naturally."

"Naturally." Jourdian rolled his eyes.

"Perhaps you should renew your courtship with Marianna Chesterton?" Emil suggested, tapping his chin. "She's a beautiful woman, and to the best of my knowledge, she doesn't have a pet and has never mentioned the circus. Every time I see her she asks about you. It's quite obvious that she believes there was more to your relationship with her than you will acknowledge. Do you know that her father confided that she has refused all other suitors, including Lord Percival Brackett?"

"Percival." Jourdian frowned a frown that nearly knit his eyebrows together as he pondered his only rival, the duke of Bramwell, an avaricious and ruthless man who had done his utmost to finish the destruction of the Amberville estate that Jourdian's father had begun.

He hadn't succeeded.

And Jourdian swore Percival would never even come close. "Tell me, Emil, is that hairy popinjay still out of sorts over the emerald mine?"

Emil smiled too. "Word has it that when he learned you'd outbid him, he locked himself in his rooms and didn't come out for a week. He cannot stand the fact that you are the richest nobleman in England and he the second."

"I've my eye on vast fruit orchards in Gloucester now," Jourdian said, still smiling. "They say money doesn't grow on trees, but the saying doesn't apply to these groves. If I know Percival, he's investigating the same orchards."

"Most likely. Moreover, I imagine he's beside himself wondering if Marianna will ever look at him the way she looks at you. When you were keeping company with her, he was a mass of red-hot rage and cold green jealousy."

Jourdian sat down in the ladder-back chair next to the window. Staring at the molded ceiling, he summoned Marianna's image to mind. "I've toyed with the idea of marrying her," he allowed himself to admit. "But she . . . There's something about her. Something . . . Carefully as she tries to hide it, she's of a grasping nature."

"A grasping nature? Do you mean that she's interested in your name and estate? *I* covet your title and fortune, too. Why not cast me aside as well?"

Jourdian took a while to answer. Not because he did not know what to say, but because it was terribly difficult for him to put his feelings into words. "You may envy my title and fortune, Emil, but I've no doubt that if I were to lose both tomorrow you would not think less of me."

Emil nodded. "True, but only because I know you would somehow earn another title and another fortune."

Unable to help himself, Jourdian chuckled.

"What is this I hear?" Emil asked, cupping his hand over his ear. "Could it actually be that I am being treated to the rare sound of Amberville mirth? A pity I cannot bottle the sound, for I feel sure I could make my own fortune selling it to the multitude of people who do not believe it exists."

"How amusing. You know, I think I heard it said that the queen is in dire need of a court jester. Perhaps you should apply for the position."

"And neglect my obligation to assist you in finding a duchess? Consider seeing Marianna again."

Jourdian rubbed his shoulder. "I'll give it some thought, but—"

"And think about Edith Hinderwell, too. She's quiet and docile. I've never seen her do anything odd. She's a plain thing, too. Although her father can afford the very best for her, her gowns are simple, and she wears hardly any jewelry. In my opinion that indicates that she cares little for material possessions."

"She indulges in superstitious nonsense. Last year at Lord Tremayne's birthday gala, I saw her gazing out of a window with such an intense expression on her face that I was certain she was seeing some ghastly occurrence. She informed me she was merely wishing on stars."

Emil moved closer to Jourdian's chair. "Come now, Jourdian, there is nothing peculiar about wishing on stars. When we were lads I taught you how to do it, and we wished on dozens of them. We collected four-leafed clovers, put pennies in our shoes, and looked for the end of the rainbow to find the pot of—"

"The stuff of *childhood*, and no wish I ever made came true. And if my memory serves me correctly I ceased to believe in such absurdities long before you did."

Emil rubbed the bit of stubble on his chin. "Well, actually I haven't quite overcome my belief in wishing on stars. Only last night, I waited for the first star to appear in the sky and wished for a mountain of gold."

Jourdian stared at his cousin. "You didn't."

Emil tipped his glass over his mouth, watched one last drop of brandy fall to his bottom lip, then licked it off. "I did."

"And do you believe that such dreams will come true simply because you wished on a hot ball of gas?"

Such sadness for Jourdian came over Emil at that moment that he had to restrain himself from hugging his cousin. "What I believe is that when one ceases to believe in wishing—"

"One dies. I know your speeches by heart, Emil."

"You may know my speeches *by* heart, but it is obvious that you have not taken them *to* heart."

Jourdian resigned himself to yet another of Emil's incessant lectures, but he couldn't stifle a yawn.

"Bored, cousin? Well, I can certainly understand why. I've stayed here at Heathcourte often enough to have memorized your monotonous routine. You awaken at seven, and bathe at seven and a quarter. You dress at precisely ten until eight, and breakfast at eight-thirty. You're in your office by nine on the dot, and—"

"You—"

"On Monday evenings your cook knows that the main course is to be leg of mutton with oysters. On Tuesdays your dinner is always sirloin of beef, served only after you have finished your partridge soup, of course. Wednesdays are lobster nights, Thursdays—"

"What in God's name is wrong with dining upon certain foods on certain evenings? The meals are all quite to my liking, and I see no reason why—"

"And you want a wife similar to your weekly food calendar.

You objected to the women I mentioned because they all want, do, or have something you consider unconventional. In a word, your duchess must be *boring*."

Jourdian bristled. "I hardly think that a wife who is simple in character is boring."

"You want a woman as indifferent to the spice of life as you are," Emil continued heedlessly. "Who not only follows your dry-as-dust routine, but who embraces the ho-hum rhythm of the Amberville household. And she'll place little importance on your name or wealth. Rather, she will devote her every waking moment to you and your children, possessing no other interests whatsoever. She'll—"

"Damn it all, Emil—"

"I know why you desire such a wife."

"And why wouldn't you?" Jourdian snapped. "You know everything else about me, do you not?"

Emil marched toward the fireplace. There he picked up a gold oval frame that contained a painted miniature of the former duke and duchess of Heathcourte.

"Barrington and Isabel Amberville," he said, holding the frame high in the air. "Isabel's love of exotic adventure is still mentioned every now and again among older members of the ton. They say Barrington indulged Isabel's every whim and took her to climb snowy mountain peaks halfway around the world. He granted her wishes to ride elephants through snake-infested jungles, hunt for long-lost buried treasure on eerie deserted islands, and sample live termites on a stick with savages who wore shrunken heads around their necks and slivers of bone through their nostrils."

"I am well aware of the details concerning my parents' travels—"

"No, Jourdian, you are not. Nor is anyone else. Your mother and father traveled so frequently that they had little time to describe their grand adventures to anyone, including you. They were gone for months at a time, and when they returned they stayed home but for a short while before leaving on yet another bizarre venture."

"Why do you do this, Emil?" Jourdian demanded. "I'm convinced that you lie abed at night with paper and pencil, jotting down all the many ways you can succeed in rousing my temper."

Emil shrugged. "A frightening task, but someone has to do it." He placed the frame back on the mantel and, with his hands clasped behind his back, he paced around the room. "Isabel's incessant craving to see the world made your own world a very lonely one. Her obsession with the unusual—which was what compelled her to make her wild excursions—gave you an intense need for the conventional. And her adoration of your father's riches made you suspicious of anyone the least bit curious over your wealth."

Emil stopped beside the sofa, picked up a pillow, and ran his thumb over the swirling embroidery. "Rebellion, that's what has driven you to become the man you are," he said softly. "Your life now is much like a revolt against uncomfortable memories. After all, a lad who is made to eat peas when he doesn't like peas is going to become a man who will never allow a pea in his house."

"Peas? That is the most absurd—"

"Perhaps, but it describes what's happened to you." With a flick of his wrist, Emil tossed the embroidered pillow back on the settee. "Don't you see, Jourdian? Everything you do is in direct defiance of something you were forced to bear as a lad."

"You have said outside of enough, Emil." Jourdian rose from his chair.

Noticing the expression on Jourdian's face, Emil realized it was not his cousin he was seeing, but the forbidding duke, a man whose cool demeanor veiled a volatile temper.

And a gravely wounded heart. "Jourdian—"

"No more!"

"Ever the bitter duke, eh? What do you have for breakfast in the mornings? A jug of vinegar?"

"Kerosene," came Jourdian's quick reply.

"I'd suggest you try lemon juice every now and again, but such a change might pull you from the culinary rut you're in." Pulling at his shirt cuffs, Emil headed for the door. "I know how bereft you will feel over the loss of my captivating company, but I must take my leave. The weather's set fair, and I'm off to the Thirlway picnic. Lord and Lady Thirlway so enjoy entertaining outside in autumn. Oh, and if I'm not mistaken, there is a cemetery not far from the Thirlway estate. Perhaps I'll find you a wife there."

Jourdian smiled. "I'll speak to the queen. I'm sure that if I recommend you, she'll hire you as her court jester."

Laughing, Emil executed a low, sweeping bow. "Good day, Your Grace. I leave you with your friends, Monotony, Dreary, and Boredom. And good day to you too, Pharaoh," he said to the cat. "I leave you with *your* friends, Vile, Hateful, and Wicked."

When his cousin was gone, Jourdian stared at the empty threshold for a moment, and then slowly moved his gaze to the gold frame on the fireplace mantel.

His parents' likenesses looked back at him. Both were dressed in the garb of Mexico, Barrington wearing a sombrero, and Isabel a gaily embroidered white peasant blouse. Both were smiling, obviously enjoying themselves immensely.

Jourdian remembered their trip to Mexico. He'd been seven then. Maybe eight. His mother had actually been given permission to fight a bull in Mexico City, a favor granted after his father had bribed the authorities with a veritable fortune. Jourdian had wanted to know everything about bullfighting when his parents returned from the trip.

But Isabel had been too busy talking Barrington into the next journey—a trip to some tropical island whose name now escaped Jourdian. There, she'd walked on hot coals with the natives and had had her nose pierced. From then on, she'd worn a ruby in her left nostril.

Jourdian never did hear about the bullfighting.

A sigh gathered in his chest. He left the room, sent orders for his stallion, Magnus, to be saddled, and was ready to ride before the stable lads brought his horse around to the manor house.

After ten minutes he was too impatient to wait any longer and stalked out of his palatial home toward the barns. A cold November wind blasted into him, ruffling his hair and the colorful mass of pansies that bloomed along the edges of the pebbled trail that led to the stables. His boots scraped through the glistening white stones, the sound grating in his ears.

Swiping at the red and yellow leaves that blew into his face and settled on his shoulders, he didn't notice the small wooden cart of pumpkins blocking his path, and walked straight into it. The vivid orange fruit tumbled to the ground, creating a course of obstacles that further tested his patience.

When he finally arrived at the barn, he saw that the groom had yet to complete the task of readying the coal-black stallion.

"Sorry, Yer Gr-Grace," Hopkins said, his stuttering made worse by the duke's intimidating bearing. "He's—he's a h-hit skit-skittish t-today. It's the snap in the air, I vow." Quickly he finished tightening the saddle girth, then handed the gleaming reins to the duke.

As Jourdian slowly worked Magnus into a pounding gallop through the countryside, he pondered his cousin's description of the future duchess of Heathcourte.

Emil had not been far off the mark.

But there was one other little vow Jourdian had made concerning his bride, one that Emil had failed to discern.

Jourdian's lips narrowed into a tight line as he dwelled on the memory of his father. Before Barrington Amberville's marriage to Isabel, he'd been one of the most powerful men in all of Europe, concentrating intently on the Amberville holdings and fortune. But marriage had changed everything. So in love with Isabel had Barrington been, he'd ignored all responsibility to the family name.

And then Isabel had died.

But even after the exotic trips and squandering of money had stopped, Barrington had continued to ignore his estate and his heir. Engulfed by sorrow, he'd locked himself away from the entire world and had followed Isabel to the grave seven years later.

Jourdian gripped the reins so tightly that his knuckles turned white. Grief had eventually killed his sire, first in mind, then in body. And love had been the reason for such profound and fatal anguish. Of those things, Jourdian was certain.

And so, whoever his very ordinary and unassuming wife would be, Jourdian had sworn not to love her.

**2**

S parkles swirling in her wake, Splendor moved away from the small mound of earth beneath which her father's glittering kingdom lay hidden. As she stepped soundlessly through the brittle fall leaves that blanketed the forest floor, her red curls shimmered down the full length of her bare body, and each of her movements sent the sweet scent of spring wildflowers into the autumn air.

She'd escaped the assembly her father had called. As the eldest princess, she knew she was supposed to pay strict attention to the affairs that affected Pillywiggin—the province of Faerie her father ruled—but such issues very nearly put her to sleep. Besides, she mused, her sister would be present at the court gathering, and Harmony could tell her everything later.

At that thought, Splendor frowned. Harmony would consent to nothing if it would not in some way benefit her. Although it was simply not in Splendor not to care for Harmony, she sometimes wondered why her tempestuous sister had been given a name that implied peace and benevolence. Why, only three days ago Harmony had taken great delight in tying a donkey's tail into a hopeless mass of elf knots. The beast hadn't seemed to care, but its poor owner had had a terrible time combing out the tangles. Harmony enjoyed tormenting humans.

Splendor could not understand why. To her, humans were the most intriguing creatures in existence.

She stopped beside a massive oak, leaned against the tree trunk, and peered down at the blades of emerald grass that barely reached her slim ankles. Little gave her more pleasure than her powers of shape-shifting. It wasn't that she minded her original size—which was about the same as the span of a large butterfly's wings—but she adored being statuesque.

She smiled a secret smile, knowing full well that her pleasure in being tall stemmed from her fascination with humans—most especially the human man who lived nearby.

Breathing deeply of the cool, woodsy air, she couldn't suppress a shiver of excitement. "He's going to be near today, Delicious," she murmured to her enchanted pet. "That handsome human who makes me glow!"

She looked down at her pet, frowned, and then grinned. A scant hour ago Delicious had been a tawny deer. Now he was a swan, standing near her feet preening his snowy feathers. "What's the matter, Delicious? Can you nay decide what you want to be today?"

Delicious rubbed his soft head over her bare calf, then returned to the task of cleaning his feathers.

Still smiling, Splendor thought of the handsome human again. She had no idea who he was, but she always knew when he would be near enough to watch. A lovely feeling passed through her, whispering that he was coming. She'd felt it from the first time she'd ever seen him, when he was a young boy and she a fairy child, and she'd watched him ever since.

Except for a period of five years, when he'd suddenly disappeared. She hadn't thought to ever see him again, but one day he'd returned, and he'd been more handsome than ever.

For as long as she could remember, she'd yearned to have him for her very own. If he belonged to her, she could keep him in her father's palace and gaze at him as often and long as she pleased instead of having to wait for him to appear. She'd grant all his wishes and give him joy as well, for she'd had more than one glimpse of the strange grief that festered inside him.

But short of stealing him away, she didn't know how to acquire such an extraordinary possession.

She floated to the edge of the forest, looked out across the fields, and continued to ponder the man she waited to see. With hair as dark as the inky black ravens that soared through the heavens and eyes the color of the sky right before a silvery rain shower, he was the most beautiful living thing she'd ever seen. And his vigor amazed her. He never lost strength the way fairies did, but could ride his huge ebony horse for hours without tiring.

He even *looked* strong, with so solid a body that Splendor was sure he would feel like a stone if she ever had the opportunity to touch him. Such sturdiness was unfamiliar to an ethereal being like herself.

She looked down at her fluid form. Her translucent skin glowed, while human skin did not. She moved in an aura of brightness. Humans cast shadows.

"And humans must be very heavy," she told Delicious. "Sweet everlasting, even wet I barely weigh more than a handful of stars."

"Splendor!" King Wisdom's voice boomed through the forest.

Splendor whirled around and saw her father, Harmony, and a host of Pillywiggin's peers standing before her. They, too, had used their powers of shape-shifting and stood as tall as she.

None were smiling at her. All were staring, some with awe, some with envy, and others with sympathy.

A vague feeling of foreboding passed through her as she watched her father stride forward. His knee-length white hair and beard fell over his round, bare body like a swath of frost, and the very ground upon which he walked began to shine like silver. "Father?"

"Splendor, you did not attend the assembly I called."

"She should be punished," Harmony bit out. "If I were her father, I would—"

'But you are not her father, I am." The king gave a great sigh, contemplating the differences between his daughters. Golden-haired, blue-eyed Harmony found her happiness in rendering gloom. Indeed, she'd done much in the way of encouraging the human fear of Faerie.

But Splendor, with her molten copper tresses and huge lavender eyes, found her greatest joy in bestowing kindness on all living things, guarding flowers and animals, and even protecting the stars that humans were forever wishing upon.

The king worried about her, for the mortal world could be a very sinister place, especially to one as innocent as Splendor.

And the mortal world was exactly where he had to send her.

"I'm sorry your mother couldn't be present to hear my all-important announcement, Splendor," he began, "but she hasn't yet returned from her mission. I believe she mentioned that her last stop was somewhere in Australia."

"Wrong, Father," Harmony stated firmly. " 'Twas America. Philadelphia, Pennsylvania, to be precise."

"Well, forgive me for my geographical error, Harmony," the king flared. "I'm sure it delighted you to correct me." Reaching out, he placed his hand on Splendor's arm. "The time has come to fulfill the betrothal made by my grandfather, Splendor."

Splendor's eyes widened as she dwelled on the extreme importance of the betrothal. Having been told the story many years before and every year since, the tale was engraved on her heart, as it was with all the Pillywiggins.

Faerie was of fragile and ancient ancestry, and over the centuries the delicate race had continued to weaken. As a result, the number of fairy babies born had steadily declined. By contrast, humans were strong and fruitful in offspring, and it had been Splendor's great-grandfather who had devised a concrete way to obtain such strength and fertility for the Pillywiggins. He'd realized that a union between a human and a fairy would result in children who would fortify the enchanted race with human vitality.

Everyone knew the union was the only way to save the kingdom of Pillywiggin, but no one had ever been aware of which Pillywiggin monarch would put into play the long-ago bargain made between Faerie and the human called Trinity. All that was understood was that by way of a dream the chosen king would know of his mission and the details concerning it.

"A dream," Splendor whispered. "You had the dream, Father?"

"Aye, a fortnight ago on All Hallows Eve." He paused for a

moment, hesitant to speak the question in his mind. "Splendor," he finally said, "has your mother . . . Did she . . . Have you had a mother-daughter talk with her yet?"

So many thoughts darted through Splendor's mind, she didn't even hear her father's question. "Oh, but how wonderful, Father! You must be terribly flattered, are you not? To be the chosen monarch . . . Delicious!" she exclaimed, bending to stroke her pet, "did you hear, sweetling? Is the Trinity male or female, Father? When will the wedding be? Which fairy will marry—"

"The Trinity is male," King Wisdom interrupted, knowing that she would chatter merrily on if he did not stop her. "And you, Splendor, are the fairy who will marry him and bear his child."

Her father's declaration so shocked Splendor that she dissolved into a swirling mist of silvery light.

King Wisdom sighed again. Ever since she'd been a child, Splendor had sought refuge from difficult situations by fading into a sparkling mist. Harmony, on the other hand, burst into flames and burned furiously until her emotions settled.

Mist and flames, the king mused. His daughters could not have been more different. A shame that Harmony did not possess a bit of Splendor's gentleness and compassion and Splendor did not possess a tad of Harmony's temper and audacity. If that were so, both would possess well-rounded characters.

Tapping his foot on the ground, the king waited for Splendor to reappear. He knew his wait would not be long, for fairy emotions came and went as quickly as the sparkle of a star.

In the next second, Splendor materialized from within her glistening haven. "Me—me, Father? *I* am to marry the Trinity?"

Harmony rolled her eyes to the heavens. "Of course, *you*! You always get everything, do you not? You're heiress to Father's throne, are you not? You'll be queen one day, will you not? Well, now you're the chosen savior of our race. The fairy who will be forever remembered as the Pillywiggin who saved us all by bringing a half-human child into our midst. And what have *I* ever gotten, I ask you? Nay a thing, that's what!"

The king rubbed his pounding temples as Harmony threw a fiery tantrum and turned herself into a spinning ball of red-hot blazes. "Harmony, please."

Gradually, Harmony cooled down until only her eyes continued to burn with anger.

The king turned back to Splendor. "You are aware of the details of my grandfather's plan?"

Words rarely failed Splendor, but now she found herself unable to reply. Only moments before she'd been fantasizing over having in her possession the handsome black-haired man who rode the huge ebony horse, and now she was to wed a man she'd never seen. Sweet everlasting, how quickly her life had changed!

"You will marry the Trinity and conceive his babe," King Wisdom reminded her. "My grandchild will be born, will mature, wed, and procreate in Pillywiggin. Of course, we cannot be certain if the babe will inherit the powers of Faerie, but just having the half-human amongst us will strengthen us. So much so that many couples in my kingdom will again begin to reproduce."

Worry replaced Splendor's surprise. How long would she be forced to stay in the human world?

The king took her hand. "Do not despair, my child. I would never permit you to remain in the human world for more time than is necessary. Never, do you understand? And do not forget that you can nay stay outside of Faerie for more than three months, anyway. You would perish if you remained in the mortal world for any longer."

As his words fell over the assembly, so did silence. Long-lived as fairies were, the subject of death was rarely broached.

"Only one thing could save a fairy from certain demise in the mortal world," King Wisdom continued solemnly, "and that is a thing called human love, an intense emotion that is born and flows from deep within the highly vulnerable human heart. This love is capable of bestowing deep, indescribable joy upon those who share it. Alas, as fairies we cannot begin to comprehend the feeling, for we lack the strength, substance, and depth necessary to bear such profound emotions.

" 'Tis a strange thing, really," he murmured. "The members

of Faerie possess great powers, but the magic of human love . . . 'Tis the mightiest force in all of creation."

All the fairies present began to ponder their ruler's declarations until Harmony's loud questions interrupted their deliberation. "What if Splendor fails to get the Trinity to marry her? And if by some frightfully slim chance he does make her his bride, what if she fails to get with child before the three months pass? Will you then send another fairy to take her place, Father? One who will most certainly succeed where she failed? Like *me*, for instance?"

King Wisdom scowled. "Harmony, take care that your envy does not turn your blue eyes green. Splendor is a very beautiful fairy. As are you," he added quickly. "There is no doubt that the Trinity will desire to make your sister his bride."

Glaring at her sister, Harmony kicked at a mound of red and yellow leaves. "If you think I'm one bit jealous, think again, Splendor. You have to *marry* one of those *humans*! 'Tis a pity you cannot simply live with the Trinity for a while and get with child without having to become his wife."

"Harmony!" King Wisdom cried. "How can you suggest that Splendor produce a child out of wedlock? My grandchild will bear his father's name, you may be sure of that!"

Harmony started to argue further, but the sound of hoof-beats in the distance cut her short.

"The time has come, Splendor," the king said, throwing Harmony a final look of displeasure. "The Trinity is near. You must swiftly show yourself to him. He will succumb to your beauty, become instantly enchanted, and you will soon become his bride."

He took her hand, started to guide her toward the edge of the forest, but then stopped. "Splendor, about the mother-daughter talk your mother was supposed to give to you . . . In order for you to conceive the Trinity's child you must . . . There are many differences between humans and fairies, of course, but—"

He broke off, noticing all the fairies were listening avidly. This was not the sort of conversation to have in front of his subjects, he realized. "Suffice it to say that the Trinity will get you with child in the same manner that fairy men sire children."

"But what is this manner, Father?"

King Wisdom heard the hoofbeats come closer. "I've no time to explain. 'Twill be the Trinity himself who will describe and perform the act."

"And . . . And as soon as I have conceived, I may return to Pillywiggin?"

"You most definitely *will* return," he declared. "You are of Faerie, and 'tis here where you belong."

"But how will I know when I have conceived, Father? Who will tell me that I am with child?"

The king smiled. "You will know, Splendor. At the very moment of conception, you will feel the creation of life take place inside you, and you will also sense the gender of the babe. 'Tis a beautiful gift all fairy women possess."

Splendor quieted then, wondering what such a miracle might feel like. But when her father began urging her to the edge of the woods, she came out of her silent contemplation and resisted with all the slight strength her fragile body held. "Father, wait! I . . . The Trinity—will he know that I am of Faerie? And if he does not, do I tell him?"

The king stopped in his silver tracks. Shrewd though he was, no member of Faerie fully comprehended human nature. "I am unsure," he admitted softly. "As I said, human emotions are different than ours, for the humans' strength and substance allow them to feel much more deeply and for much longer periods of time. However, I imagine the Trinity will learn of your lineage whether you choose to tell him or not. He might see you use your powers or dissolve into your mist. And do not forget, Splendor, that you cannot remain tall forever. Your strength will wane, and you will be forced to shrink to Pillywiggin size to regain your energies. 'Tis possible that you might feel the need to dwindle in stature while in his presence."

Uncertainty made Splendor want to seek the solitude of her mist, but she stubbornly refused to give in to the temptation. She could not help her tears, however. The tiny diamonds escaped her wide eyes and sprinkled down upon the bed of leaves.

"Come now," the king ordered.

Quickly, Splendor's anxiety vanished. She glided to the edge of the forest, Harmony and the other fairies following.

"There he is," the King whispered, pointing toward the pasture. "The Trinity. He comes in the exact manner I saw him in my dream. On his black horse in the meadow."

Splendor saw her human man riding through the field, his big black horse bringing him closer and closer to the forest. "*Him? He's* the Trinity?"

"Aye, child. He is the Trinity."

"Sweet everlasting!" Such joy filled Splendor's being that the brilliance of her glow rivaled that of the sun itself. For three whole months, the Trinity would be hers, the most precious possession she'd ever owned!

"Now, Splendor!" her father shouted. "Go now!"

She needed no further urging. Stars twinkling all around her, she swept out of the forest and skimmed over the meadow, her long hair flowing behind her like copper flames. Wanting the Trinity's first sight of her to be a perfect picture of charm and elegance, she flew in the most graceful manner she knew, one arm stretched out before her and the other held softly out to the side.

But a strong breeze upset her winsome pose, hurling her frail form through the air with mighty force.

In the next second she saw the source of her trouble. Delicious sailed at her feet. His powerful white wings stirred up a wind her slight frame could not withstand, thrusting her forward so violently that she knew she would soon be blown away. Her hair whipping around her, she began to flail her arms and kick her legs in a vain effort to regain control.

"Delicious, nay!" she shouted.

The swan seemed not to hear her. On the contrary, he stretched out his long neck and began to flap his wings with quicker, stronger strokes.

Just as she feared, Splendor blew over the meadow like a puffball in a tornado. A keen sense of helplessness overwhelming her, she closed her eyes tightly, hoped for the best . . .

. . . and crashed directly into Jourdian Trinity Amberville.

3

Jourdian saw a burst of silver light, then a flash of white before Magnus shied, bucked, and reared.

Unprepared for his horse's sudden panic, His Grace fell off the frightened stallion and toppled to the cold ground. Pain surged through his head; his thoughts swayed dizzily through his mind. He felt displaced, as if he wasn't really there but was only watching what was happening from another place.

He shut his eyes.

Stars danced before him. Not unusual, considering the hard fall he'd taken. But why did he think he smelled spring wild-flowers? The fresh fragrance was so real, it was almost as if he were lying amidst a bed of the fragile blossoms.

May flowers in November? God, his fall must have been worse than he'd realized.

He lay motionless, still watching stars twinkle. A moment later, he felt as though something pressed against his chest. It didn't weigh much, but it was there, just like the scent of wildflowers that lingered around him.

He opened his eyes and saw other eyes. Violet eyes, and they gazed at him with a combination of curiosity and pleasure. Full of sparkle and fringed with long, thick lashes, they were the sweetest, most mesmerizing eyes Jourdian had ever beheld, and he felt powerless to look away from them.

The owner of the pretty lavender eyes lay fully upon him,

and it wasn't at all difficult to discern her sex. The only thing she was wearing was the cloak of her copper hair, the alluring perfume of spring wildflowers . . .

And stars. The tiny lights shimmered all over her.

She looked like an angel.

Disbelief slammed into him. "Am—am I dead?"

She shook her head.

An angel wouldn't lie, Jourdian decided. He wasn't dead. Closing his eyes again, he strove for a plausible explanation.

Maybe he'd been knocked unconscious. Perhaps the naked, sweetly scented girl was but a dream, a figment of his senseless state. A real person wouldn't go strolling through fields without clothes on—especially on a chilly November day. A dream would also explain her slight weight. After all, she was composed of nothing but his imagination and a myriad of silver stars.

But he didn't *feel* asleep. Indeed, he was fully aware of every sight, scent, and sound around him.

What the bloody hell was happening to him?

He opened his eyes, looked at the girl, and again saw the sparkles swirling around her. Either she was a fantasy or a constellation had fallen from the sky into his arms. And since a fantasy was more believable, Jourdian realized then that he was definitely in the throes of a dream, the most realistic he'd ever experienced.

"Hello," she said.

The fragile dream spoke, and Jourdian decided her voice was softer than the stirring of a bird's wing. Her breath wafted across his chin, warm like a sunbeam, and her pale pink lips curved into a shy, lovely smile that wrinkled her small nose in a most enchanting manner.

"Your scent is supremely pleasant," she told him. " 'Tis the sort one might come upon while meandering through the woods in the winter."

Ordinarily, Jourdian would not have returned a smile given him by a naked stranger lying on top of him, but since he was obviously out cold he felt perfectly free to participate in and enjoy his dream to the fullest. Not only did he smile back at her but he lifted his hands from the ground and gently clasped her tiny, bare waist.

She was warm and soft, and her scent of wildflowers flowed through his senses like petals drifting on a gentle breeze.

"Oh," Splendor whispered when he touched her. Strength began to trickle through her limbs. Gradually the energy she'd lost during her chaotic flight across the meadow returned to her, and it was with great relief that she realized she would not be forced to shrink to fairy size to regain what little vigor she possessed.

She shifted, lifting her head from the Trinity's broad shoulder and trailing her fingers lightly across his temple. His pulse thumped beneath the tips of her fingers. A strong and steady beat, it reminded her anew of the power locked within his massive frame, and she understood then that the strength she felt flowing through her was not her own, but his.

Excitement rushed through her. Her great-grandfather and father had been right! Just being close to a human bolstered a fairy's vitality.

"You've wonderful eyes," she told him, her gaze locked with his. "There are some who believe rain has no color, but I will tell you now that they are wrong. Rain is silver and iridescent, like the wing dust of certain butterflies and moths. When you rub those wings, the dust glistens on your fingertip. 'Tis a lovely thing to see. Your eyes are such a silver, like rain and the glistening wing dust, and I do not think staring into them for hour upon hour would be a difficult task."

Jourdian thought about what she'd said. No woman had ever commented on the color of his eyes before.

"And your lips . . ." Splendor said. "Full and soft and slightly parted, and I have a glimpse of your teeth, which are as white as the water lilies that float in the pond where I bathe. You have no hair on your face. I am glad for that, for if you wore a beard I would nay have discovered the mole on your right cheek. 'Tis a mark I find quite dashing."

"You chatter," he said, grinning.

"Aye. I cannot help it. I have tried to help it, but there are so many, many things that occur to me that I fear I would burst if I could not somehow release them. Sometimes, however, I am as quiet as the falling of a snowflake. Many believe me ill when I am so quiet, but I have only been ill once in my life. A cat scratched me. He was a black cat with eyes as green as poison. My skin is sensitive, and the cat scratch caused me such torment that I took to my bed and did not rise for a full fortnight. The cat would have eaten me alive, and I'm sure that there can be no death more horrible. I do not like cats. Not at all. I am fond of hens and rabbits, however, because they don't chase me as cats do."

"Rabbits," he echoed, his mind spinning with all the things she'd told him. "Cats chase you?"

"Aye, but rabbits and hens do not."

He smiled again. He simply couldn't help it. There was something so sweet, so good about her. "Sprite," he said softly, touching one of her shimmering red curls.

She frowned slightly. Did he already know of her Faerie origins? "Why do you call me so?"

"Sprite? You remind me of one."

"You have seen sprites?"

He smiled indulgently. "No, but I'm sure they look like you. Delicate. And shimmery, with impish smiles and whimsical ways about them."

He didn't know what she was, she realized. *Sprite* was only a pet name. "I am supremely certain," she said, "that you are the most beautiful creature ever to draw breath." Her gaze caressing his face once more, she grinned at him.

And no power on earth could have kept Jourdian from kissing that dreamy, dazzling smile. Drawn to her ethereal beauty and intrinsic goodness, he gently pressed his lips to hers and knew he had never encountered such sweetness. She tasted like warm honey—literally—as if she had just partaken of the luscious substance and it yet clung to her lips.

"What—what is this you do?" Splendor whispered, her mouth still touching his.

Jourdian ended the kiss and saw true bewilderment floating within her luminous eyes. Well, she was only an illusion, he reminded himself. A beautiful and innocent chimera who had no way of knowing what a kiss was.

Far be it from him to allow her to end before he'd tutored her in the art of sensuality.

"It's called a *kiss*, and we were *kissing*."

She thought about that for a moment, but could make no sense of it. "Why do you do it?"

"You didn't like it?"

She looked at his lips again. "It didn't repulse me in the slightest."

Her answer rankled. This was *his* fantasy, damn it all, and he would dream it the way he wanted, with her writhing in his arms.

He clutched her slight shoulders and touched his lips to hers once more. A low moan escaped him as he drove his tongue into her mouth, seeking and finding more of her delectable sweetness.

Surprised though she was by his strange actions, Splendor felt filled with such incredible strength that she was certain she could fly around the world. At the very least she felt she could remain human sized for several days without having to shrink.

"Now how do you feel?" Jourdian asked smugly.

"Strong! Why, I have never been this strong! 'Tis magnificent this kissing!"

Strong? Jourdian repeated mentally. He'd rather hoped that his kiss would make her weak with desire.

Slowly, he slid his hands up the sides of her body, then moved them over her chest. Her breasts barely filled his palms, but their size didn't disappoint him in the least, for they were two handfuls of exquisite softness.

And the sudden stiffening of her rosy nipples assured him he was making sensual progress. Gliding his hands downward again, he moved her hips so that they fit into the cradle of his.

Splendor felt his loins pressing into her. Confused, fascinated, and curious, she rotated her hips over the thick, turgid feel of him. "You have become hard and hot, like sunbaked stone. And you grow in size. The way you have changed . . . 'Tis as if by magic."

"Magic?" He smiled. "No, sprite. It's your beauty that brings about such changes."

His statement made her forget to take her next breath.

"You say I'm beautiful," she whispered. "That can only mean that you have succumbed. You will now admit to your enchantment with me."

At her bold demand and imperious tone of voice Jourdian raised a brow. No one but the queen and a dream would dare to speak to him thus.

"I am waiting," Splendor said.

He decided to indulge her. She was, after all, only a fantasy. "Very well, I am enchanted, miss," he complied, smoothing his hands over the pale swells of her bottom. "Exceedingly so. But I hardly think that being enchanted with a dream will serve much purpose other than allowing me a small time of enjoyment before I wake up."

Splendor raised her head from his shoulder, her action spilling her thick hair over the side of his face. He thought her a dream? Sweet everlasting, how was she to convince him she was real?

Delicious solved the problem for her. The graceful swan descended from the sky, landed next to Jourdian's head and, with one quick motion bestowed a stinging peck upon His Grace's ear.

"Bloody hell!" Jourdian shouted.

"One cannot feel pain in a dream, can one?" Splendor asked, sliding her finger down the length of the great bird's neck. "This is Delicious. I'm sure he gave you a love bite when he nipped at your ear, but I shall nay know for certain until I have a word with him later."

Jourdian's ear stung viciously, and it came to him then that his head continued to throb, though only slightly now.

*He felt pain.*

This was not a dream! The naked girl was real, and he'd touched her breasts and derriere. He, the duke of Heathcourte, had lain in a field pawing a girl whose name he did not even know.

"Arise so that I may do the same," he commanded.

Splendor rose to her feet.

Jourdian began to stand as well, but stopped in mid-action, completely unable to take his eyes off her. He'd realized her hair was long, but he hadn't known those rich, red tresses fell to her ankles. Shining against her alabaster skin, they looked like russet flames ablaze upon freshly fallen snow. Never had he seen such glorious hair!

"You're angry now?" Splendor asked, disturbed by the way he'd ordered her to rise. "I don't understand how one can become so angry without just cause. Do you have cause that is unknown to me? If that is so, you will tell me the reasons for your anger so that I may soothe them, for I assure you nothing would give me more pleasure."

Her quicksilver chatter floating through his thoughts, Jourdian remained silent. But his gaze continued to roam down the length of her body. One pert breast was clearly visible, as was one pale, slender thigh.

Absurd though his situation was, he could not dismiss his desire.

"Will you nay answer me?" Splendor pressed.

He couldn't for the life of him remember what she'd asked him, and the loss of his wits promptly pricked his anger again. "It has never been my habit to converse with naked women while stretched out in the middle of a blasted meadow, for God's sake. Indeed, this is quite the most preposterous thing that has ever happened to me!"

He swiftly gained his feet. "Listen, and listen well," he said, his voice as low and threatening as distant thunder. "When I fell off my horse, my first thought was that I was dead. Then I decided I'd been knocked unconscious. I believed you to be a dream, and that is the only reason I touched you the way I—"

"But I am nay a dream. I am—"

"I am aware of that, and you will not interrupt me again!"

His harsh command flustered her tender feelings. No one had ever spoken to her thus. As princess royal of Pillywiggin, she was afforded the highest respect and courtesy from all her father's subjects.

She saw the first twinkles of her mist appear around her, but realized she could not dissolve right in front of the Trinity's eyes.

She wept instead.

Jourdian watched her tears fall down her cheeks and splash

to the ground. The droplets resembled tiny diamonds, and he knew a moment of guilt for yelling at her.

His remorse, however quickly it had come and gone, further piqued him. He'd never felt contrite over anything in his life, had no cause to feel a jot of guilt now, and could not comprehend why he did. "You will stop that sniveling and give me your name."

In an instant, her sorrow lifted. She felt calm again until noticing the Trinity's eyes had changed from the color of silver rain to the color of hard gray iron.

*Iron.* The metal had the power to divest a fairy of her powers, and every member of Faerie possessed a profound fear of the evil substance.

She stepped away.

"Stop backing away from me and give me your name!"

She stopped. And swallowed. And stared.

And for one fraction of a second she saw again the boy he'd once been. The boy so filled with yearning.

The boy who believed in wishing.

And then he was gone, replaced by the grim, no-nonsense man he'd become.

The Trinity needed joy, she reminded herself. He needed all his wishes granted.

"For the last time, who are you?" Jourdian flared.

"Who am I?" she answered absently, still concentrating on her memories of him.

"Very well, Miss No Name, perhaps you can tell me why you are not wearing clothing?"

"What?"

What the bloody hell was wrong with the girl? Jourdian wondered. She acted as though she was in some kind of daze. "Why aren't you wearing any clothes?"

Splendor looked down at herself, suddenly understanding how strange it was for him to see a woman without clothing. All the humans she'd ever seen wore some form of apparel, while the fairies of Pillywiggin did not possess a stitch.

"Clothing," she whispered, wondering why someone in Pillywiggin hadn't thought to suggest she don garments. "I . . . Oh, sweet, sweet everlasting!"

At her obvious distress, Jourdian knew a vague sense of alarm. Something was very wrong. He fought to remember what had happened before he'd discovered her lying on top of him, but all that came to mind was a burst of silver light and a flash of white. "What were you doing in this meadow?"

She almost answered that she'd been flying, but caught herself immediately. "I . . . Well, you see, I was . . ." Unable to think of an answer that would seem logical to a human, she bowed her head and twisted her hair around her slender fingers.

Her lack of a response deepened Jourdian's uneasiness. The girl didn't know her name, couldn't explain why she was naked, and had no idea what she'd been doing in the field. It occurred to him then that she might have had some sort of accident, one that had perhaps erased her memory.

But what could have happened to her?

He stiffened when a sudden suspicion came to him. He'd been riding through the meadow, he recalled, so angry and frustrated over his lack of a duchess that he'd not paid the slightest heed to his stallion's pace or path. In fact, he'd given the horse free rein. The burst of silver light and the flash of light . . . Obviously a bolt of lightning.

But there was not a cloud in the sky, and he couldn't remember hearing a bit of thunder. Hadn't felt a single raindrop either.

Just one sudden and inexplicable streak of lightning that had caused Magnus to shy.

Jourdian clenched his teeth. Dear God, he must have run straight into this girl! It was the only conclusion that would explain why he'd found the lass lying on top of him after his spill from Magnus's back. Why she was naked, he couldn't fathom, but he felt certain that he was to blame for her apparent head injury.

He would have to take her home with him.

Damn it all.

He stepped toward her. Unsure as to whether she would allow him to take her to his home, he clasped her elbow and gave her a stern look. "I am Jourdian Amberville, duke of Heathcourte. I am taking you to my residence, and I will not tolerate a word of argument. You will be seen by a physician who will evaluate your condition and prescribe proper treatment. Since I am accountable for whatever injuries you have sustained, you need not concern yourself with the physician's charges or any other expenditures related to your full recovery. Do you understand?"

Splendor understood only one thing—that he was taking her to his home. "Aye, Jourdian," she murmured through her smile. "I understand."

At her extreme breach of etiquette, he scowled. "I have not given you leave to address me thus. You will call me 'Your Grace.' "

"Aye, My Grace," she replied, too happy to notice his frown of displeasure.

"Not My Grace—*Your* Grace!"

"What? But 'tis what I—"

"No, it was not! You said—"

"I did not realize you had an uncivil streak."

"*Me?* I'm not the one gallivanting around in this field without clothes, and you're calling *me* uncivil?"

"I refer to your character. You've an element of rudeness in your makeup that distresses me."

Disbelief and fury blazed through him. Not daring to speak, he jerked off his coat, draped it over her shoulders, then lifted her off the ground. Her slight weight astonished him anew. She was tall, her eyes level with his mouth, and yet he felt as though he held a small child in his arms.

Not only did she suffer a head injury, but she was obviously starving, he realized. God only knew when she'd eaten last.

And yet her skin glowed. He imagined he could still see tiny stars shimmering upon her. How odd that someone as unwell as she possessed such radiance about her.

"You are taking me to your home now?" Splendor asked.

Still too angry to speak, he merely glared at her, and, holding her fragile body within the curve of his right arm, he used his left arm to pull himself into the saddle.

Just as he swung his leg over the horse's back, Splendor saw that his foot was firmly encased within the hollow of the stirrup.

The *iron* stirrup.

She shrieked and pulled her legs into her chest so that her body formed a tight ball. Shaking with fright, she then lowered her arms and opened her hands. From the cups of her palms sprays of tiny silver stars fell over the stirrups.

In the next moment, the stars faded and both stirrups dropped to the ground.

Jourdian tensed, sitting as still as a frozen pillar. Finally, he glanced down. Total mystification enveloped him as he stared at his dangling feet.

"My Grace?" Though Splendor knew his disbelief stemmed from the bit of magic she'd done, she could not bring herself to admit to her fairy powers. 'You were about to take me to your home, were you not?"

"The stirrups," he whispered, still staring at his dangling feet. "They . . . they dropped . . . just dropped off, and yet the stirrup leathers are perfectly intact. I don't understand how—"

He had no time to finish his statement. Spurred on by a touch more of Splendor's magic, Magnus took off at a full run toward the mansion, a sprinkling of silver stars glittering in his wake.

Every thought in Jourdian's mind vanished as he fought to stay mounted, a difficult task without benefit of stirrups. It was not until Magnus stopped before the manor that His Grace was able to relax.

What in God's name had gotten into the stallion? he wondered. Magnus, though high spirited, had never behaved in such a manner. And how odd that the horse had gone to the house rather than the barns. Ordinarily the steed headed straight for the water and sweet feed he knew he'd be given after a long ride.

Shaking his head, Jourdian tossed the reins to a servant, then noticed the parish vicar standing on the marble steps that led to the front door of the house. Jourdian guessed Reverend Shrewsbury had most likely come to collect a monetary contribution, a mission the man performed at least twice a month.

Wonderful, Jourdian thought dismally. After all that had happened today, a sanctimonious sermon from the long-winded man about the merits of generosity was just what he needed. "Reverend," he muttered in greeting.

The vicar's eyes widened, and his mouth dropped wide open. "Your Grace!"

The reverend's shock confounded Jourdian until he realized what caused it. Not a little embarrassment caused him to grit his teeth so hard that his jaw began to ache. Grass and dirt clung to his hair and clothes, indisputable evidence that he'd been rolling around on the ground. And the wisp of a girl snuggled against his chest gave proof that he had not been cavorting in the meadow alone.

He could only imagine what scandalous conclusions were assaulting Reverend Shrewsbury's puritanical senses.

"Who is that man, My Grace?" Splendor asked. "Why, he looks as though he just swallowed a bumblebee!"

Jourdian sighed through his clenched teeth. He managed, however, to find some semblance of control . . . until he glanced down at the wiggling lass in his arms.

His coat had slipped off her shoulders.

She was naked again.

In front of the vicar.

Bloody hell.

4

Jourdian fairly ripped the coat apart as he tried to cover the pale and perfect bosom that had captured Reverend Shrewsbury's unwavering attention. After closing the garment over the girl's breasts he thought he'd done reasonably well until he saw that the hem of the coat lay over her belly, thereby exposing the tops of her milky thighs. Not knowing what else to do, he slipped both arms beneath her, turned and lifted her toward his own chest, and prayed that all her sensual parts were now hidden.

But his well-intended action merely presented her small white bottom to the vicar's unflinching gaze. The man's eyes were so wide now that Jourdian decided they would soon pop out of their sockets and shoot across the courtyard.

His Grace remained speechless for a long moment, struggling to devise a logical explanation. But if indeed a shred of logic existed in Jourdian's mind, it was too deeply submerged beneath mental chaos to surface.

And such complete stupefaction was totally foreign to Jourdian Amberville. "The girl," he mumbled, his gaze darting from the top of her head to the vicar's face. "She— We— You— You misunderstand, Reverend. I saw a burst of silver light then a flash of white. I thought I was dead, but angels are not given to speaking falsehoods. Riding. I was riding through the meadow. The light and the flash of white . . . Lightning that I believe frightened my mount. He threw me, and I noticed stars. Hundreds of stars . . ."

His chagrin deepened when he heard himself stumbling over the most tangled explanation he'd ever given in all his two and thirty years. He, a man always in strict control of his thoughts, actions, and words, could not devise a simple interpretation of what had happened in the meadow!

"It's quite simple, really," he began again. "What happened . . . I saw stars and smelled wildflowers. November wildflowers, mind you, and they soon gave me to believe that I was either dead or caught fast in the throes of a dream-induced illusion. I don't imagine anyone would have thought differently, such was the deceiving sense of reality of the happenstance. It was only when her swan, Delicious, appeared out of nowhere and pecked my ear that I realized the dream was no dream."

He looked around, on the ground and up into the sky, but saw no swan. He did see a black and white spotted hog, however. The animal was grunting and snorting as it waddled through the chrysanthemums that edged the driveway.

Jourdian decided the animal belonged to one of his tenants. "I don't see the swan, Reverend, but I assure you it swooped out of the sky and nipped my ear."

The vicar remained silent.

But Jourdian noted that the man's look of shock was beginning to give way to an expression of censure. The reverend's erroneous speculations didn't sit well with him, and in the next moment the haughty and masterful side of the duke of Heathcourte emerged. "I regret that I am otherwise occupied, Reverend, and unable to receive you this afternoon," he declared in the ducal tone that brooked no dispute. "You will excuse me while I see to the girl's welfare."

Dismissing the vicar from sight and mind, Jourdian lifted his copper-haired charge over the saddle and carefully lowered her to her feet. Glad when the coat fell over her bare body, he then began to dismount himself, but forgot that his saddle was missing its stirrups.

For the second time in one afternoon, he fell off his horse and landed spread-eagled on the ground. A stream of choice profanities coursed through his mind, but not a one escaped. On the contrary, as if his fall from the saddle was in fact the newest and most fashionable means of dismounting among stylish members of the ton, he stood, patted Magnus's neck, and swaggered toward the door of the manor.

Adopting the same regal bearing, Splendor began to follow him, but stopped before the reverend. "I am here to give him joy," she informed the man. "Pleasure beyond anything he has ever known." With that, she continued toward the door and smiled brightly when Delicious—in the form of the black and white spotted hog—plodded up the steps beside her.

Reverend Shrewsbury stayed just long enough to watch the disheveled duke of Heathcourte, the nearly naked girl, and the snorting hog enter the mansion before scurrying toward his carriage. As he drove away, he deliberated intently on the scene he'd just witnessed and soon came to the delightful conclusion that keeping such a tale to himself would be a grave offense in the eyes of the Almighty. After all, withholding the truth was essentially the same as lying.

And as a man of God he was forbidden to indulge in the grave sin of deceit.

Absolutely forbidden.

Ulmstead had never seen the duke with as much as a hair out of place, but he uttered not a word about His Grace's soiled and disordered appearance. Nor did he comment on the girl who accompanied Lord Amberville into the manor, a girl whose bare legs were the exact shade of the white marble flooring in the entryway.

But the Heathcourte butler took extreme and immediate exception to the oinking hog who trailed behind the lass. The crude barnyard animal would surely upset Pharaoh's delicate sensibilities, which was something every Heathcourte servant struggled to prevent.

Leaving the door open, he bent and tried to swat the hairy

creature outside. "Go on with you now, you waddling ton of sausage! Out I say!"

The man's assault on her pet so horrified Splendor, that with a quick handful of stars she caused Delicious to vanish.

Jourdian turned around in time to see his butler swatting at thin air. The sight bewildered him, for Ulmstead was a man who would prefer being pitched into boiling oil than to allow his utterly proper demeanor to slip. "Ulmstead, might I ask what you are doing?"

Ulmstead dropped his arms to his sides and stared at the spot on the floor where the hog had stood. Nothing existed there now but a spot of mud.

And one tiny twinkle of light, which vanished as soon as he saw it.

The butler leaned against the wall for support and raised his hand to his shiny bald head. "Sausage," he whispered. "One second here, one second gone. Where—where did it go?"

"Sausage?" Jourdian asked.

"'Twould seem that your friend, Ulmstead, is under a bit of strain, My Grace," Splendor tried to explain, feeling bad that her magic had caused the poor man such distress. To make amends, she decided to do something kind for him.

Perhaps she would give him some hair. That would be a kind gesture. As soon as she was settled, she would gift the bald man with hair so thick that he would dance with joy over his dream come true.

Of course, she would first have to find someone deserving of Ulmstead's baldness, for she couldn't take away a human affliction without knowing where to transfer it.

Smiling, she reached out and patted Ulmstead's shoulder.

Her touch sent a stream of warmth through the butler's bony frame. He turned and looked into lavender eyes so incredibly beautiful that he forgot all about the disappearance of the hog. "Please forgive my lack of solicitude, miss," he said, returning her shining smile. "May I take your coat?"

"No!" Jourdian thundered. "She's wearing naught *but* the coat!"

"Oh!" The butler jerked his arms back to his sides. "Oh, yes! Oh, forgive me, miss! Oh, my!"

All the shouting brought the housekeeper, Mrs. Frawley, scurrying into the entryway. The rotund woman took one look at the deeply flustered butler, the unkempt duke, and the barely clad girl, and gasped so deeply that a button popped off the front of her stiffly starched gown.

The button skimmed across the marble floor and stopped in front of Splendor's foot. Without looking down, she opened her hand, wished the button into her palm, and then closed her fingers around it.

"Mrs. Frawley," Jourdian said to the astonished housekeeper, "you will calm yourself this instant and escort this young woman to the yellow chambers. Find clothing for her and see to it that she's fed. And as for you, Ulmstead, summon Dr. Osbourne." With that, he turned and started for the long and winding staircase.

Splendor watched him climb the steps. "I do not wish to go to the yellow chambers, My Grace. I prefer to go with you."

Jourdian stopped halfway up the staircase. Had he heard her correctly? "What—did—you—say?" he asked, emphasizing each of his words.

Staring up at him, Splendor knew in her heart that his terrible scowl could turn a hot sunbeam into an icicle. She couldn't fathom what she'd done to earn such a frown, and it was only with the greatest of effort that she managed not to escape into her misty sanctuary. "I said I prefer to go with you."

There it was again, Jourdian mused. Her air of authority. He'd noticed it in the meadow, and he was seeing it again now.

He didn't like it in the least. "While you remain in my house you will concern yourself with *my* preferences, not your own. And I prefer that you cooperate with my servants, who follow my instructions in a manner that you would do well to imitate."

Before Splendor could argue further, he vanished up the stairs. It seemed to her that he disappeared faster than Delicious had.

*Delicious.* Now where had she put that animal? Sweet everlasting, she'd been so frantic over protecting him from Ulmstead's swatting hands that she couldn't remember where she'd sent him!

"There now, my dear," Mrs. Frawley clucked upon seeing the lass's distressed expression. She moved toward the girl, her shock having given way to pity over the poor lass's lack of clothing and gaunt appearance. Obviously the copper-haired waif had met with some unfortunate occurrence, and the fact that the duke had brought her into his home indicated that his lordship felt an obligation to assist her.

Lord Amberville concerning himself with the needs of a female! Imagine that!

"Delicious," Splendor murmured when the plump woman arrived at her side.

"Delicious? Yes, yes, you'll have a delicious meal in just a bit. Mrs. Kearney is the Heathcourte cook, and a wonderful cook she is, too."

Splendor saw that the woman's warm brown eyes sparkled with kindness, and felt sure that the lady would help her. "Take me to My Grace at once. 'Tis supremely important that I speak to him."

Mrs. Frawley clasped her hands together in front of her ample bosom. The girl was certainly stubborn, she thought. After having received express orders from Lord Amberville to follow his instructions, she remained adamant over following her own wishes.

Oh, but wasn't this a delightful bit of excitement!

"You might see his lordship later, my dear."

"His lordship?"

"His Grace, the duke."

Splendor couldn't understand. "His Grace? But I thought he was My Grace. Is he Our Grace?"

"When speaking to him, he's *Your Grace*. When speaking *of* him, he's . . . Oh, we'll talk about that later. I am Mrs. Edna Frawley. Come with me, and we'll have you clothed, tucked into bed, and fed that delicious meal straightaway. Goodness me, poppet, you're nothing but skin and bones! Follow me, there's a pretty girl, now." Holding her hand over the gaping hole on the front of her gown, she started for the staircase.

Splendor followed, deciding the plump woman's thoughtfulness deserved to be repaid. She looked down at the button she still held in her palm.

And moments later, when Mrs. Frawley reached the upper landing of the staircase and noticed the neatly replaced button on the bodice of her dress, she fainted dead away.

⚬⚬⚬⚬⚬⚬

Dr. Osbourne examined both Mrs. Frawley and the girl Lord Amberville had brought to the manor house. "I can find nothing wrong with your housekeeper," he said when he joined His Grace in the duke's immaculate and impeccably furnished office. "She confessed to no physical malady, but only muttered something about a button. I allowed her to speak to her maids, and then gave her a sleeping draught. She should be fine by morning."

"A button," Jourdian repeated. Sitting behind his desk, he tapped a pencil upon a neat stack of business papers. "And the girl?"

"I failed to find a single bruise or other injury on her person, which leads me to believe that you did not run over her in the meadow."

Jourdian leaned over the massive desk. "I told you that after I fell off my horse, I discovered the girl on top of me. What do you think she did? Fall out of the sky?"

The doctor took off his spectacles and scratched the back of his neck. "I have no explanation. And she did not give me any further information about herself than she gave you, Your Grace. Her poor health is the sole thing of which I am certain. I don't believe I have ever seen such frailty in all my years as a physician."

"And yet she glows." Jourdian stood, walked around his desk, and stopped before the doctor. "Her skin. Didn't you notice?"

"Her skin glows?"

"Do you mean you didn't perceive an odd sort of shimmer about her?"

Dr. Osbourne's bushy white eyebrows knitted together. "I'm sorry, your lordship, but no, I didn't."

Jourdian couldn't understand it. The girl did shine, damn it all. He'd seen her twinkle with his own eyes!

"Perhaps the glow you describe was but the sun sparkling on her pale skin," Dr. Osbourne suggested. "Or perhaps your fall from your horse caused you to imagine her gleam. Your Grace, are you quite certain that you do not wish for me to examine you as well? I'd be happy to—"

"No. I told you I'm fine." Jourdian returned to his desk and sat back down. Maybe the doctor was right, he mused. Perhaps the girl's odd sparkle had been sunshine. "She'll recover, will she not?"

"It's difficult to be certain. I recommend that you continue to provide her with regular meals and a place to rest. Perhaps when her physical condition strengthens, her memory will improve and she will be able to tell you who she is, where she's from, and why she wasn't wearing any clothes."

Jourdian decided to have the girl fed ten huge meals a day and to forbid her to get out of bed. Surely such a course of treatment would hasten her recovery.

"You know, Your Grace," Dr. Osbourne said, "her attitude does give us somewhat of a hint about her. She's quite the sweetest person I believe I have ever met, but she . . . Well, her bearing is almost regal. And she snaps out commands as well as any noble person I have ever . . . Er . . . Of course, I do not mean to say that the members of the aristocracy are dictatorial—"

"Never mind that. What about the girl?"

Dr. Osbourne replaced his spectacles on the end of his nose. "I believe she is accustomed to delivering orders and seeing those orders followed. Her manner of behavior does not strike me as that of a commoner, your lordship."

Jourdian knew the physician had a point. But the girl did not seem to be of privileged birth. Her naïveté . . . her unsophisticated way of expressing herself . . .

Her artlessness was in direct contrast to the pretentiousness and insincerity so common among the ladies of the upper classes. And surely if a female member of some wellborn family were lost, he would have heard the news by now.

"I will take your observation into consideration," he said. "Good day, Doctor."

Dr. Osbourne started to leave the room. But before he passed over the threshold of the door, he turned to face the duke again. "I realize you are a busy man, Your Grace, but I believe it would be in the girl's best interest for you to keep company with her as often as possible. She asked for you several times during the course of the examination, and your visits with her might very well—"

"I am not her nursemaid."

"No. No, of course not. I only meant—"

"Moreover, I fail to see how my being with the girl could possibly have any effect on her recuperation."

"Perhaps it would have none at all, but—"

"Send me a bill for your charges. *Good day, Doctor.*"

Dr. Osbourne left instantly.

"Nursemaid, indeed," Jourdian muttered, then heard something clomping up the hall. His head aching from the aftereffects of his two falls from his horse, he looked up and saw a black and white blob shoot past the doorway. Ulmstead followed, bent over at the waist with his hands outstretched in an effort to catch the black and white blob.

"Ulmstead!"

Ulmstead came to an abrupt halt in front of the door. "Your Grace?" he panted.

"What was that thing that just tore down the corridor?"

"A hog."

"A hog?" Jourdian shouted.

Ulmstead wiped a few beads of sweat off his shiny head. "The animal entered the house with you and the girl. I tried to force him back outside, but he . . . Well, he vanished. Into thin air. A quarter of an hour ago, I discovered him asleep atop the billiard table, comfortable as you please as if he had every right to be there."

"What? How in God's name did a hog get on the billiard table?"

"I have yet to understand how the creature managed such a feat."

"Get rid of him."

"At once, Your Grace." Ulmstead turned and dashed down the hallway. "Here, piggy! Here, piggy, piggy, piggy!"

Jourdian rested his head in his hands, thinking about all the strange things that had happened during the course of the afternoon. Lightning out of nowhere, in a clear blue sky, and with no resulting thunder or rain. His stirrups falling from two thick, unsevered straps of leather. Magnus going straight to the manor rather than the barns. Heathcourte's calm and level-headed servants . . . Ulmstead swiping at thin air and muttering something about a vanishing sausage, and Mrs. Frawley losing her wits over a button. A hog sleeping on the billiard table and now scrambling around the house.

And everything had started with the girl. The naked girl who shone as if made of naught but minuscule stars. The second he'd set eyes on her, his whole life had turned completely upside down.

Who the bloody hell *was* she?

"Your Grace?"

He saw a young maid standing in the hallway. "What is it?"

Tessie jumped; the red birthmarks staining her face turned a deeper red. "Mrs. Fraw—Mrs. Frawley's in the bed."

Jourdian waited for the maid to continue, but she only stared at him with the same sort of fear she'd have exhibited if staring at a man-eating monster. "Unless you have something to tell me that I do not already know, you are dismissed."

Tessie wrung her hands in her apron, then lifted them to her face to cover the embarrassing birthmarks she knew were a flaming scarlet. "I do. I have. New information, Your Grace. I—Mrs. Frawley's in the bed, but before the doctor's medicine put her to sleep, she told me what to do. I did everything she told me, but the girl who was naked in the meadow with you won't stay in bed! She won't put on the gown I brought her, and she won't eat!"

His eyes mere slits across his face, Jourdian stalked out of the room, brushed past the maid, stormed down the corridor, and took the steps of the staircase three at a time. In short order he stood before the door of the yellow chambers.

He started to open it, but stopped himself. She was still naked, he remembered. He couldn't just burst in on her.

Unbidden, the memory of her bare beauty floated into his thoughts. He recalled the astonishing softness of her cloud-white skin, the unqualified perfection of her body.

He stared at the door as if he could see straight through it. It wasn't *his* fault she was still naked, he told himself. *He'd* sent orders for her to dress! She'd disobeyed him. Therefore, he owed her no common courtesy whatsoever. And that included knocking.

Twisting the knob, he opened the door. As soon as he set foot in the room, his sensual memories of her became reality.

She stood by the window, sunlight and her fire red hair pouring over her. Her huge violet eyes called to him as if with words, and even from where he stood he could smell her unique and captivating scent of wildflowers.

Recalling the pretty sparkle of her smile and the honey of her lips, he stepped toward her, powerless to resist her mysterious sweetness. "I've come," he began, his gaze traveling down her slender form, "to inform you . . . To tell you . . . That is to say . . ."

"My Grace?" Splendor said, scratching her arm and neck. "You've come to tell me something?"

Yes, he had, but he forgot what it was. Damn it all, what was it about the girl that so caused him to lose all train of thought, all sense of purpose?

Finally, he noticed the full tray of food on the table by the fireplace. "You did not eat, you are not wearing clothes, and you are not in bed."

"Aye, that is true."

"Why?" Jourdian blasted.

His shout startled her. Sweet everlasting, the man's shouting could put a roar of thunder to shame! "You should endeavor to control your shouting, My Grace. 'Tis evidence of your uncivil streak. And as I told you earlier, that rudeness in your makeup distresses me."

*She* was distressed? he thought. What did she think *he* was, ecstatic over the fact that he'd been forced to take her in? "Why haven't you eaten, why haven't you put on any clothes, and why aren't you in bed?"

"I asked the girl, Tessie, to bring me a soft bread and some fresh cream, but she brought me something with animal in it!" She pointed to the tray of food, scratched her shoulder, then dug at the side of her leg.

Jourdian glanced at the meat pie on the tray. "Animal?"

He didn't seem at all repulsed, Splendor noted. "Do—do *you* eat animal?"

"Well, of course I eat animal—*meat*."

Splendor shuddered. Her wonderful, soon-to-be husband actually ate animal! "I will endeavor to forgive you, but 'twill be difficult."

"Forgive me for eating meat?" Dear God, the girl was the strangest person he'd ever met! The sooner he was rid of her, the better.

"I only eat soft breads, cream, fruit, and a bit of honey."

So that was why she was so frail, Jourdian thought. With a diet like that, it was a wonder she wasn't dead.

"I do not care for those strange things over there," Splendor announced, pointing to a gleaming table across the room. "They look like flowers, but they are not."

Jourdian glanced at the arrangement of yellow silk daffodils.

"I have never encountered anything as horrible as those things," Splendor continued, scratching her elbow. "Have them removed from this room at once."

Jourdian went rigid. "I do not know who you are or who you *think* you are, but you will not order me about, do you understand? Nor will you reprimand me over my uncivil streak, as you so high-handedly put it. Moreover, you will eat what my staff brings to you, *animal* and all, you will stay in the bed, and you will wear clothing at all times."

"I cannot eat animal." Reaching around her back, she tried to scratch the area between her shoulder blades. "As for staying in bed and wearing clothing, I attempted both. Alas, I cannot wear the clothing. It irritates me." She indicated the garment.

Jourdian looked at the coarse cotton night rail draped over

the back of a chair, deciding it belonged to the maid with the red marks on her face. "You are irritated by the gown. Am I to understand that it isn't good enough for you?"

"I'm sure 'tis perfectly fine for others, but not for me."

He folded his arms across his chest. "I see. Then by all means allow me to clothe you in satin, milady. Silk, velvet, and lace."

"If you believe satin, silk, velvet, and lace will ease my distress, then I accept your offer to clothe me in such. You see, that gown and the bedding—whatever is on the bed . . . And your coat as well. Your coat, the gown, and the bedding . . . They've given me prickles that I cannot seem to soothe no matter what I do. And when one suffers from prickles, one can do naught but scratch. And I have ever so much more to do than scratch."

His mind still whirling with astonishment over her calm acceptance of his sarcastic offer of expensive clothing, a moment passed before Jourdian realized what she'd said to him. "Prickles?"

"Of a supremely unbearable sort, My Grace."

Jourdian watched as she lifted her hair and presented the whole of her bare body to his view. Alarm rolled through him.

Red welts marred her soft alabaster flesh, and blood oozed from the places she'd been scratching.

"The prickles began shortly after that doctor left," Splendor explained. She crossed to where he stood, turned, and gave him her back. "Would you scratch the middle of my back, please? I cannot reach the mass of prickles there."

"No, I won't scratch your back, and you will cease to scratch, as well. You've been digging at yourself so hard that you've made yourself bleed!"

Splendor spun to face him, still holding her thick mane of hair away from her body.

Renewed desire caught Jourdian fast, flickering through his loins like tongues of fire. He curled his hands into fists. Dammit, he had to get hold of himself! Not only was the girl covered with hives but *he* would not surrender to the demands of his baser urges. He was the duke of Heathcourte, for God's sake, not some lip-licking libertine!

And *she* was totally outrageous. Just the sort of woman he took great pains to avoid.

"Let go of your hair," he snarled. "It's the only thing you've got to cover yourself. Don't you know it's highly improper to allow a man to see your bare body?"

Splendor hadn't known. She'd thought humans wore clothing simply because they liked it. Immediately, she dropped her hair and felt it course down her frame. "If 'tis so improper for you to see my bare body, why do you stare at it so? You look at me as though I am a juicy mosquito, and you are a famished frog."

For a moment, Jourdian remained silent. How *dare* the chit question him! "I do not stare at your body, and I most assuredly do not appreciate being compared to a frog!"

Splendor could not find the energy to continue arguing with him. The itchy pain of her hives had taken a toll on her strength, and she knew that within seconds she was going to shrink to her original size.

She needed an infusion of vigor, and she needed it immediately. Reaching out, she grabbed Jourdian's hand, but the moment she took hold of his fingers she realized his touch was not enough.

There was only one thing to do.

Jourdian was taken completely off guard when she threw herself at him. Her breasts flattened against his chest and her hips pushed sweetly into his as she pulled his head down for a deep absorbing kiss that seemed to suck him dry.

Rigid, years-old domination over his own emotions evaporated like a drop of water on a scalding skillet. Breathing harshly, unevenly, and feeling his blood heat and pound through his veins, Jourdian took her into his arms and returned the kiss with a passion that nearly dropped him to his knees.

But his passion strengthened Splendor. Energy rushed through her, making her feel as vibrant as the colors of a sun-washed rainbow. In truth, she wanted the kiss to continue forever; wanted to be close to him, enveloped by his arms and his clean, woodsy scent. But since she was unsure of Jourdian's mood she knew she must end the encounter.

"I have had enough," she whispered.

His arms still around her, Jourdian lifted his head and stared down at her. "You've had enough?"

"For now," she replied softly. "But I'll need more soon. When that time comes, I shall either come to you or summon you."

He stepped away from her, his fury so great that he could not speak. She'd thrown herself at him, and he had responded to her like some randy adolescent about to receive his first taste of passion. That not bad enough, then she'd taunted him, gleefully informing him that she'd had enough!

Well, so had he.

"I want you out of my house as soon as possible," he seethed quietly. "Until that time comes you will stay in this room, following to the letter each and every instruction given to you. And I assure you, miss, that if I learn of even one circumstance of noncompliance on your part, you will sorely regret your disregard for my authority."

"I—"

"And you will never—I repeat—*never*—summon me!"

He turned then, and without a backward glance, he left, locking the door behind him.

Even after Jourdian had gone, his words lingered, hissing around Splendor's ears like angry wasps.

*I want you out of my house as soon as possible.*

Instantly, she sought the security of her mist. The glistening haze appeared around her, but before she had completely dissolved she saw a bright silver light glowing on the mantel above the fireplace. Crossing the room, she saw that the gleaming object was a candelabra.

But Splendor knew better. The beautiful candle holder was actually a fairy utilizing the powers of shape-shifting. She lifted it from the mantel and held it level with her chest. "All right, who are you?"

The candelabra became a diminutive Harmony. Sitting in

the cup of her sister's hand, she lit a fire on the end of her own finger and pressed the hot spark into Splendor's palm.

"Oh!" Splendor cried. "Harmony, why must you be so exasperating?"

"I like exasperation. I thrive on it. If I could, I'd eat it for breakfast."

Despite her annoyance, Splendor smiled. "What are you doing here?"

"Spying on you." Rising to her feet, Harmony held her arms out from her sides and walked the length of Splendor's thumb before jumping off and hovering in the air. "Why did you smash your mouth against the Trinity's the way you did?"

"His name is Jourdian Amberville, and he's the duke of Heathcourte. What I did to him is called kissing."

"What's a duke?"

Splendor thought for a moment. "I'm not quite certain, but when he told me who he was he spoke much the way Father does, which leads me to believe that a duke is of high and important social standing in the human world."

"Why did you do the kissing with him?"

"It gives me great strength." Splendor scratched at two long welts on her stomach, wishing with all her heart that she could make them go away.

But she couldn't, for although she had the power to heal others, she could not heal herself. Only another fairy could. "Harmony, you must help me with these prickles."

Harmony flew directly in front of Splendor's face and looked into her sister's left eye. "His mouth gives you strength?"

"Harmony, please make these prickles disappear."

Harmony glanced at her sister's irritated skin, then sailed across the room and alighted upon the head of a porcelain figurine that sat on the dresser. "Nay."

"Harmony, please!"

"What will you give me in return?" Harmony looked at her fingernails, blew on them, then rubbed them on her bare shoulder.

"You may have my collection of acorns. They're in my room in a big gold chest beneath my bed."

"Why would I want a lot of stupid nuts?"

"You can plant them, then watch them grow. 'Tis a good deed to help Mother Nature."

"That old crone? She and Old Man Winter are two of the meanest beings I know. Last year, Mother Nature tried to drown me with her tears. And Old Man Winter had everything I touched turn into ice. I nearly broke my tooth trying to eat a frozen apple."

"I might have done the same to you had you picked my blackberries before they were ripe and melted my snowflakes before they'd had the chance to put the weary summer to sleep."

At that, Harmony let out a peal of laughter. "My, that's rich! 'Tisn't in you to seek retribution of any kind, sister. You're too much of a ninny. You allowed the Trinity to treat you as though you were nothing more than an insect he could crush beneath his heel, did you not? He's but a human duke—whatever that is—and you're a fairy princess! *The princess royal of Pillywiggin!* If some human man ordered *me* to eat animal, I'd turn him into a slime-trailing slug!"

Splendor sighed. "I cannot very well turn my future husband into a slug, Harmony. Now are you going to cure me of these prickles, or aren't you?"

"On one condition. Give me leave to do that kissing with the Trinity."

Splendor felt a keen sense of discomfort over Harmony's request. A burning sensation, it began in the middle of her belly and spread all throughout her body. After a moment, she realized the feeling came from her unwillingness to share any part of Jourdian.

"He is mine," she said softly. "Every part of him belongs to me, including his kissing."

"I'm not trying to steal the man away from you, Splendor. I only want to taste a bit of his vigor. Why should you get all the strength? Surely he has enough for me, too!"

Still unwilling to share her long-sought-after possession, Splendor didn't reply.

"You look ugly with those prickles, sister," Harmony said slyly. "And they're bound to grow worse. Before long, you'll be one seething mass of bloody welts, and the Trinity will abhor the sight of you."

Splendor realized the truth of her sister's words. "Oh, very well. You may take a kiss from him, but it must be a short one, and you must never take another."

Smiling, Harmony threw a ball of stardust at her sister, and Splendor felt immediate relief when her itchy hives disappeared.

"So," Harmony said, "when is the wedding?"

Splendor turned away.

"I'll tell you when the wedding will be," Harmony continued. "*Never!* The Trinity isn't at all enchanted with you, Splendor. On the contrary, he wants you out of his house! And you, ninny that you are, stood right there and let him lock you in this stuffy room! Father was wrong. You're never going to become the Trinity's bride. The three months will pass, and you will have failed to conceive the child we need in Pillywiggin."

Splendor squelched her dismay and lifted her chin a bit. "I shall nay fail."

"You will. He is miserable with you here."

"He will soon be happier than he has ever been."

Harmony sneered. "We'll see."

Splendor didn't care for the wicked gleam in her sister's eyes, nor did she like the sly tone in her voice. Harmony was up to no good. "Harmony, you are devising mischief. You must leave this house now and promise never to come back. If you do not—"

She stopped speaking when the doorknob rattled.

In an instant, Harmony disappeared.

"It's me, Tessie, miss," the maid said as she opened the door and walked into the room.

Splendor watched how Tessie tried to conceal the crimson marks on her face by keeping her head bent low. "The stains on your face are a great source of embarrassment to you, aren't they, Tessie?" she asked gently.

"Aye, miss, they are," Tessie squeaked.

Umm, Splendor mused. Now she had to find *two* people deserving of afflictions—one for Ulmstead's baldness and one for Tessie's facial stains. "Perhaps they will fade in time," she offered tenderly.

Touching her birthmarks, Tessie shook her head, then held out a white bottle of skin lotion. "His Grace wanted me to bring this to you."

Splendor took the flask, opened it, and smelled its contents. The luscious aroma of sweet apricots permeated her senses.

"Lord Amberville says you need it for what ails you," Tessie added.

At the moment, hunger ailed her, Splendor mused. Her stomach growling and her mouth watering, she lifted the bottle to her lips and swallowed the fruity concoction.

Tessie's mouth dropped wide open. "You . . . Miss . . . You *drank* it!"

Splendor licked a few drops of the elixir off her bottom lip. "Aye, that is what I did, and 'twas ambrosial."

Tessie stared. No wonder the duke had decided to keep the long-haired girl locked up in the room. The miss was blooming dotty!

As fast as she could move, Tessie backed into the hall.

"Tessie, wait! I must speak with My Grace!" Splendor floated to the door just as the maid closed it. She reached for the knob, but snatched her hand away when she heard a clicking sound in the lock. The lock itself was of brass, as was the doorknob.

But the key Tessie used was iron.

Splendor drew back instantly. Standing in the middle of the room, she lifted the empty white bottle to her chest. As she caressed its neck with her thumb, a realization began to dawn on her.

Quickly, she looked down at the bottle. Was it possible that Jourdian had sent her the savory apricot drink because he regretted his harsh treatment of her? She'd told him herself that she only ate bread, cream, and fruit, and then, a short time later, Tessie had brought the drink.

He *did* care! Why, with a bit of luck it was quite possible that she would be Jourdian's bride by nightfall!

Filled with happiness and the irrepressible need to be with her betrothed, she approached the door again.

But she hesitated before reaching it. A shiver of fear passed through her as she sensed the fact that the iron key remained in the lock.

Her desire to find Jourdian deepening by the second, Splendor did what any fairy would do when locked inside a room she no longer wished to be in.

She walked through the wall.

# 5

Splendor wandered through the mansion aimlessly. One staircase led to another maze of corridors, and each corridor led to another set of luxurious rooms. Jourdian was in none of them. Indeed, she didn't come upon a single person during her search and wondered if she was the only being in the gigantic house.

Frustrated and tired after an hour of roaming, she shrank wearily into her original size and reclined inside a silver dish that sat upon the top of a lamp table in the hall, despairing of ever finding Jourdian. But a noise in a nearby room renewed her hope.

She flew into the room and saw a grand array of musical instruments in the midst of which stood a donkey. "Delicious!" she cried, floating toward him. "Where have you been?"

Delicious brayed and swished his tail.

Perching on his head, Splendor glanced at the musical instruments. How she loved music. And poetry, artwork, tapestries, and all other forms of creativity. She often wondered if humans were aware of how powerful a force Faerie truly was in relation to creativity. Did they know that when the Muse was upon them to create . . . when they felt an irresistible inspiration to write, compose, paint, sculpt, or weave, that it was because a fairy was present, urging them to produce something beautiful for the world?

'Twas the truth, whether humans knew it or not.

"Let us hear a bit of music right now, Delicious, shall we, sweetling?"

She lifted her hands and watched her magic fill the room. Silver sparkles surrounding them, the instruments of Splendor's choice began to play. Flutes and violins. Two harps and a myriad of bells.

And Splendor, with her arms held out before her, conducted the beautiful symphony. Louder and stronger she had the melody play . . .

Until a scream cut short her pleasure. Her silvery magic faded instantly, and the instruments clattered to the marble floor.

Splendor turned around and saw a terrified girl standing in the hallway.

Shaking violently, the girl fled.

"Oh, Delicious, do you think she saw me?" Splendor asked. "Or . . . Sweet everlasting, 'twas the magical music that so frightened her!"

Swiftly, she regained human size and swept toward the door. But when she reached the hallway, the girl was nowhere to be seen.

Her hair brushed over the carpet as she sailed down the corridor, at the end of which was yet another flight of stairs, which led her to yet another endless hall of rooms. Determined to find the frightened girl and somehow soothe her terror, she flew faster.

A door opened as she reached the middle of the hallway. Sure the girl was inside, Splendor soared into the room. "Girl?" she called. "Are you here? I didn't mean to frighten you. Girl?" Drifting back down to the floor, she didn't see the lass anywhere, but she did notice how large and sumptuous the quarters were.

Against the wall in front of her sat a mammoth bed covered in midnight blue. Generous swathes of the same commanding color fell gracefully from the four elaborately carved posts of the canopy.

The bed rested upon a high dais, making it seem all the more enormous. Splendor felt sure that if it were her bed, she would have to fly in order to get into it.

The rest of the furniture was equally imposing, all large and all of thick, heavy wood. The very atmosphere felt intimidating.

A powerful being dwelt here. Splendor was sure of it.

"What are you doing in here?" a deep voice demanded.

Splendor gasped with surprise, then whirled around and saw Jourdian, his hand still wrapped around the doorknob. "My Grace! Of course, this room can belong to no one else but you!" Smiling with all the joy she felt at seeing him, she glided to where he stood and cupped his cheeks with her hands. "I searched everywhere for you and became lost. I can nay remember being so lost or alone. I wasn't afraid, but I was terribly frustrated. I've found you now, though, haven't I?"

There it was again, he thought. That odd glow about her. And he knew for certain that it was not caused by sunshine. Dusk had begun to fall.

"You shimmer," he whispered, more to himself than to her.

"Only when I'm happy." She caressed the mole on his cheek with the tip of her thumb. " 'Tis so nice, this dot on your face. Like the black center in some kinds of white and yellow daisies. I hope you never wish it away."

"Daisies?"

"I must find the girl. She was so scared, and 'tis nay my practice to frighten anyone."

Jourdian saw tears gather in her eyes. He frowned. God, how her emotions changed. Only seconds ago, she was bubbling over with happiness, and now she was weeping! How was it possible for a person to slip from one emotion into another so quickly?

"I know those who do enjoy sowing fear," Splendor continued, "but I am nay one of them. 'Tis a much better thing to spread joy than to—"

"Cease this chatter." Reaching up, Jourdian pulled her hands off his face.

"My Grace—"

He slammed the door, then noticed her hives were gone. She must have used the lotion he'd had the maid take to her. Well at least she'd followed *one* of his orders, he mused irritably. "I told you to stay in your room."

She lifted her chin and one auburn eyebrow. " 'Twas nay my desire to stay in it."

Damn the chit! Did she think herself a member of royalty? "I know you understand English because that is what you speak. So why is it that you cannot comprehend the simple fact that your desires matter naught to me? I have told you to stay in the room I provided you, and I have told you to wear the clothing brought to you. Yet, here you are in my room, naked as the day you were born."

Stiff with anger, Jourdian marched to his closet, jerked the door open, and rummaged through his clothing. As he rifled through the garments, a pair of heavy black riding boots fell off a high shelf. One banged down on his head, and the other smacked his shoulder.

"Bloody hell!" he shouted, rubbing his head. Looking down at the floor of the closet, he saw the boots and couldn't understand how they'd fallen.

"My Grace, is something amiss?" Splendor approached the closet, noted Jourdian's expression of confusion and pain, and then saw a smattering of silver twinkles near the floor.

*Harmony.*

"The boots fell on me," Jourdian answered gruffly.

Quickly, Splendor surveyed the closet and the rest of the room. She didn't see Harmony anywhere, but remained certain her naughty sister had been in the closet.

"Are you hurt?" she asked Jourdian. Reaching up, she touched her fingers to the spot on his head she'd seen him rub. "I am ever so sorry such a mishap befell you, My Grace."

Her touch and the gentle compassion in her voice alleviated all traces of his pain. Indeed, he felt a profound sense of well-being. "I—I'm fine now." Turning back to the clothing in the closet, he retrieved an elegant dressing robe.

"What do you want me to do with this?" Splendor asked when he handed it to her.

Was she deliberately needling him? he wondered. The woman was bare naked, for God's sake, and she needed him to tell her what she was to do with the robe?

His irritation returned in a flash. "Why don't you just hold it for a while? The dark purple looks smashing in your hands.

Or perhaps you might throw it on the floor and walk on it. It will certainly feel soft beneath your feet."

The fact that he wanted her to feel softness beneath her feet made Splendor smile with deep pleasure. Holding the lustrous fabric before her, she began to spread it upon the floor.

Realizing she'd taken his sarcasm to heart and was about to walk on the robe, Jourdian yanked it out of her hands and held it out so that she easily could slip into it. "Put it on."

Splendor slid her arms into the sleeves, then watched as Jourdian pulled the front together and tied the sash. "Oh, 'tis glorious!" she said, rubbing her hands over the exquisite material. "What is it, My Grace?"

He'd have to have been blind not to notice how the dark purple satin complemented her lavender eyes and wondrous russet hair. It was as if the color had been created especially for her.

"Satin," he murmured.

"Satin? And what is this?" She pointed to the upper left side of the garment, where gold and silver threads were embroidered into an elaborate design.

"My crest," he answered softly.

She looked up and saw him watching her intently. "My Grace, you're staring at me like a famished frog again, and there is nay reason for you to do so now that my body is covered by this piece of satin."

His anger ignited again. At her, and at himself for gaping at her as if she were the only pretty girl he'd ever set eyes on.

She was right. He truly was acting like a famished frog, absurd though the comparison was.

"You left your rooms," he said again, stalking out of the closet. "What the bloody hell do I have to do to get through to you?"

Her smile melted into a soft frown. He was as bitter as a green persimmon.

But he hadn't always been so harsh . . .

The very first time she'd ever seen him was the afternoon she'd discovered him crying in the rose garden. He'd been but a lad then, barely taller than the rosebushes. She hadn't known the reason for his tears, nor had she understood why his grief had lasted so long, but the memory of his deep pain had stayed with her all through the years.

After that, she'd looked for him frequently, sometimes finding him waving good-bye to a man and a woman she believed to be his parents. After their coach was out of sight, he'd hang his head and kick at stones until he could find no more to kick.

She brought to mind the many times she'd watched him stare into the distance with a look of longing on his face—as if waiting for something or someone to return to him, and she pondered all the occasions she'd watched him try to learn games from another boy. He hadn't learned very well, she recalled. Nor had he possessed the same appreciation for nature as the other boy had. That lad had found something remarkable about every leaf, stone, and flower he'd happened upon.

But not Jourdian.

Splendor sighed then, finally remembering all the nights she'd seen Jourdian's silent wishes soar into the dark sky to be cuddled by the wishing stars.

Oh, how she'd guarded those stars! She'd never let a one die, but had taken special care of them so that the wishes they contained could one day come true.

"So many wishes." Slowly, she approached Jourdian, stopping when her breasts met his chest. "You've such sadness inside you, My Grace," she whispered, reaching out to lay her hand on his upper arm. " 'Tis dark and cold and almost as old as you, this sorrow, running through you like a deep tunnel in the ground. I cannot begin to imagine such profound woe."

Her perception astonished him, and for one short moment he wondered what else she'd sensed about him.

But his curiosity quickly vanished. Lord knew Emil analyzed his emotions often enough. He certainly didn't need yet another person to perform the same psychological dissection, especially this girl, who didn't know him well enough to even presume she could discern his feelings!

"Will you tell me the reasons for your woe?" Splendor asked.

He took hold of her hand, having every intention of snatching it away. But just as his fingers closed around hers, something in her extraordinary eyes stilled his action.

Something . . . a glimmer . . . not unlike the glow radiating from her skin . . .

A tender shine that sought and found a crack in his stony resolve to withstand the power of her charms. Dear God, she was a gorgeous vision to behold. Almost too beautiful to believe.

And her sweetness seemed an almost tangible thing, as if he could reach out and hold it in his hand like a measure of fine sugar.

"Sprite," he murmured. "Who are you?" Still caught fast by the soothing incandescence of her violet eyes and the aura of gentleness that surrounded her, he slid his hand through her softer-than-silk hair.

"I am called Splendor."

He knew no other name in the world would suit her. "So you remember your name now. Is there anything else you can tell me?"

She moved her hand up to the back of his neck, determined not to let this opportunity pass to tell him the things she'd wanted to tell him for so long. "I desire to give you joy, to make you laugh. I wish to be your company when you are lonely, My Grace, listening when you feel the need to speak. And if you needed silence, I would sit by your side and watch your eyes, for in them I would read your every thought. My own eyes would answer, and you would know that my thoughts were joined with yours. I would take care of you."

He stood motionless, not daring to breathe. Her gentle words sounded so strange to him, almost as if she'd spoken them in a foreign language.

But why wouldn't they?

He'd never heard anyone say them before.

"And I would grant all your wishes," Splendor vowed softly. " 'Twould make my heart sing to see you happy. And so, while I am with you I shall give you whatever you desire."

Her promise wrapped around him, and he felt as though he were being embraced by comforting arms that would hold him for as long as he cared to be held.

Being held. Comforted.

Already she had granted one of his oldest wishes.

Compelled by her goodness, which became more apparent to him with each passing second, he leaned toward her, his gaze centered on her mouth. Just as his lips touched hers he felt serenity wash through him, like a gentle wave lapping over dry sand on a hot seashore.

She softened in his arms, and small sounds came from her throat, and although his eyes were closed, he could see the light of her shimmer. And when she curled her arms around his back and squeezed him, he moaned with hunger for her, with a need so fierce that it took control of his every thought and action.

He crushed her to him, his mouth, body, even his soul devouring her warmth and tenderness the way night swallows up day. Deeper, more fierce his kiss became, and from somewhere inside him he heard his inbred awareness of proper conduct screaming for him to stop.

But he could not take heed.

Until someone began banging on the door.

"Your Grace!" Ulmstead shouted.

Fast as a slap across the face, the spell broke. Jourdian pulled back abruptly, then opened his eyes and stared at Splendor.

"Please," she whispered, "don't stop. Your kissing makes me feel so strong. 'Tis a strength I never knew before you shared it with me, and now that I have had a taste of it I don't think I can ever live without it."

God help him, he felt like pulling her into his arms and kissing her again.

He tightened his hands into fists. He'd found her only four or five hours before, and thrice he'd surrendered to . . . to . . .

To whatever irresistible thing it was she had about her. And *this* time he'd known full well she was not a dream. *This* time she had not thrown herself into his arms.

*This* time had been of his own doing.

"Your Grace!" Ulmstead yelled again.

Jourdian unclenched his right fist and pulled the door open. There in the corridor stood the butler, every bone in his skinny body shaking.

"Forgive me for disturbing you, Lord Amberville, but—"

"She's gone, milord!" Tessie screamed as she arrived, and ran straight into Ulmstead. "The girl—" She broke off when she saw the copper-haired girl at the duke's side. "I locked the door, Your Grace. Truly I did. But she . . . And the lotion! She *drank* it!"

Jourdian snapped his head toward Splendor so quickly that a sharp pain ripped through his neck. "You *drank* the lotion?"

"Your Grace," Ulmstead said, his concave chest heaving, "I am your butler. Therefore, the maids are not my concern. However, since Mrs. Frawley is indisposed, I feel I must inform you that one of the maids has—"

"You *drank* the lotion?" Jourdian asked Splendor again.

"If lotion is what the fruit elixir you sent to me is called, then, aye, I drank it. 'Twas succulent."

"Are you bereft of all sense? You don't drink it, for God's sake, you rub it into your skin!"

Splendor ran her fingers lightly down the length of her arm. "My skin?"

"The maid has left in near hysteria," Ulmstead continued as if he'd never been interrupted. "I tried my best to understand what happened to her, but all she could tell me was that she'd seen musical instruments playing of their own accord. I was about to ask her more when a donkey ran through the foyer!"

"A donkey?" Jourdian asked, so bewildered he couldn't think straight.

"A donkey sir! The beast clomped through the foyer, and then—"

"What happened to the hog?" Jourdian queried.

"I never caught the hog, your lordship," Ulmstead admitted, rubbing his bald head. "I couldn't catch the donkey either!"

"I swear on the soul of my dearly departed mum that I *did* lock the door to her room!" Tessie wailed, one hand balling up the fabric of her apron and the other clasped over the crimson birthmarks on her cheek. "I don't know how she got out!"

"She did lock the door, My Grace," Splendor said, realizing that her escape from the room might cause trouble for Tessie.

"I heard her turn the key in the door. 'Twas an *iron* key, and I will tell you now that I've a profound aversion to anything fashioned of iron. Therefore, you must rid this house of all iron without delay. I would have performed the task myself, but I've had nay the time—"

"How did you get out of the room?" Tessie asked. "How—"

A loud meow cut the maid short.

In the next moment, Pharaoh padded into the room, his long, snakelike tail swishing.

"A cat," Splendor whispered, dread skating down her spine. "And—and he says he's hungry! Sweet everlasting, he's going to eat me!"

Jourdian hadn't thought it possible for her to be any paler than she already was. But she'd become so white now that a lily would have looked dirty beside her. "For God's sake, a cat can't eat you!" Scowling, he scooped Pharaoh off the floor, then noticed yet a third person standing in the hallway near the door.

"I say, what on earth is happening here?" Emil asked, peering over Ulmstead's shiny head. "Oh!" he exclaimed upon seeing the girl standing beside Jourdian. "And who might you be, pretty miss?"

"She drank skin lotion, Mr. Tate!" Tessie yelled.

"Did you see a donkey when you came in, Mr. Tate?" Ulmstead asked. "Or a hog?"

"I found her in a meadow," Jourdian said wearily, wondering if his household would ever be calm again. "Lightning scared Magnus, and I fell—"

"Lightning?" Emil asked. "There was no lightning, Jourdian. I was outside at the Thirlway picnic all afternoon, and I assure you there was no—"

"There was lightning, Emil. And after my fall from Magnus, I found Splendor."

Emil frowned. "You found splendor in the meadow?" he asked, one eyebrow raised. "What sort of splendor?"

"She's Splendor." Using Pharaoh as a pointing stick, Jourdian gestured toward Splendor.

The cat's front paws brushed her shoulder just as he opened

his fang-filled mouth and let out a gruesome hiss. Terror nearly overwhelming her, Splendor raced out of the room.

Emil caught her and lifted her from the floor. "Here now, stop your struggling. I'll fight that heinous hellcat to the death before I let him eat you. I am Emil Tate, Jourdian's cousin. Please call me Emil."

Splendor stilled in his arms and blinked up at him. His hair was the color of warm sand, not quite gold, not quite brown, and his twinkling eyes were nearly the same color, only a bit darker. He had a beautiful, happy smile, and it created deep dimples on each of his cleanly shaven cheeks.

She knew him. He was the same boy Jourdian used to play with so many years before.

"My, but you're a bit of a thing, aren't you?" Emil said, amazed over her slight weight. He examined her face, her lavender eyes capturing his full attention until he happened to glance at her lips.

They were red, a bit swollen, and Emil recognized a recently kissed mouth when he saw one. It would seem that Jourdian had found a tad of splendor in his bedroom as well as in the meadow, he mused, his lips twitching.

"She's barely clothed, Jourdian," he said, completely unable to keep from smiling. "And what clothing she *is* wearing, I believe belongs to *you.*"

Jourdian saw that the front of the robe Splendor was wearing had parted into a low V. The upper swells of her pearly breasts were visible to anyone who cared to look at them.

And Emil, apparently, cared.

Irritation chewed through him like a voracious caterpillar. He set Pharoah back on the floor, moved toward his cousin, and took Splendor into his own arms.

Security stole over her until she noticed the cat looking up at her with hungry eyes. Her renewed horror exhausted the last bit of her energy.

Desperately, she wrapped her arms around Jourdian's neck, and kissed him full on the mouth.

Tessie gasped.

Ulmstead groped for the door frame.

But Emil merely watched.

And deliberated.

There was a donkey loose inside the mansion. And a pig.

Jourdian—a man well known for his equestrian skills—had seen nonexistent lightning, had fallen from his mount, and found a girl called Splendor.

A girl who drank skin lotion. She was practically naked, in His Grace's bedchambers, giving Jourdian a searing kiss that could have melted a glacier.

Had it been only this afternoon when he'd admonished Jourdian over his stale and overly conservative lifestyle? Emil wondered. In that short space of time, the mausoleum called Heathcourte Manor had become Pandemonium Park.

And Emil couldn't help but believe that it had been the beautiful girl called Splendor who had somehow brought the gloomy house to vibrant life.

❦

"She's leaving as soon as I have finished making the arrangements," Jourdian announced. He signed his name to the letter he'd just finished writing at the small desk in the library, then took a large swallow of straight scotch.

Seated in a large, overstuffed white velvet chair, Emil watched his cousin. "This afternoon you drank because you didn't have a woman in your life, and now you're drinking because you do have one."

"One who will shortly be gone."

"You'll throw Splendor out then? Just like that? She has no money, no clothing, and no recollection of who she is or where she's from. You are a beast of the worst sort!"

"I am not throwing her out, Emil. I will pay Reverend Shrewsbury and his wife to take her in until she regains her health." Without looking up, Jourdian folded the letter and sealed it with his crest.

"But—but you had silk sheets put on her bed, Jourdian! You ordered freshly baked bread, ripe fruit, and a pitcher of cream brought to her room! And you sent word to the seamstress in Mallencroft to deliver gowns of soft fabrics—"

"What else could I do, damn it all!" Letter in hand, Jourdian stormed across the room, stopping before one of the wall-to-wall, ceiling-high bookcases. "Anything rough irritates her skin, and I'll not have her clawing at herself or drinking skin lotion again! She won't touch animal—I mean *meat*, and if she doesn't eat something, she will be blown away by the next breeze that hits her!"

"Then why don't you just sit back and let the wind carry the little waif away?" Emil demanded, bolting out of his chair and marching into the middle of the room. "She'd be out of your life then, wouldn't she? You wouldn't have to concern yourself with her anymore, would you?"

"I have no intention of concerning myself with her. That is what I will hire Reverend and Mrs. Shrewsbury to do. The silk sheets, and bread, fruit, and cream meals are to sustain her until she moves in with the vicar and his wife. And I will have the gowns delivered to the Shrewsburys'." Jourdian handed the letter to Emil. "Be so good as to deliver this note to the vicar on your way home, will you? And tell him that I await his answer straightaway, preferably in the morning."

"I think you're making a mistake by sending Splendor—"

"Only this morning you tried to convince me to renew my relationship with Marianna, and now you're trying to match me up with a woman—"

"You kissed her."

The instant the words were out of Emil's mouth, Splendor's image burst into Jourdian's mind, so real he imagined he could see her shimmer and smell her soothing scent of wildflowers.

He struggled to erase the memories from his thoughts. Instead, he remembered his unbridled need for her and the absolutely feral way he'd kissed her.

"The famished frog," he murmured. "And the juicy mosquito."

"Mosquito? Jourdian, I think you've had enough to drink. You're beginning to sound sloshed."

Thrusting his fingers through his hair, Jourdian retrieved the bottle of scotch and sat down in the chair Emil had vacated. "She compared me to a starving frog and herself to a juicy mosquito."

"And the comparison so excited you that you kissed her."

Not bothering with a glass, Jourdian raised the bottle to his mouth and drank deeply. "And silver rain." He closed his eyes and rested his head on the back of his chair. "She said my eyes were like silver rain and the iridescent dust on the wings of certain butterflies and moths. A peculiar description, wouldn't you say?"

Emil wondered if indulging Jourdian would keep him talking. "Quite the oddest I've ever heard."

"Of course I've never seen the color of wing dust," Jourdian said, his words becoming a bit slurred. "Butterflies were your forte, not mine."

"You helped me chase one once. It was the day we raced through those wildflowers and—"

"And I found the small diamonds."

"Yes. Jourdian Amberville, finder of diamonds in the flowers and beautiful women in the meadows. She's gorgeous, cousin. Flawless skin, amazing eyes . . . And her hair! I've never known a woman with such wonderful hair."

"You're taken with her."

Emil detected a slight note of sourness in Jourdian's voice, and he stifled a smile. "I don't imagine there's a man in existence who would be immune to her charms. You have everything, don't you, Jourdian? A respected title, more money than you could spend in ten lifetimes, and now you have in your keeping a woman whom men would fight over."

"Careful, Emil. Your envy is showing."

"Since when have I tried to conceal it?"

"Never."

"She *is* beautiful, cousin. Admit it."

Jourdian admitted nothing; he drank more scotch instead. "Imagine believing a mere house cat could eat you. Her terror was genuine."

"As is mine when I'm near that cat. Why did you kiss her, Jourdian?"

Jourdian didn't answer. The truth was that he still didn't

know why he'd kissed Splendor. He simply hadn't been able to resist.

And now he couldn't forget.

Every second of his encounter with her came back to him now. He remembered sliding his hand through the tumble of red curls that fell down her back. Satin had slipped through his fingers then, warm, soft, and scented by nature.

He thought of her shimmer of happiness, the tender glow in her eyes, and her goodness, that sheer sweetness she wore the way other women wore perfume.

And he remembered her promises to him.

*I wish to make you laugh.*

"She can't make me laugh, Emil," Jourdian slurred. "Indeed, I don't find her strangeness at all amusing. She said she would try to forgive me for eating meat! What sort of tosh is that? She drinks skin lotion, too, and what of her flighty emotions? Happy, then instantly sad. Sad, then immediately happy. She goes from mood to mood in much the same way fingers flit from key to key on a piano."

*I desire to give you joy.*

Jourdian released a long, slow breath. "And what joy did she plan to give me, I ask you?" he mumbled. "She's done naught but infuriate me since I found her in the meadow. Joy. She thinks to be the woman who gives me joy? Ha! If indeed such a woman exists, she's from another world, for I've certainly never found her in this one."

Emil looked down at the letter in his hand. "You're sending Splendor away because you care about her, aren't you? Somehow, some way, she's managed to slip past your guard, and she's done it in an astonishingly short amount of time. The problem is that you don't *want* to care about her. So your solution is to send her away so you can forget about her."

Jourdian didn't answer, didn't open his eyes, didn't move a muscle.

Without a sound, Emil crossed to the fireplace and tossed the missive into the blazes.

"Good night, Jourdian."

"Good night. Don't forget the letter."

Emil left.

And behind Jourdian's chair, in the fireplace, fine ivory paper turned to ashes.

**D**ressed in the purple satin robe, Splendor sat at one end of the long dining-room table and watched Jourdian, who sat at the other end. He was so far away. And what with the two tall candelabra and the huge arrangement of flowers in the middle of the table, she could barely see him.

"You're certain you feel well?" Jourdian asked. "Dr. Osbourne ordered bed rest for you, and you did not rest at all yesterday, but only roamed about my house."

"I feel supremely wonderful, My Grace, and 'twas ever so kind of you to invite me to breakfast with you on this glorious morning."

A guilty feeling came over Jourdian; he couldn't meet her gaze. Kindness had nothing to do with his inviting her to eat with him this morning. He only wanted her downstairs and ready to leave when Reverend Shrewsbury arrived to collect her.

He sincerely hoped that she did not cause a scene when the time came for her to leave. She would stay with the Shrewsburys, and that was that.

Nodding to the servant who waited to attend him, he leaned back in his chair, then watched as the domestic filled his plate with his Thursday morning fare of fluffy eggs, buttered scones, and a steaming slice of kidney pie.

Splendor shuddered when she realized that the servant had

served Jourdian something with animal in it. Sweet everlasting, she hoped the man did not serve her the same!

"You did not have to make your bed, Splendor," Jourdian said for lack of anything better to say. "That's what the maids are for."

"Make my bed?"

"That little maid—Tessie, I think her name is. She told Mrs. Frawley that when she went to make up your bed, she found it already made."

"I didn't make my bed, My Grace, and there was nay a need for Tessie to do it, either. I didn't sleep in it." She recalled that she'd slept the entire night atop the soft and airy canopy that stretched from bedpost to bedpost. Aside from the fact that shrinking to Pillywiggin size helped conserve her energy, she'd also thought the canopy an ideal place to hide from Jourdian's cat.

"You didn't sleep in your bed?" Jourdian asked. "Where did you sleep?"

"On top of the bed."

"On the canopy?"

"I was afraid your cat would get into the room."

"And the canopy didn't fall?"

"My Grace, I weigh but little."

"But . . ." How could she have slept on the canopy? True, she didn't weigh much, but surely she was too heavy to sleep atop a length of suspended satin.

But perhaps the canopy was securely fastened to the posts, he decided. "How did you get up there?"

"I flew."

He frowned and stared and leaned over his plate. "You flew?"

"What? Umm . . . Did I say I flew? Well, what I meant to say, you see, is that I—I climbed one of the posts. I am an excellent climber, My Grace."

He could hardly believe what he was hearing, but since no other logical explanation existed that he could think of, he accepted the one she gave him. "A canopy is no place to sleep. Indeed, I have never heard of a stranger thing."

She strained her neck upward, trying to see him better over

the flowers and candelabra. " 'Twas quite comfortable, the canopy, and I see nothing strange about seeking a comfortable sleeping place. On the contrary, 'twould be strange for one to sleep in a disagreeable place when a pleasing one is within reach."

He realized he was getting nowhere with the argument, and decided to end it. After all, she would be gone shortly, and he would never have to participate in such a bizarre altercation again. Sleeping on a canopy indeed! "At any rate, I appreciate your having stayed in your room last night."

"Do you . . . *thank* me?"

Jourdian took a bite of eggs. "I suppose."

Splendor battled uneasiness. As a fairy, she spurned gratitude. "I nay wish to be thanked, My Grace. If I do something that pleases you, my reward is knowing that I have made you happy. Please do not express your gratefulness again. Besides, I did not truly set out to follow your instructions. I fell asleep, and since I do not walk in my sleep, I remained in my room."

Jourdian laid his fork down beside his plate. "Am I to understand that had you nor fallen asleep, you would have defied my instructions for you to stay in your room? You would have wandered about the house in the dark?"

"I would have gone directly to your rooms, My Grace, now that I know where they are," Splendor said, smiling when the same servant who had served Jourdian now filled her own plate with quartered apples, sliced pears, and several hot scones. "I desire to give you joy from dawn to dawn. Therefore, if I am nay with you at night, how would it be possible for me to give you nighttime pleasures?"

Shocked over what he was trying desperately not to hear, the servant dropped the glass of milk he held. The creamy liquid drenched the blue tablecloth and dripped onto the gold carpet. With shaking hands, he pulled off the thick cloth draped over his lower arm, then bent to wipe up the milk from the rug.

But he found nothing to scrub. The carpet was dry and unstained, so clean it seemed to twinkle with silver lights.

When he looked up, he saw the duke's lady guest calmly sipping a full glass of milk.

His legs trembled as he straightened. "The milk," he whispered.

"Luscious," Splendor said, and smiled. "So fresh that I imagine it only just came from the darling cow who was sweet enough to share it with me. I shall be sure to send a gift to her. A shining silver bell she can wear around her neck. I think that would be appropriate. Do you think so as well?"

The servant didn't answer. He fainted.

"What the—" Jourdian rose from his chair and rang for Ulmstead.

The fussy butler arrived instantly, carrying a baby seal in his arms. "Your Grace?"

Jourdian stared at the sleek marine animal. "You have a seal."

"I found him burrowed beneath a stack of table linens, your lordship. Oh!" he exclaimed upon spotting the supine footman. "Oh my, what has happened to poor Leonard?" He scurried over to where the servant lay and set the seal down on the floor.

Splendor seized the chance to send the seal, who was Delicious, to one of the fountains outside. "He fainted, poor Leonard," she said. She felt terrible over having so frightened Leonard, but sweet everlasting, these humans fell completely apart over the least bit of magic! How was she to live here if every twinkle of enchantment made them scream or swoon? She could not cease to use her powers. To do so was akin to ceasing to breathe.

"Splendor, you are not to discuss such things," Jourdian said when Ulmstead and two other male servants had carried Leonard from the room. "The man fainted because he could not believe what he was hearing."

Apparently the candelabra and flowers had prevented Jourdian from seeing the servant drop the milk, Splendor realized. "To what *such things* do you refer, My Grace?"

The confused tone in her voice convinced Jourdian that she truly did not understand what he was talking about. He sat back down. "You said you desired to give me joy at night. In my chambers."

" 'Twasn't a falsehood I spoke."

The room felt suddenly warm. Jourdian pulled at his collar and shifted in his chair. "This conversation is highly improper." Clearing his throat, he took up his fork again and ate a bite of kidney pie.

Bewildered, Splendor rose from her seat and moved to stand beside Jourdian's chair. Once beside him, she noticed how untidy and tangled his hair was.

Elf knots.

*Harmony.*

"Splendor?" Jourdian asked.

She would deal with Harmony later, she mused. She had to, for Harmony had already struck twice and there was no telling what other forms of pixie pranks she would employ. "Why is it improper for me to make you happy in your chambers at night?"

Jourdian's pie stuck in his throat. It took three swallows of cool water and one swallow of warm tea to get it down.

Finally he peered up at Splendor and again saw her confusion. Was it really possible that she was so naive that she did not understand the implications of going to his rooms during the night?

But then, she hadn't known what a kiss was, he remembered suddenly.

She was either the most accomplished actress ever to perform, or she'd lived her entire life beneath a rock.

He told himself he didn't care. She was going to live with the Shrewsburys, would soon be out of his hands, and so, whether her ignorance of sexuality was real or feigned, it was none of his concern.

He didn't care.

But, damn it all, how was it possible for her not to understand the impropriety of going to his room at night?

He had to know. Taking her hand, he led her out of the dining room and escorted her to a nearby parlor.

Splendor noticed the small, sunlit room was decorated in shades of springtime—delicate pinks, yellows, white, and pastel green. " 'Tis lovely, this room, My Grace. We shall dine in here rather than in that other room, which is a bit dark for my liking. And I cannot see you well while sitting at that enor-

mous table. I need to see you. Here, I could see you. Aye, we
shall take all our meals in here."

Her decree increased his curiosity over her. Who *was* she?
Why, how, and where had she acquired her commanding demeanor?

So many questions about her hammered through his mind
that his head began to ache.

"You will not dictate to me, Splendor, and never mind
about dining in this parlor. I brought you in here to discuss—
to understand if it is truly possible that you know nothing
about . . ." He rammed his fingers through his hair, then
winced. He'd never *had* so many tangles in his hair, and they'd
defied every comb and brush he'd used! "Splendor, if you do
not comprehend the consequences of going into a man's chambers at night, just what sort of happiness do you think to give
me in my bed?"

She lifted his hand to her face and touched her cheek to it.
"Whatever sort would please you, My Grace," she replied, taking careful note of the change that suddenly appeared in his
eyes. They darkened, yet there remained a strange light within
their silvery depths. "What would please you in your bed?"

The ache in his head moved much lower. Dear God, how
she aroused him. And she didn't even mean to do it!

Breathing unevenly, he walked from the door, away from
her. "Let's start from the beginning, shall we? We'll put this
matter in much simpler terms. Say you slept with me. In my
bed. What would you do there?"

She noted that the odd light in his eyes had brightened and
now resembled the sheen of excitement. "I would sleep, would
I not? What more is there to do in a bed at night?"

He stared at her for a very long while. "Hasn't anyone told
you . . . Wasn't there anyone in your life who explained . . . Who . . . Do you mean to say you know nothing at all about what happens when a man and a woman are in
the same bed together?"

His disbelief was boldly apparent to her, and she decided
that whatever all-important bed activity he was referring to
was a human thing that fairies didn't do. "Nay, My Grace, no
one has ever explained what men and women do together in

bed. But if 'twould give you joy to do this thing with me, take me to your bed and I will do it with you."

Her honesty was as plain to see as the solid oak door behind her, and he was finally convinced that she was telling the truth.

What a change she was from the other women he'd met! Most of the unmarried ladies of the ton were still maidens, he knew, but not a one of them was completely ignorant of the ways of love. Far from being unacquainted with sensuality, they flaunted their charms and flirted outrageously, and they did it with the express purpose of enticing the noblemen, some of whom were young, some of whom were elderly, all of whom itched to sample what was so blatantly displayed to them.

Splendor represented the truest meaning of purity.

And her complete unworldliness pleased Jourdian more than he cared to admit or ponder.

"Do you wish to take me to your bed?" Splendor asked, gliding across the floor to stand beside him. "There's a light in your eyes . . . 'Tis a luster that looks quite like excitement. It appeared the moment you began to speak of my sleeping with you. I will go to your bed with you now if that is your wish."

Her sweet offer to give what she didn't even understand touched a chord in his heart, one he hadn't realized existed. "No, Splendor."

She moved closer to him, savoring the strength that emanated from his body. "Please. Let me grant you this wish."

He felt the tips of her breasts smooth across his chest, and he cursed his lust, his wavering resistance. "No."

The potency of his might and vigor lured her even closer to him. She pressed herself against him and felt his vitality flow into her like a deep breath of life-giving air. "I would do everything you told me to do," she promised. "Anything, whatever you want."

Closer, closer she moved to him, and his heavily muscled thigh slipped between her legs and across her femininity.

She gasped as unfamiliar pleasure shot through her. Wanting more of the strange delight, she wrapped her arms around his waist, and thrust her hips forward, then backward, stroking herself against him with unabashed enjoyment. "Oh, My

Grace, 'tis supremely glorious this feeling that comes from your leg!"

"My leg?" Jourdian felt his lips curve with a ghost of a smile. "Splendor, the feeling isn't coming from my—"

"Don't move," she said when he tried to step away from her. "Please don't move, My Grace. Something tells me that this feeling flowing from your leg is but the beginning of something bigger. Much like a bud about to open into full blossom. Do you understand?"

He understood, all right, but her stirring against his leg was ludicrous. Shameless.

It was the sexiest thing he'd ever felt.

And one of the funniest things that had ever happened to him. His leg, he thought. She thought her pleasure came from his leg! He felt his smile grow broader.

He wouldn't laugh. No, he wouldn't. To laugh over such an absurdity was an absurdity in itself.

But his mirth defied his will, and he began to chuckle.

"Joy," Splendor whispered. "Your laughter means you are joyful, doesn't it, My Grace? Why, you must feel this pleasure too! Oh, 'tis grand that we share this delight! Let us blossom together as well, shall we?"

When she tightened her thighs around his leg, Jourdian's amusement deepened. Quite unable to control himself, he threw back his head and laughed harder than he could ever remember laughing.

"I am about to blossom, My Grace!"

Still in the throes of mirth, Jourdian couldn't decide whether to pull her away or allow her her first taste of lovemaking.

And then he heard music, a soft, quiet, faraway melody that grew a bit louder every few seconds. As if building toward a magnificent crescendo.

Splendor still clinging to him like a stubborn vine, he looked around the room. "Where is that music coming from?"

She didn't answer. She couldn't. The beautiful feelings gathering within her robbed her of her voice, her thoughts, everything but the exquisite sensations seeping into her from Jourdian's leg.

She felt her feet leave the floor and knew she was going to float right up to the ceiling. "Blossoming," she moaned.

Jourdian heard her groan something to him, but could not concentrate on anything but understanding where the strange, beautiful melody was coming from. Determined to find out, he finally succeeded in moving Splendor away from his leg, then turned to investigate the unaccountable music.

But it faded instantly.

Splendor felt the floor beneath her feet again. "Why did you stop me from blossoming?"

"Did you hear that music?" he asked, still staring all around the room.

"Music?" She pressed herself close to him and curled her arms around his back again. "My Grace, I would very much like to understand the culmination of the feelings—"

"I distinctly heard music, but it—"

"And this time I desire for you to feel the majestic feelings as well," Splendor continued. "'Tis obvious that you have never felt them as I have, for if you had you would nay have stopped us from blossoming together."

Finally, he looked down at her. He remained mystified by the inexplicable music, but knew he had to do something about the little innocent wrapped around his leg. "Splendor—"

"If you will only keep your leg still—"

"You don't understand. The feelings—"

"I was about to understand them, but you stopped. We shall begin again. Now."

"No, Splendor."

She gazed up at him, unable to understand why he didn't yearn for the pleasure the way she did. "Could it be that the feelings I felt were stronger than the ones you felt? I am unable to give you the same rapture from my leg, but if you know of another way I can bring it to you, I will gladly comply. 'Twould make me very happy to gift you with such bliss, My Grace."

Her proposition sounded through his mind just as the top of her robe parted and revealed her breasts. She was thoroughly aroused; he could tell by the way her nipples had darkened and puckered. The sight inflamed his own desire again.

He imagined what it would be like to make love to Splendor. Giving as she was, she would hold nothing back, but would yield to him everything she had to offer, everything he wanted to have.

"My Grace?"

He held himself rigid. She tempted him almost beyond his control, but he would not take her innocence, the very thing about her he found so engaging.

"No," he rasped.

"But—"

"I said no, damn it all!"

She drew away, sudden tears spilling from her eyes and dropping to the carpet. "I have wanted to make you happy since first meeting you, but all I have done is anger you. I can find no way around your uncivil streak no matter how I try!"

"Splendor . . ."

She skimmed toward the door, remembering to open it and exit like a human the moment she reached it.

And then, in a silver flash, she was gone.

Jourdian started to follow her, but something shining on the floor stopped him. Looking down, he saw bits of gleam scattered all around his shoes.

He gathered them up, and diamonds twinkled up from his palms.

Tiny diamonds.

He felt as though he'd seen them before.

Somewhere.

A long, long time ago.

---

Splendor flew down the corridor and straight through the wall at the end of it. In the next second she was outside, sailing over an ivy-drenched terrace, then a fountain, a wide, well-kept yard, and finally into a fenced pasture over which fir and sycamore branches swayed in the gentle autumn breeze. As soon as she descended, she vanished into her mist.

Within the cool and sparkling hideaway, she tried unsuccessfully to understand what it was she did and said that made Jourdian so irritable. Her father was right. Human emotions *were* different from fairy feelings. Sweet everlasting, they went quite beyond her comprehension!

She pushed her bottom lip out, pulled a long face, and indulged in a bit of self-pity. Her royal status affording her everything she wanted the instant she wanted it, she was unaccustomed to the dismal feeling of not having what she desired now—namely, Jourdian.

And what of her subjects? All of Pillywiggin was waiting for her to fulfill the terms of the betrothal and conceive Jourdian's child, and all she'd managed to do was infuriate the man.

"Three months," she whispered. " 'Tis all the time I have."

Sinking more deeply into the soothing shelter of haze, she lost track of time as she pondered the way to enchant Jourdian into wedding her.

She thought about the bed activity he mentioned. He could deny his interest in it for a million years, but she'd seen the truth in his eyes. There was something about her being in the bed with him that roused his senses. Excited him.

Whatever it was he wished to do with her in his bed, she suspected that it would not only give him joy but it would also enchant him.

Somehow, some way, she had to get into his bed with him. After he'd done to her whatever exciting thing a man did to a woman, he would marry her. She was sure of it. And perhaps then he would allow her to partake of the pleasure that came from his leg again. She certainly hoped so, for she remained curious over and hungry for the full blossoming of the magnificent sensations.

Anxious to begin her plan, she stepped out of her sparkling haze and saw that dusk had fallen. Sweet everlasting, she'd stayed in her mist nearly all day long!

"Oh! Oh, I d-didn't see ye there!" a man exclaimed. "Who might you b-be? D-don't ye know this is pr-private pr-property? B-belongs to the d-duke of Heathcourte, it d-does." He waited to see if the pretty girl would ridicule him over his stutter as so many other people enjoyed doing.

Splendor turned and saw the man who spoke to her. His clothes were soiled, straw was stuck in his gray hair, and he held a long leather strap, at the end of which was attached Jourdian's big, beautiful black horse.

She decided the man was the servant who took care of the horse. "My name is Splendor, and I assure you the duke knows I'm here. How are you called?"

He smiled when she didn't even seem to notice his stutter. "I'm Hopkins," he said, glancing at the purple garment she was wearing. He didn't know much about women's fashions, but the clothing she was wearing looked like a lounging robe. Rubbing his grizzled chin, he thought for a moment, then smiled again. "Yer the naked g-girl he found in the meadow!"

"How is it you know of me?"

"Oh, word t-travels, Miss Sp-Splendor. Not much g-goes on in that mansion that d-doesn't soon make the rounds. His lordship's b-been the t-talk of the c-county for years. Some might sp-speak ill of him, b-but not his own servants. We're loyal to him, we are, and so are his t-tenants in Mallencroft. It's where I live, Mallencroft."

Splendor warmed toward the friendly man who chitchatted in spite of his stutter. "He's good to you then?"

"I g-get my pay regular. His Gr-Grace . . . Yes, miss, he's g-good to us. B-but he's . . . Well, I mean no dis-disrespect, mind ye, b-but he's a d-difficult man, his lordship. He d-didn't used t-to b-be so st-stern, though. When he was just a lad, he'd c-come b-be with me in the b-barns, he d-did. Never said much, b-but he seemed t-to enjoy my c-company. Once he even smiled at me."

"But he doesn't smile anymore?"

"No. B-but then, he's p-perishin' sad, and p-perishin' sad people d-don't smile. I d-don't t-talk t-to him much b-because . . . well, his b-being the d-duke . . . I g-get nervous with him. B-but I d-do wish he c-could b-be happy."

Out of the corner of her eye, Splendor saw Hopkins's wish soar into the sky. She couldn't see the stars yet, but she knew the man's wish had found one. " 'Tis a good deed to wish something nice for another. You'll be rewarded for such unselfishness."

*And I know just how to reward you,* she thought, recalling his stutter.

"Have a c-care when ye go b-back to the house, Miss Sp-Splendor," Hopkins warned, looking around as if a host of spies were listening to his every word. "His lordship's knowin' no joy t-today, he's not. I c-can always t-tell when he's in a wax. He st-storms into the st-stables like a wind that could flatten anything in its p-path, and then he rides his horse as if every fiend in hell was after him. He d-did just that earlier, and rode fer hours. Sometimes after a ride like that he comes b-back put right again, but not t-today. Nay, when he finished his ride he was in a worse hump than he was b-before he left, he was, so it might b-be b-best if ye left him b-be fer a while."

Splendor closed her eyes.

*His lordship's knowin' no joy today . . .*

*No joy . . .*

Overcome with a sense of failure, she hung her head, her chin touching her chest. "I want so much to make him happy," she squeaked. "But he's so angry all the time."

"Here now, Miss Splendor, it's not as b-bad as all that, now is it? Leave His Gr-Grace to his thoughts fer a while, and he'll c-come out of it. Ye'll see. Once ye g-get t-to know him, ye'll understand he's not a b-bad sort, b-but only a b-bit stern now and again."

"Get to know him?" Splendor asked, raising her head.

"Ye have a b-better chance of that than the rest of us. Except for Mr. T-Tate. Why, stayin' in the manor house with His Gr-Grace as his g-guest . . . ye'll c-come to know more about him than we'll ever know. And once ye understand him, ye c-can g-go about makin' him happy, can ye not?"

"But I thought I *did* know him."

"Oh?" Hopkins scratched his whiskered chin. "D-do ye know what he likes t-to d-do when he's on holiday? D-do ye know what his favorite c-color is? What his favorite b-book is? What he hopes t-to accomplish with his life? It really d-doesn't matter what ye find out about him. Every little b-bit will help ye t-to make him smile."

"Aye," Splendor whispered, realizing she knew very little about Jourdian's dislikes, habits, fondnesses, and dreams.

"You're right, Hopkins. I must make every attempt to know him better. I shall ask him questions and watch what he does! I shall memorize everything about him!"

Hopkins chuckled. "Ye do that, miss— Here now, Magnus!" he shouted when the horse nudged his back and nearly toppled him over. "This is Magnus, Miss Splendor. I—I don't t-talk g-good, but His Gr-Grace's horse understands me."

Splendor longed to stroke the huge stallion's ears, but dared not. Circles of iron held together the leather straps that fashioned his halter.

"Magnus is a fine animal, b-but he's g-got a b-bit of a mean streak in him, he d-does. He b-bites."

Splendor peered into the horse's black eyes. "Why do you bite, sweetling?"

The horse nickered softly. Once, then again, and a third time.

"He doesn't sleep well at night," Splendor said. "And that makes him irritable. His stall is too close to the barn doors, you see. In autumn and winter he feels a draft at night that keeps him from getting proper sleep. In spring and summer, the firefly lights he sees outside keep him awake. Move him to a stall in the middle of the barn, where he won't feel the bite of the wind and won't see the firefly lights. Then he'll get more rest and stop biting."

"What? How d-do you know that's what's wrong with him?"

Splendor smiled. "He told me."

Hopkins's eyes opened so wide that they watered with the need to blink. The girl was demented, he realized. That, or she was . . .

Or she was fey.

"Hopkins? Is something troubling you?" Concerned by the distressed expression in his eyes, Splendor smoothed her fingers across his whiskery cheek.

At her touch, all fear, all care fell away from him and he felt a profound sense of well-being. She was good, he knew then. Sweet as an angel. "I'm thinkin' you c-could charm the b-birds from the tr-trees, Miss Sp-Splendor."

"Perhaps," she replied, her eyes twinkling. "But first I must charm My Grace. Good day to you, Hopkins."

He watched her turn and glide out of the pasture. She slipped beneath the fence fluidly, as if made of mist, and when she was on the other side, a sparrow flew down from a sycamore branch and settled on her shoulder.

Hopkins smiled. "She c-can charm the b-birds from the tr-trees, Magnus! His Gr-Grace d-doesn't stand a chance! G-good d-day, Miss Splendor!"

She waved to him and continued toward the mansion, renewed determination filling her entire being. She *would* make Jourdian happy, and leaving him to his thoughts was definitely *not* the way to do it.

Quickly, she found a lovely white-pebbled path to follow. Colorful pansies lined the stony trail, as did a few apple trees and scrawny blackberry vines. She picked three apples and pondered the dried-up berries. Brushing her hand across the wrinkled berries, she watched as they became plump and juicy once more. After picking as many as she could hold, she dropped all the fruit inside the top of her robe before returning to the house.

She arrived at the front of the manor house, and there she saw a tall, well-built man alight from a shiny black carriage. But well-built though he was, he didn't look as strong as Jourdian, and that observation pleased her in a way she didn't understand.

"Hello," she greeted him, taking care to stay away from his carriage, which appeared to have a great many iron items attached to it. "Have you come to visit My Grace?"

Percival Brackett took one look at the robe-clad girl, and didn't know whether to frown or smile. She was beautiful. Extraordinarily so.

But she was running about in a dressing robe whose top was filled with fruit. A robe, he noticed, that had the Amberville crest stitched upon it.

Interesting. How very interesting. "I am Percival Brackett, duke of Bramwell," he said, reaching up to pat his perfectly styled and combed hair.

As soon as he spoke, the sparrow flew off Splendor's shoulder and disappeared into the sky. Splendor suspected then that the man who stood before her was not kind through and through.

Peering up at him, she realized he was a handsome man. His eyes were a striking shade of green, like newly sprouted grass, and his abundance of thick, wavy hair reminded her of the color of rich, dark soil.

But his face had a pinched look that somehow detracted from his good looks. It was a look that made her wonder if he'd just smelled something terribly disagreeable. "My Grace is a duke, too."

"My Grace? Do you mean *His Grace?*"

Splendor wrinkled her nose. "I imagine he could be *Our Grace* since we are both speaking of him."

"Eh . . . Yes, I imagine so," Percival muttered, his gaze dipping down her form and catching sight of one pale calf, slim ankle, and small, bare foot.

"You are looking at me the way My Grace looks at me."

Quickly, he raised his gaze back up to her face. "And how is that?"

"Like a famished frog. As if he would like nothing better than to eat me up. And do you know that even when I am wearing this piece of satin, he remains a famished frog?"

"Indeed." Percival's mind began to whirl with the beginnings of delicious suspicions. "Are you living here with Jourdian?"

Splendor nodded and reached out to caress the leaf of a chrysanthemum. "He gave me the yellow room, but tonight I am going to sleep in his chambers."

Percival pretended to scratch his upper lip, actually hiding his huge smile. Oh, what a marvelous piece of gossip this was! "And when did you come to live with Jourdian?"

"Yesterday. I've done my best to give him joy, but I—My Grace is hard to please. I will please him tonight, though. I'm not quite certain what it is he will do to me in his bed, but his excitement fairly shone from his eyes. So I will give him pleasure in his bed. Are you coming inside? If you are, you may come with me, for that is where I am going."

Percival smiled behind his hand again. He'd come with the

hope of slyly finding out what Jourdian knew about the fruit orchards in Gloucester, but in the face of the positively scintillating news now in his possession, his business could wait.

The girl was a maiden, that was certain. The lovely little thing had no idea of what Jourdian planned to do to her.

And what of Jourdian? He hadn't bothered to discreetly settle his virgin mistress in a London town house the way other noblemen did their paramours, but had brought her directly to his country seat . . . directly beneath the noses of most all the lords and ladies of the realm, many of whom would be highly insulted over his preference for a common trollop in his ducal home rather than one of their daughters as his proper duchess.

Well, she wasn't a trollop yet, Percival amended silently, but she'd earn the nasty title tonight in Jourdian's bed. And an uncivilized little twit she was, too, running around outside wearing nothing but her lover's robe.

Percival could barely contain his glee when he realized the full significance of what he'd come to learn this afternoon.

Marianna Chesterton might yet be his.

"Will you come inside?" Splendor asked again, wondering what thoughts had seized his attention.

"No. I—I've suddenly remembered that I've no time to visit Jourdian." He pulled his watch from his pocket. "Oh my, it is nearly half past five, and I've a dinner to attend at seven! I must be on my way now, miss. It was a pleasure meeting you. A sheer pleasure."

# 7

"**M**iss Splendor has returned, Your Grace," Ulmstead announced.

Standing in front of one of the windows in his office, Jourdian turned and saw his butler waiting in the doorway with Splendor.

He drank in the sight of her, so relieved she was back and unharmed that a long moment passed before he noticed the tortoise in Ulmstead's bony hands. "Ulmstead, you are holding a turtle."

"Yes, Your Grace. I found him in the kitchen devouring a head of broccoli."

Jourdian frowned. "You found a hog sleeping on the billiard table, a donkey running through the foyer, a seal in the linens, and now a tortoise eating broccoli in the kitchen."

"Yes, your lordship."

"How have all these animals gotten into the house?"

"I'm afraid I do not know, sir."

"Put that thing outside."

"At once, Your Grace."

"Oh, and Ulmstead? Has there been any word from Reverend Shrewsbury?"

"No, your lordship."

"Be careful with the turtle, will you, Ulmstead?" Splendor asked, caressing Delicious's shell.

"Yes, Miss Splendor." With a gentle push, Ulmstead urged Splendor into the room, then closed the door.

"My Grace, what is your favorite book?"

"What?"

"Your favorite book."

She'd been gone all day and she wanted to discuss his preferred reading material! "Where the blazes have you been?"

She lifted her chin a bit. "I asked you a question first, My Grace, therefore you are obligated to answer me before I answer you."

Her audacity was not to be believed. "While my servants searched every inch of this house for you, I scoured the countryside—"

"Sweet everlasting, there is that cat! Oh, please take him away!"

Jourdian glanced at Pharaoh, who was asleep on the sill of one of the windows. "He's sleeping."

As Splendor backed up toward the wall behind her, Jourdian could actually see her fear. Her entire body trembled. Knowing he would not be able to carry on a conversation with her until he did something with Pharaoh, he marched to the window, scooped the cat off the sill, and deposited the Siamese in the corridor.

He then shut the door. "While you are in my house I am responsible for your welfare, and you've been missing for hours! Didn't it cross your mind that I might wonder where you were?"

Her fear ceased to quiver through her, but she felt he had hurt her feelings. "Did it cross *your* mind that the reason I left was because you were shouting the same way that you are now? 'Tis that uncivil streak of yours, and you would do well to take heed when you feel it begin to swell."

With great effort, he gathered patience—not because she'd suggested he do so, but because he didn't want her fleeing the house again. He'd been frantic with worry when he hadn't found her, and guilt had been his companion as he'd searched for her.

"Where were you, Splendor?" he asked, his voice cool and controlled.

Her injured feelings repaired themselves instantly, and she smiled. "In a pasture. The big one beside the stables. I was in need of solitude for my thinking time."

What was it with the woman and fields? Jourdian wondered. He'd found her in one, and now she'd spent all day in another. "You left after breakfast, and it's now five-thirty. Are you telling me that you remained in a field thinking for eight and a half hours?"

"Aye, that is what I am telling you. My Grace, I did not have to answer your question before you answered mine. However, I deigned to do so, and now, to be fair, you must answer two of mine. What is your favorite book, and do you have a color you are particularly fond of?"

"I rode all over this estate, and I did not see you in the pasture."

Splendor moved her heavy mass of hair off her shoulders. "I was in the pasture, and there I met Hopkins. You may ask him if he saw me, and he will say that he did. He is a kind and gentle man, and he says that you have smiled at him but once during all the years he has been here. Does that not make you feel a bit ashamed, My Grace?"

Now that she'd moved her hair off her shoulders, he could see the top of her robe. "What are those bulges in your robe?"

"Berries. And apples." She pulled out a plump berry and held it out. "Do you care for one?"

"No."

She pressed the fruit into his hand anyway. "If you do not feel ashamed for not smiling at Hopkins, you should, especially since he made a very special wish for you. He wants you to be happy, as do I. What do you hope to accomplish in your life? Do you prefer to bathe at night, or in the morning? Does walking through the first snow of winter please you? What do you dream about?"

"I am in no mood for a question and answer game."

"But when you are in the proper mood, do you enjoy games?"

"Splendor—"

"Would you like for me to try to make you laugh again, My

Grace? When you laughed this morning, the sound gladdened me as much as I believe it did you."

He *had* laughed with her, he recalled. And not even Emil could make him laugh the way she had.

"Do you sing?" Splendor asked. "I do. Which song would like for me to sing with you? If I do not know it, you can teach it to me. Do you sing?"

"Why are you asking me such peculiar questions?"

Smiling, she clapped her hands together. "Because 'tis the only way I can know you well."

At her answer, he felt his irritation begin to lessen. She wanted to know him well. Besides Emil, she was the only person who'd shown an interest in the man behind the title.

He watched as she sat down in the chair in front of his desk and began eating the fruit out of her robe. "What are you doing?"

"I am being your company," she slurred, her mouth full of blackberries, "because one of the things that I think will make you smile is not being lonely anymore. Am I mistaken in thinking so?"

*No*, he answered silently. "Yes," he said aloud. "You are mistaken as mistaken can be. I enjoy solitude and privacy, therefore—"

"I still do not believe I am mistaken, and shame on you for telling me such untruths."

"You will not chide me," he said tightly.

"I shall. You are in dire need of frequent admonishments. Only timely scoldings will eventually rid you of your uncivil streak."

Feeling his penetrating gaze upon her, she looked down at the top of his desk and saw a cream-colored letter. Even from where she sat, she could smell the heavy scent of roses emanating from the paper. "What is that?"

Jourdian glanced at the paper. "A letter, and don't admonish me again, do you understand? I—"

"The letter smells of roses. 'Tis from a woman. What is her name?"

"That is none of your—"

"Is it Lyrical?"

"What?"

"The rose woman's name."

"Lyrical?"

Obviously the woman's name wasn't Lyrical, Splendor realized. "Is she called Ecstasy or Sunshine? Rainbow? Is she Compassion? Peace? Is her name Decadent, or—"

"Her name is *Marianna*! All right? *Marianna*!"

"She is pleasing to the eye?"

"Splendor—"

"Is she?"

"Yes," Jourdian answered wearily. "She's pleasing to the eye."

"Why did she write you that letter?"

Somehow Jourdian managed to resign himself to the fact that Splendor's curiosity would not abate until satisfied. "Marianna is a woman I used to court. The letter is an invitation for me to join her in London for her cousin's wedding."

"And will you join—"

"I've no time. Any more questions?"

Splendor looked at Marianna's rose-scented letter one last time. As she had when Harmony had asked for one of Jourdian's kisses, she felt a burning sensation in the middle of her stomach.

Whoever Marianna was, Splendor had no intention of sharing Jourdian with her. "I shall think of more questions in a moment, My Grace. For now, please go about with whatever you were doing before Ulmstead brought me in here. I shan't disturb you, but will only be here watching you and listening if you wish to speak. Is that what you were doing?" she asked, pointing to the many stacks of papers piled on his desk.

He glanced at the papers, not a one of which he'd touched since finding and bringing her to his house. He'd never get the orchards if he didn't begin the negotiations and send out the necessary letters to his bankers and solicitors.

Dammit, why hadn't the vicar arrived yet? As long as Splendor was here, his household and routine would remain completely upside down, and he, the duke of Heathcourte, would continue to be reproached by this slip of girl who thought it her business to rid him of the uncivil streak that so distressed her.

What bloody nerve she had.

"The papers, My Grace," Splendor pressed. "Are they what concerned you before I came into this room?"

"That is the work I *should* be doing," he said, struggling to keep a tight rein on his temper lest she upbraid him again, "but not while you are in here. I prefer to work alone." He walked around his desk, sat down across from her, and placed the blackberry she'd given him beside the stack of papers. "There are many things you can do to entertain yourself while I work. You must be hungry for more than just a bit of fruit. Mrs. Kearney could prepare something for you. Some bread and honey perhaps. After you've eaten, you could read. The library is filled to capacity with books. Or you might ask Mrs. Frawley to supply you with painting supplies or some sewing. Or, you could walk through the conservatory."

"Conservatory?"

"A large room where plants and flowers are grown."

"What kinds of plants and flowers?"

He shrugged. "Plants are plants."

His ignorance of nature saddened her. "You are wrong. Rabbits, deer, and squirrels are all animals, but they are nay the same. 'Tis the same with plants, My Grace. Do you know you have a lovely patch of wood violets growing on your land? They nearly cover the forest floor, and 'tis difficult to walk among them without crushing them."

Excited by her own words, she leaned forward in her chair. A crimson apple fell out of her robe, rolled across the desk, and fell into Jourdian's lap. "And you have primrose, foxglove, yew, and willow. By the stone wall that hugs the cobblestone road there grow elm, big mounds of snowdrops, and a bank of periwinkle. You have hundreds of oak and alder, a multitude of black poplars, and oh, My Grace, so many, many cowslips that it quite delights the heart and soul to see them!"

Her enthusiasm was so great that Jourdian almost smiled. He didn't smile, however, because he realized suddenly that she knew more about his estate than he did.

Odd. "How is it that you are so familiar with what grows on

my land?" he asked, retrieving the apple from his lap and setting it beside the blackberry he'd put beside his papers.

"One need only look to see, My Grace. You have never
looked. It occurs to me that you are more impressed by what is
written on your papers."

He picked up one page and waved it through the air. "For
your information, these papers concern vast fruit orchards in
Gloucester that I am endeavoring to purchase."

"Do not buy them. Consider them next year perhaps, but
definitely not now."

He shook his head. If he waited only a few more weeks,
Percival Brackett would acquire the orchards. And Jourdian's
blistering need to make certain that the Amberville holdings
would never be subject to ruination again made it imperative
that Percival not attain as much as a leaf of the orchards.

And besides, what did Splendor know about business investments?

The woman was daft.

"This is a civil conversation we are having," Splendor said,
and smiled. "Ever so much nicer than the sort we have when
you are angry, do you not think so?"

He ignored her question. "Since you are so enamored of
plants, I suggest you visit the conservatory and leave me to my
work. You may ask one of the gardeners to accompany you."

"I assure you I will visit the plant room, but for now I will
stay here with you."

He was about to argue when he it came to him that allowing her to stay would be the perfect way to induce her to
leave. After only a short while of watching him read and sort
through his reports, she'd be bored to distraction.

He turned up the lamp and began to read. He read, and he
read. Twenty minutes passed before he let himself look up.

Sucking on a blackberry, Splendor was watching him in the
same intent manner she would have watched a juggler spin
fifty fireballs. There was simply no denying the fascination in
her eyes.

Nor was there any denying how beautiful she looked with
that dark berry pressed against her pale pink lips.

No, he told himself. He would not give in to the power of her charm again. Not now, not ever again.

Resolving to wear her down, he read for another hour before looking up at her once more.

She remained intrigued.

"How is it possible to watch someone read for almost an hour and a half and not become weary of watching?"

She thought of all the years she'd watched him. "I could never grow weary of watching you. I know of nothing else that gives me such pleasure."

Something inside him made him yearn to believe her, but common sense told him that he'd never heard such an excessive and illogical compliment. "What do you hope to gain with such flattery?" he snapped.

She sensed his rising ire, then saw proof of it when his light silver eyes darkened to the grim color of iron. "I do not understand you. All I wish to do is be with you. 'Tis a simple request."

Not a tinge of dishonesty existed in her eyes or voice, Jourdian noted. But he remained unconvinced.

His elbows on his desk, he made a steeple with his fingers, and rested his chin upon them. "Shopping," he said suddenly. Yes, shopping. All women loved spending money. Greedy and self-indulgent, all of them.

And Mrs. Shrewsbury could supervise Splendor's shopping trip.

"If you will leave me to my work," he began, "I will allow you a shopping spree as soon as I can arrange it." His gaze missing nothing, he watched her face for signs of excitement.

"Shopping spree, My Grace?"

He saw naught but confusion etched across her fine features. "Splendor, a note from me will secure credit for you in any shop in England. Mallencroft is the nearest village, but you would find more to your liking in Telford, a township about a two-hour drive from here. I'm quite sure there are several dressmakers there. The seamstress in Mallencroft will be sending a few frocks for you, but they will not be of the same quality that you will find in Telford. And if you do not care for any of the ready-made garments the dressmakers have available, you may design your own gowns and have them created especially for you."

There, he thought. Surely that would prompt a bit of excitement from her—more interest than watching him read.

"But I already have this piece of satin, My Grace."

"What? Do you mean you want nothing else?"

"Aye, that is what I mean."

Her complete lack of interest in clothes astonished him, but he remained determined to find her weakness. "What of jewels? Enough jewels to swim in."

"One cannot swim in colored rocks. And even if one could, what would be the use? They would not clean one or refresh one on a hot summer's day, would they? One could nay float upon them, either. Or drink them, for that matter."

"You think jewels are but colored rocks?"

"Is that not what they are?"

"Well . . . yes, but they're very valuable."

"Oh? Well, I do not care for jewels, but I am supremely fond of plants and flowers. You are in dire need of more flowers in your house. Most of the blooms I have seen in various rooms are not real. Do you wish me to put flowers in your home for you?"

"Whatever you like," he answered absently, still pondering the fact that she thought jewels were naught but colored rocks.

"What do you enjoy reading, My Grace? And which color are you most fond of?"

"Shakespeare's plays," he muttered. "Blue and red and green . . ."

She was lying, he told himself. No one would refuse jewels!

Quickly, he slipped his hand into the pocket of his coat and withdrew the tiny diamonds he'd found on the parlor floor. "Here," he said, sprinkling the gems in front of her. "Take them. They're yours."

She glanced at her tears. How could he give her something that was already hers?

"I can give you bigger ones," Jourdian pressed, wondering if her lack of enthusiasm stemmed from the fact that the diamonds were so small.

Splendor thought of the countless jewels already in her possession. The base of her bed was one solid emerald. The windowpanes in her room were diamond, the walls were fashioned of pearls, and the ceiling created with millions of sparkling rubies. Why, the very floors of her father's castle were made of sapphires.

True, the gems were all very pretty, especially when sunlight shimmered through their depths, but she'd never thought of them as valuable. On the contrary, they were but the materials of which the castle was built, materials gotten from the earth and from the sea.

"Nay, My Grace," she said, slipping another blackberry into her mouth. "I do not want any jewels."

She was trifling with him, he decided. Toying with him until he hit upon the exact thing she wanted from him.

Very well, he'd continue offering until he discovered her one fondness. And when he found it, he'd deny it to her. Being denied her pleasure would serve her right for dallying with him.

"How about the world then?" he queried, opening his arms as if holding the whole planet Earth. "The entire world and everything in it."

Splendor laughed. "My Grace, the world belongs to everyone, and so 'tis not yours to give."

"You misunderstand. I could *show* you the world. Take you to faraway lands and give you grand adventures."

Splendor slid one of her apples from the top of her robe and took a bite.

Jourdian saw a bead of apple juice on her bottom lip, and couldn't help but think of a dewdrop glistening upon the velvety petal of a pale pink rose. Slowly, she smoothed her tongue over the sweet droplet, and Jourdian couldn't remember ever seeing anything more sensual.

God, he thought. He had to get hold of himself. Imagine being aroused by a woman slurping fruit juice off her mouth.

"I have traveled far but once in my life," Splendor admitted, then swallowed her bite of apple, "and I do not wish to journey so far again. I'm perfectly happy here, where I am. Life is life, My Grace, and no matter where you are things are not so much different as they are the same."

*Well, I'll be damned*, he thought, staring at her. She cared naught for a wardrobe or for jewels. She had no interest in seeing the world. He'd offered her everything his money could buy, and she'd refused it all.

"Nothing," he said. "You want nothing from me."

*I want you to marry me*, she thought. *I want you to give me a child.*

"Not true," she replied out loud. "There is something I want from you."

Ahha! Jourdian mused. So she *did* have a weakness after all. "Yes?"

"I would like you to smile at your servants. Ulmstead, Mrs. Frawley, Tessie, Hopkins . . . They are all good people, as are your other servants and your tenants, I am sure. If you could manage to keep your uncivil streak in check, a smile from you would make your servants very happy. Oh, and if 'tis possible, I would like to know the gardeners who care for your plants. I am a guardian of nature as well, and I think I will like to know your gardeners."

Her announcement got his undivided attention. She was a gardener, and the fact that she remembered she was such indicated that her memory was returning. "Where are these gardens you care for?"

"Oh, they are everywhere. Wherever I am, My Grace."

"I see. And do you have a garden at home?"

She pondered the beautiful glade above her father's castle and all the wonderful and beautiful trees and flowers that grew there. "Aye."

"Where is your home?"

"Pillywiggin."

Jourdian had never heard of the place and decided it was but one of the many inconsequential villages that dotted the countryside. He resolved to study maps of the area to see if he could find its exact location. "What is your surname?"

"My surname?"

"Your second name. Everyone has at least two names, do they not?"

She cocked her head toward her shoulder and gave him a puzzled frown. "I have but one. 'Tis Splendor."

Jourdian folded his arms across his chest and leaned back in his chair. Obviously, she was illegitimate. If she were not, she would bear her father's name. "How old are you?"

"I have seen thirty-two winters melt into thirty-two springs."

It was impossible that she was of the same age as he! he thought. "You don't appear to be more than nineteen. Twenty at the most. Give me the truth."

" 'Twas what I gave you."

He sensed then that she was, indeed, being truthful, but he remained amazed by her youthful freshness. Other women her age were already trying to conceal wrinkles with heavy dustings of powder. Why, some already had the beginnings of gray hair! "Where is your mother? The rest of your family?"

Splendor ate another berry before answering. "All live in Pillywiggin."

Finally he knew where to deliver her, he mused. He wondered if he would miss her. Miss her quick, bright smile, the soft feel of her hair, her enchanting scent of wildflowers, and the innocent sweetness of her character.

More thoughts of her drifted through his mind.

And then scattered when he realized what direction they'd taken.

Miss her? He couldn't miss a person he'd known for two short days, for God's sake!

Damn it all, he was becoming as sentimental as Emil. The next thing he knew, he'd be hunting for four-leafed clovers and wishing on stars!

"I'll see to it you are safely returned to your family," he declared sternly. "You will travel in my own coach and with the protection of my name. I will also provide you with funds in the case that you are in need of further care from a physician."

Splenor dropped the berry pinched between her fingers. Desperation clawed at her. What would her father and her people say if she returned before having conceived Jourdian's child? And what of Pillywiggin? Without the half-human child in their midst, the fairies would dwindle in number until not a single one existed.

Bolting from her chair, she stretched out her arms in a pleading gesture, uncaring that her fruit tumbled out of her robe and fell to the floor. "I nay wish to return, My Grace! You cannot send me away! You cannot!"

"I promise you that I can."

"Do not force me away," Splendor begged, feeling tears fill her eyes.

Her tears bothered him immensely. He drummed his fingers upon his desk, his emotions at war.

"Please, My Grace."

Jourdian got up, walked around his desk, and stopped beside her. "Splendor—"

"Let me stay with you," she whimpered. "I want so much to stay with you."

When she snuggled next to his chest, he automatically put his arms around her slight shoulders, and he could feel her misery surge through her.

"My Grace? Will you send me away?"

How like a little girl she sounded at this moment, he thought. And yet, she was a thirty-two-year-old woman.

Thirty-two years old. Old enough to be on her own.

He realized he didn't have to deliver her back to her family; her age relieved him of that obligation.

But what in God's name was he to do with her? "Sprite," he said as gently as he could, "wouldn't you like to live with Reverend Shrewsbury and his wife? The reverend is the man you met yesterday. He and his wife live in a nice house not far—"

"Nay," she cried softly. "I do not know those people. If you send me to them, I shall not stay. No matter where you send me, My Grace, I shall not stay, but will return to you time and again."

"But—" He broke off when she curled her arms around his waist and embraced him with all the strength her delicate body held. Irresolution scrambled his every thought, and he knew he could not make a rational decision until he'd had time to think the situation through.

He'd allow her to remain with him for tonight. One more

night beneath his roof would do no harm. In the morning, he would decide what to do with her.

Yes, things would look much brighter in the morning.

* ~~~~~~~ *

Jourdian dreamed of Splendor that night.

She was in his bed, naked, warm, and cuddled in his arms. He dreamed of her scent too, so fresh and sweet, so perfect for her.

He wore no nightclothes either, and so he could feel her soft skin upon his bare chest and her slender legs tucked between his. Moonlight spilled silver over her pearly flesh, over her pretty pink lips, which quivered slightly as she breathed. Her extraordinary hair lay over his pillow, covered his sheets, and it was upon that fragrant pool of copper that he slept.

Strangely, it wasn't sexual desire that filled him while he dreamed of her in his bed.

It was a feeling of contentment, one of comfort and affection, and he remembered how he'd longed for such feelings when he'd been a lad, when there had been no one in the house to offer him such serenity.

He sighed with pleasure and he hoped the night lasted a long while and he slipped deeper and deeper into the dream.

It was the best he'd ever had.

"Jourdian, for pity's sake, wake up!"

Rudely yanked from slumber, Jourdian opened one eye.

"The hour is late," Emil declared, giving his cousin's shoulder a firm shake. "It's already half past one, and you're yet lying about! Show a leg, won't you? You've pressing business to attend to!"

"Get out," Jourdian murmured. Wanting to return to his dream, he turned to his side. "I'm going back to sleep."

"The hell you are! The entire country is talking about you, and you must do something to dispel the rumors! Reverend Shrewsbury and Percival Brackett have done a thorough job of—"

"Reverend Shrewsbury? Is he here?"

"Here?"

"The note," Jourdian replied groggily. "You took him the note I wrote to him. If he's come to collect Splendor—"

"What? No, he hasn't come to collect Splendor! I *burned* the note, Jourdian!"

"You burned it? Why?"

"Because . . . Oh, for pity's sake, I'm not here to discuss the blasted note! Damn you for a cad! You're no better than Niall Marston!"

Jourdian rubbed his hand over his face, trying in vain to understand what the womanizer, Niall Marston, had to do with the burned note to Reverend Shrewsbury.

"You've made Splendor your mistress, Jourdian, and now you must—"

"What?" Wide awake then, Jourdian sat straight up. "I've done no such thing!"

Emil ripped the covers off the bed, and there beside Jourdian lay a very naked Splendor. "What is she doing in your bed then, cousin? Chasing away any nightmares you might have? At least Niall tarries with experienced women! *You've* taken an innocent to *your* bed!"

Shock slammed into Jourdian, followed by a blow of bewilderment.

Splendor lay sleeping on the other side of his bed, her body curled up in a tight little ball, her hair her only covering.

Jourdian looked up at Emil, then down at Splendor, then back up at Emil. "It wasn't a dream," he whispered. "Twice I've thought her a dream, and twice she's proved me wrong. How did she— When did she— What the blazes is she doing in my bed?"

Emil folded his arms across his chest. "It appears as though she's *sleeping* now. The question, then, is what was she doing in your bed *before* she fell asleep?"

Jourdian jumped out of bed and threw on the purple robe he'd lent to Splendor. "Do you think I— Are you saying that I— Emil, what the bloody hell do you think I've done to her?"

At all the loud talking, Splendor began to stir and stretch and moan softly.

Instantly, Jourdian caught Emil's arm and pulled his cousin out of the room. In the corridor, the heated conversation continued. "I assure you that I didn't invite Splendor to my bed! Yesterday she took on and on about sleeping with me, but— She doesn't know— Isn't aware of what takes place between a man and a— I have *not* taken her innocence, dammit!"

"She was in your room yesterday, too, and you kissed her."

"Since when is kissing a woman a crime?"

"Now she's naked in your bed."

"I was asleep when she got into my bed, and I—"

"All right, fine. Fine. You haven't stolen her virtue. But what are you going to do about all the beastly gossip to the contrary?"

"What gossip are talking about?"

Emil shook his head.

"Stop shaking your head like some woebegone hound dog, and tell me what's so upset you! What *is* this abhorrent tattle?"

"It's about you. You and Splendor. I heard the whole of the story this morning from Godfrey Sheffield, who heard it from Sebastian Putnam, who got it from his sister, Elizabeth, who heard her mother whispering about it with Lady Holden. From what I've been able to gather, Lady Holden learned of it from Lady Culbert, who got it straight from Lady Briggs. And, as I'm sure you know, Lady Briggs is a good friend of Lady Hewlett, who, in turn, is Lady Chesterton's frequent companion. Lady Chesterton told Lady Hewlett that Marianna is prostrate with grief and that she has taken to her bed, vowing never to rise again! I *told* you she thought there was more to your relationship than you let on! Her father is incensed that you—the most highly regarded peer in all the realm—would stoop so low as to—"

"Emil . . . Wait." Jourdian's confused thoughts spun so quickly, he felt as though his head had turned into a top. "What gossip—"

"It was Percival Brackett who carried the news to the Chesterton estate late yesterday evening. To strengthen his efforts to win Marianna, no doubt. He . . . The ass called Splendor an uncivilized little twit! And Reverend Shrewsbury saw to the task of advising the local gentry. You know how obnoxiously verbose that so-called man of God is. I've no doubt he told every commoner he could find as well! The scandal is probably well on its way to London now, and—"

"What scandal are you talking about, damn it all?" Jourdian roared.

"That you've brought a country trollop to live with you at your ducal seat! Few would have raised an eyebrow if you had settled a doxie elsewhere. You could have placed her somewhere in London or in some small house near your estate. You could have gone to visit her in a cave in the middle of nowhere, for that matter. It's the fact that you brought her to *Heathcourte* that has stirred such shock. It's your duchess who should reside beneath this roof, and Splendor's presence here indicates to one and all that you prefer to live with a common strumpet than marry a woman of your own class!"

Livid with fury, Jourdian grabbed Emil's coat collar. "She is *not* a common strumpet, do I make myself clear?"

"What? Oh, for pity's sake, Jourdian, I know she's not a common strumpet! I merely repeat what is being said about her!"

Jourdian released his cousin's coat. "How did this happen? Who started this vicious hearsay?"

Emil looked straight into Jourdian's eyes. "Splendor. She told the vicar that she was here to give you joy. Pleasure beyond anything you had ever known. And she was naked at the time. Yesterday afternoon, she met Percival Brackett right in your driveway. She told *him* that she was going to sleep in your chambers and please you. During that little encounter, she was wearing naught but your robe."

Jourdian grabbed Emil's arm again. "Emil, you don't understand. The joy she says she desires to give—"

"*Desire* being the key word here."

"Listen to me! She continues to say she wants to make me happy. When she speaks of giving me joy, she means just that. Joy, plain and simple, and not the kind found in bed. She doesn't know anything at all about lovemaking. Has no idea whatsoever about—"

"Oh, come now, Jourdian. Surely she knows—"

"Nothing. She actually believed her pleasure came from my leg yesterday!"

"Your leg. I see. Jourdian, let go of my arm before you snap it in two."

"I tried to explain . . . She was stirring against my leg, and I—" Jourdian let go of Emil's arm and threw back his shoulders. "That is not the issue, Emil. The gossip being told about her is—"

"Utterly nasty, and I want to know what you're going to do about it."

"Do about it?" Jourdian glanced at his closed bedroom door, and struggled to find his composure. He shut his eyes for a moment and took a deep breath before looking at Emil again. "I will do nothing," he replied, his voice calm and cool. "The gossip will die out as all rumors do."

"They're calling Splendor your peasant whore, Jourdian. I've no doubt she's as innocent as you claim her to be, but your name suffers—"

"I don't give a damn what anyone says—"

"Then give a thought to Splendor. Her reputation is in shreds. If you keep her here, the talk will increase among the ton and the local gentry. If you send her away, she will be an outcast among the lower classes as well. Beautiful though she is, no man will look twice at her, and you damned well know it."

Jourdian walked down the length of the hall, then back again. Bloody hell. What was he going to do now?

"Marry her, Jourdian."

Jourdian stared at his cousin as though Emil had just sprouted a second nose on his face. "*Marry her*? Have you lost your wits? She's not the sort of woman—"

"Your preferences in women matter not at all now. Splendor is in terrible straits, and you are obligated to—"

"Her innocence remains intact, therefore I am not obligated—"

"The truth has no bearing whatsoever in this situation. What is of consequence is what everyone believes. And they believe the very worst. And what if her family hears? You may be sure they will not take this lightly. They'll demand marriage, and they'll have every right to take you before the courts if you do not comply."

"She is thirty-two years old, and her age absolves me of—"

"What does her age have to do with this? An unmarried woman should be able to keep her virginity and reputation untarnished regardless of her age. Should her relatives hear of this scandal, you may be sure they will pounce upon you like a pack of bloodthirsty wolves. They'll insist you make Splendor your duchess. They'll—"

"But I haven't touched—"

"So you've said, but you *have* sullied her honor, however indirectly."

Mindless of his state of dress, Jourdian marched down the corridor, turned the corner, and headed for the grand staircase. Forget tea or coffee, he fumed. What he wanted now was a straight shot of liquor, and there was a bottle right in his office.

"Dammit, Jourdian," Emil cursed, "you cannot leave Splendor to deal with this alone! She—"

"I have no intention of leaving her to deal with this sordid affair alone. I daresay she would make a worse mess of it."

"Then what will you do?"

"Obviously, she cannot remain here any longer. If you hadn't burned the note I penned to Reverend Shrewsbury—"

"Splendor spoke to the reverend before you wrote that note, Jourdian. The man already had ample gossip—"

"There are any number of locations across the country where I can settle her—"

"And if Splendor doesn't want to go where you choose to settle her, what then?" Emil asked, following Jourdian toward the winding staircase.

"I'm afraid she has little choice in the matter."

"You are most likely the only friend she'll have left once the gossip has completely spread. How would *you* like it if your only friend put *you* in an unfamiliar place and then left you there?"

"I am not her friend."

Emil seized Jourdian's arm, forcing him to stop. "Then what are you to her?"

"We are acquaintances, and nothing more."

"Even now she lies naked in your bed. I'd say the two of you are more than mere acquaintances. And your quick denial of having any sort of relationship with her whatsoever is evidence that she *is* something to you. But you're too stubborn to admit it. Or is it that you're *afraid* to own up to your feelings, Jourdian? To feel is to be vulnerable, isn't that so?"

Jourdian snatched his arm out of Emil's grasp and continued toward the stairway. "I will do what is best for Splendor, she will be forced to abide by my decision, and that is the end of it."

"I've no doubt that whatever you ultimately decide is best for Splendor will be what is most convenient for yourself. You're a cad, damn you."

Jourdian stiffened, but didn't reply. He reached the upper landing of the staircase and began his descent.

In only moments, he realized his going downstairs was a mistake.

Lady Holden and Lady Briggs stood in the marble foyer with a very flustered Ulmstead, and all three noticed Jourdian immediately.

"Your Grace," Ulmstead said, looking up at his employer, "Lady Holden has come—"

"I apologize for having interrupted your leisurely afternoon," Mildred Holden announced, taking note of the duke's lounging robe, "but I have come to extend you a personal invitation to a dinner party that I will be holding on Tuesday next."

"And I have accompanied her on her errand," Regina Briggs added.

Emil moved behind Jourdian and began to whisper. "The nosy biddies have only just invented the idea of a dinner party, Jourdian. They are here to catch a glimpse of Splendor with their own eyes."

Jourdian was fully aware of the reason behind the matrons' impromptu visit. Tightening the sash on his robe, he sent down a glare designed to intimidate the two gossip mongers.

He succeeded. Both ladies backed toward the door.

But they stopped instantly when a small voice shimmered through the foyer.

"My Grace," Splendor said, rubbing sleep from her eyes as she stood at the top of the staircase, "you are wearing my piece of satin."

"Oh, God," Emil muttered. "Jourdian, she's naked."

Jourdian did not look up at her. Rather, he kept his gaze nailed to the two women standing by the door.

He saw the unmistakable gleam of pure satisfaction in their eyes, and on their wrinkled mouths there curved malicious smiles.

*They're calling Splendor your peasant whore, Jourdian.*

Fury made him grit his teeth. Even now the two busybody harridans were probably thinking of other foul titles to give to Splendor.

Splendor, whose purity rivaled that of a newborn babe.

"You've gotten what you came for, have you not?" he snapped down at the women. "There she is, at the top of the stairs. Look at her carefully. Memorize every detail so that you can describe her accurately."

Her eyes darting from the duke to the naked girl, Mildred Holden raised one gray eyebrow. "I'm sure we have no idea what you're talking—"

"You're wasting precious time arguing, Lady Holden," Jourdian said with a sneer. "You've further rumors to spread, have you not? With such an important mission to accomplish, I suggest you be on your way. *Now.*"

They could not leave fast enough.

Jourdian stared at the door, too enraged to speak.

But voices in his head fairly shouted.

*No matter where you send me, My Grace, I shall not stay, but will return to you time and time again.*

*The ass called Splendor an uncivilized little twit!*

*I've no doubt that whatever you ultimately decide is best for Splendor will be what is most convenient for yourself.*

The voices shot through Jourdian's head like a barrage of bullets. He felt like smashing his fist into the wall.

Instead, he drew himself up to his full height and faced his cousin. "Emil," he said softly, but his voice simmered with bitterness, "bring the vicar here."

Emil nodded and smiled. Jourdian planned to confront the

holier-than-thou Reverend Shrewsbury! "I'll bring Percival as well," he said, looking forward to watching his cousin berate the two men who had caused such trouble.

"I will deal with Percival later."

"But—"

"Bring Reverend Shrewsbury. I don't care where you have to go to find him, but I want you to drag his immoral hide here immediately."

Emil started down the staircase, but stopped when a sudden thought occurred to him. Reverend Shrewsbury . . . In light of all that had happened, surely Jourdian did not still plan to send Splendor to live with the Shrewsburys! "Jourdian, what need have you of the vicar?"

"He was the first to sow the seeds of scandal. Now he can damn well put it to an end."

"Do you mean you want him to deny the truth of his own gossip?"

"It's too late for that."

"Then what would you have the man do?"

Jourdian looked up the staircase at Splendor.

She grinned at him.

The look he returned could have dried up the ocean.

"Jourdian?" Emil pressed. "What is it you want me to tell Reverend Shrewsbury?"

Stiffly, Jourdian turned away from Splendor. "Tell him he has a wedding to perform, and I want it done before nightfall."

**8**

His mood as black as his suit, Jourdian stood beside his bed and opened the large wooden box he'd had a servant bring to him. He dumped the contents onto the mattress.

Lamp glow and firelight shimmered over a mound of priceless jewelry, all of which had belonged to the Amberville women throughout the centuries. Knowing he had to give Splendor a ring during the wedding ceremony, Jourdian retrieved the first one he saw, a plain silver band with one tiny pearl as its setting.

And then another ring caught his attention, a solid gold creation set with three rows of amethysts. Picking it up, he saw how brilliantly the lavender stones gleamed, and then he compared the ring with the silver and pearl one.

What difference did it make? he asked himself. As long as Splendor had something wrapped around her finger, it didn't matter if the ring was made out of a damned horseshoe nail.

He slipped one of the rings into his pocket and headed downstairs.

Once in the drawing room, he felt as though he were attending a funeral service. What seemed like thousands of candles were lit, and the room overflowed with flowers brought from the conservatory. Even the ambiance of the room suggested a somber, rather doleful mood. The only thing missing was a casket.

But gloomy though the room felt and looked, it suited Jourdian's temper. In only moments, he would be married to Splendor, a woman he barely knew. He could not deny her loveliness, nor could he dismiss her innate sweetness, but her eccentricities did not sit well with him.

Nor did the fact that he was being forced to marry her.

"I was exceedingly happy to assist you in arranging this expeditious ceremony, Your Grace," Reverend Shrewsbury declared, clutching his prayer book to his chest. "Ordinarily, I would have insisted that banns be posted and all other customary procedures be followed; however, these are exceptional circumstances."

Jourdian did not reply.

"You are doing the right thing, Your Grace," the vicar continued. "This wedding not only frees you from the bonds of the sins you have committed, but it will effectively stop all tongues from wagging, and I . . . You . . ."

His voice trailed away when he saw the thunderous expression in the duke's eyes. That hard silver gaze crucified him to the wall as if with nails, knives, swords, and every other sharp and lethal thing in existence.

"I suggest, Reverend," Jourdian said, "that when you say your prayers tonight, you pray for your own black soul."

Reverend Shrewsbury was saved from having to reply when Mrs. Frawley scurried into the room as fast as her plump legs could carry her. "Your Grace," she panted, "Miss Splendor is coming down with Mr. Tate now, but I thought I should warn you that she refused to wear the gown that the Mallencroft seamstress delivered. The lace did not meet with her approval, your lordship, and try as I did, I could not persuade her to put the dress on."

"She's not naked, is she?" Jourdian asked, ignoring the fact that such a question was not at all decent.

Mrs. Frawley felt her cheeks heat with embarrassment. "No, Your Grace, but she . . . Well, she . . ."

"Is she wearing the purple robe?"

The housekeeper wrung her hands. "Oh, Your Grace, she wanted to wear the purple robe, but I'm afraid it's being laundered. You see, she's worn it for nearly two days straight, and I had Tessie take it to the laundress—"

"*What* is she wearing?" Jourdian demanded.

Mrs. Frawley did not have to answer. At that moment, Emil led Splendor into the room.

Jourdian could not believe what he was seeing.

Splendor was wearing one of his white silk shirts, and nothing else. Tall as she was, the hem of the garment barely reached mid-thigh, thus exposing her long, slender legs. She wore naught beneath the shirt, and he could see the dusky flesh of her nipples and the dark shadow between her legs.

Dammit, she might as well have been naked! "Mrs. Frawley," he whispered hotly, "was it not possible to at least persuade her to put something on *under* my shirt?"

Mrs. Frawley shook her head. "We tried, Your Grace, but she . . . Miss Splendor is quite the most resolute young woman I have ever known. When her mind is made up, there is simply no undoing it."

Jourdian looked at the vicar and saw that the reverend's gaze was level with Splendor's chest. Three male servants at the back of the room were watching her derriere, and Emil, damn the man to hell and back, was standing so close to Splendor that the two of them looked as if they'd been glued together. Indeed, Splendor's breast smoothed across Emil's arm with each step they took.

Ulmstead was the only male in the room who was not—in some way—enjoying her charms. The butler was much too busy trying to coax a rooster out from under a table.

Jourdian did a double take. What in God's name was a rooster doing at his wedding?

"Don't be cross, Jourdian," Emil said when he reached his cousin. "From what I gather, Splendor's robe was soiled, and the dress from the seamstress—"

"Get away from her," Jourdian commanded, pulling Splendor's hand out from the crook of Emil's elbow.

"My Grace," Splendor murmured. Tenderly, she kissed his shoulder. How right she'd been to sneak into his room last night and sleep with him! She'd given him joy. At last, she'd truly enchanted him. Proof of that was that he was marrying her.

No longer would she have to hide her identity. The wedding would free her from keeping her origins a secret. After all, in a short while Jourdian would be her husband, and as such he had every right to know that he'd married a pixie.

She wondered how to tell him.

"My Grace, I am a fairy," she might say.

Or . . .

"My Grace, the beds in your house are all quite nice, but I am supremely fond of napping inside the cup of a bluebell."

Or . . .

"Splendor!" Jourdian hissed.

Pulled from her intense deliberation, she realized he'd been speaking to her and she hadn't heard a word he said.

"You are wearing my shirt," Jourdian said, speaking down to the top of her head.

"Aye, that is what I am wearing." Rubbing her cheek on his shoulder, she moved her bouquet of yellow daffodils away from him lest the delicate flowers be crushed. "And 'tis supremely soft, your shirt. Every speck as soft as the piece of satin. You see, the dress the kind lady brought had a stiff substance on it that would have given me prickles. 'Twas a pretty shade of pink, the dress, but I could nay endure the stiff substance—"

"The lace," Mrs. Frawley supplied.

Jourdian started to take off his coat.

"I shall not wear your coat, My Grace," Splendor informed him softly, but firmly. "This is my wedding day, and I shall wear this pretty shirt."

"Splendor—"

"Do not be angry." Finally, Splendor lifted her head from his shoulder and looked up at him.

Jourdian's breath caught in his throat. Angry, frustrated, and bewildered as he was by the sheer outrageousness of his wedding, her beauty stole his every thought. He'd attended countless weddings and had seen countless brides and countless wedding gowns.

But he'd never seen a more gorgeous bride than Splendor.

No wedding creation of satin, pearls, lace, or velvet could have accentuated her loveliness the way his shirt did.

Radiant was the only word he could think of to describe her.

Her nearness . . . her warmth and beauty . . . her intoxicating scent of wildflowers . . .

Jourdian almost groaned with desire.

"Jourdian, get hold of yourself, man," Emil whispered, nudging his cousin forcefully. "There's time for that later. First you must concern yourself with marrying her."

Instantly, Jourdian drew away from Splendor and turned to face the vicar. "The vows," he snapped.

Reverend Shrewsbury pulled his gaze away from Splendor's bare legs and looked blankly at the duke. "The vows? Oh, but Your Grace, I must perform the entire ceremony from the beginning—"

"We will speak our vows and be done with this."

Reverend Shrewsbury nodded so quickly, that Splendor thought his head might come off his neck and bounce across the floor. "I shall speak my vows first," she said. Turning to Jourdian, she smiled up at him. "I promise to—"

"Splendor," Jourdian cut her off, waving away a buzzing insect that began flying around his face, "you will speak the vows that Reverend Shrewsbury puts to you."

"But he knows not what promises I wish to make to you."

"You will promise what he tells you to promise."

"I shall do no such thing. I have my own vows to make."

Jourdian did not reply immediately; he was too busy trying to blow away the persistent insect that continued to whiz about his face.

"I promise, My Grace," Splendor began, "to sleep in your bed every night. There, I shall give you the joy that I gave you last night. I shall—"

Instantly, Jourdian clapped his hand over her mouth.

"Oh, my!" Reverend Shrewsbury exclaimed, and then he studied Splendor's legs again.

"Get to the ceremony," Jourdian ordered, his hand still pressed over Splendor's mouth. "And you," he whispered down to the outlandish woman he was about to marry, "will repeat every word he says, do you understand?"

She nodded.

He dropped his hand from her mouth.

"I understand, My Grace, but I will not comply. He cannot put my promises to you on my lips, for he cannot possibly know what vows I wish to—"

"Splendor," Jourdian interrupted, "there are specific vows you must make, and you are bound by law to— Damn it all, someone get rid of this insect!" Swishing his hands around his face, he tried to catch the buzzing bug.

Splendor caught sight of the insect then. It was a hornet, its stinger out and ready to wound.

Only it wasn't a hornet.

It was Harmony, and Jourdian was about to smash her. "Nay, don't hurt her! Sweet everlasting, you're going to kill her!"

Jourdian was caught off guard when Splendor pushed at his chest. Slight though she was, she managed to get enough strength behind her shove to propel him toward the small footstool behind him.

"Jourdian!" Emil shouted when he saw his cousin topple over the stool.

Jourdian landed flat on his back. And he was still trying to catch his breath and understand what had happened to him when the hornet delivered a vicious sting right to the tip of his nose.

"Bloody hell!"

"Oh, My Grace!" Dropping her flowers, Splendor rushed to his side and knelt beside his shoulder. "Did she hurt you?"

"She?"

"Harmony!"

"Who the hell is Harmony!"

"The hornet!"

"The hornet's name is Harmony?"

"She wounded you, didn't she?"

"She stung me!"

Emil moved to assist his cousin off the floor. "Nasty fall, old boy. Nasty sting, too," he added, looking at the red swelling on Jourdian's nose.

"Shame on you!" Splendor shouted at Harmony. Deftly, she cupped her hand around the hornet, and deposited her mischievous sister into the pocket of the silk shirt.

Harmony vanished, leaving only a few twinkles in Splendor's pocket.

"You put a hornet in your pocket," Emil said, frowning.

"Aye, that is what I did, Emil. And a naughty thing she is, too."

Emil smiled, more taken with the whimsical girl with every passing moment.

"May we wed now, My Grace?" Splendor asked.

Jourdian took her hand. "Why did you push me?"

Emil laughed again. "For pity's sake, Jourdian, you were about to kill Harmony Hornet! What else could Splendor have done but push you?"

"Never mind." Jourdian faced the vicar again. "Five seconds," he fumed. "You have five seconds to marry us, and not a second more."

"Wait!" Mrs. Frawley shouted. "Miss Splendor doesn't have her flowers!" Quickly, the housekeeper swiped the bouquet off the floor. But before she handed them to Splendor, she frowned. "Silk," she whispered. "The daffodils . . . I saw her remove the flowers from the vase in her room with my own eyes. Silk."

"Yes, yes, they're silk," Jourdian snapped. "Give them to her so that we may proceed with this mockery of a wedding."

"But . . . But . . . But, Your Grace, they're not silk! Not anymore, they're not! They're . . . they're . . . *real!*"

When Mrs. Frawley's knees buckled and she began to crumple to the floor, Jourdian responded instantly and scooped the heavy woman into his arms. His arms straining with the housekeeper's weight, he carried her to a nearby sofa and gently laid her down.

"The lady who swooned was to be one of the witnesses," the vicar reminded him. "I have already written her name upon the marriage documents."

"There are plenty of other witnesses here, and you can

write their names on the documents instead," Jourdian said. He glanced at Ulmstead and the three servants who remained in the back of the room.

God, he could see the newspaper headlines now:

## JOURDIAN TRINITY AMBERVILLE, TWELFTH DUKE OF HEATHCOURTE, WEDS SPLENDOR. THE BRIDE WORE A SILK SHIRT AND CARRIED A HORNET IN HER POCKET. THE WEDDING WAS WITNESSED BY A BUTLER, THREE FOOTMEN, AND A ROOSTER.

"I'm still here to witness," Emil said, reading Jourdian's dismal thoughts. "Let's get you married, shall we?"

"Just pronounce us man and wife," Jourdian told the vicar.

"But, Your Grace, I must follow the ceremonial—"

"Splendor, do you take me for your husband?" Jourdian demanded.

"What? Oh, aye, My Grace! I do take you for my husband!"

"In sickness and health?"

She gasped. "Are you sick? If you are, you must tell me so I can quickly cure—"

"No, I'm not sick! I just want to know if you'll remain my wife if I *become* sick!"

"But why would I nay be your wife if you were sick, My Grace? You would need me more than ever then, would you not?"

Her answer melted the frown from his face.

"I take you for my husband," Splendor continued softly, smiling into his beautiful silver eyes. "I desire you for my own, and I shall endeavor to gift you with laughter and joy every day that I am with you. I shall fill your house with flowers, My Grace, and all that you desire to be blue, red, or green, will be blue, red, or green. Your wishes . . . you've but to tell me what they are, and I shall grant them. And in return I ask only for your child. Will you give me a child, My Grace?"

Her question reached inside him and took hold of his heart. He'd offered her elegant clothes, jewels, and fabulous journeys around the world. She'd rejected everything, leaving him to wonder if there was anything at all she really wanted. And now she'd made her request of him.

A child. She wanted his child.

"Jourdian," Emil prodded, "Say 'I do' and 'I will.' "

"I do and I will," Jourdian responded promptly.

"When?" Splendor asked.

"When?" Jourdian echoed. "When what?"

"When will you give me a child?"

"I . . ." He leaned down to her and whispered into her ear. "Splendor, now is the not the time to discuss such things."

"Oh? Well, when shall we discuss them?"

"Tonight," he murmured.

"Your Grace?" the vicar prompted him. "You must speak your own vows now."

"Do you take me for your wife, My Grace?" Splendor asked.

"In sickness and in health?" Emil added, thoroughly enjoying the outrageous ceremony. "For richer or for poorer? For better, for worse, for happy times and sad times, through obnoxious days and peaceful days, with hogs, donkeys, roosters, and hornets, forever and ever and ever, Amen?"

Jourdian gave a nod of assent.

"Marry them," Emil told Reverend Shrewsbury. "Hurry up!"

The vicar shook his head. "Marriage is a solemn commitment, Mr. Tate. A sacred union not to be entered into lightly, but with love. A sharing of two lifetimes together as one!" he exclaimed, raising his hands high in the air. "His Grace and Miss Splendor must swear eternal devotion. Only then will I pronounce them man and wife."

Reverend Shrewsbury's ultimatum broke the spell that held Jourdian's gaze riveted to Splendor's. He would not make this wedding more of a farce than it already was by promising to love Splendor.

He had no intention of loving her.

And as for the child she wanted him to give her . . . As well she *should* want his child! Her duty as his duchess was to provide him with an heir! Imagine his becoming all sentimental over her request for the child she was obligated to give him! Damn the woman for making him feel such sappy emotions.

He wouldn't let her do it again.

"Reverend," he whispered hotly, moving closer to the preacher so no one else would hear what he was about to say. "Might I remind you that this ceremony involves nothing remotely related to love? Your wagging tongue is one of the reasons I am standing before you tonight, and if you deny that charge, may God strike you dead. Now, I suggest that you make the final pronouncement of this ceremony without further delay. If you do not comply, you will soon be searching for another church, for the parish of Heathcourte will have a new —and more discreet—vicar."

Reverend Shrewsbury dropped his prayer book. "You cannot—"

"I assure you I can."

The hard glitter in the duke's eyes effectively reminded the reverend of Jourdian's power, and he realized then that if His Grace decided to replace him, the duke would complete the task swiftly, efficiently, and with no second thoughts. "The ring," he mumbled.

Jourdian slipped his hand into his pocket and withdrew the ring.

"Amethysts," Emil said, admiring the beautiful ring. "The exact shade of Splendor's eyes. How thoughtful of you, old boy."

Jourdian looked at the ring, then caught Splendor's gaze. Emil was right. Splendor's eyes and the sparkling gemstones were the same compelling shade of lavender.

Had he been thinking about Splendor's eyes when he'd chosen the ring?

His own mental question maddened him anew. Quickly, he pushed the ring on Splendor's finger, then glared at the reverend.

"I now pronounce you man and wife!" Reverend Shrewsbury boomed.

"Congratulations!" Emil exclaimed. He gave Jourdian a quick pat on the back, then turned to Splendor. Taking her hands, he kissed each of them. "You're fairly glowing with happiness, Splendor."

"Aye, that is what I am doing, Emil, because I am happier than I can ever remember being."

"We're family now," he told her. "And I want you to know that if there is ever anything I can do for you . . . anything you need, you've but to tell me. I'll be happy to do whatever—"

"I'm sure you will," Jourdian flared, removing Splendor's hands from Emil's grasp.

Emil smiled. "Married all of one minute, and already acting the part of the jealous and possessive husband, eh, Jourdian?"

Emil's observation rankled. Jourdian dropped Splendor's hands and turned toward the door.

"Your Grace," the vicar said, "you've yet to kiss your duchess."

"Quite right," Emil declared, still smiling. "Kiss her, Jourdian."

Noting that every gaze in the room was centered on him, Jourdian faced Splendor.

Smiling broadly, she raised her face and parted her lips in preparation for his kiss.

Jourdian bent and barely touched his lips to her forehead. There, he thought. She had his kiss, his ring, and his name. It was done.

He turned and walked out of the room.

<hr/>

"Did you find him, Mr. Tate?" Mrs. Frawley asked when Emil returned to the house.

Standing in the entryway, Emil took off his coat and handed it to Ulmstead. "No, and now it's too dark to see. Hopkins said he took Magnus and rode directly out of sight."

Mrs. Frawley looked straight into Emil's eyes, knowing she could speak her mind with him without fear of reprisal. Indeed, Emil encouraged the Heathcourte domestics to be open and honest with him. "But it's been three hours. His Grace didn't even stay to cut the cake with his bride. And a beautiful cake it is, too, Mr. Tate. On a moment's notice Mrs. Kearney managed to create the confection, and you would think that Lord Amberville would at least have one bite to show his appreciation. And what of Miss Splen— I mean Her Grace? The poor poppet. She's up in her rooms now. Alone. And this her wedding night! Oh, the poor little thing."

"She did appear rather sad, didn't she?" Ulmstead said, looking up the grand stairway. "That pretty sparkle in her eyes faded when His Grace marched out of the drawing room. How could his lordship have done such a thing?"

*Because he's a cad, damn him,* Emil answered silently. "I'll go speak to Splendor. Somehow, some way perhaps I can explain . . ." He stopped speaking. How could anyone truly explain Jourdian Amberville? The man was like an intricate puzzle whose pieces wouldn't fit together no matter how hard one tried to fit them.

Still, for Splendor's sake he had to try. "I'll go speak to her," he said again.

"And I'll have Tessie take her a bit of fruit and cream," Mrs. Frawley said.

Nodding, Emil crossed to the stairs. "Oh, Mrs. Frawley, did you ever solve the riddle of Splendor's silk flowers?"

Mrs. Frawley nibbled her bottom lip for a moment. "Mr. Tate, the only explanation I have been able to think of is that someone replaced the silk daffodils with real ones. Granted, daffodils are not in season in November, but— Well, perhaps one of the gardeners was able to grow the flowers in the conservatory or in the greenhouse. That must be the explanation, don't you agree? After all, silk flowers do not turn into real ones by magic."

"No, they don't," Emil agreed, then began his ascent up the winding staircase. In only a few moments, he stood before Splendor's door, knocking lightly. "Splendor?" he called softly, his lips pressed against the portal. "It's me, Emil. May I come in?"

Inside, Splendor flew down from the top of the canopy, changed herself into human size and, with a handful of stars, she caused Jourdian's silk shirt to float across the room and into her hands. Quickly, she slipped back into the soft garment. "Come in, Emil."

He walked into her room, and stopped abruptly.

He frowned and squinted his eyes.

Sprinklings of silver twinkled all around Splendor, as if stars had trickled down from the nighttime sky and drenched her copper-red hair and alabaster skin with their light.

She looked like an angel. Or some sort of magical being.

And Emil didn't know whether to fall to his knees or to run.

**9**

"**E**mil?" Splendor murmured.

Emil rubbed his eyes with the back of his hand, deciding he was seeing things. He was so tired. Exhausted from looking all over the damned countryside for Jourdian.

When he opened his eyes again, the silvery shine he'd seen all over Splendor had vanished.

"Emil?" Splendor said again.

"I'm sorry. I thought I saw . . . Never mind. I'd like to talk to you, Splendor, but if you'd feel more comfortable with me in one of the parlors rather than in your rooms, we can go downstairs."

She leaned her head toward her shoulder. "You are much like My Grace. He does not think it proper for a woman to be with a man in a bedroom, either. But he did not tell me exactly why, so I still am unsure. I have tried so very hard to understand him, but I cannot. Please close the door, Emil, because My Grace's cat is on the prowl. I saw him earlier, lying in wait in a pool of shadows down the hall. If only My Grace owned a rabbit or a hen rather than a cat, it would be ever so much easier to live here. Could you tell me what I did to make My Grace leave the house so abruptly?"

His mind spinning, Emil shut the door. "Splendor," he said gently, "it wasn't Jourdian's intention to marry you three days after having found you."

She nodded. "He had no choice."

"Then you understand."

"I do. He is enchanted with me, Emil. Wedding me was the only thing he could do."

Emil couldn't help but smile. Splendor was right. Jourdian was enchanted with her. But Emil knew his cousin would rather fight a lion with a toothpick than admit to being bewitched.

"Emil, do you remember all those things Reverend Shrewsbury said at my wedding?"

"Reverend Shrewsbury says a great many things, Splendor. The man has a big mouth, and it's rarely shut. Besides gossiping . . . You should hear his sermons at church. The man loves to hear himself talk, and he'd probably preach all day long if the growls of his congregation's stomachs didn't finally drown him out. I can barely tolerate him, and neither can Jourdian."

At that, Splendor began to deliberate. So the reverend irritated Jourdian, did he? So the reverend loved the sound of his own voice, did he?

She smiled a secret smile.

"What were you going to ask me about Reverend Shrewsbury?" Emil asked.

"Those vows he wanted Jourdian to make. The ones about love. Do those vows mean that there is love in my marriage to Jourdian?"

"Uh . . ." Emil walked farther into the room and sat down in a yellow velvet chair near the dresser. "I'm not the one to answer that, Splendor."

She decided to ask Jourdian instead. If, indeed, love was a part of their marriage, perhaps she could begin to comprehend the mysterious emotion.

"Are you very angry with Jourdian?" Emil queried.

She climbed onto the bed and stretched out in the middle of the soft mattress, wiggling her bare toes upon the soft yellow satin coverlet. "I was never angry with him. Anger does not come as easily to me as it does to him. I confess that I was sad, though."

"I see," Emil said, but he didn't "see" at all. "You're no longer sad?"

"I am happy that he married me. And soon he will give me a child."

*Not if he continues to stay away at night, he won't,* Emil replied silently.

"He is truly mine now," Splendor added. "I only wish I could understand him better."

Emil leaned forward in the chair and rested his elbows on his knees. "I came up here to talk to you about him, Splendor. He isn't an easy man to understand. As a lad—"

"He was lonely. He made many wishes, but then he stopped. He wept, and he yearned. Sadness was his companion. It still is."

Emil was amazed. "Did he tell you those things?"

"Nay. He speaks little of himself."

"Then how did you learn so much about him?"

She turned to her side. "I have watched him. One need only look to see."

Emil remained astonished. Splendor had learned more about Jourdian in three days than other women had been able to learn in ten years.

"He will nay allow me to make him happy, Emil," Splendor said. "And when I asked him questions that would help me to know him better, he became angry. Is he ever angry at you?"

Emil smiled. "About three hundred and sixty-four days out of the year."

"And what do you do when he's angry?"

"Sometimes I get angry right back at him."

"But I cannot get angry at him."

"And why is that?"

She moistened her bottom lip. "There are some who say my lack of aggressiveness is a fault," she said, pondering her father. "I am well aware of the fact that I am much too docile at times, but I . . . I fear I simply do not know the way to summon true anger."

"You should learn."

Splendor thought perhaps she would take lessons in aggressiveness and anger from Harmony. Surely there was no better teacher in the world.

"Practice on Jourdian," Emil suggested, then smiled. "You needn't fear him, for I assure you his bark is far worse than his bite."

Splendor frowned. She'd seen animals bite before, but never humans. She'd never heard humans bark either, for that matter.

"You don't always have to return his anger, however," Emil continued. "Sometimes he might need your compassion. Or a smile. Sometimes a hug. Let your own emotions tell you how to react."

Splendor knew her shallow fairy feelings would not aid her in her dealings with Jourdian.

"Of course, you must give thought to your own self as well," Emil said. "You don't always have to be so concerned about Jourdian that you ignore your own happiness. If he's not behaving as he should, by all means tell him so. If it is *you* who need the smile, compassion, or embrace, advise him. There are many men in the world who couldn't care less about their wives' contentment, but they are fools in my opinion. Granted I'm not married, but I believe that when a man takes the time to see to his wife's needs and wants, he'll be all the happier for it."

Splendor digested that bit of information carefully. If she told Jourdian exactly how she wanted him to behave, he would be all the happier for it.

And she so wanted him to be happy. "Very well, Emil, I shall tell him what I expect from him when next I see him."

"You do that. And don't let him cow you, Splendor. I understand that it's difficult for you to be angry at him, but it doesn't take true anger to stand up to someone. All you need is a bit of courage." Emil almost laughed when he thought about Jourdian being told how to behave by his delicate little wife. "And tell him about yourself. It's all well and good that you want to know him better, but let him know you better, too."

Splendor understood then that she'd been right in her decision to tell Jourdian about her Faerie origins. "I shall tell him about myself when next I see him."

Emil started to nod, but then shook his head. "Well, tonight's your wedding night, and not really the time for much talking."

"What will Jourdian and I do then?"

"What?" Good heavens, Emil thought. Jourdian hadn't exaggerated when he'd said Splendor knew nothing about lovemaking!

Emil didn't know whether to envy his cousin or feel sorry for him. "Jourdian will know what to do tonight," he answered lamely. "And tomorrow will be soon enough for you to begin telling him about yourself."

"Very well. But since he's not here, will you tell me more about him now?" Splendor asked.

"You're already acquainted with his dark side." Emil rose and walked to the window. There he watched shadows play in the moonlight on the terrace. "But there's another side to him as well. Jourdian may seem cold and uncaring, but . . ."

"He is neither cold nor uncaring."

"No. If not for him, I might still be living in a dilapidated cottage in the nearby village of Mallencroft, eking out a miserable living just as my father was forced to do."

"Oh? What did My Grace do for you?"

Without realizing his actions, Emil crossed the room and sat down on the bed with Splendor. "When I first met Jourdian I was the uneducated son of an equally ignorant tenant farmer, completely unacquainted with the sumptuous lifestyle of England's elite. I'd see their elegant carriages rumble by, but other than that I knew nothing about them. One fateful day, however, I happened to overhear my mother talking about the fact that she was first cousin to the duchess of Heathcourte. Isabel was Her Grace's name, but she wasn't always a duchess."

"What did she used to be?"

"A peasant. She was born and raised in a shabby cottage in Mallencroft much like the one I grew up in. Her name was Isabel Brockett."

"Brockett? But who in Jourdian's family was a Trinity?" Splendor asked, rubbing her hand across the yellow satin bed coverlet.

Emil wondered how Splendor had known of the name Trinity, until he realized she must have read it on the marriage certificate. "Jourdian's middle name is his great-grandfather's surname. Virgil Trinity. Virgil's wife was Pegeen. Their daughter was Abbie Trinity, Isabel's mother."

Curious to know more, Splendor sat up and moved closer to Emil. "How did Isabel meet Jourdian's father?"

Emil shook his head. "I'm not certain."

"Perhaps he was riding his horse, and she was out strolling. They met on the road on a bright day. Birds were singing all around them, and maybe there was even a fawn watching from the woods."

Emil grinned. "Perhaps. All I know is that when Barrington first saw her, he fell instantly in love with her. At least that's what I heard my mother say. Isabel really was a beautiful woman. She and Barrington were married shortly afterward, and Isabel left Mallencroft to live here in Heathcourte Manor."

He leaned against the bedpost. "From the bits and pieces I was able to gather, Isabel was always a flighty, self-seeking sort who never resigned herself to her poor social status. She longed to leave Mallencroft, see the world, and indulge in exotic adventures. I'm not altogether sure she even loved Barrington. But she certainly adored his wealth and the way he spoiled her. As the wealthiest peer in the realm, he was able to grant her every whim. Had she been a more compassionate person she would have had little problem convincing him to aid her destitute family in Mallencroft. But once she became his duchess, she severed all ties with her relatives."

"She was a frosty woman."

"Frigid. Shortly after her marriage, her father died, and her mother passed away only a month later. Isabel did not attend either funeral. She was too busy in London, spending Barrington's money."

A knock at the door interrupted his story. Tessie entered then, carrying a tray laden with fresh fruit, warm bread, and a pitcher of rich cream.

Splendor took the tray, set it on the bed, and reached for the maid's hand.

Tessie drew away. She had yet to understand how Splendor

had escaped from the room three days past, nor could she reconcile herself to the fact that Splendor had consumed a bottle of skin lotion.

Duchess or not, Splendor was a trifle balmy in Tessie's opinion. "Hope you enjoy it, Your Grace," she forced herself to say.

"I am certain I shall," Splendor replied, sensing the maid's trepidation. "And how kind it was of you to bring the food, Tessie." Quickly, she reached for Tessie's hand again, this time succeeding.

At the duchess's touch, Tessie felt an odd warmth travel from the tips of her fingers all throughout her body. A sense of peace came over her, one of calm contentment, and she grinned so broadly that she felt her ears move. "It was my pleasure, Your Grace." Smiling, she executed a small curtsy and then left the room, quietly closing the door behind her.

"The stains on her face embarrass her," Splendor told Emil.

"I know. I've seen her try to cover them with her hands. A shame there isn't a way to remove them."

Splendor smiled. "Are you hungry, Emil?" She slid the tray toward him.

For a while, they feasted upon the succulent fruit and warm bread.

"Please continue with your story, won't you?" Splendor asked.

"Of course. Where was I?" Emil thought a moment. "Oh, yes. Well, a year or so after Barrington married Isabel, Jourdian was born. It surprises me that Isabel stayed home long enough to give birth to him. She and Barrington were rarely home. They traveled all over the world up until the time Isabel died when Jourdian was eleven. Jourdian spent the majority of his childhood with his governesses, tutors, and the servants. Until I found him."

"And you were his first friend. 'Tis a supremely sweet thought."

Emil smiled a faraway smile then, pondering the day he'd first met his cousin. "When I first learned that I was related to the duchess of Heathcourte, I recalled she had a son. I didn't know how old he was, but I couldn't wait to see the aristocratic cousin I never knew I had. I really didn't hope to meet him face-to-face, but I thought perhaps I could catch a glimpse of him. So, I sneaked onto Amberville lands, and Lady Luck went with me—"

"A wonderful being," Splendor said.

"I beg your pardon?"

"Lady Luck. She's supremely marvelous. Why, think of how dismal the world would be without the good fortune she spreads!"

"Uh . . . Yes. Yes, quite right," Emil responded, and laughed. God, what a fanciful woman she was! A sheer delight to be with.

"You were saying, Emil?"

"What?"

Splendor bit into a piece of soft bread. "You sneaked onto Amberville lands, and Lady Luck went with you."

"Yes, and not ten minutes after setting foot upon the Heathcourte estate I discovered a well-dressed lad walking along the edge of a dense forest."

"Jourdian," Splendor whispered.

"Lonely Jourdian."

"Poor lonely Jourdian."

"Lonely, yes, poor, no. His suit of clothes cost more than my mother spent on food for a year. I summoned up my courage, walked straight up to him, and told him the entire story about how he and I were related. He was just as surprised to learn he had a cousin as I had been. He was nine and I was eight then. We met frequently after that. I tried to teach him childhood games, but he never caught on well. Still, I think he enjoyed trying to learn. And after we'd played for a while, he tutored me in all the classroom subjects he studied with his private school master."

Splendor nodded, remembering seeing the two of them romping through the meadows and reading books together.

"The duke and duchess never knew Jourdian and I were meeting," Emil continued, watching Splendor pour a glass of the heavy cream. "But I confessed to my own parents. And when they learned how lonely Jourdian was, they encouraged me to continue seeing him. My mother even knitted him a pair of stockings, and Jourdian wore them until they were threadbare. I remember thinking how odd it was that he preferred the homemade stockings to the ones he already had, which were of the finest quality. Now that I'm older, I understand that he liked my mother's stockings better because she'd taken the time to make them especially for him."

Splendor tried to comprehend what Emil said. "My Grace likes things made especially for him?"

"Well, they mean more, don't you think so?"

Splendor didn't know what to think, and soon decided that delight over specially made things was a human emotion she was incapable of feeling. "Tell me more, Emil."

Her interest in Jourdian pleased Emil very much. "As often as he could without getting caught, Jourdian would slip food from the Heathcourte kitchens and bring it out to me to take home to my family. He gave me many of his clothes and shoes, and once he gave me a set of solid gold candlesticks that he'd pilfered from right beneath Ulmstead's nose. My father sold the candlesticks in Telford, and the money kept us warm, dry, and fed for months."

Splendor grinned. She remembered the bright summer day when Jourdian had carried the candlesticks to a small structure built near one of the estate gardens. That was the day she'd chased the snakes out of Jourdian's path. If she hadn't forced them away, he'd have walked right on them.

"As I said, Isabel died when Jourdian was eleven," Emil went on softly. "Jourdian wept uncontrollably, but do you know? I don't believe he cried because his mother was gone, but for all the years of days and nights she could have been with him but wasn't. He never tired of listening to me tell stories about my own loving mother, and while I envied him his wealth and high social status, he coveted the affectionate relationship I had with my parents. He—"

"Why did you not take him to your home so he could enjoy your mother and father?"

"I used to beg him to come to Mallencroft to meet them, but he never did. He was probably right not to go. Someone would have recognized him, and then word might have gotten back to Isabel, who would have most likely found a way to keep him from ever seeing me again."

"How frigidly frosty of her."

"A regular ice maiden," Emil agreed. "When she died, Jourdian did everything he knew how to do to establish a relationship with his father, to no avail. Barrington withdrew into a world of grief after Isabel's death. He neglected his son and his estate, which had already begun to fall to ruin due to Isabel's excessive spending and the fact that Barrington was not in residence long enough to see to his holdings. Sorrow finally killed the man when Jourdian was seventeen. The funeral buried Jourdian's last hope for a loving relationship with his sire."

"A loving relationship," Splendor whispered, yearning to understand what such a thing was like.

Emil stuck his finger in the cream pitcher. "Jourdian left Heathcourte soon after the funeral," he said, licking the cream from his finger, "and with what was left of the Amberville fortune, he attended universities in Cambridge, Paris, Strasbourg, and Seville. He was even in Athens for a while, studying philosophy at the University of Otho. I didn't see him again for five long years, and when he returned he was different. He—"

"The five years," Splendor repeated, remembering those years when she hadn't seen him. "Away studying. He must have learned a supremely vast amount of things."

"Yes, but when he returned, he'd become hard and resolute. And when he set about repairing the damage done to his inheritance, he was ruthless in his dealings. Especially with Percival Brackett, the man you met yesterday."

"That is the man who sets a great store by his hair. He patted it as though each touch filled him with great joy."

"He's an eel who thinks he's a whale."

At Emil's description of arrogance, Splendor laughed.

"Percival, like his father before him, harbored deep resentment toward the Amberville name," Emil explained, smiling when he saw Splendor drink deeply of her glass of cream. "A resentment born of greed and jealousy. The Bracketts had always been the second wealthiest family in England next to the Ambervilles, but they'd always desired to be first. Excluding the royal family, of course. For a time—while Barrington squandered his fortune on Isabel and while Jourdian was out of the country studying—the Bracketts *were* the richest in the land. Indeed, they managed to acquire many of the Amberville holdings. And when Jourdian returned to his ducal lands, Percival wasted little time making sure Jourdian was made aware of the fact that the Bracketts had had a part in the destruction of the Amberville estate."

A deep frown scored Splendor's forehead and wrinkled her nose. "Percival deserves to be punished."

Emil chuckled. "Jourdian has been punishing that narcissistic dandy for ten long years. Every time some sort of promising business venture presents itself, Jourdian beats Percival to it, a fact that has made Percival Jourdian's one and only enemy."

"What is a narcissistic dandy?"

Emil folded his arms across his chest. "The eel who thinks he's a whale. According to Percival, he's all the go. But he *does* feel threatened by Jourdian."

Reaching for a plump red grape, Emil got back to his story. "As I said, almost as soon as he returned from his studies abroad, Jourdian began to rebuild the family fortune and regain society's respect for the family name. Your husband has a sixth sense when it comes to investing, Splendor, and within only one year's time he not only brought the Amberville estate back to its original financial status, he'd increased the family fortune several times over. And I watched him do it. My parents had both died while he was abroad, and he moved me right into Heathcourte with him for a while."

Emil paused then, his poignant memories affecting him deeply. "As a nobleman to be reckoned with by that time, he then set about carving out a place for me in society. Me, a common peasant . . . Jourdian took me to London, to every aristocratic gathering held. Members of the ton might have wanted to reject me, but they didn't dare insult Jourdian. It was difficult for me at first because I sensed that most of the aristocracy merely pretended to hold me in high regard. But, as I'm sure you've noticed," he said with a smile, "I am exceedingly handsome and personable. My looks and charismatic personality soon won everyone over, and I have been welcomed into society's bosom ever since."

Splendor returned his smile. "He has been very good to you."

Emil sobered. "*Good* does not begin to describe how he has been to me."

Hearing Emil's voice tremble, Splendor looked intently into his eyes. "His being good to you . . . Why does that make you sad?"

He looked at her curiously, unsure how to answer such an odd question. "Haven't you ever been deeply touched by someone's kindness toward you? So affected that you . . . It's not sadness. It's . . . it's profound gratitude. And affection. And an overwhelming sense of tenderness. It seems to pull at your heart."

Splendor strained to understand. "Does it hurt when your heart is pulled?"

He couldn't believe she was so completely unfamiliar with the emotion he was trying to describe. "That is only a figure of speech. The heart is not really pulled. It only feels that way."

Splendor remained confused. "And that is how love feels as well?"

His disbelief soared. "Are you saying you don't know what love is?"

"I—"

She was quickly silenced when the door opened and banged into the wall.

Jourdian filled the threshold.

"My Grace!" Splendor cried, her smile reaching from ear to ear.

Jourdian kept his cold gray gaze frozen to his cousin's face. "Emil, what the bloody hell are you doing in bed with my wife?"

Not realizing or remembering that he'd *joined* Splendor on the bed, Emil did not reply. He looked at Splendor, then at the mattress and canopy, and finally back at Jourdian. "I— She— You left, so I—"

"So you thought to take my place in her bed?"

"*What?* Jourdian, for pity's sake—"

"I don't recall giving you leave to stay here tonight."

"I would be in my own home in my own bed if I had not

spent the entire evening trying to hunt you down." Emil rose from the bed, nodded to Splendor, and crossed to the door. "You're in a black mood, cousin," he murmured. "Don't take it out on Splendor."

Jourdian's foul mood darkened further. "Am I to understand that you have appointed yourself her guardian angel?"

"That's as good a description as any I can think of."

"I see. In that case, you may sleep in the next room. There, you will be sure to hear her screams. Good night."

After one last look at Splendor, Emil quit the room.

Jourdian closed the door. "You are never to allow a man into your bedchambers."

"Then what are you doing in here?"

"I refer to other men. As your husband, I have the right to come in here as often as I am inclined."

"Very well. Will you join me, My Grace?" Splendor asked, gesturing toward the tray of fruit, bread, and cream.

When she leaned forward to reach for a bit of pear, Jourdian received a brief, but extremely enticing glimpse of her breasts.

His breakneck ride through the countryside had not eased his fury, but it had helped him to resign himself to his fate. He knew he could do nothing to change his situation, and although he was livid, he could not resist the damnable power Splendor had over him.

"I will, indeed, join you, Splendor, but not in dining."

She finished her pear, then drank more cream. "If you nay wish to eat, then what is it that you would like to do with me?"

He saw a drop of cream clinging to the left corner of her mouth, and ached to kiss it away.

"My Grace? I asked what it was you wanted to do with me."

"What men and women do in bed, Splendor."

She saw that luster in his eyes again. That gleam of excitement she'd seen yesterday, and she knew that whatever it was he wanted to do in the bed with her would make him very happy. "Aye, My Grace, but please remember that I do not know what men and women do in bed."

Unbuttoning his shirt, Jourdian sauntered toward her. "The time has come for you to learn . . ."

**10**

An unfamiliar feeling came over Splendor as she watched Jourdian take off his shirt. She'd been in awe of his strength for many years, but as she watched the play of hard muscle in his chest and arms now, she felt a mysterious but pleasurable sense of anticipation wind through her.

"I am looking forward to something," she murmured when he arrived before her. "Something . . . The power in your chest and arms makes me want to lick my lips the way I sometimes do when I am hungry and about to eat something of which I am supremely fond."

At her description of desire, Jourdian almost smiled. "I suppose that's one way of explaining how you feel, but I assure you that your feelings will deepen before we're finished."

She wiggled on the mattress. "That is not possible."

"Yes, Splendor, it is."

"My feelings do not run as deep as yours."

He took her statement as a dare, and knew he would meet the challenge with ease. Already she was squirming on the bed, and yes, she truly *was* licking her lips.

But the drop of cream still remained at the corner of her mouth.

He tossed his shirt into her lap.

His action intensified her feelings of want. She lifted the shirt to her face. It was still warm with the heat of his body, and its fragrance was of nighttime air. Of trees and fresh soil and moonbeams and starlight.

And another scent as well.

The smell of a man. A strong man. It was a dark scent, a potent one.

It was Jourdian's scent. It called to her as if with a husky, mesmerizing voice, and her need for the inexplicable something swirled and warmed inside her until she could think of nothing else but fulfilling her hunger for it.

"My Grace," she whispered.

"Jourdian," he corrected her.

She gave a slight nod. "This yearning I feel . . . And this thing men and women do in the bed together . . . The feeling and the bed activity are somehow related, are they not?"

"How astute of you to come to that conclusion."

She fidgeted on the mattress again. "I am ready for you to show me what men and women do in the bed now."

He removed his boots and stockings, and stretched out upon the bed. "We've got all night. I'm going to show you just how much more ready you can be. Now, come here."

Splendor lay down beside him and placed her hand on the swell of muscle beneath his nipple. "Jourdian," she murmured.

He liked the way his name sounded on her pretty pink lips. Liked the airy resonance her soft voice lent to it.

Her fresh scent of flowers aroused him further. He moved closer to her, and when his face was almost touching hers he licked the drop of cream from her lip and tasted her honeyed sweetness as well.

"This is very nice, lying here on the bed with you," Splendor said. Sighing with contentment, she raised her leg and draped it over his thigh.

He began to throb with need for her. He wanted to bury himself inside her, take her fast, wildly.

He would go slowly. Somehow, he would find the will to control himself.

"Oh, how sweet," Splendor said through a smile.

"What are you doing?" Jourdian asked when she pressed her hips into his leg.

"I'm—"

"Stop that," he ordered, in no mood to resist his desire for her any longer. He'd wanted her since first setting eyes on her in the meadow, and he would not be denied now.

"But Jourdian, I only want—"

"I know exactly what you want, Splendor, and I've told you before that it doesn't come from my leg."

"Then from where does it come?"

"I'm trying to show you."

"You are not trying quickly enough, Jourdian. If something is important, it must be done with the utmost speed, and you are taking your time—"

"Cease this chatter. What we are about to do has little to do with talking, and everything to do with touching." He began to unfasten the buttons on her shirt.

She moved his hand away and held it tightly. "You told me that 'tisn't proper for a man to see me without clothing. Granted, you saw me naked this morning, but that was because you took my piece of satin. 'Twas nay my fault, but yours."

"It's permissible for me to see you without clothing now because I'm your husband. Let go of my hand."

She released his hand and allowed him to continue the task with her shirt buttons. "And do you enjoy seeing me naked, Jourdian?" she asked, hearing her breath tremble when his knuckles brushed her nipple.

He cupped his hand over her breast. "I do. Now be quiet."

"Your touch sends heat through me, as if you were made of fire."

"I'm glad to hear that." Slowly, he slid the shirt off her shoulders. "Take your arms out."

"You are glad that I am so hot?"

"Yes, now take your arms out of these sleeves."

"I was going to suggest we open those doors and allow the night air to cool us."

"I want you hot, Splendor, and no night breeze is going to cool you. Now, if you don't take your arms out of these sleeves right now—"

Before he could finish, she pulled her arms from the sleeves.

And then she lay naked before him. "God, you're beautiful," Jourdian whispered.

She saw him staring at her body as if tonight were the first time he'd ever seen it. "You have seen me without clothing before, Jourdian. Why is tonight different?"

He slid his hand over her waist and rested it upon the gentle crest of her hip. "Before tonight, I could only see you. Tonight I am going to touch you. Touch every part of you until there is no doubt in your mind about what men and women do together in bed. And when I'm finished," he added, pressing a light kiss to her shoulder, "I'm going to do it all over again."

"My heart is beating like a hummingbird's wings."

A smile quirking the corner of his lips, Jourdian sat up and lifted her into his lap. Leaning over her chest, he took one rosy nipple into his mouth.

"Jourdian, I am certain that I have caught fire."

"Not yet, sprite. But I promise you that you will." Circling his tongue over the soft, puckered flesh of her nipple, he moved his hand from her hip, across the top of her thigh, and over the silken swell between her legs.

"Sweet everlasting, what is this you do to me?" Splendor cried.

He buried his face into the soft valley between her breasts, and when he spoke his lips caressed her skin. "I do what you tried to do for yourself."

"Oh, Jourdian, you were right," she moaned. "The pleasure does not come from your leg, but from your hand!" She raised her hips higher, more firmly into his palm.

Her head fell over the crook of his elbow, her long russet hair pooled upon the yellow coverlet, and it was upon that soft bed of copper shine that Jourdian laid her down again. Continuing to caress her breasts with his lips and tongue, he moved his hand lower, his fingers slipping over the softness of her femininity and into the warm moisture of her desire.

"You, too," Splendor whispered, squeezing the masses of muscle in his upper arms. "Let me do this to you, too. Show me the way. This feeling you give me . . . 'Tis a pleasure of which I cannot partake alone, Jourdian, but one I would like to share with you."

Her sweet generosity stirred his emotions. A soft, gentle feeling came over him, transcending his desire and making him want to please her more than he ever had another woman. "Later," he managed to tell her. "Let me show you first."

"That is your wish?"

"It is."

She granted his wish, and lay still and quiet.

But her silence did not last long. The moment Jourdian slid his fingers between the satiny folds of her womanhood, she cried out loudly.

"Shh! Do you want Emil to hear?"

Splendor didn't care who heard her. The only thing that mattered was finding release from the sweet ache caused by Jourdian's fingers. Again, she cried out, this time louder than before.

Jourdian realized he had to hurry, lest she bring the entire household running. He stroked her faster, and as he did, another sound joined her loud cries of pleasure.

Music. The same enchanting melody he'd heard in the parlor yesterday.

"Jourdian, please!" Splendor shouted when his intimate caresses slowed.

"But that music—"

"Don't stop," she panted, grabbing his wrist.

Despite the fact that Jourdian could not understand where the strange but beautiful music was coming from, he continued his endeavors to gift Splendor with her first taste of ecstasy.

Louder and louder the music became.

"Sweet everlasting!"

He knew she'd reached the peak of pleasure when her entire body began to tremble.

The music reached its crescendo as well, playing so loudly that it fairly shook the walls.

"Jourdian," Splendor whispered, still quivering as bliss rushed through her. It was a tempest of profound sensation, this thing that held her fast, and Jourdian was at its center, holding her there, lifting her higher and higher still until at last the most beautiful pleasure she'd ever known swirled through her.

"I have opened completely," she gasped. "Like a bud

spreading its every petal to the warmth of the sun, I have blossomed beneath the touch of your masterful fingers."

Jourdian knew he'd never heard such a dramatic description in all his life. He continued to caress her until she stilled and sighed. As soon as he knew she was replete, he started to comment on the music again.

But he no longer heard it. Quickly, he rose from the bed.

And so he didn't see that Splendor had risen completely off the mattress and hovered above it. By the time he turned to face her again, she'd floated back down to the bed.

"Jourdian, I have never known such pleasure existed."

"Existed," he mumbled. "That music, Splendor . . ."

"If this is what men and women do together in bed, Jourdian, I should like to do it morning, noon, and night."

"Yes. Yes, of course," he answered absently.

"Is something amiss?" Splendor asked.

"That music—" Damn it all, he was going to find the source of the music right now! He crossed to the door, opened it, and stepped into the dimly lit hall. "Get in the bed. I'll be back shortly."

When he vanished down the corridor, Splendor donned her silk shirt and followed him.

"I told you to wait in the room," Jourdian flared when she arrived by his side.

" 'Twas nay my wish to stay in the room, Jourdian. 'Twas my wish to go with you."

"You—"

The opening of a nearby door cut him short. "I say, is the wedding night over already?" Emil asked as he walked out of his room into the hall, tying the sash of the dressing robe he was wearing. "What are the two of you doing out here?"

"Emil, did you hear music a short while ago?" Jourdian asked.

"Music?" Emil frowned, smiled, then neared his cousin. "No, but I can certainly understand why you did," he murmured next to Jourdian's ear. He cast an appreciative glance in Splendor's direction. "The wedding night must have been a smashing success for you to have heard music, old boy."

Jourdian scowled at his cousin. "I tell you, I heard music.

And I heard the same inexplicable melody in the parlor yesterday morning."

"You've been working too hard, Jourdian," Emil replied, clapping his cousin on the back. "You should go on holiday. At the very least, you should take a few days off and indulge in a bit of sport."

Splendor grasped her husband's arm. "What sort of sport do you enjoy, Jourdian?"

He sighed with irritation. "I am not going on holiday, and I do not have the time for sport. What I want to do is understand where the blasted music is coming from!"

"Oh, hello, Tessie," Splendor said, suddenly spotting the little maid a short distance down the hall. "What are you doing?"

Tessie approached with a tall stack of towels in her arms, and bobbed a quick curtsy. "Begging your pardon, Lord and Lady Amberville, but what with the wedding this afternoon I didn't quite finish my work on this floor. I'll be through in only a moment."

"Did you hear any music?" Jourdian asked her.

"Music? No, your lordship."

"He heard music," Splendor explained. "An inexplicable melody, and now he is determined to find its source."

With wide eyes, Tessie looked up and down the hall, at both walls, and then at the ceiling. "Music from nowhere," she whispered. "Ghosts." She dropped the stack of towels.

They landed on Jourdian's bare feet.

"Ghosts!" Tessie wailed. "Oh, Your Grace, Heathcourte must be haunted!" Tears streaming down her birthmarked cheeks, she continued to wail.

"There are no such things as ghosts," Jourdian snapped at her. "And you will calm yourself this instant."

Splendor took hold of Jourdian's arm again. "You are supremely wrong, Jourdian. There most certainly are such things as ghosts. I've seen many of them."

"Oh!" Tessie sobbed again. She fell to her knees, still cupping her cheeks.

"There, there now, Tessie." Emil tried to calm the frightened girl. "His Grace won't allow the ghosts anywhere near you, will you, Jourdian?"

"There are no ghosts!" Jourdian roared.

"I will be happy to go through the house in search of ghosts," Splendor offered. "If I find any, I will see what I can do to force them to leave. But really, Tessie," she said to the wailing maid, "most ghosts are quite benevolent. Chances are if Heathcourte is home to spirits, they are kind ones you needn't fear."

Jourdian rolled his eyes. "Oh, of all the—"

"Of course, Heathcourte might house goblins," Splendor ventured. "Goblins truly are wicked, and if I find any I will be forced to summon aid to rid the house of them, for goblins are surely the most stubborn creatures in existence. Is that what you wish me to do, Jourdian? Look for obstinate goblins?"

He could do nothing but stare at her for a full minute. "That is the most ludicrous thing I have ever—"

"Perhaps you have brownies," Splendor thought aloud suddenly, tapping her finger on her chin. "A brownie is a hairy little man about twenty-five inches high. He likes to adopt houses, and when he adopts one he will look after that home."

"Splendor," Jourdian said, "please—"

"A brownie emerges at night to do work left unfinished by the human workers. All one must do to coerce him to do such chores is leave a bowl of creamy milk out for him, perhaps with a bit of bread and honey. But we must be careful not to insult a brownie in any way, for if we do he will punish us by shouting out our secrets for all to hear. He might destroy our clothing, pinch us while we sleep, or he could even beat us."

"Beat us?" Tessie cried. "Oh! Oh, Lord protect us!"

"That is enough!" Jourdian shouted. "Splendor, one more word out of you, and I'll—"

"Very well," she complied. "Just tell me if you want me to search the house for ghosts, goblins, or brownies. You know, we will recognize a brownie straightaway because some have no fingers or toes. Others have no noses. I will look for Heathcourte brownies, Jourdian. 'Tis the very least I can do in return for the supreme pleasure you just gave to me—"

"No," he interrupted before she could describe their love-making to Emil and Tessie.

"What of your own pleasure, Jourdian?" Splendor asked. "Did you not say that first you would show me—"

She broke off when she saw Jourdian's cat creep out from within the shadows down the hall. "The cat," she whispered. "Jourdian, he is hungry."

"Good night," Jourdian said to Emil and Tessie as he kicked the towels off his feet. Taking Splendor's hand, he led her back down the hall, leaving his cousin to deal with the hysterical maid and the stalking Siamese.

Once back inside Splendor's room Jourdian shut the door and turned on his bride.

"Are you not going to find the source of the music you heard?" she asked before he could say a word.

"Forget about the damned music. It must have been my imagination. You—"

"Oh, do you have a good imagination? I so admire creative minds. Musicians, writers, poets, weavers, sculptors, painters . . . All are precious and needed in this world, is that nay your opinion as well, Jourdian?"

"I am not going to discuss creativity of the mind, damn it all! I want to talk to you about—about . . ."

Bloody hell. What had he been going to talk to her about? Damn her for always making him forget what he wanted to say.

Shoving his fingers through his hair, he tried to recall what it was she'd said or done in the hall that had so angered him. After a moment, he finally remembered.

"For God's sake, why must you speak of such things in front of others, Splendor? What you said in front of Emil and Tessie was—"

"I did not think that talking about ghosts, goblins, and brownies was such a terrible thing, Jourdian."

"I refer to what we did in bed! What we do there is private, do you understand?"

She didn't understand. "Is what we did . . . Did we do something wrong? Is that why you do not want anyone to know?"

Reminded anew of her complete ignorance of the subject of sexuality, Jourdian took a deep breath. "No," he said calmly, "we didn't do anything wrong. We're married. But talking about our bedroom activities is totally inappropriate."

Nodding, she returned to the bed and lay down, her head propped upon a mound of yellow-satin-covered pillows. "I begin to see. 'Tis a secret."

"Fine. It's a secret."

"Is it a secret because Emil and Tessie have never heard of what we did in this bed? Are they as uneducated in the subject of bedroom activities as I was? If that is so, Jourdian, then we are obligated to enlighten them, for I assure you that my ignorance of the bed activity was a source of great frustration for me until you finally illuminated my benightedness. Would we nay do the same for our friends? Would we nay—"

"Nay—I mean *no* we would not! And if you think for one second that you now know everything there is to know about lovemaking—which is what the bed activity is called—then you are sadly, sadly mistaken. There is more, Splendor. Much more. Indeed, I have barely begun to tutor you in the art."

" 'Tis an art, this lovemaking?"

"Yes, and I'll not have you speaking of it with anyone but me!"

Staring at him, she remembered the advice Emil had given her earlier. "I do not need to become angry to confront you. I need but a bit of courage."

Jourdian watched her rise from the bed and cross the room, her hair like a shimmering cascade of flame. When she stood before him, she tilted her chin up and raised one auburn eyebrow.

"I have found sufficient valor to inform you that I do not care for the way you behave, Jourdian. I want you to be happy, and if you see to my needs and wants, you will be happier. Tonight is nay the time for talking, so I will refrain from telling you about myself. However, I shall take this opportunity to ask that you cease shouting at me, cease losing your patience, and cease treating me as though I were naught but an insect you could crush beneath your heel. Moreover, I ask that you embrace me at least fifty times a day and that you gift me with twice that many kisses. I also ask that you join me in bed for the art of lovemaking as often as I wish. That is, as soon as you have finished teaching me everything there is to know about it. As I ponder what you said, it occurs to me that there might be a few aspects about the lovemaking art that don't appeal to me. If that should prove true, I would not want to do them. Now, what say you to my requests?"

His gaze enveloped her like a dark shadow devouring a patch of sunlight. "What say I?" He reached for her waist and pulled her straight into him. "I say, Splendor," he said, his lips a whisper away from hers, "that you will like all the many things I teach you about lovemaking, and you will most assuredly want to do them."

"That is not for you to say," she murmured shakily, feeling that same sense of warm anticipation he'd made her feel earlier. "You cannot know what I like and what I do not—"

"I will know, Splendor."

"But—"

His kiss drank the rest of her words, his mouth settling over hers in a possessive manner he didn't care to think about at the moment. His need for her burning through his blood, he thrust his tongue between her lips in a rhythmic motion, deeply, relentlessly, and with a silent demand that she reciprocate in kind.

She obeyed instinctively, and slipped her own tongue over his bottom lip. Timidly at first, but when she felt his hands sweep under her shirt, smooth over her breasts, down her belly, and over her bottom, she responded with a boldness that surprised her, plunging her tongue into his mouth and pressing her hips directly into the hot, hard bulge at his groin.

The fire in Jourdian's blood grew with unbearable intensity. With one fluid motion, he swept Splendor into his arms and strode toward the bed. There he laid her on the mattress.

"Jourdian, I cannot find the words to tell you how strong I am feeling at this moment. Your kiss filled me with such—"

"The shirt," he whispered. "Take it off."

She slipped out of the garment and held her arms out to him.

"I'm going to undress now," he warned her softly, his gaze

pinned to her face. "Completely." Carefully, he studied her expression for signs that would tell him she was afraid or unwilling.

He saw nothing on her lovely face but joy. It shone from her smile and glowed from her eyes.

He unfastened the front of his pants, then rolled the waistband down over his hips. As he slowly revealed himself to Splendor, he waited for her to move her gaze from his eyes to his loins.

She watched only his eyes.

Jourdian removed his pants and undergarments, sure that when he was totally naked she would take at least one furtive glance at his sex.

"Are you afraid, sprite?" he asked when she did not examine his full length.

"I feel fear only when your light silver eyes become the color of hard gray iron."

"Look at me," he ordered sharply.

" 'Tis what I am doing, Jourdian."

Determined that she would see every inch of him before he continued with the bedding, he lifted his knees upon the mattress, one on each side of her hips, and straddled her. He took her wrists then, placing her palms on his thighs. Slowly, he pushed her hands higher until her fingers slid into the thick black mat of hair that shadowed his loins.

"Look at me," he demanded again. "All of me."

Seeing his command echoed within the silver blazes in his eyes, she lowered her gaze. Down his muscled arms and his corded chest. Over the flat expanse of his belly.

And finally to his masculinity. "What is this magic you possess, Jourdian, that you can change the appearance of your body?"

He saw a hint of curiosity in her eyes and heard a whisper of confusion in her soft voice, but she showed not a shred of anxiety. It was yet more proof that she had no idea of what he was going to do to her.

Gently, he clasped her right hand and curled her fingers around his turgid arousal. "It doesn't make you shy to see me this way, Splendor? To touch this part of me?"

Lost in the hard, powerful sight of him and the warm, thick feel of him, Splendor didn't reply. Her curiosity rising, she moved her hand upon him. Up to the velvety tip of him, then down to the base of him.

She'd never seen fairy men look this way before. This way . . . stiff and erect. " 'Tis much like a thick, fat cattail, isn't it?"

Her outlandish comparison stunned him into a moment of disbelieving silence. One second he felt insulted, and then he knew an instant of amusement.

He smiled, but resisted laughter. He'd been forced to marry Splendor, he sternly reminded himself. He was still furious.

But mirth continued to rise through his anger.

He was about to make love to his bride, for God's sake. Now was not the time to laugh.

He couldn't help it. Laughter rumbled in his chest then spilled from his lips, causing his shoulders to shake and the bed to bounce.

"You are laughing," Splendor said. " 'Tis a supremely joyful sound, Jourdian, one with which you should gift the world often."

He leaned over her, supporting himself with his hands beside her cheeks. For a second, he could do naught but stare at her beauty. The limpid violet pools of her eyes, the rosy softness of her lips, and her magnificent hair, which lay spread around her like a huge red halo.

The mellow firelight in the room cast a golden hue to her milk white skin, but he could still detect her sparkle. That odd but lovely glow she wore over her body like a shimmering silver veil.

"Jourdian?"

He felt her hand boldly traveling down his manhood again. Once more, he wondered about her casual inspection of him. "Splendor," he murmured, "I have accepted as true your unmitigated innocence, but what I cannot understand is your absolute composure at this moment. You act as though you have seen hundreds of naked men in your lifetime. Can you explain that, sprite?"

She blinked up at him. Humans wore clothing, she reminded herself, and her poor show of response over Jourdian's nakedness had struck him as quite peculiar.

Her mind spun like a dandelion puff whirling in the wind. "I— Every trace of you pleases me, Jourdian. Your arms as much as your face. Your face as much as your hands and legs and feet. I see you in your entirety. Is it wrong for me to be pleased by the whole of you? Or would you have me choose favorite elements of your body? Should I prefer your lips because of your kisses, or should I favor your hands because of the delicious pleasure their touch gives to me? I could fancy your arms because they feel strong when wrapped around me.

"Or," she added, her voice softening as her fingers caressed the velvet length of his masculinity, "I could choose *this* part of you as the best liked. I will endeavor to be partial to whatever part of your body you desire, but in truth I would rather be pleasured by all of you, for I did not marry this hot, hard aspect of you, nor did I marry your face, arms, legs, chest, or feet. I married you, Jourdian, the man, the whole man from top to bottom."

He knew there existed some manner of argument to her explanation, but he'd be damned if he could figure out what it was. On the contrary, the words she'd used to justify her calm acceptance of his nudity made him feel foolish for questioning her in the first place.

Still, he had to make some sort of comment. "A cattail, eh?" He glanced down at himself, and decided to accept her comparison as a compliment. Many years had passed since he'd taken the time to look at a real cattail, but if his memory served him correctly, they were none too small.

"Jourdian, I realize you are about to tutor me in the art of lovemaking, but I would remind you of the one thing I asked of you at our wedding this afternoon." Gently, Splendor tugged at one of the midnight locks of hair at the nape of his neck, then drew her finger along the chiseled crest of his cheek. "A child, husband. 'Tis what I asked of you, and you said that we would discuss my request tonight."

"We'll do more than discuss your request, wife," he answered huskily. "We will seek to fulfill it."

His reply so thrilled her, that she squealed with pleasure.

"And will we strive to fulfill my wish for a child now, or after you have schooled me in the art of lovemaking?"

"During."

She did not question him. Her father had told her Jourdian would know what to do, and she trusted that her husband did, indeed, know. "Then I am ready to conceive your child."

The instant the words were out of her mouth, she felt and saw an immediate change come over Jourdian. Every muscle visible to her tensed, grew, and his jawline hardened as if he were clenching his teeth. His breathing became labored and uneven, and a fine sheen of perspiration broke out over his forehead.

He lowered his massive frame upon her and, keeping his weight off her by propping himself up on his elbow, he covered her mouth with his own. Kissing her slowly, deliberately, he slipped his hand between her thighs. His fingers glided through the slick petals of her femininity and delved gently into her wet heat.

"Jourdian!"

His name on her lips heightened his blistering need to bury himself inside her. Assured that she was well prepared to receive him, he nudged her thighs apart with his knee, knelt between them, and grasped her hips.

"Wrap your legs around me, Splendor," he instructed.

The smoldering tone in his voice licked at her senses like fire. She curled her trembling legs around his waist, and felt the hot crown of his masculinity caress the hidden entrance to her body.

Hidden? she repeated silently. No part of her was hidden from her husband's hot, consuming gaze.

"Splendor, I'm going to be inside you in a moment," he tried to make her understand. To emphasize, he pushed into her ever so slightly.

Her eyes widened in alarm. "Jourdian, you don't mean to—"

"Yes."

"But . . . But 'twill not fit, husband!"

"It will, and I promise to give you the pleasure again, Splendor. Only this time, I'll feel it with you."

She summoned back her trust in him and lay still, hardly daring to breath as she waited for him to do this fairly impossible thing to her.

He tightened his hold on her hips, more than a little worried about the pain he was about to cause her. He'd never lain with a virgin before, and angry though he remained over the circumstances of their marriage, hurting his fragile bride was the last thing in the world he wanted to do.

Quickly, he thought. One swift thrust, and then he would do everything he knew how to do to transform her pain into the pleasure he'd promised her.

He took a deep breath and drew his hips back in preparation to drive them forward.

"Jourdian?"

His breath rushed from his lungs. "Splendor, for God's sake," he whispered raggedly. "I cannot wait any longer."

"But I only want to know one thing." She placed her hands on his belly, her thumbs rubbing over his navel. "When you do this lovemaking to me, does it mean that you love me?"

No sound did Jourdian make as her softly spoken question hit his ears. Indeed he could have sworn that the very beat of his pulse had ceased.

Love.

The emotion could tear to pieces the heart of a young boy and turn a strong and powerful man into a simpering fool. "Bloody hell."

The harshness in his voice scraped over her nerves like millions of thorns. She looked into his eyes—eyes as frigid and fierce as frozen daggers. She'd seen him angry several times since she'd met him in the meadow, but she knew it was not mere anger she was seeing now.

It was rage.

Truly frightened, she saw the first sparkles of her mist appear around her, and knew she would fade right in front of him.

But just before she surrendered to the irresistible pull of the glistening vapor, she saw Jourdian get off the bed and yank his pants on. He stormed out of the room without a word, slamming the door so hard that two paintings fell off the wall.

And the fairy princess he'd married wept diamonds and dissolved into a circle of shimmering haze.

**11**

Splendor's first thought when she awakened the next morning was to confront Jourdian. Sweet everlasting, she had so much to say to him. Not only was she determined to learn the reason why her mention of love had so infuriated him last night, but she was also intent on following Emil's advice. She would tell Jourdian about herself.

Today, this morning, her husband would learn that his pet name for her was an accurate description of who and what she was.

"I truly *am* a sprite, Jourdian," she practiced while donning the silk shirt she'd worn to her wedding. "A pixie, an elf, an imp . . . I am a fairy, husband, the princess royal of Pillywiggin."

She left her room and headed toward Jourdian's chambers, where she assumed he'd slept last night. His rooms were on the third floor of the mansion, and she flew up two long flights of stairs to arrive there.

Upon entering the long corridor, she saw the door to his chambers was open.

But it was Emil, not Jourdian, who stood inside.

"Emil, where is Jourdian?" she asked, stepping into the room.

He couldn't look at her. Instead, he stared at the ceiling. "Gone."

"Gone downstairs?"

"No, gone from this house. He left, Splendor. Ulmstead said he departed before dawn."

"But where did he go?"

Finally, Emil looked at her and hated the dejected expression he saw on her face. Damn Jourdian Amberville to hell and back, he seethed. How could the man leave his bride the day after their wedding? "I don't know where he went, Splendor, but I'm sure he won't be gone long. He'll be back. You'll see. He'll be back before you've even had time to miss him."

"I already miss him."

When he saw a suspicious glitter in her eyes, he moved to embrace her. "Don't cry," he murmured, patting her back. "Please don't cry."

A few more of her diamond tears sprinkled down to the floor before she stopped weeping. "I would like to be alone for a short while, Emil. Here, in Jourdian's room, where all his things are."

"Of course." He released her, and tweaked her nose. "I'm going home this morning, but is there anything I can do for you before I leave?"

"Nay," she said, and smiled. "Is there anything I can do for you?"

He felt like hugging her again. She was undoubtedly the sweetest person he'd ever met. "Yes. Be happy."

"I am almost always happy, Emil."

How true, Emil thought. Most of the time, she really was happy. What a fool Jourdian was to walk out on such a treasure. "I'll be back to visit you tomorrow."

"I shall look forward to seeing you."

When Emil was gone, Splendor shut the door. No sooner had she done so when the room filled with bright silver light.

And in the next second, a human-sized Harmony appeared. "Who is that man, sister?" she asked while floating on her back some six feet above the floor. "I saw him at your wedding yesterday, too. Oh, Father told me to tell you that he's glad you're married. You're to let him know the instant you're with child so you can come home to Pillywiggin. Are you with child?"

"Nay."

"When will you be?"

"I am not certain."

"How does one get with child? I asked Father, but he told me to ask Mother. Mother, however, is gone on one of her missions, as usual. She's been home but one time since you left, and she only stayed a little over an hour before she flew off again."

"She's very diligent with her missions. She must be."

"How does one get with child?" Harmony asked again.

Splendor raised her hands up by her shoulders in a gesture of ignorance. "I still do not know." She drifted off the floor to join her sister in the air. "I am supremely glad to see you."

Harmony flew to recline on the mantel, knocking several crystal knickknacks over in the process. The decorations fell to the marble hearth and splintered into millions of bits.

Quickly, Splendor cast a handful of stardust over the broken sit-arounds, and in moments the knickknacks were whole again.

"What a good-deed doer you are, Splendor," Harmony spat.

"Harmony, you must help me."

"Nay. I'm mad at you. Mad as mad can be because you spoiled my fun yesterday at your wedding. Really, Splendor, a few hornet stings—"

"You are mad at me?" Splendor smiled broadly. "Oh, 'tis precisely the sort of aid I need!"

"For me to be mad at you? Splendor, I think you have been with these humans too long. You are becoming demented."

Splendor floated nearer to the mantel. "I want you to teach me how to become angry."

Harmony's laughter burst through the room. " 'Twould be far easier for to me to teach a bull to play a harp!"

"Will you try?"

"Nay."

"But—"

"Who was that man in here with you?"

Anxious though she was to take anger lessons from Harmony, Splendor knew her sister would not be denied answers to any questions she might ask. "He is Emil Tate, and he is Jourdian's cousin."

"It does not hurt my eyes to look upon him."

"Aye, he is handsome, isn't he? A dear and kind man he is, too."

"A dear and kind man he is, too," Harmony repeated, imitating Splendor's soft, gentle voice. "How nauseating." Arms curled around her belly, she bent over at the waist and pretended to be sick to her stomach.

"Harmony, I rarely ask favors from you, as you well know. But—"

"Ha! Just four days past, you had me rid you of those prickles. These petitions of yours are becoming a habit, Splendor. And in case you've forgotten, *I'm* not the family wishgranter. *You've* won that revolting little title."

Splendor descended back down to the floor and sat down on a small stool across the room. "If I'm to make Jourdian happy, I must know how to become angry at him. He is angry often, and Emil says I should learn—"

"Who cares if he's happy or not? Honestly, Splendor, is there no end to your obnoxious goodness?"

Splendor chose her words carefully. "Speaking of his happiness, Harmony . . . I must ask that you cease tormenting him. You tied his hair into elf knots, didn't you? And when you stung him yesterday at the wedding you caused him pain. And when you threw his boots on his head the other day, you—"

"I'd rather hoped to knock him unconscious when I smacked him with the boots, but the man has a head as hard as a stone wall."

"But why must you bedevil him so?"

Harmony set herself on fire and burned a large black hole on the wall above the mantel. "Because 'tis what I do, sister," she said when she'd ceased to blaze. "I sow fear and gloom, and you sprinkle kindness, generosity, joy, and all that other sort of rot."

"Will you help me learn how to become angry?"

"Nay."

"But why?"

"Because I don't like helping. I'd rather be the reason why one *needs* help."

Splendor realized she was getting nowhere, and decided to try another tactic. "Very well, sister, I shall endeavor to find someone else to teach me the art of fury. It pains me to have to do so, for I know full well that there is no one on the face of our dear Mother Earth who understands and demonstrates rage as skillfully as you."

Harmony ran her hand down her long, golden hair. "I *am* rather marvelous at it."

"Supremely so."

"No one can fly into a faster fit than I."

"No one," Splendor agreed, suppressing a smile. "And such impressive fits they are, too, Harmony. Why, if I learn to fly into fits even half as well as you, I shall be satisfied." She rose from the stool and glided toward the door. "I must be on my way, sister. 'Twill take me a while to find someone given to frequent bouts of anger. Adieu."

"Wait," Harmony called. "I suppose I could teach you a few of my tricks. Not all of them, mind you, but a few."

Triumph soared through Splendor like a bright star shooting through a midnight sky. "And may we begin today? Now?"

"The sooner, the better. Your sickening sweetness 'twill take days and days to sour. Now, if the Trinity were to shout at you and then throw a rock at your head, what would you do?"

"I would dodge the rock and then tell him not to throw any more at me."

Harmony rolled her eyes. "I can't believe what a ninny you are. Nay, Splendor, you would catch the rock, throw it back at him, and hit him right between the eyes. You would shout a terrible name at him, and then you would turn him into a slime-trailing slug. A lovely touch then would be to put your heel over him and threaten to smash him into a glob."

"But—"

"You could change him back into a man after he's learned his lesson."

"Very well, Harmony, but how do I summon the *anger* necessary to perform such a ghastly deed?"

Harmony pointed to a spot in the air and flicked a bit of

stardust from her finger. Instantly the spot in the air became a tiny spark. "Think fire. The Trinity shouts at you or does something equally stupid, and a tiny spark ignites inside you. The longer and louder he shouts, the bigger and hotter the spark becomes, until finally . . ."

Splendor watched the small spark in the air become a huge ball of twisting red-hot fire.

"That's anger, Splendor. That's what it feels like. Like fire, and then it bursts from inside you. You strike out, like a hungry flame about to devour a dry and brittle leaf."

Splendor watched in horror while the fireball swept around the room, setting ablaze everything in its path. Flames seared the thick carpet, consumed furniture, licked up the draperies, and swallowed up Jourdian's bed. "Sweet everlasting, Harmony, stop!"

Waltzing through the walls of fire, Harmony glared at her sister. "You certainly know how to spoil all the fun, don't you, Splendor?" Frowning, she waved her hand upward, and a thick sheet of stars and rain fell from the ceiling, dousing all the fire and returning every burned thing back to its original immaculate state.

"Fire," Harmony said. "You must think fire, for anger burns through one much like flames."

"Fire," Splendor whispered.

"Try it now."

"But I've no one to become angry at."

"You have me."

"But you've done naught to make me angry."

"You're right. Well, I'll think of something to anger you with later. For now, let us chat, shall we? Actually, there *is* something I've been meaning to tell you. Something I think it only fair for you to know."

"And what is that, sister?"

Harmony smiled. "I'm going to take the Trinity away from you, Splendor. I've never had a human for my own and, as much as I hate the creatures, I still want one. And I've chosen the Trinity. I'll allow him to get you with child and all that, but he will be mine, not yours. I'm going to keep him in a bottle in my room and feed him gnats."

Splendor's first impulse was to submit to the peaceful refuge of her mist, but she stubbornly fought the temptation. "I will nay allow—"

"I do not recall asking your permission, sister. The Trinity will be mine, make no mistake about it."

Although the room was chilly, Splendor began to feel warm. Not outwardly, but inside. And the warmth steadily grew in intensity until she felt hot. Very hot.

As if she were on fire.

"Nay, Harmony," she said, hearing her own voice simmer.

"Aye, Splendor," Harmony taunted. "Mine, mine, mine. The Trinity is *mine!*"

"Nay!" Splendor shouted as loudly as her lungs would allow. "If I catch you anywhere near him, Harmony, I'll—I'll—"

"You'll what?" Harmony pressed.

"I'll put you in an iron box!"

The very mention of the word *iron* caused Harmony to shrink to Pillywiggin size. Several minutes passed before she recovered from her fear. "That was fine, Splendor. But you wouldn't really put me in iron box, would you?"

Instantly Splendor regretted her terrible threat. "Oh, Harmony, no! I would never do such a thing! Surely you know that I would never hurt my own sister! Surely you know that I—"

"All right, all right, you don't have to overdo it. But why did you threaten me with iron?"

Splendor wrung her hands in her hair and fought back tears. "You must forgive me. I was worried. Supremely upset. You said you were going to take Jourdian away from me, and I—"

"I know what I said, but I didn't mean it. And it didn't look to me that you were merely worried, Splendor. If I didn't know better, I'd say you were angry. At the very least, you were immensely irritated. And this is only your first lesson in anger, so immense irritation is a good start. With a little more practice you should be able to heat that irritation into true fury."

Splendor recalled the hot feeling she'd experienced when she thought her sister planned to steal Jourdian, put him in a bottle, and feed him bugs. "Oh, Harmony, you taught me so quickly."

Harmony flew toward her sister and alighted upon Splendor's shoulder. "I am an expert at ire. A genius with wrath. The leading connoisseur of hostility. A veritable virtuoso at rage."

Splendor removed her sister from her shoulder and held Harmony in her hand. With her pinkie finger, she stroked Harmony's tiny cheek. "You are teaching me anger, dear sister, and so I shall teach you kindness and gentleness. I shall instruct you in the art of generosity and—"

"Satan save me, I think I'm going to be sick."

And right before Splendor's eyes, Harmony turned herself into a rock and pitched herself through the sparkling window.

*❦*

"She's done naught but read since the duke left Tuesday last, Mr. Tate," Ulmstead said, standing in front of one of the duke's office windows with Emil, Mrs. Frawley, and Tessie. He paused a moment to calm the squirming chipmunk he'd discovered in a closet and now held in his hands. "An entire week of reading nothing but Shakespeare."

Emil pulled back the velvet draperies and peered through the glass. There in one of the estate gardens was Splendor. Sitting in a mass of ground ivy and the fiery pool of her hair, she was bent over the thick book in her lap. "What's that black garment she's wearing?"

"Another of His Grace's dressing robes," Tessie replied, she, too, watching Splendor through the big window.

"She looks as if she's in mourning," Emil said. "Doesn't she have anything else to wear?"

"She spilled cream on the purple robe, sir," Mrs. Frawley said. "And I was able to talk her out of wearing any more of His Grace's shirts."

Emil frowned. "She's been here for almost two weeks, and

still has nothing to wear. I thought some gowns had been made for her."

Mrs. Frawley sighed. "She can't abide the fussy adornments on any of the gowns the Mallencroft seamstress has delivered. The lady returned for them two days ago and promised to bring back plainer dresses. It would seem the duchess has simple tastes."

"And much pride and courage," Ulmstead added. "Another bride might have wept for days upon the abrupt departure of her groom, but not Her Grace. She's putting on a good show of contentment, smiling, laughing . . . I even heard her singing yesterday. And a lovely voice she has, too."

"But it's *only* a show, mind you," Mrs. Frawley declared. "The poor lass is hiding a broken heart, you can be sure of that. No woman could accept her husband's abandonment without a bit of grief. Especially Her Grace. She truly cares about the duke. Why, she told me herself that the reason she's been poring over Shakespeare's works is because His Grace told her he enjoyed the stories. I imagine she hopes to impress him with the fact that she's read his favorite books."

Emil watched Splendor turn a page in her book, but knew there was little chance of her impressing his cousin with a bloody thing if Jourdian didn't come home from wherever the blazes he'd gone off to.

Damn the man. Not only was he the richest, most powerful aristocrat in England but he also possessed a wife almost too beautiful to believe. Hundreds . . . No, *thousands* of men would envy him.

And what did the misbegotten cad do? "Leave," Emil thought out loud. "He just mounted his horse and left. Without as much as a fare-thee-well."

"You've found no leads to his whereabouts then, Mr. Tate?" Tessie asked.

"No, but I'm wondering if he might have gone to Briarmont."

Ulmstead thought about Briarmont. Another of the duke's four country estates, it was but half a day's ride from London. "Will you look for him there, sir?"

"I will if he doesn't come home soon. But I hesitate to

begin an extensive investigation for fear the whole countryside will learn that Jourdian left his bride the day after their wedding. Lord knows *someone* must protect them from yet more vicious gossip."

"A wise and loving decision you've made," Mrs. Frawley said. "His Grace is blessed with you for a cousin, Mr. Tate. And one day you'll make some sweet young girl a fine husband. A fine one, indeed."

Emil smiled a crooked smile. "I'll see Jourdian settled first, thank you very much."

The foursome watched Splendor for a while longer before Emil spoke again. "You're more than likely right about her, Mrs. Frawley. Even as we watch her, I bet she's memorizing Shakespearean lines she can quote to impress Jourdian."

"Has my office become spy headquarters?" a deep voice asked from across the room.

Emil and the three servants turned from the window and saw Jourdian standing on the threshold.

"Your Grace," Ulmstead, Mrs. Frawley, and Tessie greeted him in unison.

"When I arrived there was no one to meet me at the door," Jourdian said. "Now I find my butler, housekeeper, and upstairs maid staring out of a window. Am I to understand that the three of you have forgotten your duties during my absence?"

"No, Your Grace," Mrs. Frawley quickly replied. "We were only watching Her Grace—"

"They're concerned about Splendor," Emil interjected hotly.

"And spying on her from my office window will calm their worries," Jourdian answered sarcastically. He glanced at the three pale-faced domestics. "You are dismissed."

They hurried out of the room.

"Where the devil have you been for the past week?" Emil demanded.

Jourdian strode toward the liquor cabinet and poured himself a liberal portion of brandy. "Briarmont."

"I thought as much. If you hadn't come home, I was going to go drag you back."

Jourdian chose to ignore that particular tongue lashing. "I

went to Briarmont to finish the paperwork concerning the Gloucester orchards," he lied. The Gloucester papers, he thought. God, he hadn't seen them, much less worked on them, in over a week.

"You've got more on your plate than your damned investments now, Jourdian. You've got a duchess to see to, and you could have finished your perishing paperwork here at Heathcourte."

"My house has become a circus."

"How dare you leave Splendor for an entire week!"

"She must accustom herself to my absences. I'm gone often, as you well know."

"But you left her the day after your wedding."

Jourdian took a long swallow of brandy. "A wedding that was forced on me."

"You're a cad."

"So you've said."

Emil walked away from the window and stopped in front of his cousin. "Splendor has been reading Shakespeare all week because you told her you enjoyed the plays. It's likely she's trying to memorize lines with which to impress you."

"Then I must act duly impressed when she recites them, mustn't I? I'll applaud."

"She's trying to make you happy."

Jourdian drank the rest of his brandy.

"You're afraid," Emil announced. "If you allow your feelings for Splendor to continue to grow, you might turn out like your father, isn't that right, Jourdian? In your mind, Barrington's love for Isabel was the man's downfall."

"Emil—"

"You're going to hurt Splendor."

"Splendor is not your concern."

"*Someone* must watch out for her feelings."

Jourdian slammed his glass on the liquor cabinet. "Your easy camaraderie with Splendor doesn't sit well with me. Stay away from her."

"You won't be her companion, but you won't allow anyone else to keep her company either, is that it? You'll keep her here at Heathcourte the way one would keep a porcelain doll behind glass. You'll glance at her every now and again, but other than that, you'll do everything you know how to do to pretend she doesn't exist."

Jourdian strode to his desk and sat down. "I never said I forgot her while I was at Briarmont."

"You missed her?"

"I wondered what new manner of trouble she was causing in my absence and what I would be forced to do to repair the problems."

"You're a—"

"Cad," Jourdian supplied.

Emil marched to the door.

"Where are you for?" Jourdian called.

Slowly, Emil turned and glared at his cousin. "I'm going to be with Splendor. You already believe the worst about my relationship with her, so it will do me no harm to give credence to what you believe. Stay here in your bloody office, poring over your bloody papers, and I'll go charm your lovely wife. She sits in the ivy garden right outside this room. Cheery-bye."

Quickly, Emil left the room and raced down the hall. In the entryway of the mansion he opened and slammed the door, but didn't exit. Instead, he hid behind a marble pillar, and waited.

Seconds later, Jourdian stalked into the foyer and stormed outside.

Emil smiled.

Jourdian proceeded around the outside of the house toward the ivy garden, sure he would find his cousin flirting with Splendor. It occurred to him that he was again acting the part of the jealous husband that Emil had accused him of portraying at the wedding, but in the next moment he dismissed that possibility.

He was simply protecting what belonged to him. Emil could go out and get his *own* wife, damn it all. The duchess of

Heathcourte would not be touched or ogled by any man but her husband!

Shortly, he arrived at the ivy garden, but Splendor and Emil weren't there. Thinking they'd gone for a stroll, he began to search for them. Vast though the grounds were, no small area escaped his scrutiny. Finally, after well over an hour, he spotted Splendor near the forest. Book in hand, she was alone.

He stopped to watch her.

A swift autumn breeze teased her long, flowing hair and picked up the black satin folds of the dressing gown she wore. She seemed to float, for no sound did she make as she walked along the edge of the glade.

Jourdian knew he'd never seen a more graceful woman than she.

He pondered his trip to Briarmont. He'd ridden across the miles as if every fiend in hell were trying to catch and drag him into the perpetual fires of damnation. But swift though Magnus was, the stallion could not outdistance his master's demons. The devils caught up with Jourdian at Briarmont, reawakening his rage over Splendor's request for love, and kindling his guilt for leaving her only hours after their wedding night.

Why had he thought about her every moment he was away? Was it because almost every leaf he saw reminded him of her autumn-kissed hair? Because every delicate cloud in the sky brought to mind her pearly skin? Because every soft sound of nature he heard prompted the memory of her innocence?

Or was it because he missed the way she made him smile and laugh? He hadn't smiled once since he'd left her, much less laughed. In truth, he'd been utterly lonesome at Briarmont, and many times during his stay there the memory of her sweet chatter sang through his mind.

Jourdian continued to watch her. A small thorny plant caught the skirt of her robe as she strolled, pulling the garment away from her long, slender legs.

He remembered how those gorgeous legs felt wrapped around his waist.

Lust, he mused. Perhaps he'd thought about Splendor and come home to her because she remained a fire in his blood he hadn't yet quenched. Even now, as he watched her meander near the forest, desire for her burned through him.

He would bed her today, he decided. Now, as soon as he could get her into his bedroom. And if she dared to mention love again, he would make his feelings on the subject clear to her immediately.

He started to call to her then, but stopped when she paused beside a large tree, laid her book down, and curled her arms around the thick, rough tree trunk. It looked to Jourdian as though she were embracing the tree.

She looked up into the tree branches and lifted her hand. A tiny yellow bird with a bit of twig in its beak fluttered down and landed in the palm of her hand. Another bird, a red one, swooped down and alighted atop her head.

She laughed then, and the sound of her laughter sang through Jourdian's senses. Enchanted, he watched as she reached for the red bird on her head and brought the creature close to her face. It rubbed its soft head against her chin and chirped merrily when she caressed its feathered belly.

"Look there," Jourdian heard her say. "We've another friend here now."

Astonished, Jourdian saw a doe come out of the woods. He saw Splendor kneel on the leaf-strewn forest floor, and the lissome deer walked straight into her open arms. The birds still in her hands, she embraced the doe's slender neck, and she laughed again, gently, and with such absolute contentment that Jourdian smiled.

"Splendor," he called softly.

The birds sailed back into the trees, and the deer bounded back into the woods.

Slowly, Splendor turned and looked behind her.

There stood Jourdian, late afternoon sunshine dancing through the waves of his ebony hair. He wore a tight pair of riding breeches that clung to every ripple and bulge in his lower torso, and his long-sleeved ivory shirt was unbuttoned at the top, revealing a V-shaped portion of his muscular chest.

Hunger for him assailed her, and now she knew exactly what she hungered for. "Let us go to the bedroom, shall we, Jourdian?"

Her question pleased him enormously. Innocent though she was, she possessed a simmering passion just waiting to be ignited. "No 'hello, husband' first?" he teased her.

"Hello, husband." She smiled.

The brilliance of her grin fairly blinded him.

"Why did you leave me, Jourdian? I missed you supremely."

He shuffled his feet in the grass, then stopped himself. What had he to feel bad over? He could go wherever he pleased, whenever he pleased, and Splendor would have no say so over the matter! "I had some business to attend to. And you would do well to accustom yourself to my traveling."

"I shall accompany you when next you leave. But *you* would do well to understand that I believe you work overly much. Sadly, however, you do not know how to play."

He changed the subject. "I saw you with the animals," he said, walking toward her. "I've never seen anyone entice birds from the trees and deer from the forest. The creatures showed no fear of you at all. Wild animals. Unafraid."

When he stood in front of her, she laid her hands on his shoulders. "I told you that 'tisn't my practice to frighten. The birds and the doe hadn't cause to fear me, for they knew I'd nay harm them."

Jourdian picked up a thick lock of her hair and watched the vibrant strands slip over his fingers like red satin ribbons. "And how did they know not to fear you?"

"Because they are animals. And animals have the gift of sensing who will hurt them and who will not."

"The animals fled at my approach."

" 'Tis something for you to ponder in times of solitude."

Jourdian couldn't suppress yet another smile. "Touché." He glanced into the woods. "Can you bring the animals back?"

"Aye." She faced the shadowed forest again and made cooing sounds.

The yellow finch and redwing returned to her immediately, one settling on her hand, the other on her shoulder. The doe, however, approached more cautiously, her big round eyes centered directly on Jourdian.

"She's frightened of you," Splendor said. "Kneel before her, Jourdian."

"Kneel before an animal?"

" 'Twill make you shorter than she and less intimidating."

Before this day he'd knelt before royalty only. Now he knelt before a deer.

"Hold out your hand, Jourdian, palm up, and make a soft noise for her."

He held out his hand and whispered, "Come here."

The doe joined Splendor and the birds. "She knows you're master of these lands," Splendor said, caressing the deer's ears. "And she thinks you cruel."

"Cruel? I've done nothing to her."

"You have. Your estate workers will nay allow her to eat the berries that grow in various places in your yards. They have chased her and her friends away. Several times they have thrown stones at her. You employ the workers, Jourdian."

"But I didn't know my gardeners weren't letting her eat . . ." He stopped speaking, frowned, and stared at Splendor. "You act as though you speak and understand the deer."

"I do. I can communicate with all animals. I understand plants, too."

"Plants. I see."

"Plants speak to those who listen. The ivy in your ivy garden is very happy where it is, but the chrysanthemums at the front of your house are distressed because they are soon going to drown if your gardeners do not reroute the rain that pours down from your roof and balconies."

"Distressed chrysanthemums. Of course. Splendor, shall we return to the house? I think you've had enough sun for one day."

"And shall we go to the bedroom, Jourdian?"

"Directly there without stopping once."

Gently, she released the birds, bid the doe farewell, and retrieved her book of Shakespeare. Looping her arm through the crook of Jourdian's elbow, she grinned up at him. "I have been reading your Shakespeare."

"And have you enjoyed his works?" he asked, leading her toward the manor house.

"Last night I longed to walk out on the balcony of my room, but of course, I couldn't because—"

"You are off on a tangent, Splendor. I was asking about Shakespeare."

"Aye, that is what you were asking about, Jourdian, and I am trying to tell you. Last night I longed to walk out on the balcony, but I could not because 'tis made of iron. I have asked you to rid the house of iron, but you have not heeded my request. You must be more mindful of my needs, Jourdian. I will overlook your inconsideration this time, but beware of the fact that I am learning the art of anger and will not hesitate to demonstrate my newly found skills.

"And so," she continued without pause, "I could not walk on the iron balcony last night. Instead, I opened a window, leaned out, and said, 'Jourdian, Jourdian, wherefore art thou, Jourdian?' "

"Wherefore . . ." Jourdian could hardly think straight, what with all her chatter bouncing through his mind. "Why have you such a strong aversion to iron?"

"I will tell you later."

He escorted her past the ivy garden and around to the front of the house. "I want to know now."

"But you will not know now, Jourdian, because I am not going to tell you until later. Romeo and Juliet are my favorite characters in this book. Do you like them as well?"

"Yes. Splendor, I'll not have you disobeying me, do you understand? If I tell you to do something, you must do it at that precise moment without hesitation. Your unwillingness to explain your aversion to iron—"

"And do you like Hamlet, Lady Macbeth, and the three witches, too?" Splendor asked as he assisted her up the steps that led to the front door of the house. "I liked the part in *Macbeth* when the three witches stir the cauldron and make the prediction that Macbeth will first become the new thane of Cawdor and then king of Scotland. 'Double, double toil and trouble.' 'Tis what they said, Jourdian."

"I know, Splendor." Jourdian opened the door and led her inside. "Now, about the iron—"

"I've a surprise for you. I think 'twill make you very happy. I will give it to you in the bedroom."

"What is it?"

" 'Twill not be a surprise if I tell you, Jourdian. But, suffice it to say that this surprise is going to give you supreme pleasure."

"And you'll give it to me in my bedroom?"

"Aye, that is where I will give it to you."

Jourdian had to restrain himself from bedding her right there in the entryway. He looked up the long, winding staircase. It was only the first flight of stairs he would have to climb before arriving at his chambers on the third floor.

"What is this look of exasperation on your face, Jourdian?"

"It's a long climb to my bedroom, sprite. And anxious as I am to receive your surprise, I wish we were already there."

Splendor took a quick, deep breath. The time had come, she thought. He'd made a wish. She'd been going to wait until she'd given him his surprise before telling him about her enchanted origins, but now was as good a time as any to reveal her identity to him.

"Your wish is granted, husband." She opened her hand, out of which streamed thousands of tiny silver lights.

And in the next moment, Jourdian found himself standing in the middle of his bedroom.

**12**

lack jawed with disbelief, Jourdian stared at his room as if he'd never seen it before. He didn't speak, didn't move, didn't breathe.

"Jourdian?" Splendor took his hand and squeezed it tightly. "You know that name you call me? Sprite? Well, 'tis a good name for me. An accurate one."

He didn't reply. He couldn't.

He could only gawk at the room. Every single item from the carpet to the ceiling, had changed color. The walls were a bright red; the windows were now of green glass. All the wood furniture was blue.

The whole room was red, green, and blue.

And in every available nook, cranny, and crevice . . . on and inside and over every accessible spot, there grew a plant. Dozens of them. Some sort of red flowering vine twisted up the posts of his bed and around the closet door. Huge yellow roses spilled down tables, off the fireplace mantel, and over the floor. Thick rows of multicolored wildflowers edged the four walls, and a small evergreen tree grew atop the dresser.

Nothing was planted. Nothing was in a container, and nothing stemmed from dirt.

The plants sprang directly from the floor or from furniture.

"Jourdian? Did you hear what I said?"

Still speechless, he walked backward until his legs met the

chair behind him. He sat down. "I had only a splash of brandy earlier in my office. I'm perfectly sober."

Splendor glided toward his chair. "I am glad that you are not hysterical. Mrs. Frawley and poor Leonard both fainted when they witnessed my magic, and Tessie was afraid of me until I touched her with a bit of peace. Ulmstead was frightened when I made Delicious disappear, but I am going to give him some hair soon as a secret apology for scaring him. I am also going to rid Tessie of the marks that mar her face, and Hopkins of his stutter, but first I must—"

"Sober," Jourdian repeated, his gaze still sweeping around the room. "But one second I was in the foyer, and now I'm—"

"You wished to be here in your bedroom, Jourdian. I told you I would grant your wishes, and 'tis what I did when I brought you up here. And you said I could fill your house with plants. I have not done the rest of the house yet, but only your room. And what of your favorite colors? You said they were red, blue, and green. I did a bit of redecorating while you were gone. Do you like your room? Everything is red, blue, and green. Even your clothes."

She drifted toward one of his dressers, opened a drawer, and withdrew a pair of stockings.

Jourdian saw his socks were blue. Not dark blue, but light blue, like a spring sky.

"And look here, Jourdian." Splendor crossed to the closet and selected two suits, one crimson red, the other grass green. "I've changed the color of all your shirts, shoes, neck cloths, outerwear, gloves, and hats, too. All in your favorite colors! Everything I have done in your absence . . . 'tis the surprise I had for you. Are you not pleased, husband?"

"No, I'm asleep. I have to be asleep."

Splendor joined him by his chair again. "You are awake." She reached out and pinched his arm.

He felt the sting. "I'm awake." His heart was beating so fast, he wondered if he would soon collapse and die.

"Aye, Jourdian, you are awake. And I am a Pillywiggin fairy. Pillywiggin. 'Tis the name of my father's kingdom, which lies beneath the floor of the woods near the meadow where we met."

Slowly, he looked up at her. His thoughts twisted, tangled, and knotted in his mind, and he could not think coherently. "A fairy," he mumbled.

Memories returned to him. Childhood memories he hadn't thought of in many long years. He saw Emil in his mind, and his cousin was but a small boy.

*Wouldn't it be grand if we found a fairy, Jourdian?* Emil had once asked. *Fairies live all over England, you know. They have sparkling wings and carry wands.*

Jourdian continued to stare up at Splendor, his thoughts still jumbled beyond control. "No wings," he muttered. "You don't have a wand either."

"I do have wings, husband, but I do not wear them often because they are so hard to keep clean. Dust catchers are what they are, and if you have ever cleaned dust off a fragile pair of fairy wings without tearing them, you understand my frustration with them. And Father will nay allow me to give the task to the servants. He says we must all learn to clean our wings ourselves. So, I do not use my wings much. I can fly supremely well without them. And if I grow weary—which is often, especially if I must fly over a long distance—dragonflies make excellent mounts.

"As for wands," she continued. " 'Tis naught but a myth that fairies carry wands. The Pillywiggins simply open their hands or stretch out their fingers, and magic flows."

"A fairy," Jourdian said.

"A fairy princess. And in answer to your earlier question, I fear iron because that particular metal can take away a fairy's power. One touch . . . Just one touch of iron will forever divest me of my magic."

Jourdian felt dizzy, as though he'd turned around and around and around too many times. His mouth was parched, and he couldn't seem to get a deep enough breath to fill his lungs.

"My father is King Wisdom of Pillywiggin," Splendor added. "My mother is Queen Pleasure, and my sister is Princess Harmony. 'Twas she who tangled your hair, dropped the boots on your head, and stung you at the wedding. I must warn you now that she will take a kiss from you, Jourdian. I promised her she could have one when she rid me of the prickles, and I cannot go back on my promise. But 'twill be a short kiss, and she will nay take another. Exasperating though she can be at times, I have never known her to break an oath."

Jourdian closed his eyes and held his head in his hands. He wasn't drunk, and he wasn't asleep. "Splendor," he whispered, the small sound an effort to make, "how did I get into this room?"

"I brought you here."

"How?"

"With magic."

Jourdian said nothing, but only continued to hold his head in his hands. Minutes ticked by, during which time he concentrated intently, using every shred of logic he had.

Finally, his common sense began to chase away his disbelief and untangle his raveled thoughts. "Paint," he murmured. "Yes, of course. You simply painted the furniture, walls, and ceiling. And you ordered green window glass in my absence. And the plants . . . You created an illusion. It only *appears* as though the plants are growing out of the floor and furniture."

She looked around the room. "Nay, the plants are growing from the floor and furniture. But magic causes them to believe they are growing in dirt. They are under a spell, Jourdian. 'Tis called fairy thrall. Anything done with fairy magic is called fairy this or fairy that. A ship stranded out at sea might have her sails filled with a sudden gust of fairy wind. A tender plant dying of thirst might be quenched with fairy rain. The magic of Faerie is very powerful."

Jourdian lifted his head and stared up at her again. "Trickery. Magician tricks, nothing more."

"Magic."

He bolted from the chair and grasped her arm. "How did you get me up here?"

"Magic."

"Damn it all, Splendor, I want the truth."

"Damn it all, Jourdian, 'tis what I gave you." She smiled up at him. "I am not given to cursing, but do you not think cursing goes well with anger? I am learning anger, as I told you earlier. Go ahead, husband. Do or say something that might irritate me, and I will show you how well I am doing with my anger lessons."

She was deranged, he thought. A madwoman, fit to be locked away forever.

But even if she was crazy, that still didn't explain how he'd come to be in the room so quickly.

Maybe *he* was insane, too. "My mind," he whispered. "I've lost my mind."

"You have lost naught but a willingness to believe in magic."

"I have never believed in magic!"

"You have. As a child. You made wishes on stars, and if you did not believe in magic you would nay have made those wishes. They are all still there, your wishes. I have guarded your wishing stars all these years. Indeed, only one has fallen from the sky. That mishap occurred when I had taken to my bed after the cat scratched me. 'Twas my mother who spotted your fallen star, but she did not have time to retrieve it. She was on one of her missions that night. But she told me where I could find it. I traveled very far for that star. Do you remember that I told you that I had journeyed far only once in my life? That was the time. Your star . . . 'Twas in a rice field in China, Jourdian, and I put it back in the sky."

Jourdian was sober now, but he decided that within a half an hour he would be drunker than he'd ever been in his whole life. He stormed toward the door.

"Where do you go, Jourdian?"

"Downstairs to drink myself into complete oblivion."

"I do not wish for you to go downstairs and drink yourself into oblivion. You may do so later, but for now you will remain here with me."

He spun to face her. "Ever since I met you in the meadow, you have attempted to order me about. I am the *duke of Heathcourte*, for God's sake, and you will not command—"

"And I am the *princess royal of Pillywiggin*." Splendor touched the top of her head, and in the next instant she was crowned with a glowing circle of diamonds. "I am not altogether certain what a duke is, but I do not believe I am mistaken in thinking my rank is a bit more exalted than yours. Especially since I will one day replace my father on the throne, and be queen."

He stared at the glittering headpiece she wore. "How did you do that?" he asked incredulously. "The crown . . . And how did you get me from the foyer into this room?"

"How many times must I tell you, Jourdian? I am a fairy, and I used magic to—"

"Enough of that nonsense, Splendor! There are no such things as fairies! And if you don't tell me how you've accomplished all this amazing trickery, I'll—"

"No such things as fairies? But Jourdian, you are looking at a fairy. And I must tell you that you are vexing me by shouting at me."

"Oh? Well, why don't you use your—your *fairy magic* and send me into a pit full of snakes?"

Splendor didn't care for his sneer or the taunting sound of his voice. "A supremely marvelous suggestion." She tossed stardust straight into his face.

He choked and sneezed, and a fraction of a second later, Jourdian could see nothing but blackness. Cold and dampness seeped into him, and from all around him came ominous hissing sounds. Something slithered over his feet; something else brushed his lower calves.

A soft silver light appeared then, illuminating the rocky walls around him. He bowed his head and looked down.

His knees almost buckled.

Hundreds of serpents surrounded him; all were poisonous. He saw rattlesnakes, corals, and kraits. Adders, vipers, copperheads, and black mambas. So many snakes that they seemed to be one slinking mass of venom.

A cobra fell on top of him and twisted around his shoulders, its hood fully flared, its long tongue flicking in and out of its open mouth like a whip. Sweat streamed down Jourdian's face.

"Is this what you had in mind, Jourdian?" Splendor asked from within the orb of soft silver light.

He heard her voice coming from above his head, but he didn't dare look up for fear that the slight motion would agitate the seething body of serpents.

She floated down so he could see her.

Jourdian saw her stepping all over the snakes, and yet the serpents ignored her completely. This had to be a nightmare, he thought. Yes, he'd felt the sting of Splendor's pinch, but pinch or no pinch, this situation was unreal. Inconceivable.

He reached up, grabbed the cold, scaly body of the cobra, and threw the heavy snake off his shoulders. No sooner had the serpent left his hands, when every snake in the pit bared its fangs and lunged toward him.

Jourdian opened his mouth to scream, but before a sound escaped him, he was back in his bedroom, safe and sound, without as much as one snake scale anywhere near him. He continued to shake, and sweat still poured from his forehead, stinging his eyes.

"You did not truly believe I would allow any of those snakes to bite you, did you, Jourdian?" Splendor asked, curling her arms around him.

A long while passed before Jourdian calmed sufficiently to move or speak. He felt suddenly tired. Exhausted. He stumbled to the bed, sat on the soft mattress, and reached for one of the bedposts for support.

Like a small, weak flame, the truth trembled through his mind. He saw its light, he felt its burn, but he still didn't want to believe it.

And yet he had no choice. "The snakes . . . No nightmare could have been that real."

Splendor noted that his voice was as hollow as a reed. "Jourdian—"

"And no human magician could have performed such an impossible feat." Jourdian took a deep breath, assailed by a sense of realization so pressing that he felt his shoulders sag. "You . . . truly . . . are . . . a . . . fairy."

"Aye, husband, that is what I am."

"A fairy." Willing his legs to work, Jourdian rose from the bed and slowly paced around his red, blue, and green room. He paused beside his dresser, fingered one of the evergreen's boughs, then glanced at the tree's trunk, which stemmed straight out of the wooden surface of the dresser.

"Jourdian, I am nay an evil elf," Splendor tried to reassure him. "You've nay a need to fear—"

A loud and fierce growl on the other side of the door interrupted her.

"Delicious," Splendor said.

"Your swan?" Jourdian had never heard a swan growl, but now he knew firsthand that stranger things could happen.

Splendor opened the door.

A grizzly bear stood in the hall, swinging its great head from side to side, slobber spraying from each corner of its tooth-filled mouth.

"Delicious," Splendor greeted him. "Come in, sweetling."

On its huge back legs, the bear ambled into the room.

Splendor closed the door, and rubbed her hands down Delicious's fat, hairy belly. "Jourdian, one other supremely tiny thing I must tell you . . . Delicious is not a swan. He's . . . Well, he is anything he chooses to be. Since we have been here with you, he has been a hog, a donkey, a seal, a turtle, a rooster, a chipmunk, and now he is a bear. He came to be with me when I was but a fairy child, and I named him 'Delicious' because he is deliciously wonderful.

" 'Tis a sweet story how he came to be with me, Jourdian. I was in the pond in yonder woods, lying upon a lily pad and basking in the sun. In the next moment I fell into the water. Ordinarily I swim well, but that day I could not because when I fell into the water I became entangled in a bunch of underwater plants. I nearly drowned, husband. Delicious was a fish at the time. A pretty fish, all silvery and with wonderful black eyes and thick, O shaped lips. He saw me struggling in the water plants, and he nudged me back to the surface."

She hugged the huge grizzly bear who was Delicious. "He saved my life that day, and I have had him ever since. He was born a cockroach, but was not happy with his lot in life. After all, Jourdian, what use to the world are cockroaches? But he happened upon a witch one day. She set out a dish of sweetened water for him. He would not touch it. She was old, frail, and thin, the witch, and Delicious thought she needed the sugar water more than he. To reward him for his consideration and kindness, the witch cast a spell over him that allowed him to be whatever sort of animal or insect he wished. Delicious could not make up his mind, so the witch gave him unlimited choice throughout his lifetime."

Jourdian didn't bat an eye. He walked to the window. The green window.

He recalled that Emil had wanted him to court Caroline Pilcher.

He had refused because Caroline owned a pet python. Caroline also wanted to perform equestrian stunts in a circus.

Splendor owned a pet that could be whatever it wanted to be. And she rode dragonflies.

Emil had wanted him to woo Edith Hinderwell.

He'd declined because Edith wished on stars.

Splendor didn't wish on stars. She *guarded* them. She'd flown all the way to a rice field in China to retrieve one that had fallen from the sky.

Jourdian pressed his forehead to the cool, green pane of the window. A normal wife, he mused. He'd wanted a simple, unassuming, ordinary, plain, conventional wife.

"And the duchess of Heathcourte is a fairy," he said in a choked voice.

"A Pillywiggin, to be precise," Splendor added.

He turned away from the window. "I didn't want to marry a Pillywiggin," he ground out between gritted teeth. "I wanted a plain woman! A *human* woman! And what did I wed? A wing-wearing, stardust-throwing, wish-guarding, dragonfly-riding *fairy!*"

In an instant, Splendor's mist appeared and surrounded her. Jourdian's rejection of her made her ache; she dissolved into the sparkling haze, covered her face with her hands, and sobbed.

For a moment, Jourdian stood transfixed, struggling to comprehend what he was seeing. His wife had just been swallowed up by glittering fog. "Splendor?"

No answer.

"Splendor?" Jourdian approached the bright cloud and gazed into it, trying to find some hint of the enchanted female who was his wife. "Splendor, come out of there!"

Several minutes passed before she stepped out of the mist.

"You dissolved," Jourdian whispered.

"You made me sad. When I am extremely upset, my mist appears and embraces me. But I do not remain sad for long. I cannot. Fairy emotions, you see, are not as deep as human emotions."

Jourdian had heard of people crawling into their "shells" when distressed, but he'd never met anyone who faded into mist.

Of course, he'd never met a fairy, either.

He rammed his fingers through his hair, then saw shining droplets clinging to Splendor's cheeks. More twinkled from the palms of her hands. "Those are no ordinary tears, are they?" he demanded. "The diamonds I found on the parlor floor after you cried and fled the room . . . You cry diamonds! It's no damned wonder you didn't want the jewels I offered you! You can cry a gleaming mountain of them all by yourself!"

Battling despair again, Splendor could only nod.

Jourdian strode to the door. His hand on the knob, he looked over his shoulder. "I am going downstairs now, Splendor, to think and to drink until I cannot think anymore."

"But Jourdian, I do not want for you to go down—"

"It's my wish. Do you understand? *I wish* to go downstairs, and I do *not* wish to be disturbed!"

Instantly Splendor ceased to argue. Sighing, she lifted her hand toward him.

Jourdian saw a trail of silver stardust floating toward him. He tried to dodge the magic, but the enchanted lights caught and swirled around him.

A second later, he was downstairs in the room his mother had called the tea room. Kicking a dainty footstool out of his way, he stormed out of the room and strode to his office. "The tea room," he muttered, grabbing a bottle of scotch off the liquor cabinet.

He looked up at the ceiling as if he could see straight into his upstairs chambers. "I didn't want a cup of blasted tea, damn it all! If you're going to send me from room to room to room to room, the very least you could do is send me to the ones I want to be in!"

Not bothering with a glass, he tipped the bottle of liquor to his lips and swallowed until lack of air forced him to stop and take a breath. And then he drank more.

And more.

"An annulment," he murmured to the scotch bottle as he stared down at it. "We've not consummated the marriage, and so there is no possibility that she carries my child."

He opened a bottle of brandy. Slumping into his office chair, he pondered the idea of the annulment. "I've grounds for it," he slurred. "I'm not married to a human."

But how would he explain his reasons for wanting an annulment?

*Reverend Shrewsbury, my wife is a fairy princess, so please annul my marriage.*

He shook his head. Revealing Splendor's origins wouldn't get him an annulment. It would get him locked in an insane asylum for the rest of his life.

"Bloody hell."

Jourdian started on the brandy, and an hour later a drunken stupor numbed him to all feelings. He longed for unconsciousness, but just when he was at the verge of falling asleep he saw her.

Splendor. He couldn't miss her. She moved toward him in a nimbus of brilliance.

"I do not imagine I am going against your wish not to be disturbed," she whispered. "In your state, nothing could disturb you. Go to bed, husband."

Jourdian saw her lift her hand above his head. Her starry magic rained over him, and he wasn't surprised when he then found himself out of his office chair and tucked into his bed. And sloshed as he was, he didn't argue with the fairy who'd put him there.

He simply rolled over and sought the blessedness of sleep.

**13**

**W**hen Jourdian awakened, bright afternoon sunlight stabbed through his eyelids and his head throbbed with such intense pain that he wanted to scream.

But he dared not. Even the sound of his own breath intensified his misery. "I'm going to die," he whispered, wincing from the effort to speak.

"Die?"

Splendor's voice startled him, for he'd thought he was alone. "Don't move," he managed to tell her. "This bed is already rolling as if tossed on a stormy sea."

She sat up and poked her finger into his shoulder.

"Ouch, Splendor."

"Jourdian, I but touched your shoulder."

"My skin hurts. My teeth hurt. God, even my *hair* hurts."

"What is the matter—"

"I told you not to move. Any second now my head is going to burst wide open."

Gently, Splendor laid her palm over his temple. "There, there," she cooed. " 'Tis gone now, the pain."

Jourdian opened his eyes, astonished to realize the pain truly was gone. He felt fine.

But why wouldn't he? His little fairy nurse had cured him with her fairy medicine.

At that thought, he groaned, turned to his side, and found

himself nose to nose with a porcupine. He didn't have to think twice to know the quilled creature was Delicious.

"Jourdian, you slept all night and half of this day. Might we indulge in the art of lovemaking now?" Splendor drifted off the bed and hovered above him, her hair pouring down all over him and Delicious. " 'Tis what I told you I wanted to do when you found me near the woods yesterday afternoon. Oh, and I would also remind you of your promise to get me with child."

He sat bolt upright, his swift action tossing the porcupine, Delicious, straight off the bed and onto the floor. "A child," he whispered. Tilting his head back over his shoulders, he reached up, took Splendor's wrist, and pulled her back down onto the bed. "You're a fairy."

"Aye, that is what I—"

"So, what's my son going to be? A damned leprechaun? A troll?"

She gasped. "You insult me. Trolls are horrible, ugly, and evil beasts who—"

"Then what is my son going to be?" Jourdian demanded.

"Half-human, half-fairy. And he may or may not inherit the powers of Faerie."

Wonderful, Jourdian seethed. It was possible that the thirteenth duke of Heathcourte would turn out to be an elf.

He vaulted out of bed. Barefoot and naked, he crossed the plant-filled room.

Floating in the air behind him, Splendor followed.

And when Jourdian turned back toward the bed, she was right in front of his face. "God!"

"What?"

"You scared me!"

" 'Tis nay what I meant to do, husband. I only wanted to—"

"Don't fly after me like that, damn it all!"

She wafted to the floor. "Jourdian, the night after our wedding, I asked you to cease shouting at me."

He left her where she stood and walked back across the room, looking over his shoulder to see if she was sailing behind him.

She remained where she was, beside his dresser and the

evergreen that grew from it. "Your habit of shouting at me is—"

"I am not going to discuss my shouting habits, Splendor." He grabbed the black dressing robe he'd seen her wearing the day before, and yanked it on. "I have barely had time to reconcile myself to the fact that my duchess is a creature of enchantment, and now I must dwell on the prospect that my heir will not drive about the countryside in a gleaming carriage, but upon the back of a damned dragonfly!"

At his continued shouting, Splendor felt a warmth flare up inside her. Hotter it became, and she realized it was the beginning of anger. She drew back her hand.

Jourdian had no time to avoid her magic. The silver light sped across the room, coating him from head to toe.

He opened his mouth to shout again, but found he could not part his lips.

"You cannot shout at me again, Jourdian," Splendor informed him, "because I have sealed your lips. I will gladly loosen them, but first I shall have your promise not to raise your voice."

He saw fire, but short of wringing her slender neck, he couldn't think of a single other form of retaliation.

Splendor folded her arms across her chest and tapped her bare toes on the floor. "I am waiting."

He gave a sharp nod of his head, and more stardust fell over him. Lifting his hands to his mouth, he rubbed his fingers all over his lips. "Don't you *ever* do that again, Splendor. And put some clothes on, damn it all!"

"Do not shout at me again. And as for clothing . . . Well, now that you know I am a fairy, I shall tell you also that neither I nor anyone in the Kingdom of Pillywiggin wears clothes. We are a naked race."

"Oh, is that so? Well, this is not the Kingdom of Pillywiggin. This is Heathcourte, here we wear clothes, and don't you dare glue my lips together for shouting, do you understand? I *wish* for you not to do it!" He marched to his closet and withdrew a red silk shirt.

"Red," he spat. "What in God's name am I to do with a red shirt? Put my clothes back the way they were!"

"Nay."

"No?"

"Nay, because you are rousing my irritation again." Splendor cast a wave of silver stars toward the closet.

Jourdian cringed, just waiting to fall into another snake pit, to have his lips sewn together, or perhaps to be turned into a rabid dog or some other sort of disgusting beast.

Nothing happened to him, but his clothes were changing color at the rate of every two seconds. Yellow, turquoise, violet, mauve, pink, orange . . . Every possible color in the world washed over his clothing, changing each and every garment from hue to hue to hue.

Jourdian threw the shirt he held down on the floor. In an effort to find one shred of patience, he silently counted to ten. "Stop those colors, Splendor. I *wish* for you to stop them this very instant and return my clothing and this room to their original states. And get rid of all these confounded trees, vines, flowers, and bushes!"

Her lips pursed, Splendor obeyed.

Jourdian looked around, satisfied that everything was back to normal. "Now, wife, sit down."

"I do not wish to—"

"But *I* wish it."

"You take advantage of my willingness to grant your wishes, Jourdian," she said, but complied by taking a seat in a nearby chair.

He ignored her chastisement and concentrated on his child, his heir. He couldn't allow the name of Amberville to die out, not even if it meant bequeathing his title and estate to a half-human with magical powers.

And yet . . .

"Splendor," he began, "about the child. I—"

"You will give me one, will you not?"

Another wave of despair rushed through him. He walked away from the bed. To the window. Back to the bed. Then to the fireplace. "How— What— You— I— Splendor, I'm afraid I have no idea how to get you with child."

"*What?* But you are supposed to know how to make a baby!"

"I *do* know, damn it all! But— What I mean is . . . I know how to make love to a woman. A *human* woman. Hell, for all I know, I might not be able to get you with child at all! Humans and fairies . . . Maybe they don't even mix!"

"Oh, but they do, Jourdian! I promise you they do! 'Tis one thing of which I am supremely certain!"

He believed her. "All right, but how do fairies . . . What are the sexual habits of fairies?"

"Sexual habits?" Splendor wrinkled her nose. "I am afraid I do not understand."

"How do elves make love? Do they even *make* love?"

"Indulge in the art of lovemaking?"

"Yes. Do they?"

Her shoulders slumped forward. "How can I answer that, husband? You have yet to make love to me, so there is no possible way I can know if the activity is something fairies do."

He rubbed the back of his neck. "Do you remember what I almost did to you the night after our wedding?"

She thought. And thought.

"You said it wouldn't fit, Splendor."

"Oh, that. Yes, I remember."

"It *will* fit, as I told you that night. And when I'm deeply inside you, I'll spill—"

He stopped explaining. *Would* he fit inside her? Dear God, how was he to know? Maybe fairy women were different. Splendor was so fragile. So slight. What if she couldn't accommodate him? What if he hurt her badly?

What if her body was simply not meant to accept his, and he killed her?

The possibility nearly scared *him* to death.

"What are you going to spill inside me, Jourdian?"

He turned to the fire and kicked a stray piece of kindling into the dying flames. "We haven't reached the point in this conversation to talk about *that* yet. Splendor, how do Pillywiggins create fairy babies?"

Splendor began to weep. "I do not know," she whimpered. "Sweet everlasting, I thought *you* would be able to tell me!"

He turned and watched diamonds cascade into her lap, more wealth than most people earned in a year. "You thought I would be able to tell you? How the hell can I tell you, Splendor, when I'm not a Pillywiggin fairy!"

"Oh, Jourdian, this is terrible," Splendor cried. "I trusted you to know how to get me with child, but you are as ignorant as I!"

"I am not! Were you a human woman, Splendor, I would be bedding you at this very second, make no mistake about that! But what if fairies don't make babies the way humans do? What if I use the human way to get you with child and then I hurt you? For God's sake, what if I kill you?"

"What is bedding?"

"Making love!"

"You are shouting again."

"I don't know how to make love to my own wife! Given that, would you have me laugh, dance, and make merry?"

"You—"

"Look," he said, walking toward her chair, "I must make love to you to get you with child. At least, that's what I would have to do with a human wife. But—"

"Oh, Jourdian—"

"Don't cry again," he ordered. "We'll figure it out. We'll just go slowly, that's all. We'll experiment. And I'll stop in a second if—"

"But I have just *this* second figured it out." Splendor rose from the chair and placed her hands on his hips. "If making love to me . . . or *bedding* me will get me with child, then the answer is simple. I did not understand the two were related until you told me. Humans and fairies procreate in the same manner, husband. 'Twas the one thing my father told me.

"And so," she continued, reaching inside his robe, "you will put yourself inside me, spill, and I shall conceive."

Jourdian felt her soft, warm hand fondling his sex. He wasn't ready to respond to her caresses. Didn't want to bed her. Not until he'd had some time to gather his thoughts and fully surrender himself to the circumstances fate had dealt him. After all, it was only yesterday when he'd discovered his wife was a fairy. And it was only moments ago that he'd learned that his son might very well be more of a Pillywiggin than an Amberville.

No, he was not prepared to make love to her. Not yet.

He started to step away from her, away from her hand and the delicate fingers that stroked him. But he couldn't. And it wasn't Splendor's magic that kept him from doing so.

It was his own reaction to her beauty. In despair though he was over her relation to Faerie, he still could not deny that she was, without a doubt, the loveliest female he'd ever beheld.

He lifted his hand, cupped her breast, and felt himself harden in her palm.

"The cattail returns," Splendor murmured. She parted his robe and lowered her gaze. "Why does this happen to you, Jourdian?"

Before he could answer, the room became awash with a bright silver glow. In the center of the ceiling burned a red-orange ball of fire.

Jourdian watched the flaming orb descend. "What the devil—"

"I want to see the cattail, too," Harmony announced as she doused her blazes.

Jourdian stared at the naked woman.

"This is my younger sister, Harmony," Splendor said.

He continued to gawk at Harmony for a moment before looking at Splendor. "Your sister . . . She was fire."

"Aye, that is what she was."

Harmony laughed. Shocking humans into speechlessness had always been one of her favorite pastimes. "Care to see more of my magnificent talents, human?"

Within a swirl of silver enchantment, she became a pink velvet chair. A skeleton whose bones moved as if waltzing at a ball. A tall marble pillar. A Samurai warrior; a long, black whip; an emerald-encrusted gold box overflowing with rubies and pearls; a tattered straw hat; and finally a majestic white unicorn with a wreath of fragrant coral roses around her neck.

Then she became herself again, human size.

Jourdian was too stunned to speak.

"Harmony, you are a show-off," Splendor said. "Jourdian, Harmony used her powers of shape-shifting to turn herself into all those things."

He nodded as if her explanation made all the sense in the

world. "Shape-shifting." He wondered if Splendor possessed the same powers, but before he could ask her he saw Harmony sail toward him.

She wrapped her frail arms around his back and pushed her lips to his mouth with all the energy she had.

Totally shocked, Jourdian could not react immediately.

"Harmony, that is enough!" Splendor shouted.

His broad chest heaving with fury, Jourdian thrust Harmony away.

"Strong," Harmony whispered, her gaze riveted to Jourdian's lips. "Oh, Splendor, you were right! I am filled with such strength that I feel I could spin the whole of the Earth upon the tip of my little finger! This kissing . . . 'tis glorious, sister!"

Splendor felt as though she'd eaten something terribly disagreeable. A sour taste filled her mouth, and her insides cramped with a burning ache.

The sensation was much like anger, but something more as well. Whatever the emotion was, it had erupted the second she'd seen Harmony's lips touch Jourdian's.

She scowled, and when she spoke her voice shook with displeasure. "Glorious as it is, Harmony, you have had your kiss, and you may nay have another. Jourdian's lips belong to me, as do all his kisses, and I'll not have you —"

"So you've said," Harmony spat. "Fine. I shall find another human man to do this kissing with. Now, before I return to Pillywiggin, let me see his cattail."

Anxious for her sister to leave, Splendor started to pull Jourdian's robe to the side so her sister could see.

Jourdian snatched the robe from her hand and pulled it back together. "For God's sake, Splendor!"

She cocked her head toward her shoulder. " 'Tis only Harmony, Jourdian. My sister. She's never seen a cattail—"

"Well, she's not seeing mine!" He glared at the fairy who was Splendor's sister. Harmony didn't resemble Splendor at all, he thought. While her hair was just as long and thick, it was golden blond, and her eyes were the color of fiery sapphires.

She was quite beautiful, but there was something about her . . . Something . . .

Jourdian knew instinctively that she was trouble.

He pushed his shoulders back, irritated by her abrupt arrival in his personal quarters, the liberty she'd taken by stealing a kiss, and her mischievous nature. If gentle-hearted Splendor could send him into a pit of snakes, he didn't want to *think* about what Harmony could do.

He wanted her out of his home. "I don't recall extending you an invitation into my rooms. Into my *house*, for that matter."

Harmony raised a delicately arched brow. "I do not recall seeking an invitation. I go where I wish, and I do not need or want the approval of some cattailed human."

Jourdian narrowed his eyes, his dislike for Splendor's sister growing steadily. "Leave."

Her actions so fast they were blurred, Harmony pitched a handful of glitter at him.

Jourdian disappeared.

"Harmony!" Splendor cried, clasping her cheeks with her hands as she stared at the spot where Jourdian had stood only a moment ago. "Oh, sister, what have you done?"

Harmony began to braid a long lock of her hair.

"Harmony!"

"I did what I've advised you to do twice."

For a moment, Splendor was confused. And then comprehension fell on her like a stone wall. "Nay! A *slug*, Harmony?"

"Slime-trailing," Harmony added. "You'll find him outside. 'Tis where slugs belong. But I didn't bury him in the dirt, though. He's out in the open so you may spot him easier. 'Twas thoughtful of me not to bury him, was it not?"

"Out in the open." Splendor gasped. "Sweet everlasting, sister, what if a bird eats him!"

Harmony finished plaiting her hair, then tossed the thick braid over her shoulder. " 'Tis a possibility. I suggest you go rescue him from such a grisly fate."

"But where is he?"

"I told you. Outside. Are you losing your hearing, Splendor?"

"Where outside?" Splendor demanded. *"Where?"*

Harmony smiled. " 'Tis for me to know, and you to find out."

Splendor burned inside. Hotter than ever before. Throwing herself forward, she tried to grab and shake her sister.

But Harmony vanished, leaving naught but a few silver twinkles in Splendor's hands.

"Harmony! Come back this instant and tell me where you've put Jourdian!"

Nothing. No sound, no Harmony.

Terrified for Jourdian's safety and mindless of her naked state, Splendor soared through the wall and flew over the vast estate. Her fear grew, her eyes filled with tears, and the tiny diamonds sprinkled over the land, catching sunlight within their prisms as they fell through the air.

Heathcourte boasted of dozens of gardens, and she had no idea which one to explore first. There were probably hundreds upon hundreds of slugs in the cultivated patches of earth over which she sailed!

She would have to search through them all. One by one.

Until she found her husband's slimy trail.

As Emil alighted from his coach in front of Jourdian's manor, a flash of red in a nearby garden of dense bushes caught his attention. Thinking the movement that of a large bird, he proceeded toward the steps of the house.

"Emil!"

He turned, his eyes widening when he saw Splendor standing among the thick plants. She was as naked as the statue of the nude woman she stood beside, and her face, arms, and hands were covered with dirt. "Splendor, what in heaven's name are you doing?"

She motioned him toward her, and when he arrived he took both his arms into her muddy hands. "Emil, you must help me! I have looked in no fewer than thirteen gardens!"

He didn't miss her hysteria. Not only did she sound totally

panicked, but she was paler than he'd ever seen her, and her entire body was quaking.

Quickly, he removed his coat and assisted her into it. "What are you looking for?"

"Slugs. I have found a wealth of them, but none is—"

"Slugs? But why? Where is Jourdian? Does he know you're out here looking for—"

"I will explain later, Emil. For now, you must help me find slugs. I will continue searching through this garden, and you will search in others. Save every slug you find, and when we are finished looking through every garden, I will examine each slug we collect."

"But—"

"Here is a sack." Splendor curled her arm behind her back, released a few silver stars, then grabbed hold of the burlap sack that suddenly appeared in her hand. Quickly she gave the bag to Emil.

"Splendor, I don't understand—"

"Please," she begged, gazing into his eyes with all the desperation coursing through her frame. "Just do as I ask, Emil."

He did. And hours later when he joined Splendor near one of the estate fountains, he handed her a sack half full of slimy slugs. "And now, Splendor," he said, brushing his dirty hands over his pants legs, "tell me why I performed this outrageous chore."

She dumped his slugs into the massive pile of the ones she'd found. On the ground she began sorting through them. "I shall tell you, that I promise, Emil, but first we must find the slug with the black dot on its face."

"A black dot."

" 'Tis a mole."

"A mole. Of course. How terribly silly of me not to have realized that myself."

"Sit down here with me and help me find the—"

"The slug with the black mole on its face."

"Aye! And we must hurry because my strength is quickly waning. This day has taken a supreme toll on me, Emil!"

Bewildered beyond belief, but hesitant to further upset the panicked Splendor, Emil sat down on the grass and picked up a slug. Bringing the creature closer to his eyes, he looked for a black dot on the slimy little face. "This one hasn't as much as a freckle."

"Then put it back in the sack. We mustn't mix them up or else we will find ourselves examining the same slugs over and over again."

Emil deposited the moleless slug into the bag, and continued to help Splendor inspect the others. A short while later the sack was full, and not a single slug they'd analyzed had had a black dot on its face.

"He's not here!" Splendor cried. "He's still loose somewhere!"

"Who?" Emil seized her shoulders, deeply concerned over her rising agitation. "Splendor, who—"

"Jourdian!"

"Jourdian?"

Splendor didn't reply. A hawk had caught her attention. The great bird circled in the sky a few times before switching direction and sailing down toward the mansion. Closer it flew. Closer, nearer to one of the second-story balconies.

Something was on that balcony, Splendor realized. Something the hawk wanted.

A sixth sense told her exactly what that something was.

She flew to her feet, raised her arms, and threw her magic with all the strength she had. The silver stars shot toward the manor, reaching the balcony the same time as the hawk did.

*"Jourdian!"* Splendor screamed.

And then he was there, hanging off the balcony and swatting at the hawk that was pecking at his head.

"My God!" Emil shouted. "Oh, dear God!"

"Splendor!" Jourdian yelled. "The hawk! I can't hold on!"

Skimming toward him, Splendor drew back her hand to toss more magic at him, but did not release the stars in time.

Jourdian fell off the balcony and landed in the thick hedgerow that lined the side of the manor house.

"Jourdian!" Splendor and Emil cried in unison.

They reached him just as he was struggling to remove himself from within the thick branches of hedgerow. Leaves and small sticks stuck out of his hair, his black dressing robe was torn in various places, and a bird bite bled on his forehead.

Emil looked up at the balcony. "Jourdian, what in God's name were you doing on that balcony?"

Jourdian glared at Splendor. "I was hanging on it, Emil. But first, of course, I crawled up the side of the house. Out of the ivy garden. And once on the balcony I almost became supper for a damned hawk!"

Emil could not utter a word. Confusion and disbelief fairly consumed him as he pondered the day's events. Splendor and her slug hunt. Jourdian hanging off a balcony and now shouting that he'd almost been eaten by a hawk.

He wondered if the duke and duchess had been drinking.

"Jourdian," he finally said, "what do you mean you crawled up the side of the house?"

Jourdian didn't take his angry gaze off Splendor for a second. "I mean just that. I crawled up the side of the house. If you don't believe me, look for yourself. I left a slimy trail in my wake!"

"Jourdian, I am supremely sorry," Splendor murmured. "We did our very best to find you in one of the gardens, but—"

"Emil almost stepped on me, damn it all!"

"But he did not step on you, and you are all right now, are you not?" Splendor asked. Gently, she touched the hawk peck on his forehead.

The wound vanished, but Jourdian's fury did not. "Splendor," he growled, "if I *ever* see that malicious sister of yours again, I'll—"

"Kiss me, husband," she whispered, feeling herself tremble as the last of her energy drained from her body.

Jourdian frowned. He'd just fallen off a balcony after almost being devoured by a bird of prey, and she wanted him to kiss her?

"I am dwindling," Splendor tried to make him understand. "Kiss me now, for I've nay the strength to take a kiss myself."

Jourdian saw her sway on her feet and reached for her immediately. His arms embraced thin air.

"I am here, Jourdian," a small voice called from below.

Jourdian looked down. There, standing on a smooth, white pebble was a very naked, very tiny Splendor.

"Jourdian," Emil whispered. "Splendor . . . She's—"

"A fairy," Jourdian announced, still staring down at Splendor.

"A fairy," Emil repeated. His legs shaking, he grabbed his cousin's shoulder for support, to no avail.

Jourdian watched Emil crash to the ground, right next to where Splendor stood.

She laid her tiny hand on Emil's earlobe. "He fainted, Jourdian. Poor Emil."

Jourdian didn't say a word. Summoning patience and resignation he had never realized he possessed, he picked his family up off the grass.

And then the utterly proper duke of Heathcourte walked around to the front of the manor, up the steps, and into the house, his unconscious cousin slung over his shoulder and his wee wife in the pocket of his robe.

"**A** fairy," Emil said, lying on the sofa in the blue salon, nursing a stiff shot of brandy. He'd gotten over his initial shock, but remained totally astonished by the fact that the newest member of the Amberville family was also a member of Faerie. "A real live fairy."

Jourdian slammed his fist down on the arm of his chair. "How many times will you say that? You've been repeating those same words since you came out of your swoon a half an hour ago. Can you think of naught else to say? For almost two decades you have made it your business to give me advice, and now I find myself married to a fairy, and you babble like an idiot."

Emil sat up, set his brandy snifter down, and swiped his hair away from his eyes. "A fairy. You married a fairy. With my own eyes . . . I saw her shrink. I cannot believe—"

"Well, you had better believe it! She threw me into a snake pit, sewed my lips together, and then her sister, Harmony, turned me into a slime-trailing slug! If that's not proof enough—"

"I believe you, Jourdian." Shaking his head, Emil rose from the sofa and began to walk around the room. "I find it terribly difficult to believe, but I do believe you. It all makes sense now . . . all the strange occurrences. Splendor's flowers at the wedding. She changed them from silk into real ones. The hornet—Harmony, her sister. And when I visited her in her room that night after you left, she glowed. Stars fell all around her, and I thought her an angel or some magical creature. I remember being uncertain as to whether I should run or fall to my knees before her. Ultimately, I decided my exhaustion was causing me to see things."

"You do realize that you cannot tell a soul about Splendor, do you not?"

Emil stopped beside the small ornate fireplace. "Do you think me daft? I would be locked away until the end of my days!"

Jourdian rested his head on the back of his chair. "The same possibility occurred to me."

"Where is Splendor, by the way?"

"Still in my pocket." Jourdian looked down at the tiny bulge in his dressing robe pocket, which lay over his thigh. "She fell asleep in there. I touched her with my finger to wake her up, but she's sleeping so hard that she didn't move or make a sound."

Emil frowned. "Are you sure she's not . . . dead?"

"No, she's not dead! Can't you see her breathing?"

Emil crossed to Jourdian's chair and leaned down close to his cousin's thigh. Sure enough, the tiny hump in the dressing robe pocket moved up and down in a rhythmic motion. "Let me see her."

"No."

"Just a peek. It's all quite fascinating, you know, her being one of the Wee Folk, and all. Just a glimpse of her, Jourdian."

"No."

"Why ever not?"

"Because she's still naked, damn it all!"

"I've seen her naked before."

Jourdian closed his eyes. "You and half of England."

"She has no clothing."

"Not yet, but she will soon. I purchased an entire wardrobe for her while I was away at Briarmont. On one of those days, I rode into London and hired the entire House of Brenn."

"What? Mme. Brenn employs over a hundred seamstresses."

"One hundred and eleven."

"You hired them all?"

"The entire house. Haste is of the essence. With a mass of seamstresses sewing for Splendor, I imagine her wardrobe is almost complete and will be delivered any day now."

"But how could you order clothing without Splendor along for a fitting?"

"Her forehead is level with my mouth, and she's waif-like. That's what I told Mme. Brenn."

"What about shoes?"

"I ordered dozens of shoes in different sizes. Surely one size will fit. Everything I'm having made is soft, simple, void of any decoration whatsoever, and I thought I had done quite well. A pity I did not think to order clothing for a woman as tall as my thumb."

Emil smiled. "Do you remember when I suggested we look for fairies on these very grounds, cousin? It was years ago, and you refused to indulge me. You sat by a stone wall with your books in your lap, and you watched as I searched high and low for evidence of—"

"I didn't believe in them."

"And now you are married to one. Jourdian, you have dirt between your toes." Emil stared at Jourdian's bare feet. "I've never seen you so filthy."

"I was a slug, Emil. And I've yet to bathe since carrying you and Splendor into the house."

"Ah, yes. Jourdian Amberville, the slug of Heathcourte."

"I fail to see the humor—"

"My reference to your slovenly state was a compliment. Dirt becomes you, cousin. You should wear it more often. Why do you suppose Splendor shrank the way she did?"

His eyes still closed, Jourdian shrugged his shoulders. "All I know is that she lost her strength. I never had the opportunity to question her further because she fell asleep. I have, however, realized a correlation between her losing her strength and the vigor she apparently receives from kissing. She's mentioned that frequently since I met her."

"I see. What else do you know about her?"

Jourdian opened his eyes. "She's a princess. The princess

royal of her father's kingdom of Pillywiggin. One day she'll inherit the throne."

"She'll be Queen Splendor? Jourdian, that means you'll be the prince consort of Fairyville."

"Pillywiggin," Jourdian corrected his cousin. "And I am no such thing."

"You will be when Splendor becomes queen."

"She's my duchess. Not some future queen."

"She outranks you. I suppose we should both be bowing to her."

"Emil—"

"What more do you know about her?"

"She says our son might very well inherit her powers," Jourdian said, and sighed. "My heir. An elf."

"I'll stand as a very proud godfather at his christening. It matters naught to me what the little chap is, I'll love him, pointed ears and all."

"My son will not have pointed ears!"

"How do you know?"

"Splendor doesn't have pointed ears!"

"But perhaps someone in her family does. I've seen paintings of elves, Jourdian, and many of them possess pointed—"

"That's enough!" Jourdian stood, careful not to allow his robe to sway overly much.

"Your son will be a king one day, cousin. He'll inherit the fairy throne from Splendor. He'll be both king of Pillywiggin and the duke of Heathcourte. Imagine that."

"How is it that you can accept this bizarre situation with such aplomb, Emil?"

Emil sat down in the chair Jourdian vacated. "Because things are as they are, cousin. You married Splendor, and she cannot help being what she is any more than you can help being what you are. What possible good would it do for me to become as agitated as you are?"

Jourdian stalked to the window, looked out of the pane for a brief moment, then turned away. "You can accept her being a fairy because you are given to fantasy in the first place. A grown man who continues to wish on stars is—"

"Splendor is no fantasy, Jourdian," Emil said, rising from his chair to retrieve his brandy. "She's real. Just as real and alive as you and me. She eats and sleeps. She breathes and—"

"And flies, and fades into mists, and cries diamonds, and shrinks, and—"

"And has successfully pulled you out of the sucking depths of your monotonous routine." Emil sipped the brandy, stared at his cousin, then burst into laughter. "God, this is rich! Only about a fortnight ago, you expounded on the fact that you wanted a duchess whose middle name was 'Ordinary' and you've gone and wed a pixie!"

Before Jourdian could form a retort, he felt Splendor moving in his pocket. "Emil, give me your shirt. She's waking."

"My shirt?"

"How many times must I tell you she's naked!"

"Oh." Emil set his brandy down again, removed his shirt, and handed the garment to Jourdian.

"Now turn your back," Jourdian instructed his cousin. "And be quick about it."

Just as Emil turned to face the opposite wall, Splendor sailed out of Jourdian's pocket. Jourdian saw a circle of bright silver appear around her. He watched warily, unsure of what to expect. "Splendor?"

The circle became larger, and so did Splendor. When she stood tall before him, Jourdian fairly ripped Emil's shirt apart in an effort to put the garment on her. "I can do naught to change the fact that you're of a naked race, Splendor, but as your husband I demand that you cease flitting about without benefit of clothing."

She looked at the robe he was wearing. The sash had come loose, and she saw everything he owned from the waist down. "You are not fully dressed either, Jourdian. Indeed, I can see your—"

"Never mind." His fingers flew over the buttons on her shirt. "How could I dress with you asleep in my pocket?"

"Why didn't you awaken me?"

"I tried, but you wouldn't budge. And I was afraid to take you out because I didn't know where to put you! You were so . . . so . . ."

"Tiny," she supplied. "Now you know why I fear your cat."

Pharaoh, Jourdian thought. As if he didn't have enough to fret over, now he had to worry that the Heathcourte feline might eat the Heathcourte duchess!

"I'll give Pharaoh to Mrs. Frawley," he announced. "She can keep him in her cottage." Quickly, he finished buttoning Splendor's shirt. "All right, Emil, you may turn back around. She's dressed."

"Splendor," Emil said when he saw her. "You're a fairy."

She smiled. "Aye, that is what I am, and Jourdian is going to give his cat to Mrs. Frawley."

"I've never known a fairy before."

Splendor laughed. "I had never known humans, either. But I have been with you and Jourdian many times. Indeed, I watched the two of you grow into men even as I grew to become a fairy woman."

"You didn't tell me that," Jourdian said.

"There are many things I have not told you, Jourdian."

He watched her walk to the window across the room. Golden sunbeams mingled with her silver glow and illuminated her violet eyes. She looked like a living, breathing jewel, and Jourdian was so struck by her radiance that a long while passed before he realized he was staring at her like a man who had heretofore been surrounded by ugliness and had just come upon his first glimpse of true beauty.

"Jourdian?" Splendor said.

Her silken voice coaxed him from his daze. "Now is as good a time as any for you to tell me a few of the things you haven't told me before," he said. Wondering what other surprises she had in store for him, he took a seat on the settee.

"Tell us a bit about fairies and their history," Emil said, sitting down beside his cousin on the small sofa.

"Fairy history?" Absently, Splendor twisted a lock of her hair around her wrist, pondering her origins. "We are somewhere between men and angels. There was once a time when we lived in peace among mortals, and fairy sightings were frequent—"

"There was an old woman in Mallencroft who swore she'd seen one when she was a lass," Emil said. "She said she'd become terribly lost in the forest that grew near her childhood home. When night fell, she began to weep. A sparkle of light appeared, dancing all through the darkness, and when she followed the bit of gleam it led her straight out of the woods. She was sure it was a fairy."

"Emil, stop interrupting," Jourdian chided. "Splendor, please continue."

Splendor winked at Emil. "As I said, fairy sightings were not uncommon, but men destroyed the tranquillity by planting large fields and building fences, highways, villages, and cities. Where there had once been wilderness, there then existed the proof of men's need for boundaries. The wild, untamed world was beaten into submission, and the realm of Faerie began to weaken. My race became elusive then. 'Tis why fairy sightings are now few and far between."

She reached for a spray of silk fern. As she pulled the greenery from its crystal vase, stars—like dew—appeared on the artificial leaves, and the fern became real in her graceful hand.

She smoothed the supple plant across her cheek. "Faerie is a lovely world, and is better than the mortal world by one marvelous tad. The sun that shines in Faerie is one tiny tad warmer and brighter than the sun that shines upon the mortal world, and our moonlight is one tiny tad more silver. Our blossoms smell one tiny tad more aromatic than yours, our fruit is one tiny tad sweeter and juicier, and our breezes one tiny tad cooler. Even our snow is one tiny tad whiter than yours. 'Tis the same with all else in Faerie. By that one tiny tad of superiority, one is aware that one has left the human world and passed into the realm of Faerie."

"I'd like to go there one day," Emil said, totally fascinated by Splendor's story.

"Make that wish on a star," Splendor advised, "and perhaps you will see it granted one day."

"He's made so many wishes on so many stars that there aren't any stars left for him."

"Not true, Jourdian," Splendor disagreed. "There are enough stars for every person in the world to make millions of wishes."

She took a step to the left so that she stood right in the middle of a shining pool of sunlight. "As you can see, fairies have nay a shadow," she said, pointing to the spot on the carpet where her shadow should have been. "When we walk, we make nay a sound. With a touch of our finger and a sparkle of our eyes, we can cause all care to fall away from men. 'Tis called fairy charm, and I have used the charm thrice since I've been here, once on Ulmstead, once on Hopkins, and once on Tessie. They were afraid of me, and I do not like anyone to fear me, for I would never harm another living being."

"You threw me in that snake pit," Jourdian reminded her.

"But I did not allow the creatures to hurt you." She glided away from the window and approached the settee. " 'Twas I who chased the snakes out of your path the day you almost stepped on them, Jourdian. You were a boy then. And—"

"The diamonds," Jourdian murmured. "The ones I found in the meadow when I was a child—"

"My tears," Splendor confessed.

"Now I understand why the diamonds I found on the parlor floor looked so familiar. I *had* seen them before."

"Once upon a time," Splendor agreed.

Emil leaned forward. "Do you think you could cry a few tears now, Splendor?"

"Emil, if you don't mind," Jourdian admonished.

"Sorry," Emil muttered, but he didn't feel at all apologetic. "Of course, you don't have to weep now, Splendor. But if you should shed a few expensive tears in the future, just leave them where they lie, and I shall be happy to clean the floor of them."

Jourdian shook his head, then turned his attention back to Splendor. "Why did you cry in the meadow that day so many years ago?"

"Because the two of you had crushed the flowers. I guard them, you see, and they are very precious to me. I have nay an objection to the picking of blossoms as long as the plant itself stays healthy. Many times it is good for plants to have their blossoms plucked. But when you and Emil raced through the field that day, you crushed the flowers, killing many of them. 'Tis why I wept."

"I'm sorry," Emil said, and this time he meant it. "But I didn't know—"

"I know you didn't," Splendor said, "but now you do. Take care that you do not commit such murders again."

Properly chastised, Emil nodded.

"You were a good boy, though, Emil," Splendor added sweetly. "Do you remember the elder tree you used to climb? The big one that grew near the pond where there were many, many ducks?"

The memory returned to Emil instantly. "I spent hours in that tree. Do you remember too, Jourdian?"

Jourdian shook his head. "You climbed hundreds of trees, Emil. They all looked the same—"

"Oh, but they are not the same, husband," Splendor declared. "Especially that elder. That tree was home to Elder Mother, a powerful spirit who is very protective of her home. Emil, when I saw you climb the tree the first time, I feared for your safety, for if you had angered Elder Mother in any way, she might have caused your family's livestock to die of sickness, or . . . or . . ."

"Or what?" Emil pressed, filled with a morbid fascination over what his fate might have been.

"She might have killed you."

Emil swallowed hard. "Killed me?" he repeated, his voice quivering.

Jourdian rolled his eyes. "For God's sake, Emil, the tree mother didn't kill you. You're alive. Besides, how can a tree mother kill anyone?"

"*Elder* Mother," Splendor corrected. "And she can kill by any one of various means, Jourdian. There are many in the world of Faerie who do her bidding, and Emil might have been tickled to death by a killmoulis, which is an especially homely brownie. A killmoulis has an immense nose, but nay a mouth. When he eats, he must stuff his food up his nostrils. 'Tis a disgusting sight to see. But Emil, do you know why Elder Mother did not summon a killmoulis to come tickle your last breath from you?"

"Why?" he whispered.

"Because you did not pick her elderberries. And you showed supreme consideration by not stepping on any of her new growth. Had you done so, you would have crushed the tender leaves, which would have released her rage. She was quite fond of you, actually."

Emil lapsed into silence, pondering the countless times he'd climbed into the elder without realizing the deadly peril.

"Elder Mother didn't care for *you* at all, Jourdian," Splendor announced then.

Jourdian frowned. "But why? I never climbed into her branches at all, much less ate her berries."

"True, but you paid her nay a hint of attention. 'Twas as if you did not even see her standing there. Once, when you were beneath one of her branches, she tried to win your notice by bending a branch down and caressing your face. You only swiped her leaves away. You spurned her that day, Jourdian, and from then on she has said you are an arrogant and heartless being."

At that, Emil burst into laughter. "Here you thought only *human* women were vying for your attention, Jourdian, and now you find out that the *tree* women were as well!"

Jourdian was about to declare the entire conversation ludicrous when he realized that such ridiculous discussions would occur every day for the rest of his life. Splendor was an elf, and there was no avoiding her whimsical chatter or stories of enchantment. "Fairy tales," he murmured.

"I used to watch you weep, Jourdian," Splendor said, reaching out to toy with his thick ebony hair. "I kept you company during those sorrowful times. You did not know I was with you, but I was there, husband. Indeed, I was with you on many occasions when you thought you were alone."

Jourdian remembered all the lonely hours he'd spent walking around on the estate, either waiting for Emil to arrive or missing Emil when he'd left. And all the time, Splendor had been with him.

The thought comforted him, somehow eased the dreary memories.

"I would stay with you until you went into this house," Splendor continued. "And then I would return to Pillywiggin and yearn for the next time when I would see you." She knelt beside his legs and took his large tanned hand into her small pale one. "You have been my fascination for many years, but I never once dreamed that a day would come when I would not be forced to wait for you to appear. When I would be able to speak to you and hear you answer me. When I could touch you and feel you touch me back. When I could give you joy and see you return it to me. I am happy here with you, Jourdian."

He sat in silence as her sweetness—like some joyful, carefree dancer—waltzed through him.

He'd given her little, he mused. No clothing as of yet, and her wedding ring was but a bit of gold and amethyst. She cared naught for his title, for her own was grander. Indeed there was no material possession he could bestow upon her that she did not already have.

And yet she was happy.

With him. Simply to be with him.

A coldness inside of him began to melt then, dripping away like sun-kissed frost.

He wondered why it was that Splendor had come to be with him now. Now, after so many years of watching him from afar. "Why—"

"Are you happy with me, too?" Splendor drew his fingers toward her mouth and smoothed his thumb across her lower lip.

He saw the unmistakable glow of hope in her lavender eyes, and felt a none-too-gentle nudge of Emil's elbow in his side.

Shifting on the sofa, he tried to think of what to say to Splendor. Was he happy with her? But how could he know? She was beautiful, yes, and sweet and gentle, but he'd been forced to marry her. And then he'd learned she was a fairy.

She was an elf, dammit, and he'd sought the most ordinary woman in existence! How could he be happy?

But he didn't feel miserable. Indeed, there had been several occasions during which he'd actually enjoyed himself with Splendor. She made him laugh. And many of the things she told him touched him with serenity.

Did that mean he was happy with her?

He really hadn't had the chance to find out yet, he realized. Ever since he'd met her, one chaotic thing after another had occurred.

He hadn't even made love to her properly yet.

The thought poured fire into his loins. He fidgeted on the sofa again, painfully aware that his dressing robe would do little to conceal his growing arousal.

"I believe," he said softly, "that we should tidy up and have a bite to eat now." Still holding Splendor's hand, he stood.

Splendor rose as well and curled her arm around his waist.

The feel of her breast against his chest deepened his desire. All he could think about was getting Splendor upstairs. "Emil, if you will excuse us?"

"I can provide you with sustenance, Jourdian," Splendor said, "and we can bathe after we sup." With a spiral of stars, she laid a small table with a gold platter of fresh fruit, several silver dishes of soft breads, a pot of golden honey, and a crystal pitcher of cream.

His stomach growling, Emil was the first to the table, anxious to see what sort of splendid foodstuffs Splendor's magic had produced.

A wave of disappointment caused him to frown when he saw the simple meal. "I don't suppose you could conjure up some venison, could you, Splendor? Smothered in mushrooms and onions? A bit of woodcock would be quite tasty as well. Roasted, if you please, with a side dish of—"

"No animal." Splendor shuddered.

"She means meat," Jourdian explained, his impatience to bed his wife growing by the second.

"Aye, that is what I mean, Emil," Splendor said. "I shall be glad to give you anything but animal."

"Anything?" Emil asked.

"Anything you wish."

Her reply catapulted Emil over the years, back to the time when he went to bed hungry, when his thin frame shook with cold and he had no coat to stave off the chill.

When he had nothing more than his dreams and his wishes.

"Gold," he whispered, remembering his fondest wish of all. "I wish for a mountain of gold."

Stars twinkled, and there in the middle of the room sat a hill of gold nuggets, the top of the pile touching the ceiling.

For a moment, Emil couldn't move, couldn't speak. As a child, how often had he wondered what a mountain of gold looked like? Now he knew, and the little boy inside him laughed with joy.

He ran toward the huge stack of wealth and began to throw himself upon it.

"Splendor, get rid of that gold this very instant!" Jourdian thundered.

In a silver flash, the gold vanished, and Emil fell directly to the floor. He staggered to his feet and glared at his cousin. "Jourdian, for pity's sake—"

"She will not be granting your wishes, Emil, and that is that," Jourdian declared.

"You're selfish, that's what!" Emil tried to straighten his collar before remembering Splendor was wearing his shirt. "The wealthiest peer in all the realm and now you have your own fairy! A gorgeous one at that! And I cannot even see my wish granted for a bit of gold!"

"A *bit*?" Jourdian returned. "My God, Emil, that was almost enough gold to fill an ocean!"

Splendor touched her husband's shoulder. "I only sought to make your cousin happy, Jourdian. Why did it so displease you that I granted his wish?"

"Because I know him well enough to realize that if I allowed you to grant one wish, he would think of a thousand more."

"Stingy, that's what you are!" Emil exclaimed. "You've no need for a mountain of gold because you already have a hundred times that much! I, on the other hand—"

"How would you explain the gold, Emil?" Jourdian asked coolly.

"It wasn't my intention to show it to anyone, cousin."

Eager though he was to take Splendor to bed, Jourdian knew he had to deal with the situation with Emil. If he didn't, the man would wish for the world, and Splendor would accommodate him. "Very well, Emil. You would hide it, and you would never spend it."

"I didn't say that. What good is possessing wealth if I cannot enjoy it?"

Jourdian folded his arms across his chest. "What would you buy?"

Emil rubbed his palms together. "A new coach to start with. And finer horses as well."

"Snow-white horses with polished black hooves!" Splendor suggested.

"Yes, yes," Emil said. "And a wardrobe. I'd purchase a whole new wardrobe that would be the envy of Prince Albert himself! Oh, and a larger house, and a ship. An entire *fleet* of ships—all mine, all harbored and waiting to sail me to wherever I might decide to go."

"I see," Jourdian drawled. "Is that all?"

"I'm certain there's more. If you will be good enough to give me paper and pencil, I will list all the many things I would buy."

With a wave of his hand, Jourdian dismissed Emil's request for writing materials. "For now, let's discuss the coach, horses, princely wardrobe, house, and fleet of ships, shall we? Tell me, Emil, what would you say when people began to notice and question your sudden windfall of wealth?"

"What? Er . . . I'd tell them that I'd done exceedingly well with my various investments."

"Aye, that is what he would tell them, Jourdian," Splendor said, her palms itching to release the magic that would grant Emil's wishes.

"Come now, cousin," Jourdian chided. "You know as well as I that such lucrative investments never remain secret for long. Why, almost as soon as they prove profitable, the entire business world learns who began them, where, when, how, and why. Think carefully, Emil, and you will realize that such an explanation will not suffice."

" 'Twill not suffice, Emil," Splendor said. " 'Twill not suffice at all."

Jourdian crossed to the table, picked up a ripe orange, then set the fruit back down. "Such a sudden fortune might very well lead people to believe that you came by the wealth illegally. And if you were accused of a criminal activity, you could not resort to telling the truth, now could you? As you said earlier, such an admission would get you permanent lodging in an asylum for the insane. So, it would seem that you would have two choices—prison or an asylum. Now, do you still want the mountain of gold?"

Emil turned to Splendor. "How about a harem? My own private bevy of beautiful women?"

Splendor looked at Jourdian.

He shook his head.

"All right," Emil said, "no harem. Just one woman, then. A beautiful princess like Splendor. A princess next in line for a throne. And once I'd married her, I'd be prince consort! Think of that, Jourdian. I'd finally have the title I've always—"

"No."

"Very well," Emil conceded, but not about to give up, "no princess. An heiress, then? Just one simple little heiress who will inherit the biggest fortune in the world?"

Jourdian crossed to where Splendor stood, took her hand, and led her to the door.

"All right, forget about women," Emil said as Jourdian and Splendor stepped into the corridor. "How about a money tree?"

"No," Jourdian said. He looked at Splendor. "You've created a monster. He'll dwell on naught but wishing now."

"Oh, Jourdian?" Emil called as his cousin began to escort Splendor down the hall.

Jourdian stopped and turned around. "Whatever it is, the answer is no."

Emil glared. "I wasn't going to make another wish. I just remembered why I drove over here to Heathcourte in the first place. So much has happened since my arrival, that I quite forgot to give you the news."

"And what news might that be?"

"You're going to love it." Emil smiled smugly. "Lord and Lady Holden are holding a dinner and dance a fortnight from Saturday. I happened to meet Lord Holden yesterday afternoon, and he told me that you and Splendor are invited. The invitations will be sent out tomorrow, which is why you haven't received yours yet. It would seem that most of society will be turning out for the affair, as all are anxious to meet your bride. Your wedding is the story of the decade."

Jourdian could not begin to imagine what manner of chaos

Splendor would cause at such an elegant function. What if she turned her roast beef into pears, or shrank while dancing on the ballroom floor? What if she became distressed in some way? Her blasted mist would come and swallow her up.

And if her sister, Harmony, decided to attend the affair as well . . .

"We will not be accepting," he stated firmly.

"The affair is being held in your honor, Jourdian. It would be in very bad form for you to send your regrets."

"Be that as it may, we will not be attending." Refusing to argue further, Jourdian led Splendor down the hall.

"Please may we go to the dinner and dance, Jourdian? I so adore dancing, and I would very much like to meet your friends. I am certain they could tell me many things about you that I have yet to discover, and I would ever so much enjoy—"

"No."

"But why?"

"Because I said so."

Splendor bristled. "You are dominating me, Jourdian. In Pillywiggin, I am—"

"I know what you are." He stopped at the end of the hall and aimed his gaze straight into hers. "You are a princess there, but this is not Pillywiggin. This is my home, and I am master here. And you, as my wife, are bound to do as I say."

"You cannot take away my title—"

"Nor can you take away mine. I am willing to accept your magical background, Splendor, but do not push me any farther than I am inclined to go. You are my duchess, and you will remain with me here at Heathcourte. Since you will not be returning to fairyland, your royal title has no significance any longer."

She bit her bottom lip. He didn't know. She'd never told him that she would indeed be returning to Pillywiggin. It had never occurred to her to tell him!

He was, after all, only the man chosen to sire the child for Pillywiggin, and she'd never once pondered the idea of staying with him after she'd conceived his child. She needed his baby, and in return she would do everything she could to lift his inner sorrows and bring him joy.

But she *would* return to Pillywiggin.

She had to tell him so. "Jourdian," she said, her voice wavering slightly.

"Yes?" He fairly snarled the word.

She saw his eyes change color. Their silver shade deepened into the frightening color of iron, and she quickly decided to keep her secret for a while longer.

"Yes?" Jourdian growled again.

"Nothing," she murmured. " 'Twas nothing, husband." To keep him from seeing her distress, she gave him a huge grin.

Her pretty smile softened his temper instantly. He pulled playfully on one of her auburn curls, then turned to open a narrow wooden door that led to an old musty staircase.

"I have never seen these stairs," Splendor said as she began the climb up the steps.

"They'll get us upstairs just as quickly as the grander ones in the foyer."

Splendor smiled. "And is this the reason why you have chosen this isolated staircase, Jourdian?" She reached down and gently grasped his manhood, which jutted completely out of the parting of his robe.

Her caress drove him almost over the brink of control, and each breath he took was a struggle to draw into his lungs. Stopping midway up the steps, he tugged Splendor into his arms, pressed her against the wall, and leaned into her. "Keep touching me like that, Splendor, and I will forget all mode of decorum and take you right here in the stairwell."

"Take me where?"

Her untarnished innocence kindled yet more desire, deeper, hotter, so intense he began to sweat. "I'll take you to heaven on earth. I'll make love to you."

Deep, tickling excitement floated through her. "You promised me pleasure," she whispered. "You said that making love would bring me the same pleasure I found with your leg and your hand. Is that the heaven on earth?"

He closed his eyes and buried his face in the nest of fragrant hair on her shoulder. Every muscle in his body strained as his need for her built. "Yes," he rasped.

"Aye, Jourdian. Here, then. Here in the stairwell. I am hungry for the pleasure, and I can no longer wait to understand how you will fill me with yourself. Take me to this earthly heaven of yours. Take me now."

He felt his sex throb against her warm, flat belly. He was clenching his teeth now, and already his hips were moving back and forth in the timeless rhythm of mating. Sliding his hand into her hair, he grasped a handful of flame and pulled her head back.

He took her mouth the way he wanted to take her body. His tongue drove between her lips, again and again, deeper each time, and he willed her to know that the invasion of her mouth was but a hint of the greater, more intimate invasion to come.

His chest heaved, and his eyes glittered when he pulled away from her. "Virgin." He spoke the word with a hot whisper. "Were you not a virgin, Splendor, I would freely give in to the powerful temptation you present to me now. But I'll not consummate our marriage in some clammy stairwell. I'll have you on satin, wife, with your hair, your legs, and your maddening scent wrapped around me."

When he took her hand and began back up the steps, Splendor's knees were so weak that she stumbled.

Immediately, Jourdian lifted her into his arms and carried her the rest of the way up the small, dim staircase. At the top, he opened the door, turned a corner, and proceeded up a second stairwell.

Finally, he arrived at his own hall. Blood and lust pounded through his taut frame as he strode toward the door to his bedroom. The heavy oak portal was slightly ajar.

One kick opened it; another closed it.

"Look around, Splendor," Jourdian demanded. "Is she here?"

"Who?"

"Your sister. Is she here? Disguised as a lamp or a handkerchief or a puff of dust or something?"

Concentrating intently, Splendor surveyed the room, her narrowed gaze touching each and every part of it. She neither saw nor sensed anything that alerted her to Harmony's presence.

"We are alone, husband. Pleasure me now."

Jourdian groaned a response she couldn't understand and advanced to the bed. "The shirt," he told her as he laid her down upon the mattress.

Stars twinkled all over her, and the shirt disappeared.

So did Jourdian's robe and all the grime he'd accumulated during his stint as a slug. He looked down at his clean, naked body, and saw a dusting of silver lights shining upon his skin. "I could have bathed and removed the shirt by myself."

" 'Twould have taken you too long. Cease this torment, Jourdian, and ease this ache inside me."

Many pleas had been put to Jourdian, but never one as sweet. He lowered himself to the bed and pulled her into the hot, hard curve of his body. "I'm not going to stop tonight, Splendor," he warned, his hand gliding along the inside of her thigh. "Do you understand? Nothing you do or say is going to stop me from making you my duchess in every true sense of the word."

In answer, Splendor took hold of his hand and slid it over and into the essence of her femininity. "You cannot stop what you have yet to begin . . ."

**15**

She heard a primal sound, low, guttural, like that of a hunger-driven animal rumble in Jourdian's throat as he captured her mouth with his own and drove his tongue inside. He nipped at her bottom lip, and she felt a flash of discomfort, then another surge of pure passion. "Emil said that your bark was worse than your bite," she whispered into his mouth. "I thought only beasts bit, but you just snapped at my lip."

He smiled a smile that filled his eyes with silver blazes of desire. "I plan to do more than snap at your lip, wife. I'm going to devour every inch of you."

He pressed his hand against the inside of her wrist. Slowly, his fingers traveled upward, skimming across the warm, soft cup beneath her arm, and then coming to a burning halt over her breast. Ending the kiss, he took her other breast into his mouth, nibbling and laving at the crinkled velvet of her nipple. And then he suckled, pulling more of her into his mouth as if he would swallow her whole.

"Jourdian, sweet everlasting." She felt hot, bright, and wild, her need for him almost lethal in its intensity. Lightning, she thought. Aye, it was lightning that flashed over her skin and delved into her body. Arching into Jourdian, she sought more of her lover's heat, more of the scorching excitement his touch sired within her.

There was an uncivilized scent about him, a feral one, male, so powerfully masculine that her breath caught in her throat as she pondered his strength. Boldly, she flicked her tongue over his shoulder, savoring the salty tang, the arousing taste of a man whose body was consumed by desire. The feel of Jourdian, the texture of his skin, and the hard coils of muscle beneath it played further havoc with her emotions, and she heard the silent thunder of her blood as it pounded through her veins.

Everything about him sent streams of sensation throughout her body. She surrendered completely to him, parting her legs when she felt his fingers brush through the hair between her hips. Closer those magic fingers went, closer to the quivering flesh at the heart of her femininity. She felt him unfold her womanly softness. Gently—oh, how gentle yet skillful his fingers were—he spread her slick, sensitive petals, and found a tiny pearl of flesh that trembled beneath his touch.

She cried out his name, a sweet oath, and then his name again, and again, and again until the name of Jourdian sounded throughout the room like a silvery aria.

Music accompanied the song she sang. A gay and completely enchanting melody, it swelled as Splendor's cries became louder.

Jourdian needed only seconds to finally comprehend the mysterious symphony. She was a fairy, he reminded himself. A fairy in the thrall of passion.

When sensual joy was upon her, Splendor made music.

Jourdian had never imagined anything more beautiful.

A thread of tenderness wove through his desire, enhancing his resolve to pleasure her thoroughly. He moved his hand a bit lower and began to circle his thumb around the most intimate opening of her body. "Splendor," he said softly. "Feel how you weep for me."

"Weep?"

He moistened her inner thigh with the dew of her own desire. "Here," he whispered, circling his thumb upon her again. "Here is where you weep."

When full comprehension dawned on her, her excitement deepened. "And will you dry the tears, Jourdian?"

"Nay." He smiled slowly. "I'm going to bring you more."

He entered her then, just a bit, with a finger, and then he

slid another inside her as well, pumping them slightly in rhythm, slightly in depth.

"More," Splendor begged, her eyes closed tight, her forehead creased as she concentrated intently on the pleasure she knew was yet to come.

God, Jourdian thought, as her joyful music grew louder. She was so tight, so hot, so wet. He wanted to plunge himself inside her. Wanted that tightness, that heat, that moistness to squeeze him, set him afire, and drench him with ecstasy.

His rigid sex pulsated next to her hip. He ground it into her soft skin, pushed his fingers more deeply inside her, and knew that the bliss he would soon find within her beautiful body would eclipse any he'd ever experienced.

First, however, he had to concern himself with her virginity. The thought worried him until a sudden possibility came to him.

Perhaps fairies didn't feel pain the way humans did. The prospect was highly soothing.

He noticed that her music softened, almost stopping completely when he slowed his intimate caresses. Soon, he would give her cause to play her joyous melody again. "Splendor," he murmured, "do fairies feel pain?"

"I feel nay a bit of pain at this moment, Jourdian, only a pleasure that would certainly blossom if you would touch me with your fingers—"

"I didn't ask if you were feeling pain now, sprite." He kissed the warm crest of her cheekbone. "I asked if fairies feel pain."

"Jourdian, put your fingers deeper—"

"Splendor, I will have your answer to my question before I continue."

She huffed with impatience. "Aye, husband. Fairies feel pain. Do you nay remember when I told you about the cat that scratched me? I took to my bed and stayed there for a full fortnight."

Jourdian moaned inwardly. If a mere cat scratch had kept her in bed for two whole weeks, he couldn't even imagine what losing her virginity would do to her. "Listen to me, Splendor," he said, trying to keep his voice calm and steady. "I want you to try your very hardest to lie still, do you understand? No matter what magical thing you might be tempted to do when I—when I begin to make love to you, don't do it."

When he moved above her and straddled her hips, she aimed a confused expression into his eyes. "What are you talking about, Jourdian? What magical thing do you think I will be tempted—"

"I don't know." He watched a tinge of worry come into her eyes, and hated himself for making her feel nervous. But he couldn't just ram himself inside her like some unfeeling animal! Couldn't just break through her virgin's shield without giving her some hint of warning! She'd hate him for that.

And something deep inside him rebelled violently against the prospect of Splendor hating him.

"Jourdian?"

"You might want to disappear, or something, Splendor. Perhaps your mist will appear and you'll want to dissolve into it."

"But—"

"Just don't do any of those things, sprite. Lie still, and I promise to make the pain go away. I promise, Splendor, and I do not go back on my word, not ever."

"Pain." She spoke the word as if testing to see what sort of flavor it would leave in her mouth. "Pain, Jourdian?"

"It will be swift, and I'm going to hold you tight and still, all right? I'll hold you in my arms, and I won't move again until you're ready."

"But you said this making love would bring me the pleasure—"

"It will." He leaned down to her, his hands touching her, caressing her, trying desperately to work magic of their own so she wouldn't fear him.

He murmured something to her she didn't understand, but it didn't matter. She felt his soft voice vibrate upon her neck. His big, strong hands moved beneath her to stroke her back and her bottom, and she knew he was trying to comfort her in a wordless way.

"Your legs," Jourdian said, straightening his torso so that he was once again upright over her hips. "Lift them, sprite, will you do that? Curl them around my back, like this."

His hands behind her knees, he raised her legs, and smiled

encouragingly when she encircled them around his back. Slowly, softly, but then with increasing pressure, he grasped her hips, pulling her closer to him, into him, directly against the moistened tip of his manhood.

She gasped sharply.

Jourdian frowned. "I haven't done anything yet."

"I am merely preparing myself, Jourdian. Practicing, if you will. Pain is not an easy thing to accept, and I want to be ready for it when it comes."

Jourdian clamped down on a fresh wave of worry. He pulled his hips back, then arched them forward and upward so that the crown of his staff glided smoothly between her tender folds and over her soft, sensitive female jewel. She began to pant and she made mewling sounds, and he repeated his sensual caresses until she began making her joyful music once more.

The exquisite melody filling his room and his senses, Jourdian touched the crest of his arousal to the hollow cleft of her sex. He shuddered with imprisoned need and stretched slightly into her.

He'd never wanted anything more than he wanted her.

"The pleasure," Splendor panted. " 'Twill be yours as well."

God, how her sweetness touched him! "Yes. We'll share it, sprite."

He read a royal command in her eyes then. *Hurry*, it demanded. "Yes, Your Royal Highness," he acquiesced.

He grasped her hips more tightly, his fingers pressing into the soft flesh of her bottom, his pulsing hardness easing up farther inside her. With his own eyes, he told her he was sorry.

One quick, solid thrust broke through her taut maiden's veil. She bucked wildly beneath him; he settled his full weight atop her body and gathered her in his arms to keep her still.

Her warmth, her tightness . . . the very silk of her presented a challenge that tested every shred of his will, every bit of his determination and patience. Absolute lust, a primitive and a basic element of the man he was, made him yearn to drive into her over and over again.

But another side of him, a person he was only just beginning to know, forced him to subdue his base instincts. This was Splendor beneath him, his wife, and some profound and caring emotion hitherto unknown to him compelled him to lie still and give her all the time she needed to fully accustom herself to the feeling of having him so deeply inside her.

"Splendor," he whispered. With his entire being, he regretted having hurt her. She lay still now, but he wondered what she was thinking.

He waited to see if she would seek some manner of revenge against him. Buried to the hilt inside her impossibly tight sheath, he closed his eyes, ready to be turned back into a slug or to be tossed back into the pit of snakes. Or perhaps she would disappear, and in his arms there would be naught but air and a few folds of the bedspread.

Nothing happened.

He opened his eyes, and what he saw fairly strangled him with deeper remorse.

A mass of innumerable white diamonds flashed upon the dark blue satin coverlet and Splendor's copper tresses. Even as he looked at the glistening jewels, more slipped from Splendor's cheeks.

"I'm—I'm so sorry, sprite," he choked.

Splendor clung to silence as she waited for the pain to subside. The sharpness of it receded quickly, but a dull, throbbing ache remained. She felt too tightly stretched, too full, and was afraid to move.

Jourdian, she thought, the mere sound of his name in her mind somehow easing her discomfort and apprehension. How strange this was . . . holding his body deeply inside of hers. No longer were they two beings, she realized.

They were one, joined in the most intimate way she could imagine.

Suddenly, the ache that lingered within her no longer mattered. She felt stretched, yes, and so full, but how beautiful this union, she thought. How completely wondrous it was to receive and accommodate a part of Jourdian in such a sensuous and glorious way.

"Our joy," she whispered up to him. "You promised."

With a gentle touch, he brushed away several diamonds that clung to her long, sweeping lashes. His forearms lying beside her, he lifted his upper torso from her and moved his hips slightly, cautiously, prepared to stop in a second if she wept or winced again.

But her beautiful face glowed with a silver sheen of happiness, and her lovely lavender eyes twinkled with excitement. And when she timidly raised her hips to meet his, he knew without question that he no longer had to hold his desire in check.

Giving free rein to his passion for her, he withdrew from her in preparation to drive back inside.

"Jourdian, you cannot mean to end this so quickly!" Splendor cried when she felt his thickness leave her body.

"Splendor, we've only just begun." He pushed into her again, pumping his hips firmly and steadily, drawing in and out of her depths with a rhythm and pressure he knew would again bring back her pleasure.

His own bliss began almost instantly. Straining to hold back, he realized he'd never come so close to losing control. "Let me hear your music, sprite," he coaxed her, "and I'll waltz you straight into heaven."

She had no idea what music he was talking about, nor did she care. The only thing that mattered to her at the moment was the delicious sensation that mounted within her. The pleasure was different now than before. More gratifying, richer, and deeper, and she knew in her heart it was because Jourdian was a part of her, and she a part of him.

She caught his rhythm, the timing of his powerful thrusts, and her hips rose and fell in the cadence he set. It surely was a dance, she realized, this stirring making of love. A waltz as Jourdian had said, and she didn't miss one exquisite step.

He lunged into her faster then, and she felt him become harder and thicker than he'd been before. The base of his masculinity pressed firmly, yet gently across the outer regions of her female flesh, and the heat of his loins burned her with blazes of pleasure.

She dug her fingers into the rock-hard planes of his back, and imagined him swirling her along a path of stars. "Jourdian," she panted, "I am about to—"

"I know, Splendor. I know."

"We are going to float," she warned him, her bliss heightening. "Toward heaven."

He no longer heard anything but the ethereal music of her joy. Louder the melody became, reaching its crescendo and reverberating through his bedchambers with all the force and magnificence accomplished by a hundred-man orchestra.

Closing his eyes, Jourdian yielded to the power of his own release then, moving faster and faster, harder and harder, driving into Splendor with a force that hurled him straight into the same bliss that caused her to writhe and cling beneath him. Deep, bone-melting pleasure flamed through his loins, spreading fire through his torso and limbs, searing even his thoughts and setting aflame the very heart of his soul.

He stiffened, every part of him hardening and straining as he felt the burst of his seed stream into Splendor's depths. The very real sensation of floating came over him. Floating . . . on a wave of rapture that carried him higher and higher toward the heaven he'd promised her.

*Splendor.*

He tried to call her name, but his continuing ecstasy made speaking impossible.

*I knew it,* he tried to tell her. Yes, he'd known it would be like this. Had sensed it even before tonight. Her innocence, her sweetness, and her giving nature had made their lovemaking the most incredible experience of his entire life.

*Splendor.* Her name described perfectly the gift she'd given to him. He wanted to say something tender to her. Something gentle.

But he could not. The words would not come.

"Heaven," he whispered to her.

"Aye," she whispered in return. "But I suspect we will come down before we get *that* high."

Her strange reply made him open his eyes and look at her face.

He saw more than her face.

He saw the floor, about six feet below. Turning his head, he saw the ceiling, about two feet above.

He and Splendor were, indeed, floating. They'd come right off the bed and were drifting through the room. His first reaction was shock, but his surprise quickly faded. Anger never rose, either. He was, after all, married to a fairy, and therefore had to accustom himself to such strange goings-on.

"I don't suppose it would do me a bit of good to tell you to get us down from up here, would it, Splendor?" he asked as they glided above the fireplace mantel.

"I cannot get us down until my pleasure has completely waned, husband. I still feel soft tremors, especially when you move."

"I see." He moved a little more for her, wincing when he bumped the back of his head on the ceiling.

She made music of sensual joy, he mused again.

She floated on waves of sensual bliss.

Making love with Splendor would never be boring.

❦

"Did I please you, Jourdian?" Splendor wanted to know the second the leisurely flight around the room came to an end and they'd floated back to the bed. "Did I give you joy?"

His body still on top of hers, Jourdian rolled to the mattress. "Are we going to fly about the room like that every time we make love?"

She sat up and leaned over him, her hair spilling red fire over his chest. "I nay mean to do it, husband. 'Tis something that simply happens when I am consumed with such ecstasy. You felt the rapture too, did you not?"

He'd felt it all right, so much so that his heartbeat had yet to return to normal. "You pleased me very much," he said, pulling her down and holding her close.

She shimmered with happiness. Finally, she'd given Jourdian true joy. "Will you kiss me?"

"Why? Do you feel like you will soon shrink?"

"Nay. I just want a kiss. I like kissing."

With his fingers, he tilted her chin up, then touched his lips to hers. He kissed her languidly, as if he had all the time in the world. Lightly, he traced the outline of her lips with his tongue, all the while playing with the thick copper curls that lay spread all over the bed and his chest.

"Did I hurt you very much?" He picked up a handful of the costly tears she'd shed earlier and sprinkled them over her flaming red hair.

"Aye, you hurt me, Jourdian."

Her honesty was painful to hear. "I'll never hurt you again."

"If you do, I shall nay mind because I know now that there is supreme pleasure after the pain."

"No, Splendor, you don't understand." He shifted to his side so he could look into her eyes. "There is pain only the first time. Once you have known a man, your body is never so tight again. The next time I make love to you, you will receive me easily, sprite."

"You have opened me."

"Yes."

She lapsed into silence for a moment, but kept steady hold of his beautiful silver gaze. "I felt you spill, Jourdian. Felt the hot burst of you. 'Twas your very essence, was it not?"

He laid his hand over her flat belly, wondering if even now his son had been conceived. "Yes, it was my essence, and it mingled with yours. That's how a child is created. With a part of each of us."

She had not conceived. She knew she hadn't. "Let us continue to make love until we create the child. Every day . . ."

"Every night, every morning," he promised her.

"Now?"

"So soon?"

"We will not get the child if we do not keep our essences mingling, Jourdian."

He smiled. She spoke as if she were an expert on the subject of conception. "How right you are, wife."

She slipped her hand between his legs to fondle him, and discovered him soft and pliant. "Jourdian," she said, looking down at him, "this is the most pitiful cattail I have ever seen."

He tried to feel insulted, but could only feel amusement. "Splendor, I lose strength, too. Almost the way you do." He tried to make her understand. "After a session of lovemaking like the one we just had, I'm bound to be a bit drained."

She nodded slowly, then squirmed upward to kiss him passionately. Pressing her lips against his, she plunged her tongue inside his mouth.

Taken aback by her boldness, but certainly not opposed to it, Jourdian returned the kiss with the same ardor with which she'd begun it.

After many long, delicious moments, Splendor raised her head. "There," she said, smiling. "You are infused with fresh energy now, are you not?"

"Look for yourself."

She lowered her gaze. The sight that met her eyes caused her to laugh out loud. "Oh, Jourdian, I have never seen a cattail grow as quickly as yours! And 'twas not done with a hint of fairy thrall!"

"No, but with a wealth of fairy beauty."

She saw the sheen of desire come into his eyes, and sighed with delight when he gently pushed her back down to the mattress and knelt between her parted thighs. Only when he lowered himself upon her and she felt him begin to penetrate her did she tense and experience a small tremor of anxiety. "Jourdian . . ."

He felt her quiver beneath him and watched her ball her small hands into fists, but he didn't stop. He'd told her he wouldn't hurt her again, and now he would give her solid proof. Slowly, heated inch by heated inch, he slipped into her.

Splendor's fists uncurled. She felt him slide deeper and deeper inside her, stretching and filling her like before, but there came not a shred of pain. "No pain, Jourdian."

"Not ever again, Splendor."

He made love to her slowly, with long, leisurely strokes, pacing their lovemaking in such a way as to build her pleasure bit by bit. When he heard her music and sensed she was at the brink of release, he bridled her fulfillment by changing the rhythm of the movement of his hips. Thus, he kept her hovering somewhere between mere delight and total ecstasy.

Only when he saw the color of her eyes deepen from lavender to a dark purple did he indulge her longing for completion. He heard her music reach its majestic zenith and felt her silken femininity tremble around him.

Off the bed they rose, and Jourdian found his own release just as they floated beneath the chandelier. Cool crystal prisms skimmed lightly down his back as hot sensual bliss flamed through him.

He didn't know how long he and Splendor glided through the room, nor did he care. Holding her tightly to him, he sighed with deep contentment and closed his eyes.

And when Splendor brought them back to the bed, Jourdian was already fast asleep. With a dash of silver stars, she placed him under the covers with his head in the middle of a mound of satin pillows. Joining him there, she settled herself close to him and watched his face as he slept.

He was so beautiful that her heart leapt within her breast. And the memory of his lovemaking . . . the way he'd held her, whispered to her, kissed her, and brought her such tantalizing joy . . .

She knew that if she lived to be a thousand years old, she would never again know the same profound happiness that she'd found with Jourdian Amberville.

A thousand years, she mused. She had only three months.

He began to speak in his sleep. Murmured something she didn't comprehend. She remembered other things he'd said. Things she had understood.

*Nothing you do or say is going to stop me from making you my duchess in every true sense of the word.*

Lifting her hand, she caressed the mole on his cheek with a touch as light as a baby's sigh. He had made her his duchess, she mused. He'd married her, then filled her with his essence. A truer thing she couldn't imagine.

*You are my duchess, and you will remain with me here at Heathcourte.*

His declaration beat through her mind like a hard, violent rain, flooding her with a bereft feeling she'd never experienced in all her life. She felt as though she was losing something. Something precious to her, something she would not have back again.

She'd never lost anything before.

The sadness that welled within her then was the most profound emotion she'd ever known. And it remained inside her. Wasn't shallow, didn't fade.

It grew, and it made her heart hurt.

And for the first time since she'd met Jourdian in the meadow, she pondered the day when she would leave him.

# 16

**W**hen Jourdian awakened the next morning, the place beside him was cool and empty. Rubbing the last remnants of sleep from his eyes, he sat up and looked around the room. "Splendor?" He got out of bed and walked into the middle of his chambers. "Splendor?"

Wondering if she'd dwindled in size, he began looking inside every small container he could find: vases, bowls, dishes, a deep fold in one of the velvet drapes, even inside his hats.

After a while of searching in vain, he decided she was downstairs, perhaps with Emil, granting wishes right and left. God, there was simply no guessing what he might encounter when he found his overly wishful cousin and exceedingly generous wife.

He didn't bother to ring for his valet, but chose his clothing himself, laid it out on the bed, and then proceeded into his bath, a large and elegant room done in white marble and accented with fixtures of pure gold.

As soon as he stepped into the room, he heard splashing sounds coming from behind the white silk screen that stood in front of the sunken bathtub. "Splendor?"

He heard a female voice speak. But the voice was low, muffled. "Splendor," he called again.

Wondering why she didn't answer him, he walked across the room and behind the screen.

He stopped short. And frowned.

A woman knelt beside the tub, her hands immersed in the water. She was garbed in a gown that Jourdian's quick mind recognized as typical of the eleventh century.

Mindful of his nakedness, he hastened to find a towel and wrap it around his hips. Dressed thus, he joined the woman behind the screen again. "Who are you, and what are you doing in my bath?" he demanded in the ducal tone that intimidated most people who heard it.

The woman didn't look up, but only continued to swish her wrinkled hands through the water.

"Madam," Jourdian snapped, "how did you get in here?"

She drew her hands out of the water, and stared at her right palm. Her face set in grim lines of determination, she began to rub that palm with her other hand. " 'Out, damned spot! Out, I say! Out, damned spot! Out, I say!' "

Jourdian reeled with disbelief that quickly turned into precise comprehension. Spinning on his heel, he marched out of the bath, dressed with utmost haste, and headed downstairs.

"Where is Her Grace?" he demanded when he encountered Ulmstead on the second-floor staircase.

Ulmstead struggled to hold on to a long, velvet sash at the end of which was tied an irritated llama. "Sir, I found this llama in the reception room downstairs. It raced up here, where I was finally able to catch it. Forgive me for using this drapery sash as a rope, Your Grace, but it was a matter of necessity. Now, however, I cannot get this animal to walk down these steps. A llama! This is quite the most preposterous creature I have found yet!"

Jourdian glanced at the llama he knew was Delicious, then looked back up at the bewildered butler. "Uh . . . I heard that a circus has been traveling through this area. The llama more than likely escaped from the carnival."

"A circus?"

"Ulmstead, have you seen Her Grace?"

"I haven't seen her, your lordship," the butler panted, his bony face taut with strain as he battled to keep the llama from going back up the stairs. "But it could be that she's with Mr. Tate, who is breakfasting in the morning room."

Jourdian left Ulmstead to deal with Delicious, and wasted no time getting to the morning room, a sunny apartment with a huge bay window.

Emil sat at a small round table in front of the window, his breakfast laid out before him. "Good morning, cousin," he said, toasting Jourdian with a cup of steaming tea. "Slept in this morning, did you? It's ten and a quarter, and you're usually up by seven and in your office working by nine. My, but your ho-hum routine has changed since you wed."

Jourdian noted the leftover fruit on the plate across from Emil's and the glass that was half full of cream. "Where is Splendor?"

Emil sipped his tea, then set the cup back on the delicate saucer. "She finished eating and said she was going for a stroll. But I've company in here, so you needen't worry about my being lonesome."

Jourdian frowned. "What company?"

Emil pointed to the corner of the room behind Jourdian. "Those charming women have been keeping me thoroughly entertained."

Jourdian wheeled around, certain he would see a harem of beautiful, voluptuous females.

He saw three hags with stringy white hair, pointed chins, and eyes like bits of lit coal. Hunched around a big black pot, long sticks in their gnarled hands, they stirred something that steamed from the cauldron.

And they chanted. " 'Double, double, toil and trouble.' "

"The witches from Macbeth," Jourdian seethed. "Emil, why did you allow Splendor to—"

"She's not my fairy, cousin. She's yours. I have no right to tell her how to use her magic. Besides, I think it rather fascinating to be able to meet Shakespearean characters. And those witches are really perfectly harmless, Jourdian. They've done naught but stir their pot and chant since Splendor conjured them up."

Too furious to answer his fanciful cousin, Jourdian left the room and stormed directly outside. Stalking all around the grounds, he looked everywhere for his wayward wife. Only when he neared one of the rose gardens did his search slow and finally stop.

A tall figure moved amidst the roses. But it wasn't Splendor. It was a man, a bearded man. His hands clasped behind his back, he paced, and his face registered deep, grim contemplation. " 'To be, or not to be: that is the question,' " he said as he walked among the roses. " 'Whether 'tis nobler in the mind to suffer the slings and arrows of outrageous fortune—' "

" 'Or to take arms against a sea of troubles, and by opposing end them?' " Jourdian finished for him. He drew in a deep, shuddering breath. "Hamlet," he fumed aloud. "Lady Macbeth in my bath, the three witches in my morning room, and Hamlet in my rose bushes! What more, Splendor?" he shouted, uncaring that she might be too far away to hear him. "Who else am I going to come upon, damn it all!"

" 'To die: to sleep,' " Hamlet continued.

"Listen," Jourdian said to him, "I want you out of my garden and back in your book in two seconds, do you understand me? And take Lady Macbeth and those cauldron-stirring witches with you! What if someone sees you out here? How the bloody hell would I explain—"

" 'No more,' " Hamlet said, " 'and, by a sleep to say we end the heartache and the thousand natural shocks that flesh is heir to, 'tis a consummation devoutly to be wish'd.' "

Ramming his fingers through his hair, Jourdian tramped away to resume his search for his incorrigible fairy wife. He'd taken only a few long strides before spying a lovely dark-haired maiden leaning over one of the second-story balconies, her ample bosom nearly spilling out of her gown.

She spoke. " 'O Romeo, Romeo, wherefore art thou, Romeo?' "

His eyes mere slashes across his face, Jourdian stared into the hedgerow beneath the balcony, already knowing who he would see. Sure enough, there stood Romeo, gazing up at Juliet with all the love in the world in his eyes.

" 'Deny thy father,' " Juliet continued, " 'and refuse thy name. Or, if thou wilt not, be but sworn my love, and I'll no longer be Capulet.' "

"You'll no longer be *alive* as soon as I find Splendor!" Jourdian shouted up to her.

Again, he set off to look for Splendor. A half an hour of looking seemed like half of eternity to him, but he finally found her standing near the pavilion. As he neared her, he realized she wore naught but a silk shirt and a bit of cream around the edges of her mouth.

Well, at least the pavilion was situated near the edge of the woods, well away from the house. The chances were small that any of the estate workers could see her here. But dammit, when would her clothes arrive?

"Splendor—"

"Jourdian!" she greeted him gaily. "Oh, husband, do you know that I almost stepped into this pretty white edifice?" she asked, gesturing toward the pavilion. "But just as I began to step into it, I realized it is put together with iron nails! How many times must I tell you that iron—"

"Lady Macbeth is in my bath trying to wash a damned spot of imaginary blood from her hand, the three witches are watching Emil eat in my morning room, Juliet is hanging off a balcony, Romeo is loitering near the hedgerow, and Hamlet is ambling through my rose garden trying to answer the question of to be or not to be!"

"Aye, that is what they are all doing."

"I want those characters *not* to be, Splendor, do you understand me? *Not to be!* Get rid of them right this very second!"

"But—but you like Shakespeare and his characters!"

"Not enough to live with them, I don't!"

"Jourdian, you are shouting at me."

"That I am, wife, and if you dare to throw me into that snake pit again, I'll—"

"You will what?" She folded her arms across her breasts and lifted her chin a few notches.

Jourdian saw a dare in her amethyst eyes. "Do you challenge me, Splendor? Do you think that because you can do magic that I am going to cower before you?"

"You—"

"Do your worst. Here I stand, completely vulnerable before

your powers. But I promise you this: Short of killing me, you will not escape—"

"*Kill* you!" The very thought misted Splendor's eyes with the sheen of diamonds. "Jourdian, I would never—"

"No?"

"*Nay!*"

It was Jourdian's turn to fold his arms across his chest. "Then I've nothing to fear, do I? Get rid of Lady Macbeth, the witches, Ham—"

"I will not kill you, Jourdian, but I will—"

"Then do it. Do what you will."

"I could turn you into a slug, just as Harmony did," she warned.

"Fine. I'm ready."

"Do not tempt me."

"I'm more than tempting you, Splendor. I'm daring you."

"How would you like to be plunged into the North Sea? With sharks?"

His heart skipped a beat, but his face remained expressionless. "Do it."

" 'Twould be effortless to fill the shoes you wear with scorpions."

One by one, he lifted both his feet. "Fill them."

She stared at him for a long moment. " 'Tis trust you show, Jourdian. I am glad that you are not afraid of me. Glad that you know I will nay cause any harm to befall you."

He felt his frantic heartbeat slow. "Are there any more fictitious people in my house and gardens? If I go to my barns, will I see King Lear and Othello in the tack and feed rooms? Is the master here as well? Is he, Splendor? Did you put old William Shakespeare himself in my office perhaps?"

"Do you wish for him to be there?"

"*No!* Send those characters back to their appropriate pages in the book!"

She floated to him. "I wanted to make you happy. I thought you would enjoy—"

"You thought wrong. Now, for the last time, get rid of those characters. I *wish* for you to do so, and I *wish* for you to grant my wish right now."

Her lips thinned in displeasure, Splendor waved her hand toward the manor house, which, for a moment became completely encased in a cloud of silvery magic. "They are gone, and you are uncivil. By gifting you with a few of Shakespeare's characters, I had so hoped to make you smile and laugh. And yet you saw fit only to shout."

Jourdian realized how truly upset his shouting had made her when he saw her misty haven begin to appear around her. Before she could dissolve, he took her hand and pulled her away from the shining haze. "You are not going to disappear every time we have a disagreement, Splendor."

She looked up at him. "But 'tis what *you* do, Jourdian. When you become angry or in some way upset, you get on your horse and ride away. What is the difference between disappearing into mist and riding away on a horse? Both are means of escape from difficult situations, are they not?"

He knew she had a point, but he'd be damned if he'd concede. "There is a big difference between disappearing into a fog and riding away!"

"But you ride away into the country and disappear."

"On a *horse*, not on a cloud of *mist*!"

"The ends are the same. You vanish from sight. Uncivil is what you are, Jourdian. Uncivil for shouting and uncivil for continuing an argument that you know full well I have won."

Patience didn't come easily, but he managed to find a thread of it. "Listen to me, Splendor," he said quietly, and took hold of her slight shoulders. "You rouse my temper easily because . . . I didn't know what you were when I married you. I . . . The woman I was looking for . . . She . . . You're different, and I—"

"Jourdian," Emil called as he arrived. "I'm off now, cousin. Many thanks for your hospitality, and a pox on you for not allowing me any of my wishes. Splendor," he said, picking up her hand and kissing it lightly, "a pleasure to see you, as always. I'll come again soon, and when I do it will be with the fervent hope that my selfish, stingy cousin will permit me a few wishes."

Jourdian rolled his eyes. "Emil, this conversation was over last evening. I will not discuss it—"

Before he could finish, a sphere of fire burned a black hole upon a patch of grass on the side of the pavilion. In the next instant, Harmony stood on the charred spot, her bare legs still engulfed in blazes.

"Oh, God," Jourdian muttered. "Just what I need after the morning I've had."

"Who . . ." Emil began, but was so mesmerized by the woman's naked beauty that he could not think of the rest of his words. "Who . . . Who . . . Who . . ."

"Oh, how supremely amusing, Emil!" Splendor exclaimed, and smiled. "You sound exactly like an owl!"

Emil continued to gawk at the nude woman. The gold of her hair rivaled spring sunshine. Her eyes were the bluest things he'd ever seen, her lips impossibly pink. And her breasts . . .

He swallowed. Hard. God almighty, her white breasts were the most beautiful he'd ever seen. And her legs! He could only imagine how the pale silk of her legs would feel beneath his fingers and palms.

But beyond her beauty, there was something else about her. Something that seemed to drift toward him, into him, and curl around his heart.

It was a bond, he realized. Yes, he felt an immediate bond with her. It didn't matter that he knew not her name or anything else about her. There existed a natural affinity between them, stronger than anything he'd ever experienced.

Emil had always wondered if falling in love at first sight was possible. Now he knew it was. "Who is she, Jourdian?" he whispered so faintly that Jourdian could barely hear him.

"She's trouble, that's who," Jourdian answered, glaring at Harmony. "T-R-O-U-B-L-E. Her other name is Harmony. She's Splendor's sister, and you would do well to stay as far from her as possible."

Harmony returned Jourdian's glare. "I understand that you have nay a fear of my honey-sweet sister, human, but I think you forget that the last time you angered *me* you became a slimy bit of bird food."

Splendor laid her hand on Jourdian's arm. "Do not anger her, Jourdian. Her temper is hotter than the heart of the sun."

"Her hot temper matters not at all to me. I want her off my land," Jourdian flared.

Harmony raised one golden eyebrow. "I live on this land, human."

"This land belongs to *me*."

"You do not own Pillywiggin."

"If it's on my land, I do."

"How dare you," Harmony warned.

"Jourdian," Splendor said. "Harmony. Please."

Harmony turned to the man standing beside Jourdian. As her gaze met his, her stomach fluttered. She could not seem to look away from him.

His unruly hair was the color of hay, almost the same hue as hers, but not as bright. He had large round eyes like old gold coins, and as she peered into them she thought she saw a smile in each of them.

He grinned at her. Looking at his teeth, she thought of the fences some humans liked putting around their homes. White. Strong. Straight. Yes, the man had fence teeth.

He was tall, appeared to be every bit as strong as Jourdian. Harmony's stomach fluttered again, then she felt her feet leave the ground by a few inches.

Such proof of inner joy had never happened to her before. "Splendor says you are her husband's cousin," she said to him, and saw the smiles in his eyes widen and flash.

"Emil Tate," Emil introduced himself. He had to restrain himself from pulling her into his arms and kissing her breathless. Somehow, he thought, he had to make her understand they were meant for each other. That destiny had finally brought them together.

Completely perplexed by the strange connection she felt with Emil, Harmony was determined to ignore the feeling. "I do not like your cousin, Emil," she said, pitching another dark look in Jourdian's direction. "And since you are related to him, I do not like you, either."

"Oh, but I'm not like Jourdian at all," Emil declared. "I'm kind and considerate."

"Kindness and consideration," Harmony began, "are two qualities that churn my stomach."

Emil nodded. "Mine too. That's why I have been trying to become contemptible and boorish."

"Emil, for God's sake," Jourdian said. "Why are you trying to impress this evil-minded—"

"He tries to impress me because he has more intelligence in his head than you've in yours," Harmony spat out.

She raised her hand, and before Jourdian realized her intentions, stardust clung to every part of him. Clenching his jaw and his fists, he waited in silent apprehension to see what she'd turned him into.

But nothing happened. Looking down at himself, he saw the same man he'd been only seconds before.

"What's the matter, Harmony?" he asked, sneering. "Are your powers weakening?"

The instant the words were out of his mouth, he felt the eerie sensation that someone else was speaking the exact words at the same time as he was. The other voice sounded close, right next to his ear.

"Jourdian," Emil murmured. "Oh, my!"

"Now, Jourdian," Splendor cooed, trying her best to sound calm, "there is nothing to worry about. I will undo what Harmony—"

"What has she done?" Jourdian asked, again hearing his words being spoken by another person. And yet, he thought, the other voice sounded exactly like his own. "Would someone please tell me what she's done?"

Emil stared at his cousin. "You have two heads."

"*What?*" Jourdian turned his head to the right, then to the left.

Shock nearly knocked him off his feet. There, on his left shoulder, sat another head, a replica of his own.

The mouth on the head smiled. "Hello, Jourdian," it said. "I'm Jourdian."

Harmony burst into laughter. "Two heads, human! When you had only one, you didn't possess the intelligence of a brick. So, I have found it in my generous heart to bestow upon you another head. Now your intelligence has doubled. If I cared for gratitude, I would have your thanks."

Quick as a wink, Splendor dusted Jourdian's second head

with her magic, and her husband was once again a one-headed man.

Jourdian felt his left shoulder, and when he was satisfied that the second head was gone, he took a menacing step toward Harmony.

Splendor grasped his arm. "Good-bye, Emil. Good-bye, Harmony." In a burst of silver, she and Jourdian disappeared.

Emil stared at the empty spot where they'd stood. "Where—"

"She rescued him," Harmony said, "because she knew he was about to become a lamb in a den of starving wolves."

"Is your magic as powerful as Splendor's?"

Harmony floated into the air, lying on her back as if reclining on a soft sofa. "Whatever she can do, I can do better."

Emil stared so hard that his eyes began to sting. Harmony's hair fell away from her body like a shower of pure gold, revealing the full length of her flawless form.

"What do you gawk at, human?" Harmony demanded when she caught him staring at her.

"You . . . I . . . You're very beautiful," Emil murmured. "And it's still difficult for me to accustom myself to the sight of unclothed women out in broad daylight."

At his compliment, Harmony fairly purred. Still in the air, she turned to her side. "Why do you humans cover your bodies? Are you ashamed of how you look without all those clothes you wear?"

"Certainly not! It's just that humans are more sensitive over certain parts of our bodies."

"Which parts?"

"Uh . . . The private parts."

"You are not answering my question, human. Which parts are so private?"

Emil felt color wash over his smoothly shaven cheeks.

"Very well," Harmony said, drifting back to the ground, "since you will not answer me, you must show me."

When he saw stardust shooting toward him, Emil lifted his arms in front of his face and ducked as if fending off a brace of battering fists. But the fairy magic caught him easily and quickly divested him of his clothing.

He stood before Harmony then, just as naked as she was. "Dear God!" Struggling to hide his bare body, he covered his loins with his hands, ran into the pavilion, and hid behind the swing that hung suspended from the roof.

"Ah, so you *are* embarrassed," Harmony said. She approached the pavilion, but drew swiftly away when she sensed all the iron that was nailed into the structure. "Come out of there, human."

Emil knew it wasn't wise to disobey a fairy, especially one as hot-tempered as Harmony. But nothing—not even fear of fairy punishment—could induce him to leave his spot behind the swing.

Nothing but a bit of magic.

In a second, he was standing back on the grass in front of Harmony. Keeping his hands over his loins, he looked all around, dreading the possibility of seeing any of the Heathcourte gardeners. "Someone is going to see . . . The gardeners. They're going to see me!"

Harmony floated nearer to him, so close that she could feel his warm breath on her cheek and smell the spicy scent he wore.

An odd warmth passed through her. Warmth and that equally peculiar flutter again. "These gardeners . . . do they have something different on their bodies than you do?"

"No, but—"

"You are the same as they?"

"Yes, but—"

"Then why do you care if they see you without your clothing?"

Lost within the depths of eyes that were as blue as the heart of a flame, Emil couldn't answer. Her nipples brushed his bare chest, and her left leg touched his.

And no longer could he hide his male parts from Harmony's view.

"The cattail," Harmony mused aloud, looking down at his stiffened masculinity. "*This* is what had Splendor so enthralled?"

"What?" Emil gasped. "I assure you that Splendor has never seen me—"

"I refer to her husband's cattail. But tell me, what is so special about these cattail parts of you?"

Emil realized then that Harmony was just as innocent as Splendor had been. Oh, how he longed to be the man to tutor her in the passionate arts of love.

But he remembered himself instantly. "It's indecent for me to have this conversation with you, Harmony. You should ask your sister."

At that, Harmony burst into a spinning globe of fire. She shot around and around the pavilion, leaving a trail of black smoke in her wake.

Amazement caused Emil to forget his naked state. "My God," he whispered, watching as she cooled down and again became the beautiful fairy she was. "Did that little display signify that you're angry?"

"I burn when I am upset. Darling little Splendor dissolves into cool mist."

Emil detected a sour note in her lovely voice. "Why are you upset?"

Harmony pulled a big tarantula out of thin air and stroked the creature's hairy back with the tip of her finger. "She is always first. She learned about human cattails before I, did she not? She's first in line for the throne, too. She gets everything, aye, that she does, and 'tis grossly unfair."

Emil began to comprehend the strange, but profound closeness he'd felt toward her the moment he'd seen her. "It's hard being second, isn't it, Harmony?" he asked, his voice brimming with sympathy and understanding.

Harmony pushed back her bare shoulders and turned away from him. "I do not know what you mean, human."

"I think you do." He reached out and fingered one of the sunny curls that shimmered down her back, wondering warily if he might draw back a nub. "And I know precisely how hard it is."

She wanted to show further indifference and push back her shoulders again, but curiosity made her turn to Emil and look into his eyes. "What do you know about being second?"

Emil was careful to keep a safe distance. She still held the wicked-looking tarantula in her hand. "I'm second, too, and there are times when I covet what Jourdian has. His wealth is the stuff of dreams, and his title is one of the most respected in all of England. It's impossible not to feel a bit of envy."

Harmony nodded. "Aye, 'tis impossible."

"But there's nothing we can do about our situations," Emil pointed out gently. "I can never be the duke of Heathcourte, nor will I ever possess a fortune similar to his. And you, Harmony, will never be Pillywiggin's queen."

Harmony began to burn again, but she quickly cooled when a sudden thought entered her mischievous mind. "I could put your cousin somewhere where no one could find him. I would take great delight in doing such a thing to him. And if he were lost to the world, you could have his title and his fortune, could you not?"

"No! For God's sake, don't do anything of the sort!"

"But you want what he has."

Emil's pulse raced erratically. If Harmony caused Jourdian to disappear from the face of the earth, he'd never forgive himself for inadvertently putting the idea in her head in the first place. "If I could, would you have me get rid of Splendor so you could have the throne?"

"You cannot."

"But if I could, would you wish for me to do it?"

"Nay."

"Why not?"

"Because she is my sister."

"And you love her."

Harmony had no idea what love was. "I—"

"And I love Jourdian," Emil continued smoothly. "Just because I crave the things he has, doesn't imply I'd harm him in anyway. And it isn't only Jourdian. There was a boy in the village where I grew up who had the most wonderful white pony I'd ever seen. It had big dark eyes, a thick tail that brushed the ground, and a ribbon of black streaking down its face. I wanted that pony with all my heart, but I'd never have hurt the boy or stolen the animal away from him. The boy was my friend."

Harmony remained silent.

But Emil knew he'd gotten through to her. Jourdian, for the

time being, was safe from her vicious magic. "You know," he said, "you'll find me a ready listener if you should ever feel the need to talk about your feelings at always being second. I assure you I'll understand everything you tell me."

A tender emotion tried to come to Harmony, but she stubbornly tamped it down. "And I assure *you* that I will never need a human for anything."

"Oh?" Recalling Jourdian's explanation about how kissing revitalized Splendor, Emil rubbed his thumb over his bottom lip. "What about the need for strength? An infusion of vigor into your fragile body?"

"Vigor," Harmony repeated, her gaze locked on his mouth. "Get rid of the spider."

Too excited to realize she was obeying his command, Harmony tossed the tarantula into the air, where it promptly disappeared.

Emil spread open his arms. "I've more strength than you would know what to do with. If you want it, come and get it."

She flew into him, wrapping her arms around his neck. Emil reached up into the shining mass of her hair, twined his fingers through the golden silk, and held her steady for his kiss.

Gently, as if she might come apart in his arms, he touched his lips to hers.

But Harmony would have none of his tenderness. She fairly smashed her mouth into his, seeking every bit of the energy he could offer her.

What she sought, Emil gave. He kissed her deeply, passionately, and when she began to shimmer in his embrace, he knew he'd succeeded in gifting her with the vigor she craved.

And he knew also that she'd given him a desire that would never be satisfied by any other woman, fairy or human. He would have her for his own, he vowed. No matter what he had to do to make her his, she would belong to him.

"Had enough?" he asked when she floated out of his arms.

"I do not think I can ever have enough of this kissing!" Harmony cried, her entire body aglow with joy and power.

"I like that answer. Now, would you be willing to give me something in return? A few wishes, perhaps?" Well, after all, Emil mused, if Splendor couldn't grant his wishes, he might as well see if Harmony would. And there would be nothing Jourdian could do about it.

"I am not the wish-granter in my family," Harmony informed him crisply. "My ninny sister, Splendor, is."

"But you can grant wishes."

"Aye, but I shall not."

"At least give me my clothes back."

Harmony pondered his request. It went against her grain to perform any sort of good deed, but for reasons she could not understand, she felt inclined to do this one for Emil. With a flicker of silver, she dressed him back in his clothing. " 'Tis all I am willing to do for you. Do not ask me for anything else."

Emil's shoulders slumped. "What a stroke of ill luck," he grumbled. "I've finally found a fairy of my own, and she won't grant my wishes."

"A fairy of your own?" Harmony laughed. "I do not belong to you, human!"

"Not yet," Emil whispered, watching as she turned herself into a ball of fire and burned into nothingness. "But you will, Harmony. Yes, you definitely will."

For the next several days, Jourdian found himself constantly looking over his shoulder. Harmony's sudden and obnoxious visits set him on edge, and every time he turned a corner or walked into a room, he expected to see her burning in front of him.

But it was Splendor who followed him, who joined him in each room he entered. She even rode with him, though not on Magnus, for there remained the problem with the iron stirrups.

She rode alongside the great stallion, mounted on a blue-green dragonfly. Jourdian wasn't at all pleased to see his tiny wife sailing around on the back of an insect, but he soon decided it was the only solution to her yearning to ride with him.

Still, he wanted her to have and ride a horse. And since he didn't care for the idea of her riding bareback, he began to devise various means to overcome the dilemma with iron.

As she'd promised she would, Splendor became his steady company, smiling and chattering throughout the course of each day.

And melting in his arms at night.

Gradually, Jourdian began to question how he'd endured so many years of relative solitude. So accustomed to Splendor's presence did he become, that when she left his side for even a moment he wondered where she'd gone and when she'd come back.

He also wondered what she'd be wearing when next he

caught sight of her. Her clothing had arrived from London, and she took great delight in changing into various gowns whenever the whim to do so swept through her capricious fairy mind.

Of course, she didn't change clothes the way human women did. She simply sprinkled her stars, and voilà! She was wearing another dress.

"Do you like this gown, Jourdian?" she asked one evening as they enjoyed a late supper in the privacy of their bedchamber. "Does this blue not remind you of an April sky in the morning?"

He looked up from his plate, blinked, and gave her a slight frown. "Not five seconds ago you were wearing a dress you said made you think of a lightning bolt. Silver-white, you said it was."

"Aye, that is what I said it was, but I grew tired of it."

"You had it on for all of six minutes."

"I am supremely fond of this blue one."

Jourdian leaned over the table and caught fast hold of her sparkling, ever-moving gaze. "I'm glad you're enjoying your new clothes, but every time I look at you, you're wearing a different color. It almost makes me dizzy."

She swallowed a bite of strawberries. "I have always liked the rainbow, Jourdian, and now I have found a way to imitate it."

Flustered though he was, he couldn't help a smile. Leaning back in his chair, he watched her, pondered her. True, she was totally opposite of what he'd hoped to find in a wife, but there was something so sweet and genuine about Splendor that he often forgot to remember that she was not the perfect duchess he'd vowed to have.

*Perfect duchess.* How many times had he thought about those words in the past ten years? Thousands of times, he was sure. And when he'd thought of them, other words followed. Words like conventional and plain. Dutiful, ordinary, meek, and normal.

He'd never thought of words such as sweet or generous. Kind hearted, joyful, or caring.

"I don't suppose you have ever slid down a rainbow, have you, Jourdian?" Splendor asked, reaching for a warm, soft roll.

He pushed his empty plate away, and took a long sip of port. "No." But his mind was on another topic altogether. Sweet, generous, kind hearted, joyful, and caring, he mused again. Those were the things he thought about Splendor. But what did she think about him? It was curiosity that made him want to know, of course. Curiosity, and nothing more.

She'd said he was handsome, and she liked the sound of his laughter.

That's all she'd said. All the good, anyway.

Beyond those things, she thought him rude and uncivil. Had made that perfectly clear to him.

He wondered if she had any other feelings for him.

Curiosity was a beast. He supposed he ought to fight it back, but he didn't want to. The questions concerning her feelings for him loomed in his mind, too great to ignore now.

"Jourdian?"

He shook himself mentally. "I'm sorry. I wasn't listening."

" 'Twas as if you were in another place, another time. Is something troubling you? If so, perhaps I can help."

There it was again, he mused. That generosity and caring that felt like a warm hug to him. "I was only thinking. About my work." God, what a lie, he thought. What work? Oh, he'd read through some interesting reports and answered letters and inquiries, but he'd ignored his real work, the business concerning the Gloucester orchards. He hadn't been able to concentrate on the deal, what with Splendor's smile and happy chatter distracting him.

Tomorrow, he thought. First thing in the morning, he would complete the transaction.

"I asked you if you wished to slide down a rainbow with me, husband. 'Tis supremely wonderful, the feeling of gliding down a swath of misty color."

Gazing at her over the rim of his glass, Jourdian drank more port. "It sounds interesting, but I believe I'll give it a miss."

Splendor nibbled at her bread. "Harmony kissed Emil. And Emil kissed her back."

That bit of news took Jourdian unaware. "When did this happen?"

"Last week. The day I brought the Shakespearean characters to life. Do you remember when I transferred us into the house after Harmony gave you two heads? Emil and Harmony remained outside together. 'Twas then she kissed him and he kissed her back. She took his clothes off, too, and he hid his cattail behind his hands. Harmony told me everything. She visited me yesterday, but 'twas a quick visit, Jourdian, and she did not make mischief. She only wanted to know when Emil would be coming back to visit you. Since I did not know, I could not tell her."

Jourdian made a mental note to confront Emil when next he saw his cousin. Emil was more than likely trying to acquire a fairy of his own, and the very notion alarmed Jourdian immensely.

Emil and a fairy. God, there was no way in the world to guess what would result from such a combination.

"If I made a wish of you, would you grant it for me, Jourdian?"

He set his glass down. "What sort of wish?"

"First you must agree to grant it."

"I will not agree to grant a wish before knowing what that wish entails."

"Then I'll nay ask it."

"Fine." He picked up his glass, pushed away from the table, and ambled over to the fireplace.

He didn't care what wish she wanted from him, he told himself. Whatever it was, it would probably irritate him, so it was better that he didn't know what she wanted.

*What she wanted.*

Besides a child, she never wanted anything from him. Never asked him for a thing.

Still, only a fool would promise to give what he didn't know he would be forced to give.

What did she want? he tried to guess. Had she changed her mind about jewels and trips abroad? Did she desire more clothing?

Since she'd never asked him for much, he realized that

whatever it was she wanted now must mean a lot to her. It would probably make her very happy to receive it.

Jourdian wanted her to be happy. She'd twisted his life inside out, but he simply couldn't help wanting her to be happy.

"All right, Splendor, I'll grant your wish," he said abruptly, turning from the hearth to look at her. "Now, what is it?"

"Why did you decide to grant my wish so suddenly?"

"Would you have me not grant it?"

"Nay."

"Then I suggest you ask it before I think better of your request and deny it to you."

She rose from her chair and began to float around the room. Watching her, Jourdian realized she was performing the fairy version of pacing. She was nervous, he understood then, and his curiosity over her wish intensified. "Splendor, I'm waiting."

She stopped beside the bed and trailed her fingers down the midnight blue canopy.

"Do you want me to make love to you?" Jourdian asked, wondering if that was why she'd stopped by the bed.

"I always want you to make love to me, Jourdian, but 'tisn't the wish I would put to you now."

"Then what—"

"Might we go outside? 'Tis a beautiful night, husband. See how the moon paints the earth with her silver," she said, pointing toward the moonlight on the terrace. "And look how many stars—"

"It's almost midnight," Jourdian interrupted after glancing at the clock on the mantel.

"An enchanting hour."

"It's cold outside."

"I promise you will be warm. Please, Jourdian."

A midnight walk on a cold December night, he mused. "Very well."

And then he was there, outside beneath the moon and the stars, strolling hand in hand with Splendor. She'd taken them into an intricate maze of hedgerow, he noticed, and he could hear night creatures buzzing and chirping from within the thick branches.

A bit of frost sprinkled the hedgerow leaves with pretty patterns of sparkling white, and yet he didn't feel the chill in the winter air. He wore nothing but pants, a shirt, and shoes, but he was warm.

Warmed by fairy thrall.

His feet crunched into brittle leaves and snapped twigs as he walked, but Splendor's gait was as quiet as the fall of a single snowflake upon a still and glassy pond. With the exception of her violet eyes and hair of flame, she was almost the same color as the moonlight that spilled so beautifully upon her. Pale, she was, ethereal, angellike.

And she was his.

Tenderness thrummed through him, a soft emotion that caused him to stop and take her into his arms. He kissed her, a whisper of a kiss, as soft as the light in her eyes, as gentle as the sound of her sigh.

"Your wish," he murmured. "What do you want, sprite?"

" 'Tis not something I can hold in my hand."

His curiosity deepened.

" 'Tis an explanation I seek, Jourdian. One that I have yearned to have since the night of our wedding."

He drew away from her, but clasped her wrists. "What do you want me to explain?"

She gazed into his eyes, eyes whose silver rivaled that of the moonglow. "Love," she said softly.

He let go of her wrists and all the tenderness he'd felt only moments before. Spinning on his heel, he left Splendor and her questions behind him.

They all caught up with him. "Jourdian, why did my mention of love that night so infuriate you?"

He walked faster.

Splendor began to fly. Behind him, and then beside him. "Jourdian?"

With long, irate strides, he searched for the maze's exit. As a boy, he'd known exactly where it was, for it was within this very network of dense bushes that he and Emil used to hide from the Heathcourte servants. Many years had passed since then, but his memory had not dimmed.

In only moments, he left the maze and stalked toward the house. He'd traveled only several yards before a shower of silver fell around him.

Loath to know what magic Splendor had performed, he shut his eyes and damned her to hell and back.

But when he opened his eyes, he found her much closer to heaven than to hell. She sat on a cloud, high in the night sky and against a backdrop of twinkling stars.

And he sat on the cloud with her. With the aid of the moonlight, he saw the roofs of his house and his barns, all hundreds feet below.

Apprehension snaked through him. How was it possible to sit on a cloud? "Magic," he mumbled. "Damn it all, Splendor—"

"Jourdian, I brought you up here so you cannot escape me."

Determined to best her, he moved toward the edge of the cloud. "I could jump."

"Aye, that is what you could do, and then you would fall."

"You'd save me. You'd throw your stardust at me."

"I might miss."

He leaned back into the puffy whiteness, then noticed the cloud was drifting. Already, his house and barns were gone from sight. "We're moving."

"A breeze blows our cloud, but do not worry."

He was sitting in the middle of the sky, sailing over the English countryside on a damned bit of vapor, and she told him not to worry? "Bloody hell."

Splendor tilted her head toward her shoulder. "Has it ever come to your notice that you say ' bloody hell' and I say ' sweet everlasting'?"

"There are far more drastic differences between us than our epithets."

"Jourdian, what is it about love that so distresses you?"

When he turned his head to look at her, she saw misery in his eyes. Saw it as clearly as she saw the huge full moon above. "Do you resist speaking of love because in truth you nay know what it is? I thought all humans knew what love is."

"I never said I didn't know what it is."

"I have heard it said that love brings indescribable joy to those who feel it."

Joy? Ha! "Get us off this cloud and back into the house."

"I do not understand any of this, Jourdian. Love should fill you with deep happiness, and yet—"

"I *wish* for you to take us back down to land!"

"I shall grant your wish, Jourdian, when you have granted mine."

Fury burned the voice from his throat. He could do naught but sit there and glower at her.

But Splendor looked beyond the glint of rage in his eyes, and she saw his simmering bitterness and that agonizing sorrow.

Plants growing in his room would not ease his bitterness, she realized then. Decorating his home in his favorite colors and bringing fictitious characters to life would not lift his grief.

Only a clear understanding of his problems with love would give her the means with which to kill his pain.

"I cannot help you," she whispered achingly. "I am powerless to give you the succor you need."

"I do not recall asking you for help," Jourdian retorted.

She did her best to ignore the spite in his voice. "Do you know why I cannot help you?"

"No, and I do not care . . ."

"Your pain is somehow connected to love. And I, Jourdian, cannot feel love. 'Tis why I have asked you so many questions about it. My emotions are not as deep as yours, for as a fairy I lack the substance you have. Compared to you, I am like a puff of misty air or the quick twinkle of a star. I shimmer, but blow on me, and I vanish. Consequently, the supremely profound feeling of love is something I will never know. Therefore, I have no way of comprehending your misery, much less alleviating it."

Her admission stunned him. Only a short time ago, while they'd still been in their bedroom, he'd wondered what feelings she harbored for him.

He knew now that whatever they were, they had nothing to do with love.

Splendor . . . incapable of love. An ironic twist of fate, he mused. He *wouldn't* love her, and she *couldn't* love him.

"All I wanted to do was give you joy," Splendor squeaked, and pressed her face into his shoulder. "And now I realize that I cannot, for you will nay be happy until you have faced, fought, and conquered whatever monster it is that dwells inside you. The beast will eat you alive, and I can do naught but stand by and helplessly watch. Not even my magic can save you. I—I am so very sorry, Jourdian!"

She began to sob into his shirt, and Jourdian saw a mass of her diamonds fall over his legs and sprinkle down toward earth. "Splendor, don't cry. Don't—"

"I cannot help it."

Her fragile body quaked, and he knew the pitiful sound of her cries would make angels weep. He was no angel, and the burst of compassion he felt for her at that moment nearly knocked him off the cloud. She wept for him, he realized. Cried her precious diamond tears because she wanted to help him and could not.

Instinct began to shout at him, his intuition telling him in no uncertain terms that no other woman he might have married would have cared about him as much as Splendor did. Perhaps it was true that her emotions were not as deep as those of humans, but what feelings she possessed she gave with all her heart and soul.

Something welled up inside Jourdian at that moment. Rose from a place so deep he could not understand where that place was.

He forgot his anger. Couldn't even recall why he'd been angry with her in the first place. "Splendor," he said quietly, his arms enfolding her, "whatever resentment I carry inside me has nothing to do with you. Things happened . . . A very long time ago, things—"

"A very long time ago," Splendor murmured, her mind racing. "Aye, when you were a little boy."

"Yes, and—"

"Emil told me your parents were always gone." Little by little bits of comprehension began to come to her.

"Emil's mouth is as big as Reverend Shrewsbury's."

"The two people you used to weep for *were* your mother and father. I was right about them. You loved them, didn't you, Jourdian?"

Jourdian sighed heavily, knowing that if he did not submit to Splendor's interrogation, she would keep them in the sky forever.

He swept a handful of cloud into his palm and tossed it into the air. Its gentle flight into the distance somehow eased his tension.

"Jourdian?"

"Yes, Splendor," he said quietly, "I loved them."

She waited for him to tell her more, and her wait seemed as endless as the sparkling night sky. "Please tell me the rest. I would nay ask if I did not care."

He didn't know whether it was the possibility that he would spend the rest of his life floating around in space or the fact that he truly needed to talk about his childhood, but her poignant entreaty coaxed memories to his lips. "I was fascinated with them," he began softly, a bit hesitantly. "My mother was very beautiful, and when I was little she seemed like a jewel to me. She glittered, both outwardly and inwardly, always laughing, always wearing flash and bright colors. And my father . . . He was a very distinguished-looking man, tall, broad shouldered, and with a short gray beard that I always wanted to touch but never did."

"Why didn't you touch it?"

Jourdian smiled a sad smile. "I was afraid . . . Well, perhaps fear wasn't what I felt. Intimidation might be better. Touching his beard didn't seem like something I should do. I was in awe of him. Authority and power touched everything he said and did, and I wanted to be just like him."

He paused a moment before continuing, watching a star shoot across the heavens. Stars had always been so far away. Now he was so close to them he could feel their heat, just as he could feel the heat of flames in a fireplace. "I longed to be with my parents. It seemed to me that I was always at Heathcourte, where nothing wonderful ever happened, and they were always away from Heathcourte, where every wonderful thing in the world could happen."

"Why did you not go with them when they did wonderful things away from Heathcourte?"

Jourdian shook his head. "I was only a lad, and would have been in the way. Moreover, I had to learn to be a duke. Had to study academics and etiquette. I couldn't have learned such lessons on some deserted island where treasure was buried. Nor could I have learned them in a native jungle or in a bullring in Mexico. So I was forced to stay home with a mass of highly intellectual schoolmasters and proper-minded governessess."

"But your parents always came back to you and Heathcourte."

"And they were gone again."

"Aye, then they were gone again," Splendor said, recalling all the times his parents had left the mansion so soon after having arrived.

"Even after my mother died, Father remained gone. He closed himself away from everyone and everything, and he never opened himself again. A few years later, I buried him alongside my mother."

"I know."

"Emil told you."

"Aye."

"What else did that loquacious cousin of mine say?"

"Do not be angry with him, Jourdian," Splendor chided gently. " 'Twas Emil's longing to help me understand you that compelled him to tell me about you. He loves you."

"I know he does, Splendor," Jourdian whispered.

"He told me how he met you. How sad and lonely you were, and how the two of you became fast friends. He described your mother as a woman who longed for every expensive and exotic thing life had to offer, and he said that your father was happy to accommodate her."

She drifted off the cloud and hovered in the air in front of Jourdian. "You never felt your love returned, did you, Jourdian? Not by your mother or by your father. Your father was too involved with your mother, and your mother was too involved with getting everything she wanted. And . . . And even after your mother was gone, your father still did not love you. He could not love you because . . . your mother took all the love when she died. And then your father died, too, and when he did your last chance to feel a parent's love died as well."

Jourdian nodded, but didn't elaborate. There was more to the story than Splendor had guessed. There was also the fact that his father's love for Isabel had turned Barrington into an absentminded fool.

"Oh, Jourdian," Splendor said, wafting close enough to him so that she could cup his cheek in her hand. "Now I begin to understand why the mention of love makes you ache."

He wondered if she really could understand. Did her fairy emotions allow her to comprehend that love was not pure happiness? That it had a dark side as well? Could she grasp the fact that love could blind a man to all else and destroy him?

"Jourdian?" Splendor said, feeling a strange wave of emotion in her heart. "I yearn to soothe you, but—"

"It isn't your responsibility to soothe—"

"Aye, 'tis my responsibility, Jourdian," she whimpered, diamonds flowing from her eyes again. "I swore to make you happy, and I—"

"You have, Splendor. You have."

She saw starlit honesty in his eyes. "But how? What have I done?"

The desperation in her voice gripped him. He reached for her, pulling her out of the air and into his lap. "You make me laugh. When one laughs, doesn't that mean one is happy?"

She brushed diamonds off her face and nodded.

"You're very beautiful," Jourdian added. "That makes me happy. And at night, you're ecstasy incarnate in my arms. What man wouldn't be happy with that?"

He wanted to tell her more, but knew not what else to say. Still, there *was* something more. Something deeper, something even more special than her amusing character, her beauty, and her passionate lovemaking.

Whatever that special something was, it floated through his emotions just as he now floated high in the night sky.

Before he realized his own intentions or actions, he was kissing her.

Wildness erupted inside her when his tongue flicked across the center of her lips then teased the corners of her mouth.

Gently, he urged her onto her back, pulling her closer and closer until her body was molded to his. Enveloped by the cloud and his masculinity, Splendor curled her arms around him, her palms sliding over and pressing into the sleek coils of muscle in his back.

She felt his hand slide beneath her gown.

And then it stilled. "You wear nothing but a thin chemise beneath this dress," Jourdian said, his smoldering gaze burning into hers.

"Aye, that is what I have on beneath this dress. I know what you are going to say, but—"

"So you read my thoughts now, do you?"

"Aye, and I know that you are going to scold me for not wearing the undergarments. But I do not like them. They are too much to wear, husband, and make me feel too heavy."

He didn't question her further. Her lack of underwear made his sensual task all the easier.

"The stars are watching us, Jourdian," Splendor whispered, watching the stars peeping down from the sky.

"Let's give them something to really watch, shall we?" he suggested, his lips still clinging to hers.

Again, she felt his hand move over her legs, sweeping over her inner calves, nudging her thighs apart, and beckoning forth all the passion she held within her writhing frame. His skilled fingers sought and found the heart of her femininity, but not long did they remain there. She moaned in protest when he withdrew his hand and ended his kiss.

"Will we stop so soon, Jourdian?" she demanded.

He saw her eyes glittering with the fury of desire. The sight made him laugh a deep, husky laugh. "Stop, Splendor? Deny myself my first opportunity to make love on a cloud bed in the middle of a midnight sky? Surely you jest."

She saw him work at the fastening of his pants, then watched his beautiful maleness spring free from within its confines. Joyfully, she opened her arms to receive him.

Jourdian knelt between her slim ankles and leaned forward to taste and lick at her belly with the tip of his tongue as if she were a succulent sweet. He sampled her navel, each of her hip bones, and then nuzzled his lips into the auburn silk at the apex of her thighs.

When his mouth dipped even lower, Splendor closed her legs and captured his head between them. "Sweet everlasting, Jourdian, will you taste me there?"

He lifted his gaze to hers. "Is that a mere question, or a passionate plea?"

"Both," she said, her voice as soft and hot as the rustle of a flame.

"Then the answer is yes to your question and to your plea."

Blood flooded his loins when she opened her legs wide to receive him in the incredibly intimate fashion with which he planned to take her. He'd thought to begin gently, softly, but his first taste of her drove his lust straight through the wall of restraint.

His tongue slid inside her, then almost withdrew completely before he thrust it upward again. Listening to her gasps of surprised pleasure, he moved his upper lip over the hidden bud of her desire, and smiled inwardly when her quiet moans of bliss were overwhelmed by the powerful music of her joy.

He loved her thus for many long moments, his tongue delving, withdrawing, plunging into her over and over again until at last he could ignore his own desire no longer.

Rising, he tunneled his hands beneath her bottom, lifted her hips off the cloud, and embedded himself inside her with one long, deep stroke. Not a thread of control would come to him, and he ground his hips into hers with wild urgency.

He heard her music play louder, stroking the starlit heavens with its beautiful melody. Off the cloud he felt Splendor rise, he with her. There was naught but night air beneath them now, and the experience of floating among the lofty celestial bodies was the most incredible Jourdian had ever known.

"Jourdian," Splendor cried softly.

He felt her inner muscles tense around him, squeezing from him his own powerful climax. Higher she took him, higher into a world of dazzling sensation.

And together they found ecstasy in a heaven full of stars.

"Dear God, Splendor," Jourdian panted. He raised his upper torso and saw that the entire sky was ablaze with dancing lights. Earth was but a round and distant sphere, and the moon rose up before him, a tremendous white orb, intimidating and awesome at once.

He wondered if he could reach out and lay his palm upon its cratered surface.

He decided to try.

He held out his arm. His body tensed, his fingers straining, stretching.

And he touched it. The glorious moon.

He, a mere human had caressed the moon.

A feeling of wonder enveloped him, a sense of magic, and he realized suddenly that all the many marvelous things he might have missed as a child were nothing, nothing at all, measured up to making love in the nighttime sky and feeling the moon beneath his palm.

And it had all happened because of Splendor.

"Jourdian?" Her mind and body filled to the brim with him, Splendor embraced him as tightly as her strength would allow. "I wish that I could love you," she whispered into the moist hollow of his shoulder. "I know that if I could, I would love you as you have never been loved before."

Her wish was Jourdian's own.

And the moment he realized that poignant truth, one solitary star set apart from all the rest, embraced his wish and grew so bright that all the other stars in the sky paled in comparison.

**18**

"*What?*" Harmony shouted, standing within the crackling blazes in the fireplace of the yellow chambers. "What do you mean you are going to learn to love him?"

Splendor ignored her sister's astonishment, and continued to calmly stroke Delicious's cold, scaly back.

The green lizard blinked its black eyes closed, gave a reptilian sigh of pleasure, then turned himself into a baby elephant. He lumbered toward a small table across the room upon which sat a porcelain basin. Dipping his thick, gray trunk into the bowl, he sucked up water, then commenced to spray it over his body, the carpet, and the wall.

Shaking her head over her pet's antics, Splendor returned her attention to Harmony. "I mean exactly that, sister. I am going to discover the secret to loving, and I am going to love Jourdian. 'Tis an emotion I long to feel and understand."

"But why do you want to know what love is? We've nay a need for it in Pillywiggin."

Splendor pondered her husband. "This is not Pillywiggin. 'Tis Heathcourte, and while I am here I must concern myself with human things. Love is a human thing, hence Jourdian needs to have it."

"Who cares what that man needs! Splendor, you are here to conceive his child, not give him some heartfelt emotion unknown to Faerie."

Splendor wasn't certain she knew how to make Harmony understand something she barely understood herself. "I am still trying to conceive the child, sister. I have nay forgotten my duty to Pillywiggin. But I care about Jourdian. If I can make him happy, 'tis what I will do."

"But you cannot love no matter how hard you try."

Splendor meandered to the window and watched a trio of sparrows frolic over the terrace. "Love is mighty, Harmony. You heard Father say so. If 'tis truly the most powerful force in creation, then it can surely work its magic on me."

"That is nonsense." In a puff of black smoke, Harmony emerged from the fire flames and assumed human form. "Father's fury will know no bounds when he learns what you are planning. He—"

"How will he know?" Splendor asked, turning from the window.

Harmony shook her head. "Is there so much sickening sentiment in you that you've no room for brains? I shall tell him, of course!"

Splendor had already pondered that possibility. "And if you do, I shall tell him that you have been cavorting with a human of your own. You know full well that the only reason Father sent me to Jourdian was to conceive a child. You have not been sent to any human, Harmony, and yet you—"

"I have been with Emil but thrice!"

"Thrice? Besides Jourdian's courtyard, where else have you been with Emil?"

Harmony's gaze darted around the room while she tried to decide whether to be honest, or not.

"I can always ask Emil," Splendor warned.

"He came to visit the Trinity two days ago," Harmony admitted, "but he preferred to be with me. I saw him get out of his carriage. When I called to him he followed me into the woods. And he followed me of his own will, Splendor. I did not use magic to beckon him."

"I see. And what did you do in the woods with him?"

"That kissing," Harmony confessed, caressing her lips with two fingers and remembering how soft Emil's mouth had felt upon hers. "And we did it again this morning. 'Twas near the stone wall that edges the Trinity's land."

"You just happened to spot Emil there, too."

Harmony shook her head. "Yesterday in the woods, I told him to go there and wait for me."

Splendor left the window and crossed to where her sister stood. "Why are you fond of being in his company?"

"He listens to me when I speak of the fact that you get everything and I get nothing. He understands."

Splendor nodded a slow nod. "You hate humans. But there is nay a hint of hatred in your voice when you remember Emil."

"I do hate him," Harmony flared, tiny yellow blazes leaping into her blue eyes. "But I need his kissing to feel strong, and I like to complain to someone who gives me his ear. When I grumble in Pillywiggin, no one hears a word I say. But even so, I do not like Emil. I hate him with all the passion in the universe. I am only using him for what he can give me and do for me."

Harmony was lying, Splendor knew. "Do you think he loves you?"

The question took Harmony off guard. "What is love?" she queried without thinking. "How does one recognize it?"

Splendor gave a deep, long sigh and floated to the bed. There she brushed her fingertips across the satin coverlet. "I do not know the answers to those questions."

"Then how will you love the Trinity?"

"When I discover the way, I shall tell you. Then you can practice on Emil."

Harmony pondered her last meeting with Jourdian's cousin. "Do you know what Emil did this morning? I were nay paying attention to my own actions, and I wandered too near to his horse. Emil threw himself at me, tossed me away, and so startled his mount that the steed kicked him in the belly. He lay on the ground, quite out of breath, and I thought for a moment that he had died. When I saw he was alive, I was furious that he had pitched me away as though I were naught but a bit of rubbish. But when he showed me his saddle and I saw all the iron on it, I understood why he had cast me away."

Splendor thought Emil's rescue of Harmony a beautiful story. "And the horse kicked him. Emil suffered pain for you, Harmony. I think he must love you."

Harmony began to smile, but caught herself in time. What was the matter with her? she wondered angrily. If she didn't take care, she would soon become as simpering as her ninny sister! "I hope Emil loves me. Aye, I hope he does. And I shall spurn his love! Throw it back in his face like a stone that will bruise and make him bleed! And I am going to tell Father that you are—"

"Three times you have been with Emil," Splendor said, suppressing a smile. "Father will see that as three times too many." She paused to allow her words to sink into Harmony's devious mind. "Are we in agreement then, sister? We shall keep each other's secrets?"

Harmony's long golden hair became yellow tongues of fire, flickering down her body and sending sparks all over the carpet. "If you were not a fairy, I would lock you within the frigid depths of the moon and never let you out."

"But I am your sister, and so you will not imprison me in moon ice. What I feel certain you will do is keep my secret, just as I shall keep yours."

"You cannot love the Trinity, Splendor. 'Tis impossible. He is unlovable. He is a mean person."

Splendor smiled. "You are a mean fairy. It seems to me that the two of you should get along supremely well."

"You offend me, sister. Compared to me, he is no more harmless than a drop of dew!" Harmony shrank into Pillywiggin size, not because she had to, but because she wished to recline upon a powder puff that lay on the dressing table.

A bit of powder yet clung to the puff, making her sneeze four times. Wiping her nose with the back of her tiny hand, she looked up at Splendor. "Why do you seek to fulfill that ghastly man's need for love?"

Splendor took a seat on the velvet stool in front of the vanity. She took a pinch of powder between her fingertips and trickled the fragrant dust over Harmony's tiny frame. "Because I believe my love would be like medicine to him."

"He is sick?" Harmony asked hopefully, then sneezed again. "Cease sprinkling me with that powder, Splendor."

Splendor rubbed the powder on her fingers onto the top of her wrist. "His heart is sick."

"His heart? Bah! You talk more like a human every time I see you."

"Oh, Harmony, do you really think so?"

"The comment was an insult, sister."

But to Splendor it was a compliment. She was beginning to think and speak like a human.

Surely she could learn to love.

Splendor didn't go to Jourdain for her love lessons. She understood enough about him now to know that he would have been little help to her. True, he had shared his thoughts and memories with her the night they'd made love amidst the stars, but she sensed a lingering unwillingness within him, a hesitancy to reveal any more than he already had.

But during the next few weeks, Splendor discovered that there were plenty of other humans in and around Heathcourte who possessed no such hesitancy to talk about love. Mrs. Frawley, she soon learned, was in love with the subject of love.

"Love is what keeps our world alive," she told Splendor one bright morning while supervising the upstairs maids with their tasks.

"Alive?" Splendor asked. "Oh, Mrs. Frawley, would you please put that horrible beast out of here?"

Mrs. Frawley fairly smelled the duchess's terror, then saw Pharaoh sitting on a velvet chair in the corridor, his sable tail swishing. "Oh, it's only His Grace's pet cat. Granted Pharaoh's a devil at times, but he . . . My goodness, how did he escape my house? I distinctly remember locking him in the kitchen this morning before I left . . ."

"Please," Splendor whispered, her back to the wall. "Make him go away."

Mrs. Frawley shooed the Siamese off the chair, whereupon the cat hissed and disappeared down the hall. "There now. He's gone. I'll take him back home with me when I leave this evening."

Splendor gave a weak smile. Pharaoh wasn't going to stay at Mrs. Frawley's house, she knew. The look in the beast's eyes told her that he fully planned on returning to the mansion time and time again.

"Let's return to the subject, shall we?" Mrs. Frawley asked. "Love is to humans what rain and sunshine are to flowers, my dear," she explained, forgetting that the "dear" little Splendor possessed one of the most sought-after titles in all the land.

"Do you have a lot of love in your life?"

"Indeed I do. I have loved my Mr. Frawley for forty-six years. I married him when I was sixteen, and with each year that passes our love deepens. He's a quiet man, Mr. Frawley, but he has no need to speak often. I read his thoughts as well as I read words written on a page."

Her yellow silk gown swishing softly, Splendor followed the housekeeper into one of the guest rooms, where two maids were busy dusting and polishing furniture. "But how did you come to love your husband, Mrs. Frawley? Did you have to do something special to feel such adoration for him?"

Mrs. Frawley feigned a nonchalant demeanor, but in her heart she knew the duchess wanted to love the duke. The thought filled the housekeeper with deep delight. "I didn't do anything to fall in love with him. It just happened." She paused a moment to reprimand a young maid who had missed a wealth of dust on the mantel. "I met Mr. Frawley in the village where I was born and was instantly attracted to his good looks. A more beautiful smile you have never seen, and when he gifted me with that smile for the first time, I nearly swooned."

Splendor thought about Jourdian's smile and how happy it made her to see it. Was that happiness the beginning of love?

"Mr. Frawley began to court me soon enough," Mrs. Frawley continued, smoothing the dusky pink coverlet on the bed. "Oh, what merry times we had. We danced, and we had picnics. We strolled and held hands, and I began to miss him terribly when we weren't together. He felt the same. That was when we knew we were meant to be together."

Splendor remembered how many times she'd missed Jourdian. Even before she'd known who he was, she'd missed him when she hadn't seen him out riding.

"Mr. Frawley and I were wed shortly thereafter, and by the next year we had a son," the housekeeper recollected. "A daughter followed, and then two more sons. Our children are grown now, with families of their own, and now I have eleven grandchildren to love. Why, love is the reason why I don't live here in the manor house. His Grace's father offered me a lovely room when I first came to work here, but how could I leave my dear Mr. Frawley?"

"But what *is* this love you have for Mr. Frawley?" Splendor pressed. "What does it feel like? What does it do to you when it comes?"

A wave of pity came over Mrs. Frawley. Poor, poor Splendor, she thought. The lass had never known love.

Mrs. Frawley hoped fervently that if the duchess came to love the duke that his lordship would love Splendor in return. Love wouldn't come easily to the duke, however, for he was a man who had known naught but the unfortunate side of the emotion.

Still, there was nothing wrong with wishing for the duke and duchess to find love, and Mrs. Frawley wished for it with every fiber in her rotund body.

"Love is a deep attachment to someone, poppet," she explained gently. "It creates a profound caring inside you, a caring for the person you love. Love is the sharing of laughter and tears, and of struggles and worries. Love is helping each other. It is a very strong bond, and it holds two people together through good times and bad. When you truly love someone, the love you feel is stronger than any other emotion you are capable of feeling, and it assists you in dealing with anger, frustration, grief, and even fear. It's a gift to be cherished and protected."

"A profound caring," Splendor murmured, nodding her head. "A bond, the sharing of joy and sadness. A gift."

"Yes. All those things, and much, much more. And I

hope to have another forty-six years of happiness with . . . with . . ."

When Mrs. Frawley's voice softened and then faded away on a trail of what sounded like fear and sadness, Splendor touched the housekeeper's hand. "Is something amiss, Mrs. Frawley?" she asked, then noted the woman's eyes mist with tears.

Mrs. Frawley dabbed at her eyes with the corner of her stiffly starched apron. "He will be fine, I'm sure, Mr. Frawley will. But he has been quite ill for almost a month. The doctor says his heart is weak and that there is nothing that can be done for him."

"Nothing? Do you mean he might . . . 'Tis possible that he might die?"

Mrs. Frawley couldn't answer, couldn't bring herself to admit that frightening possibility. "I cannot lose him," she whispered. "I just cannot lose him."

"You mustn't stop hoping," Splendor said softly. "Mustn't stop wishing for his health to return. 'Tis the saddest thing in the world when people cease to wish."

"You're right," Mrs. Frawley agreed. "And I have not stopped hoping, wishing, or praying. I must have faith that Mr. Frawley will recover, mustn't I? Yes, that is what I must do."

Splendor smiled, and spent the next several days deliberating upon Mrs. Frawley's explanation before seeking out yet more information.

Ulmstead was the next Heathcourte employee to be cornered by the inquisitive and determined duchess. But before the butler could answer her questions, she was forced to wait until he caught and put outside the skunk he'd found asleep in one of the china cupboards.

Splendor watched him place the creature on the stoop outside the front door, ready to intervene should he harm Delicious in any way.

He didn't, but simply urged the skunk on its way with a gentle farewell and a soft touch of his hand.

"What do I know about love, Your Grace?" Ulmstead asked. He closed the door, brushed skunk hair off his spotless black coat, and folded his bony hands in front of his chest. So the duchess wanted to love the duke, did she? he mused. Well, he was more than glad to assist her in any way that he could. And he would pray every night that His Grace would see fit to love the duchess in return.

"I have never been married, Your Grace, but I did love once many years ago. Beatrice was her name, and I shall never forget her."

"Would you tell me about the love you had for her?" Splendor entreated.

Ulmstead smiled fondly. "She didn't know I loved her. It was a secret love, for she was promised to another. I met her when I was of the age of three and twenty. Her father had employed me as a domestic in his house. The family was of the gentry, Beatrice the eldest daughter. I had ample opportunity to be near her, to hear her speak, and to see her smile. She was a gentle person, always very kind to me, very considerate. There were times when I wanted to tell her I loved her, but I never did. When she married a wealthy neighbor, I was happy for her."

"Happy for her?" Splendor echoed, completely bewildered. "But how could you be happy when the woman you loved married another?"

Ulmstead smiled again.

And Splendor noticed that although his smile was sad, his eyes glowed with inner joy.

"When you love someone, you want the best for that person," Ulmstead explained. "I had naught to offer a woman of Beatrice's station. Her husband provided her with everything she could want or need, and he loved her as she loved him. Yes, I was happy for her. Happy that she had found love and joy."

Splendor realized that sacrifice was a part of love. At times, people freely relinquished important or precious things for the benefit of a loved one.

She laid her hand on Ulmstead's concave chest, directly over his heart. "You are a dear man, Ulmstead."

Ulmstead would have blushed to the ends of his hair if he'd had any. "Happy to be of help, Your Grace."

Splendor wasted no time in finding her next source of information.

"Love?" Hopkins asked. Standing beside one of the barns in a splash of December sunlight, he rubbed his grizzled chin and smiled. "My wife's b-been g-gone fer tw-twelve years, Yer Gr-Grace, b-but I've still g-got my memories. Her name was Jane, and t-to this d-day I've never seen a pr-prettier g-girl. She was a b-bit of a thing, she was, her head b-barely reachin' my chest. Her hair was yellow like fresh st-straw, and her laughter made the whole world a b-better pl-place t-to b-be."

Lost in his recollections, he absently ran his hand over the rough planks of the barn. "I knew I loved her when I st-started feelin' like there was a light inside me whenever she looked at me. I felt a gl-glow d-deep d-down. Here." He laid his hand over his heart.

"Sayin' g-good-b-bye to her was the hardest thing I've ever had t-to d-do, Yer Grace," he continued softly. "She g-got a fever, and I was with her when she d-died. I held her cl-close in my arms, and when her heart st-stopped, the light in mine went out. It's never b-been lit again."

Splendor saw tears gather in his bleary eyes. "Would you rather not have loved her?" She tried to understand. "If you had not loved her, you would not be sad right now."

"Not loved her?" Hopkins repeated disbelievingly. "If I had it all t-to d-do again, I'd change nothin'. Lovin' Jane g-gave me thirty-one years of happiness. A man would have to be insane not t-to want so many years filled with love and joy. Why, I vow that one *d-day* of love is b-better than an entire *lifetime* without it."

One day of love was worth more than a lifetime without it? Splendor thought, her brow creased with astonishment.

Hopkins looked up into the sky toward heaven, where he was sure his beloved Jane was waiting for him. "I would have d-died fer her, fer Jane, aye, I would have at that. When she sickened, I would have t-taken her pl-place on that d-death b-bed."

Splendor's amazement intensified. Hopkins would have given his very life for the woman he loved. Died for her.

Sweet everlasting, there was nothing at all in Faerie that had the value of love.

Christmas had never been a festive time of the year at Heathcourte. The duke had little time for what he deemed frivolous traditions, and so, with the exception of a few pine boughs here and there that the servants managed to hang, and the goose dinner Mrs. Kearney insisted on preparing, the twenty-fifth of December had always been a day like any other.

Until Splendor learned of its significance from Mrs. Frawley, Ulmstead, and Tessie. The sly servants took full advantage of the possibility that Splendor might be able to talk His Grace into a real Christmas, and shamelessly filled the duchess's head with visions of a gaily decorated tree, big red velvet bows, and mounds of beautifully wrapped gifts.

All Hallows Eve was the only day celebrated in Faerie, for that last day of October was the time of the year when Faerie enchantment reached its peak of power. When Splendor realized that Christmas was an enchanted time of the year for humans, she was determined that Jourdian would have his Christmas. But she didn't seek His Grace's permission like the domestics had been sure she would.

She simply brought Christmas to Heathcourte without mentioning her plans to a soul.

The house was as the house always was when everyone sought their beds on the night of the twenty-third. And when they awakened on Christmas Eve, every Christmas tradition they'd ever heard of graced the mansion. All staircases, fireplace mantels, and door frames were adorned with fresh, spicy-scented evergreen boughs, complete with bright red velvet bows and streamers and clusters of silver jingle bells. White, crimson, and emerald candles sat lit in every room, alongside bowls of clove-studded oranges and peppermint candies. A lifesize Nativity scene, complete with manger, lambs, the proverbial donkey, a host of angels, and a huge star brought Christmas into the courtyard.

And Christmas trees abounded. Each servant found one in his or her room, and Mrs. Kearney discovered one in her kitchen. The live trees stood in Jourdian's office, his library, bedchambers, two sitting rooms, and the grand entryway, and each tree was trimmed with strings of plump cranberries, tiny white candles, lacy snowflakes, and shining silver stars.

The servants were amazed by the beauty and authenticity of the snowflakes and stars.

"Such fine lace," Mrs. Frawley said, admiring the snowflakes that graced the tree in the foyer. "Why, the snowflakes appear so real that I could swear they feel cold."

Tessie nodded. "And the silver satin stars . . . I've never seen such glowing satin. And they're warm, nearly hot to the touch."

"Perhaps because they hang near the lighted candles," Mrs. Frawley guessed.

Only Jourdian and Emil knew that the snowflakes were not made of lace, but of real snow that fairy thrall kept frozen. And the stars were not of silver satin. They were real, and they twinkled with the magic of the fairy who'd borrowed them from the sky.

Emil was delighted over the Heathcourte Christmas, but Jourdian's first impulse was fury. How could Splendor have taken Christmas into her own stardust-filled little hands and created a situation he was at a loss to explain to the bewildered servants? Didn't she realize that her magic had to be elucidated somehow?

Emil came to the tenderhearted Splendor's rescue by inventing an answer to all the questions. "Lord and Lady Amberville wanted to surprise the household," he lied merrily to the staff. "While everyone was asleep, Their Graces had a host of villagers from Mallencroft come and decorate all through the night. The villagers barely finished before dawn."

The servants accepted the falsehoods and thanked the duke and duchess profusely. And much to her complete astonishment, Splendor didn't mind the gratitude. On the contrary, all the sincere thanks she received warmed her inside and made her feel twice as happy over having given the glittering beauty of Christmas to Heathcourte.

Her willing acceptance of gratitude was yet one more proof that human ideals and emotions were finding a dwelling place within her fairy heart, and the knowledge so thrilled her that every time she thought about it she floated several feet off the floor.

"You are not still angry at me for touching the house with a bit of enchantment, are you, Jourdian?" she asked on Christmas Eve night as she, Jourdian, and Emil sat before the fire in one of the sumptuous sitting rooms. "I had no another way to decorate, and I so wanted to give you a real Christmas. And Mrs. Frawley said that Christmas is an enchanted time of the year, so I did not think that a sprinkle of magic would be unfitting."

Looking at her, Jourdian noted that her lovely face was not as pale as usual, but was flushed with joy, and her gorgeous violet eyes shone more brightly than all the burning stars on the tree. She seemed . . . so alive tonight. Alive and . . . Well, she seemed different. As if there was more to her.

As if she had somehow become less transparent, he thought. She retained her shimmering glow, yes, and she still had no shadow. But for some odd reason Jourdian couldn't explain, she was more corporeal. More substantial.

She couldn't seem to keep still, popping up from her chair every five minutes or so to touch the tree, fiddle with the greenery and bows looped on the mantel, and check each tiny flame on all the many candles. She ate four clove-oranges and so many peppermint sweets that Jourdian was sure she would soon double over with a stomachache. She even tied a thin red satin ribbon around Delicious's scrawny neck. The fickle animal had chosen to be a bat for Christmas, and hung upside down from one of the drapery cornices.

No, Jourdian thought in answer to Splendor's question. He wasn't angry. Not anymore. After all, Emil had eased the staff's confusion, and all was well with the domestics.

Looking around the ornamented room, he discovered he felt happy. He had no memory of such a grand Christmas. His parents had always celebrated the holiday out of England, and although the servants had tried to give him a small Christmas, those Christmases were nothing compared to the one Splendor had given him.

He watched her while she sat in her chair. In a completely unladylike action, she crossed her legs in front of herself on the chair, exposing her bare ankles. She'd wear naught but a chemise beneath her gowns. Shoes she refused altogether. Jourdian had refrained from arguing with her about her skimpy attire, for he felt lucky to have convinced her to dress at all.

Lost in her beauty, he continued to observe her. Nervous excitement running through her, she began to fiddle with her hair, making braid after braid, and then unbraiding them all. She played with the fringe on the chair pillow, stuck her fingers between her little pink toes, and blew bubbles in her glass of cream.

How like a small girl she was tonight, he thought. And how strong was his desire to hold her in his lap, stroke her soft cheek, and whisper sweet words to her.

"You did a superb job, sprite," he said, then sipped his brandy. "But you know? Christmas wouldn't be Christmas without presents."

Splendor gasped. "Do you . . . Jourdian, do you mean we do not have to wait until tomorrow to open the gifts?" she asked loudly.

"I don't imagine you *can* wait that long, Splendor."

Up from her chair Splendor popped again, her lavender silk dress and long copper hair whispering around her long legs. Giggling all the way, she glided over to the tree and retrieved three brightly wrapped boxes.

"Who's the other one for?" Jourdian asked when she'd given him one box and Emil another.

Splendor looked at Emil, who turned quickly away and brushed specks of nothing off his coat sleeve.

"Harmony," Jourdian guessed suddenly. "That trouble-making sister-in-law of mine is coming!"

"Now, Jourdian, calm yourself," Splendor cooed. "I invited Harmony because 'tis Christmas, husband. I thought to share this special occasion with her because, like me, Harmony knows nothing of it."

"Really, Jourdian," Emil chided. "It *is* Christmas, and Harmony *is* a part of your family now. And I'll see to it that she behaves herself."

At that, Jourdian's eyes narrowed slightly. "I've been meaning to ask you about your relationship with that witchy elf, but you have made yourself scarce. It's been weeks since you were last here. Could it be that you have found more enjoyable company elsewhere, and is it possible that said company's name is Harmony Hellion?"

"She is not a hellion!" Emil swiftly rose from his chair and hurled a furious look toward his cousin.

"No?" Jourdian asked. "Then what is she, Emil?"

"She's . . . She's highly spirited, is what. Misunderstood and in dire need of someone to care about her feelings. And you would do well to understand, Jourdian, that I will not sit here and permit you to slander—"

"How often do you see her?" Jourdian queried.

"Every day now, and I've thoroughly enjoyed each second in her company."

"She doesn't turn you into anything?" Jourdian wanted to know. "Doesn't give you extra heads?"

Emil smiled smugly. "No. She likes me better than she likes you."

" 'Tis true, Jourdian," Splendor announced. "Although Harmony professes to hate Emil, she has worked none of her magical mischief on him. Out of habit she's been tempted, but she told me that for some reason beyond her understanding she simply cannot make herself torment him the way she can you."

"I see." Jourdian drank more brandy. "And how many wishes have you had Harmony grant for you, Emil?"

Emil's frown turned into a sheepish expression. "None. Not

that I haven't asked, mind you, but she refuses to grant a single wish. She claims that wish granting would make her more like her benevolent sister, and although she's made great strides in controlling her penchant for spreading gloom, granting wishes remains one fairy talent she declines to utilize."

At that bit of news, Jourdian's deep dislike of Harmony began to lessen. "Perhaps she is not as bad as I previously thought. It would seem that she possesses a wealth of sense, actually."

Emil had no chance to form a retort.

The Christmas tree became consumed with wild blazes. The flames burned violently for a few moments before dying as quickly as they had ignited, leaving the tree as fresh and supple as it had been moments before.

No one in the room showed the least bit of surprise, for all knew that that fiery-tempered Harmony had arrived. She sat perched on one of the cranberry strands, Pillywiggin size and naked.

"Harmony," Jourdian called from his chair, "I will consent to allow you to join us this night, but I must insist that you clothe yourself."

"I must insist as well," Emil said, determined that Jourdian not see Harmony's naked glory, which he considered for his viewing only. Not that he had touched her in any ungentlemanly way. He had not. Respect was what she deserved, and respect was what he gave her.

Quick as a bee, Harmony zipped off the cranberries and flew to stand on the top of Emil's head, her tiny feet disappearing into his unruly hair. "I do not need your permission to stay here," she informed Jourdian, her voice as crisp as a piece of burned toast. "Nor must I follow your demand that I dress. And if you continue to order me about, you will soon find yourself in the hot sand of the Sahara desert in the guise of a cactus."

"Harmony, please," Splendor pleaded.

"Don't forget who you threaten, Harmony," Emil advised. "Jourdian is my cousin." He reached up, gently curled his hand around her body, and took her off his head. "And if you don't put something on, I shan't give you the Christmas gift I've brought for you," he said, holding her in front of his face.

Instantly, a black satin gown draped Harmony's tiny form. And then, within a swirl of silver, she shifted her shape into human size and stood before Emil. "Give it to me! Give me my gift!"

"Black," Jourdian mused aloud, looking at her somber gown. "Not quite in keeping with the season, but much better than nothing at all."

"Harmony," Splendor said, "I told you to bring gifts tonight. Did you nay bring any, sister?"

Harmony nodded. "I want mine first, though."

Jourdian almost reprimanded her for acting so spoiled, but thought better of it. It was Christmas, after all, and he found it in himself to demonstrate the true spirit of the holy occasion.

He rose from his chair and crossed to the tree. "This is for you, Harmony," he said, slipping a red and white package out from beneath the tree.

She fairly grabbed it out of his hands. Viciously, she tore off the paper, and saw that Jourdian had given her a book. "A book?" she whined. "I do not like to read! I should pitch you into the mouth of an erupting volcano for giving me such a useless Christmas gift!"

"Harmony," Splendor admonished. "I am supremely ashamed of you!"

"As am I," Emil said. "You are acting like a brat."

Before Harmony could reply, Jourdian took the book from her and pointed to the title. "I think you'll like this book."

She glanced at the title. "*A History of the World's Worst Villains*," she read aloud. "Villains?"

Jourdian nodded. "The most nefarious criminals ever to walk the face of the earth."

"Oh, how wonderful!" Harmony cried, her entire face beaming with joy. "I will read this book from cover to cover and memorize every word!"

"I thought as much." Jourdian couldn't help but smile. He'd known full well that Harmony would seize the chance to delve deeper into the aspects of evil.

"I have this for you, Harmony," Splendor said, handing her sister a red oblong box with a green bow tied around it.

When Harmony opened the box, its contents shone so brightly that Emil and Jourdian were forced to shield their eyes. Only after a long moment could they bear to look at the gift again.

Laughing with utter delight, Harmony held the shard of lightning as one would hold a spear.

"Lightning," Jourdian murmured.

"Aye, that is what it is, husband," Splendor said. "When we were small, Harmony used to have a lightning bolt as a toy. But Father took it away from her when she hurled it into the pond in yonder woods and nearly burned away all the water. Mother Nature sent a quick and violent rain to replenish the water before the fish and other pond life succumbed, but Father would nay give the lightning back to Harmony."

Jourdian nodded as if the explanation were the most mundane he'd ever heard.

" 'Tis a marvelous gift, sister," Harmony said, twirling the lightning in her nimble fingers, fascinated by its deadliness. "And I promise not to dry up any more ponds. Your gift from me is there." With the fiery bolt, she pointed to a tremendous wooden chest.

Within the chest, Splendor found masses and masses of acorns. "Oh, Harmony, you dear, sweet thing!"

"Acorns?" Emil asked.

"She collects them so she can plant them properly," Harmony explained, slipping the rod of lightning into the bodice of her midnight gown. " 'Tis an obnoxiously kind thing to do, but Splendor cannot help her goodness. She was born with the malady."

"A joyful Christmas, Emil," Splendor said, pressing a large yellow satin drawstring bag into Emil's hands.

Emil found a tiny tree inside the bag. Planted in a sterling silver box, it bloomed tuppence. "A money tree!" he exclaimed.

"Aye, that is what it is, Emil," Splendor said, then saw Jourdian frown. "But 'twill not grow a fortune for you," she warned. "Only a few tuppence a week. That is all right, is it not, Jourdian?"

He supposed a few tuppence a week would do no harm.

Emil set the tree down and presented Splendor with the gift he'd brought for her.

She gasped with delight when she saw the tiny music box. Its base was created with mother-of-pearl, and on its top a small golden fairy with a silver wand in her hand twirled in rhythm to the lively melody.

"I found it in a jewelry shop in Telford last month," Emil said. "When I saw the fairy's pretty smile, I thought of you."

Upon hearing Emil compliment Splendor, Harmony's eyes blazed with anger. "Do you think her smile prettier than mine?" she demanded.

"Both of you have pretty smiles," Emil assured her. "And when you settle down, I shall give you *your* gift."

Instantly, Harmony cooled off, the flames in her eyes dying to a mellow sparkle. Deep inside, she hoped fiercely that Emil's gift to her was bigger and better than the one he'd given to Splendor.

Emil knew precisely what she was thinking, and because he knew the reasons for her jealousy, he'd chosen her gift with utmost care.

When Harmony opened the box he handed to her, she pulled out a heavy gold satin cape. Encrusted with rubies, diamonds, topaz, and sapphires, and with thousands of gleaming threads of red, yellow, and orange shooting through it, it resembled a solid sheet of wild flames. Indeed, the slightest movement caused the fabric and jewels to blaze with burning beauty.

Emil took the shimmering garment from her and placed it around her slim shoulders. "I know jewels mean little to a fairy," he murmured near her ear, "but to humans this cloak is worthy of . . . a queen."

"A queen?" Harmony smoothed her hands down the fire-like mantle. She might not ever be a queen, but Emil's gift certainly made her feel like one. "I am very pleased with this gift, Emil. It has great meaning."

"I hoped that it would." Emil kissed her full on the mouth.

Watching Emil and Harmony, Jourdian realized just how much his cousin loved Splendor's sister. It was not the kiss that proved Emil's affection, but the gift. Jourdian's experienced eye told him that Emil had spent a fortune on the cloak. Each of the countless jewels on the cape was of the finest quality, and there was no doubt in Jourdian's mind that Emil had exhausted his savings on the creation of the incredibly expensive garment.

A fact that made Jourdian's gift to his cousin all the more significant. "Emil," he said, "this is for you. Merry Christmas."

Emil took the cream-colored paper Jourdian handed to him. The paper was rolled into a tube and tied with a red ribbon. Completely unable to guess what the paper was, Emil opened it quickly.

His eyes widened; his heart nearly stopped.

The paper was the deed to the Egyptian emerald mine Jourdian had purchased months before. "Mine?" Emil asked. "The mine is mine?" The questions were naught but squeaks, for Emil could barely talk so great was his astonishment.

Jourdian laughed. "Yours. I thought it better for you to receive a fortune legitimately than to have it appear out of thin air, which is a wish I know you have not yet let go of."

"Thank you," was all Emil could say, but his voice overflowed with emotion. "I—I'm afraid my gift for you isn't nearly as magnificent."

Perhaps Emil's gift was not as magnificent as an emerald mine, but Jourdian was deeply touched by the thought behind the present.

The gift was a leather-bound diary, its cover tattered and stained, its pages fragile and yellowed. It was Emil's diary, one he had begun the day he'd met Jourdian so many years ago.

Jourdian scanned the pages, moved by the passages that related Emil's affection for him. And as he turned more and more pages, he noted that Emil's handwriting, spelling, and grammar improved steadily, solid testimonial of the long hours Jourdian has spent tutoring his cousin in academics.

"I didn't want you to forget," Emil said. "Those years. Those days. We had such fun then, Jourdian, and I—I didn't want you to forget."

When Jourdian held out his hand for a handshake, but then embraced his cousin instead, Harmony looked on in sheer wonder. What she was witnessing was love, she realized. The emotion was evident in the gifts Emil and Jourdian had exchanged, the way they'd spoken to each other, and the warm hug they shared now.

And Harmony finally understood her sister's intense desire and determination to learn about and experience the profound feeling. Love *was* a magical emotion. A magic more powerful than anything she'd ever imagined.

Harmony wanted to know that magic. Wanted it to surge through her like a mighty whirlpool in the depths of the sea. And she wanted to feel that love before Splendor did. As usual, she wanted to be first.

"I have a gift for you, Emil," she blurted out, hoping with all the strength she possessed that he would like what she'd selected for him. " 'Tis there in the corner."

Emil looked in the direction of the corner and saw a big green box around which swirled a myriad of silver stars.

And it was moving.

Filled with boyish curiosity and excitement, Emil rushed to open the box, but as soon as he touched it he discovered the box was naught but an illusion. It disappeared before his very eyes . . .

And there stood a pony. A snow white pony with a thick tail so long that it brushed the floor. The animal had big dark eyes, and a thin ribbon of black streaked down its face.

Only Emil understood the significance of the gift. The pony was a replica of the one he'd wanted as a child, the one his friend had owned in the village of Mallencroft.

Turning, he gazed at Harmony and gave her a smile so full of love that words could not get past it. He opened his arms, laughing when she flew into them. "I think perhaps we shall take our leave now, Jourdian and Splendor," he said, anxious to be alone with Harmony.

"Wait!" Splendor looked all around the room. "Harmony, will you not give Jourdian a gift?"

Still in Emil's arms, Harmony frowned. She'd brought Jourdian a gift, yes, but for some irritating reason, she no longer wished to give him the box of black widow spiders.

"Harmony?" Splendor pressed.

"All right!" Her mind spinning with gift ideas, long moments passed before Harmony realized what the perfect gift would be. "My present to you, Jourdian," she began, unable to believe she was actually going to speak the next words on her tongue, "is a solemn promise to never use my magic on you again. No longer need you fear me, and I swear this oath upon Faerie itself."

Her gift given, Harmony tossed a fistful of stardust into the air. In a flash, she, Emil, the white pony, and the box of black widow spiders vanished.

Splendor slipped her hand into Jourdian's. "I hope you know how supremely difficult it was for Harmony to give you that gift, husband."

"It was the best I've gotten tonight."

"Oh, but you have not seen mine." She gave him a soft package.

When Jourdian opened it, he found a pair of bright red woolen mittens with blue and green stripes running through them. One was big enough to fit a giant, the other small enough to fit an infant. The big one had four fingers and no thumb, and the tiny one had two thumbs and a gaping hole on the palm.

But Jourdian didn't care. What mattered was that Splendor's gift was not made of magic. She'd knitted the gloves with her own hands. And that meant more to him than any gift she ever could have given to him.

"I started making the mittens the day after our wedding," Splendor informed him. "Emil told me that handmade gifts were very meaningful. Mrs. Frawley gave me the yarn and a bit of instruction. The needles she tried to give me were of thin iron, so I was forced to make a replica of them out of silver. I do hope you like the gloves, Jourdian, for I worked very hard on them."

His kiss told her exactly how much he liked her gift, and when he lifted his mouth from hers, she was a solid mass of gleaming joy. "Let's go upstairs, shall we, Splendor?"

"But—but . . ."

"But what?" Jourdian asked, squelching the urge to laugh at the bereft look on her face, an expression of disappointment he knew stemmed from her belief that he had not gotten her a Christmas gift. "Is something the matter, sprite?"

"Nay," she whispered, but diamonds dripped from her eyes and her glistening mist began to appear around her.

"Before you hide away in your haze," Jourdian said, "would you like to see what I got you for Christmas?"

Her tears vanished immediately, as did her mist. "Aye, that is what I would like to see!"

From behind the tree, Jourdian retrieved a very large box, and placed it at Splendor's bare feet.

Too excited to find the patience to open it with her hands, Splendor opened it with silver magic. And when the stars of enchantment faded away, she saw a beautiful saddle and bridle.

"There's not a shred of iron anywhere on them," Jourdian told her. "I had the saddle maker substitute another metal."

Splendor touched the bright metal parts of the saddle and bridle. They were made of pure gold.

"There's a new horse in the barns," Jourdian said. "A lively chestnut mare whose coat reminded me so much of the color of your hair that I bought her on the spot. We can ride together now, sprite, and you can bid your dragonfly farewell."

"Oh, Jourdian, may we go see the mare?"

"Can it wait until morning? That way you'll have another Christmas gift when you wake up."

She started to argue further, but quieted when she saw the naked desire in his eyes. "Aye, husband, the mare can wait. My passion for you cannot."

He lifted her into his arms and frowned. "You weigh more than you used to."

"I do?"

He bounced her in his arms a few times, testing her weight once more. "You do. Have you been eating more?"

"Oh, Jourdian, do you know what I think is happening to me? I am becoming more like a human! Harmony said I was beginning to speak and think like a human, and when the

servants thanked us for Christmas I did not mind their gratitude at all. And now you say I am heavier."

Staring into her eyes, Jourdian recalled that earlier he *had*
noticed she seemed less airy and more substantial. "Is it possible for a fairy to become human?"

"Nay, but it must be possible for a fairy to absorb a measure
of human qualities. What other explanation is there?"

None that Jourdian could think of. "Does this mean you
will gradually stop using your magic?"

His question gave Splendor pause. "Is that what you want?"
she asked softly.

"I . . ."

Splendor without her magic. As he deliberated upon that
thought, Jourdian realized that without her magic, Splendor
wouldn't be Splendor. Such a thing was akin to a rose without
its scent.

"You are who you are, sprite," he replied. Kissing the tip of
her nose, he walked toward the door, although he knew he
would never reach it. Sure enough, in the next second he saw
a cascade of stars and then found himself in his bedchambers,
Splendor still in his arms. A smattering of more fairy thrall
swiftly divested them of their clothes.

"Patience is definitely not one of your virtues, Splendor,"
Jourdian said, chuckling as he carried her to the bed.

"Wait." Splendor looked all around the room. "Would you
please make certain that horrible cat is not in here?"

"Pharaoh lives with Mrs. Frawley now, remember?"

"Aye, I remember, Jourdian, but that is nay a correct thing
to remember. The cat does not stay where he should."

Anxious though he was to make love to his wife, Jourdian
knew the evening would go nowhere if Splendor wasn't positive that Pharaoh was not in the room. Gently, he laid her on
the bed, then began a thorough search for the blue-eyed feline
that so terrified her.

After only a few minutes of looking, he found the cat asleep
in the closet. Pharaoh hissed ominously as his owner deposited
him in the hall and shut the door.

"You're safe now, Splendor," Jourdian said, and then joined
her on the bed. "Safe from everyone but me."

Splendor's joyful music filled the room almost the second Jourdian's lips captured hers and he began to drink of the honeyed sweetness of her mouth. He kissed her endlessly, leisurely, his hands tracing every curve, hollow, and line of her body, a flawless body no man but he had ever touched.

He stroked her hair, then nibbled at her earlobe, and his breath was hot on her flesh. His tongue left wet swirls on the silk of her breasts and her pebbled nipples, and his fingers sent fire through her loins when they dipped between her thighs and toyed with the jewel of her femininity.

"I want to touch you, too," Splendor murmured.

She didn't have to ask twice. He rolled to his side, and nearly came up off the bed when she closed her delicate hand around his engorged manhood.

"Hard," Splendor whispered, then moved her hand down to the dark pouch that hung beneath his pulsing arousal. She cupped his softness, weighed it in her hand, and marveled over the hard-soft contrasts of his body.

"I have heard your sensual sounds when we make love, Jourdian," she said softly, still caressing his turgid length. "I have smelled your scent, and have felt and seen every part of you. But one thing I have not done is taste you . . . as you have tasted me."

His gaze swept to her mouth. God help him when that mouth, those soft, sweet lips touched him, he thought. Already a rush of bliss raced through his frame, and she'd done naught but warn him of her intentions!

He watched her lower her head toward his hips, saw how her fiery hair fell around him in luxurious pools. Her beauty increased his anticipation, and when he finally felt her tongue flicker across the crown of his sex, he squeezed great handfuls of the bedspread in his fists, closed his eyes, and called out Splendor's name in a voice that blazed with rising pleasure, hotter desire.

She smiled, suddenly realizing the power a woman could have over a man. Jourdian was the strongest being she'd ever known, and yet now, as she parted her lips and took him deeply into her mouth, he was a man who had completely surrendered to her will.

With her mouth, she began to imitate the motions of love-making, taking him well past her lips and then almost out again. Over and over again she repeated the sensual actions, relishing the feel and taste of him.

"Splendor."

The torment she heard in his voice stopped her abruptly. Lifting her head, she cast a worried expression into his molten silver eyes. "I have given you pain!" she exclaimed, hating herself for not taking more care with his beautiful and sensitive maleness.

"Yes," Jourdian answered huskily. "I suffer an ache that would have been quickly alleviated had I not stopped you when I did."

"What? Oh. I am sorry, Jourdian, but I was so fascinated by my own actions that I did not realize how difficult it was for you to quell the spill of your essence."

"I don't care to keep it quelled, Splendor." He lay still for a moment, thinking. "I want to watch our lovemaking," he finally said.

"Watch? Do you mean with mirrors?"

Mirrors? he thought. A highly entertaining idea, but one he would save for another time. "Straddle my hips the way I do yours."

She obeyed, anxious to know what he had in mind.

Jourdian reached down and took hold of his straining arousal. Lifting it upward, he positioned it between Splendor's thighs, directly at the sweet, moist entrance to her body.

He raised his gaze to hers again. "Now sit down and take me inside you."

Trembling with excitement, Splendor lowered herself onto him, crying out with pleasure when she felt his hardness slip into her depths. Yearning for all of him, she started to push her hips down with one strong motion.

But Jourdian caught her waist and held her so that she couldn't move. "Careful. Go slowly, Splendor. This is going to be deeper than what we've done before. Much deeper, and I want you to stop if you feel any discomfort."

Her eyes wide with wonder and bright with the light of passion, Splendor took him more slowly, feeling him sink into her inch by glorious inch. And when he was totally embedded inside her, she felt stretched to her limit, filled to her capacity.

"Sweet everlasting, Jourdian," she whispered, her whisper a short pant. " 'Tis supremely magnificent to possess you so completely!"

"It doesn't hurt?"

"Nay."

Jourdian smiled a slow, easy smile. "Then I would have you ride me, wife."

"Ride you?"

He didn't explain with words. He showed her instead, moving his hips in a circular motion he knew would create tremors of pleasure deep inside her.

"Oh," Splendor breathed. "Oh, Jourdian."

"Ride, wife. Ride."

She did. Rotating her hips all the while, she rose higher on to her knees, felt Jourdian almost slip out of her, then impaled herself on him again and again and again.

"God, you are so beautiful," Jourdian rasped. He watched avidly, hungrily, as she pumped herself with him. Her head fell back over her shoulders, her wildfire tresses licking at his thighs.

"Look," he told her. "Look and see what it is to make love, Splendor."

Still circling her hips, she bent over at the waist so that she, too, could see the sight that so captivated him.

She watched their lovemaking. Saw his thick manhood slide into her and out of her, almost leaving her completely. And when he surged upward again, she saw herself open and stretch to accommodate his width and length.

Never had she imagined such a wondrous and profoundly beautiful thing. The way a man loved a woman and the way she accepted his loving . . .

The thought had barely floated through her mind when she saw Jourdian begin to smooth his thumb over the wet, inner flesh between her moist thighs. "Sweet—"

"Everlasting," he finished for her, his voice searing into her. He began to arch his hips toward her, driving into her with strong, urgent thrusts, and when Splendor felt him swell inside her, she knew he was about to reach the very peak of ecstasy.

"Splendor," Jourdian groaned, and exploded inside her.

Her passion crested wildly, and as Jourdian gave her his seed and listened to the powerful melody of her sensual joy, he watched her. The muscles in her belly and thighs rippled. Her eyes were closed, her lips parted, and from her throat came breathy moans that increased his pleasure tenfold.

Their flight around the room began in the next moment. Off the bed they rose, drifting around the room as if borne on a summer breeze.

"I like the way you ride, wife," Jourdian whispered, losing his hands within the mass of her copper hair.

"I have an excellent mount," she quipped in reply.

They wafted back toward the bed, and once under the sheets, Jourdian gathered Splendor in his arms and pressed soft kisses all over her cheek until he became too sleepy to do so any longer.

"Merry Christmas, milady," he whispered groggily.

"Merry Christmas, My Grace." Her body curled next to his, Splendor shut her eyes and waited for slumber to claim her.

But her eyes soon opened again. Wide. She couldn't stifle a small gasp of surprise when a delicious heat flooded her lower abdomen. She felt warm inside, illuminated, as though she sheltered a tiny flame deep within her.

A tiny flame . . .

A tiny life.

he had conceived Jourdian's son. She couldn't have been more certain of the child's gender if she were holding him in her arms.

Only seconds before the little being had been naught but a thought, a wish, and now he was alive, real, and cradled safely inside her. Her fingers trembling, Splendor laid her hand over her belly, awed by the fact that her babe dwelled just beneath her palm. Hers and Jourdian's son.

Quickly, she lifted her head so she could see her husband. "Jourdian," she said softly. "Jourdian."

He was sleeping too deeply to hear her.

She poked his shoulder.

He didn't move.

In the morning she would tell him, she decided. For now, throughout the night, the precious secret was hers alone.

Lowering her head to Jourdian's chest again, she smiled, wondering what her baby would look like. Would he have eyes the silver of rain or the lavender of wood violets? Would copper crown his head or midnight black? Would he inherit the powers of Faerie, or would he be human?

Who was the little boy she carried?

Almost giggling with joy, Splendor looked up at Jourdian once more, her eyes touching each part of his magnificently sculpted face. As she watched him sleep, she called to mind their lovemaking. Their Christmas. She remembered how she'd met him, how he'd taken her here to Heathcourte, and she recalled his frequent bouts of fury, the beautiful sound of his laughter.

She pondered their night in the starlit heavens, all their verbal battles, and their rides upon his land, he on Magnus, she on a dragonfly.

She remembered everything about him. Everything she knew, everything they'd shared.

She knew his thoughts before he spoke, sensed his emotions before he demonstrated them. She missed him when she wasn't with him. His happiness was hers, as was his sadness.

She felt attached to him, as if she were sewn to him with unbreakable threads. And she was so happy with him. Happier than she'd ever realized she could be.

Only two months had passed since she'd met him in the meadow, but she knew that those two months were worth more than all the years she'd lived without him.

Deep and powerful emotion streamed through her. It stemmed from her soul and twined through her heart like a tender vine bursting from the ground and twisting around its surroundings.

Jourdian's heartbeat pulsed beneath her ear, rhythmically, the sweetest sound in the world. Splendor sighed deeply . . .

And knew with every fiber of her being that she loved him.

She flew out of the bed and hung in the air above Jourdian's sleeping form, her body glowing so brightly that the room appeared filled with afternoon sunshine.

She loved Jourdian. *She truly loved him!* Somehow, some way, the magic of the human emotion had worked its wonderful enchantment on her.

She thought her heart would literally burst with joy.

"First our son," she whispered down to her husband, "and now love. Has there ever been a happier night in all the history of the world, Jourdian?"

Completely unable to contain her elation, she began to fly around the room with all the speed and grace of an eagle. Brilliant stars rained down from the ceiling, and the very walls began to shine like polished silver.

And then, abruptly, the stars vanished and the walls ceased

to shine. Splendor's flight slowed, stopped. She floated down to the floor, her face ashen, her frame shaking.

Her joy killed by a stabbing realization.

She loved Jourdian. But in a month's time she would have to leave him. She couldn't stay here in the human world. If she tried, she would die.

"Die," she whispered, the word wafting toward the bed where Jourdian lay sleeping. "Aye, and with me would perish our unborn child."

*Their* child. The babe was Jourdian's as well as hers, and she would have to take the child away from him, away to Pillywiggin.

Diamonds slipped from her eyes and poured to the floor. The betrothal, she thought. The long-ago bargain with Virgil Trinity had been a callous one on her great-grandfather's part.

She understood that he had sought desperate measures to save his race, but he had not considered the emotions of the Trinity descendant who would sire the special child. Had not given thought to how the chosen human man would feel over the loss of his babe.

But she hadn't either, Splendor realized. In her desire to conceive, she'd been as insensitive and heartless as her great-grandfather, never pondering the fact that Pillywiggin's gain would be Jourdian's loss.

That she hadn't understood love when she'd first come to Jourdian ceased to matter. She knew what love was now, and so she was able to understand that the spiriting away of his son was going devastate Jourdian.

She couldn't tell him about the babe. He had every right to know he'd sired a son, and she couldn't tell him.

Deep, silent sobs brought her to her knees. Her father's description of love was only half right, she realized miserably. It was true that the emotion bestowed deep and indescribable joy. But there was another side to love. A dark side, and that side rendered anguish.

Splendor dissolved into her glistening mist.

But for the first time in her life, the soothing haze brought her no comfort.

Sitting at the dining-room table with Splendor by his side, Jourdian watched his wife carefully. When he'd awakened, he'd found her standing in front of one of the bedroom windows, gazing through the pane of glass. She'd professed to have slept little. After that she hadn't said much at all and, much to his confusion, she'd been avoiding looking at him.

He laid his hand over hers. "Are you sure there's nothing wrong, sprite? You're unusually quiet this morning."

She stared at her plate as if the fine piece of china were the most interesting thing in the world to look at. "Nay," she whispered. "All is well."

*All is well.* The lie made her eyes sting with tears. She quickly blinked the diamonds away before Jourdian could see them.

"Reverend Shrewsbury has arrived, Your Grace," a servant announced as he came into the room. "The reverend requests a very brief meeting."

Jourdian felt a flash of hostility. The vicar had more than likely come to do bit of spying on him and Splendor. Of course, he would use the excuse of having come for a Christmas contribution.

Christmas, Jourdian thought. He could not send Reverend Shrewsbury away on this holy day. "Show him in."

Moments later, the vicar walked into the dining room. "Your Gr-Graces. Merry Ch-Christmas t-to you."

Jourdian had never heard the talkative man stumble over his own words before. After many years of hours-long sermons in church and continuous gossiping throughout the vicinity, the vicar had developed a strong and skillful tongue. "I take it you have come to collect a contribution, Reverend?"

The reverend shook his head. "I've c-come to t-tell you that I will no longer b-be ab-able to c-continue with my p-position as vicar of Heathc-courte. I . . . For some st-strange and unfortunate reason, I seem t-to have lost my ab-ability to sp-speak pr-properly. As vicar, I am t-to g-give a sermon every Sunday, b-but I c-cannot pr-preach with the st-stutter I have ac-acquired."

Listening to the man stutter, Jourdian felt a shred of pity for him. But only a shred. The man's speech impairment would effectively slow his rapid-fire gossiping. Jourdian was glad for that since more than a few people had suffered the results of Reverend Shrewsbury's sowing of slander.

"I will see to it that you receive an ample retirement fund, Reverend."

"Thank you, Your Gr-Grace. Farewell and once again, Merry Chr-Christmas."

"What do you think of that, Splendor?" Jourdian asked when the vicar was gone. "One of England's sharpest tongues has lost its cutting edge."

"Aye," she murmured, avoiding his gaze again.

Deciding to leave her with her thoughts for a bit, Jourdian looked up and saw Ulmstead standing by the sideboard. The butler held a tiny sand crab in one hand, and with his other hand he was rubbing his head.

Jourdian wondered if the man had some sort of itchy head rash. "Ulmstead, what are you doing?"

Thrilled to have the duke's attention at last, Ulmstead smiled. "I am smoothing my hair, Your Grace," he announced proudly, then winced slightly when the sand crab pinched his thumb.

"Your hair. I see." But Jourdian didn't "see" at all. What in God's name was wrong with everyone? Splendor wouldn't talk, and Ulmstead was smoothing nonexistent hair!

"Yes, my hair, your lordship," Ulmstead said. He left his spot by the heavily laden sideboard, approached the table, and bent over so the duke could see his head.

Jourdian couldn't believe what he was finally seeing. There, on Ulmstead's head, was a layer of deep brown fuzz. It certainly wasn't long enough for the man to brush, but it was hair all the same.

"It truly *is* hair, Lord Amberville!" Ulmstead exclaimed. Beaming, he reached up to pat the fine dark fluff again. "I noticed it at the stroke of midnight last night, and I . . . Oh, forgive me, your lordship. I don't mean to go on so."

"Please continue."

"I really am terribly excited," Ulmstead blurted out. "Your Grace cannot imagine how I have missed my hair. I began to lose it when I was but a young man. Seeing it grow back is like a wish come true! And I've not a single strand of gray. One would think a man my age would have gray hair, wouldn't one? And yet, my new hair is the same color as it was when I was young!"

A wish come true, Jourdian repeated silently. His gaze slid to Splendor. One look at her face told him exactly what she'd done.

" 'Tis Christmas Day, Ulmstead," she said, evading Jourdian's eyes and looking instead at the grinning butler. "Truly an enchanted time"—she paused while a footman scooped fruit onto her plate—"so why would your wish nay come true? And I am supremely certain that your new hair will continue to grow and thicken."

Ulmstead slipped the sand crab into his pocket and continued to rub his fuzzy head. "I—"

"He is well, Lady Amberville!" Mrs. Frawley shouted as she burst into the room. "Mr. Frawley is well at last!" She arrived at the table, her large frame quaking with happiness.

"Mrs. Frawley," Jourdian said, a tad displeased with her loud and unseemly behavior.

She bit her bottom lip. "Pardon my outburst, Your Grace, but my husband has been unwell for over a month. His heart was so weak that the doctor was sure he would soon pass away."

"I'm sorry to hear that," Jourdian said, leaning back in his chair as another servant filled his plate with thin slices of rare beefsteak and eggs topped with rich, melted cheese and glistening sautéed onions.

"Oh, but he is well now, your lordship!" Mrs. Frawley announced. She took the duchess's hand and squeezed slender fingers with her own plump ones. "He is up and about, Lady Amberville. The clock struck twelve last night, and out of the bed he rose, demanding food and drink as quickly as I could prepare it for him! And this morning he danced through the house with me, celebrating Christmas, good health, and another forty-six years of wedded bliss! Oh, your ladyship, it's a wish—"

"Come true," Jourdian said, glancing at Splendor again.

"I am supremely happy for you and Mr. Frawley," Splendor said softly.

"You may spend the day with your husband, Mrs. Frawley," Jourdian announced, "for there will be no housecleaning done at Heathcourte today. You may have a day of leisure as well, Ulmstead."

"Oh, but before you go, please leave the little crab with me," Splendor entreated.

"Of course, Your Grace," the butler replied. "I found it swimming around in a basin of water in the kitchen. It must have arrived at Heathcourte along with yesterday's delivery of fresh fish." He pulled the crab out of his pocket and set it beside the duchess's glass of cream.

Delicious scurried sideways to the edge of the table and promptly fell off.

"Tell Tessie and all the rest of the servants that they, too, may have this day to themselves," Jourdian added. "A joyful Christmas to all of you."

For a moment, the domestics simply stared at the duke, astonished by his unusual generosity. And then, in an instant, the dining room cleared of all servants, each of them anxious to indulge in Christmas festivities with their families and friends.

"That was a very kind gesture, Jourdian," Splendor complimented him.

"Yes, but did you notice that I waited until we had received breakfast before dismissing them?" He hoped to make her smile with that comment, but she merely picked up her sterling silver fork and began pushing grapes, orange sections, and cherries around on her plate.

"Splendor, something's not right with you, and I want to know what it is. Last night you were happier than I have ever seen you. Dancing and floating all around. Giggling, smiling, and enjoying your first human holiday. And here it's Christmas Day, and you act as though your world has shattered into a million bits."

Shattered, she mused. An accurate description of the state of her heart.

She forced herself to meet his concerned gaze. "Might we go see my mare, Jourdian?"

"Is that what's bothering you? The fact that you haven't seen your second Christmas gift?" He stuffed three bites of eggs into his mouth, tossed his napkin to the table, and rose from his chair. "We'll have a morning ride," he said, assisting Splendor out of her chair. "I doubt it will be as pleasurable as the one we enjoyed last night, but we'll give it a go."

Without a word, Splendor followed him upstairs and changed into a blue velvet riding habit.

"Will you ride barefoot?" Jourdian asked upon seeing her naked toes peeping out from beneath her heavy skirts.

When Splendor slipped into the soft leather boots he'd bought her, Jourdian knew there was something very wrong with her. Until this day, she had adamantly refused to wear as much as a pair of stockings on her feet.

"Splendor," he said, grasping her shoulders, "I insist that you tell me what it is that has you so distressed."

She forced herself to meet his penetrating gaze. "I told you I slept little last night, Jourdian," she said lightly. "I am simply weary."

"Would you rather not ride this morning?"

"I want to ride."

She still didn't seem very enthusiastic, Jourdian noted. Wondering if a kiss might lend her a bit of sparkle, he drew her close and slanted his mouth over hers.

Splendor knew his intentions, but the strength his kiss gave to her would not change the fact that she would soon be forced to leave him and take away his son.

"You're not shining," Jourdian stated gruffly.

"Shining?"

"You always shimmer when I kiss you."

Sweet everlasting, would the man never cease questioning her? "I'm—"

"Tired."

"Aye." With much effort, she smiled at him.

He saw straight through her forced grin, but could think of

no way to make her tell him what was bothering her. And the fact that she was hiding something from him disheartened him.

Hoping her new mare would make her happy, he escorted her downstairs. "Look, Splendor. It's snowing," he said the moment they walked out of the house and saw the frosty bits drifting down from the sky. "The first snow of the year on Christmas Day. It makes one feel like smiling, don't you agree?"

She wiped snowflakes off her lashes. "Aye."

"Then why aren't you smiling?"

Again, she feigned a happy smile.

Again he knew she was pretending. "I thought you liked nature."

"I do."

Her continuous lackluster behavior was beginning to wear down his patience, and he felt a prick of irritation. Saying nothing more to her, he led her to the stables. "Saddle the duchess's mare, Hopkins. And make certain to use the saddle and bridle I sent down earlier."

"Yes, Yer Grace," Hopkins answered, his voice raw and rasping. Quickly, he led the beautiful chestnut mare out of her stall. "She's a fine horse. Young and spirited, yet so gentle that a child could ride her. I've spent all mornin' with her." He laughed. "I feel like a lad with a new toy."

He stroked the mare's sleek neck, wondering when the duke and duchess were going to notice that his stutter was gone. "I hope Yer Graces can hear me all right. I'm a bit hoarse this mornin'. The bells in Mallencroft woke me up last night at midnight. I laid in bed grumblin' about all the noise, and then I spent the rest of the night talkin' to my dog. So many hours of one-sided conversation made me hoarse, it did at that."

Jourdian had never heard Hopkins talk so much. The man's stutter usually kept him quiet.

The man's stutter . . . What stutter?

Another wish come true, compliments of the Fairy of Heathcourte, he mused. "I imagine that anyone who suddenly lost his stutter would indulge in incessant talk."

Hopkins grinned. "It's gone, Yer Grace. I've stuttered since

I first learned to talk as a child, I have, and now the stutter is gone. It's a bloomin' miracle." Singing, he led the mare down the length of the barn where he and three stableboys quickly began to saddle and bridle her.

"Reverend Shrewsbury," Jourdian murmured, still watching Hopkins. "The vicar was stuttering this morning. Did you give him Hopkins's stutter, Splendor?"

"Aye, that is what I did."

"Is that how fairies help people with physical maladies, by transferring the problem to someone else who deserves it?"

"Aye, that is how we do it."

Jourdian started to nod, but stopped. "Do you mean you gave Mr. Frawley's weak heart to someone?"

"Nay. A weak heart could kill its recipient. I would never do such a thing. Mr. Frawley was cured by another power. An almighty power who heard Mrs. Frawley's prayers."

"What about Ulmstead's hair? And have you taken away the birthmarks on Tessie's face?"

"I have not found anyone who deserves Tessie's red marks, but Ulmstead's bald head now belongs to—"

"Here she is, Yer Grace," Hopkins said as he returned with the mare. After handing the duchess the reins, he left to ready Magnus.

"Your mare's name is Autumn Fire," Jourdian said, "which is the exact color of her coat and your hair, Splendor. I'd hoped you would like her, but you didn't even smile when you saw her."

"I am pleased with her."

He saw not a single sparkle in her eyes, and her lack of enthusiasm hurt.

And angered him. He'd done everything he could think of to lift her sagging spirits, and she hadn't responded. Well, fine! If she wanted to continue to sulk over reasons she refused to share with him, that was just dandy with him!

He turned and walked out of the barn. "Enjoy your ride."

"You will not ride, Jourdian?"

"I don't believe I would enjoy the company."

He marched toward the manor house, his anger growing

with each step he took. What the bloody hell had happened to Splendor between last night and this morning?

Damn the woman for not confiding in him. For not giving him the chance to alleviate her worries. Her sadness. Her fear, or whatever the bloody hell her problem was. She'd forced him to talk about *his* troubles, hadn't she? Yes, she had, but now that it was time for her to reveal the reasons for her own distress, she refused to comply!

He arrived at the house and went directly to his office, determined not to give Splendor another thought. Taking a seat in the chair behind his desk, he started to sort through a pile of business reports when a sealed letter caught his attention. The missive was sealed with a crest he recognized immediately as Percival Brackett's. Dark foreboding slithering through him, he ripped the letter open and saw that it was dated December twenty-fourth. Yesterday.

Fury knotted his stomach as he read the lines of flowing script.

> *Jourdian,*
>
> *I had thought to convey my best wishes to you upon the event of your wedding, but I now believe such well-wishing unnecessary. Apparently you are so enjoying matrimony that you have elected to spend more time with your bride than on your investments. Were that not so, my acquisition of the Gloucester orchards would not have been as simple to achieve.*
>
> *A Merry Christmas to you and Lady Amberville.*
> *Cordially,*
> *Percival Brackett*

Slowly, as if he could squeeze blood from the paper, Jourdian crushed the letter into a tight ball. "He got the orchards," he fumed aloud. "From right beneath my nose, he got them!" Ramming his fingers through his hair, he bolted from his chair and stalked across the room, kicking a footstool out of his way. At the window, he felt sorely tempted to slam his fist through the sparkling pane of glass.

There was no good reason for Percival's having acquired the lucrative fruit orchards.

None but one.

Jourdian clenched his teeth so hard that his entire head began to pound. He'd been acting the part of a besotted fool since marrying Splendor. No, since *before* then, he amended. Since meeting her in the meadow. Yes, from the moment he'd looked into her eyes while lying sprawled in that blasted field, he hadn't been able to keep his mind on a single thing but her.

Thoughts of his father came to him. Memories of Barrington's love for Isabel.

"Love," Jourdian muttered. The very sound of the word grated in his ears and renewed his determination to keep the ruinous emotion at bay.

He took a deep breath and pushed back his shoulders. Things were going to change, he swore. Change drastically. No longer would he neglect his work, his responsibilities as the duke of Heathcourte. He'd toiled unceasingly to repair the damage his father's obsession with Isabel had caused to the Amberville name and holdings, and he'd be damned if he would allow yet another woman to endanger them again.

As soon as Splendor returned from her ride, he would make it blatantly clear to her that she was not to disturb him in any way, shape, or form. He didn't need her smiles, her laughter, her company, or anything else he'd been foolish enough to enjoy in the past.

He needed but one thing from her.

An heir.

✦

Splendor reined in Autumn Fire beside a cold, bubbling stream that coursed through the woods that surrounded Heathcourte. After dismounting, she caressed the mare's velvety ears and allowed the horse to drink of the fresh, sparkling water.

She thought about her ride. Hopkins had once told her that whenever Jourdian was upset or angry, he took Magnus out for a gallop through the countryside and the wild ride usually soothed Jourdian's temper. In the hope that such a ride would do the same for her, Splendor had raced Autumn Fire all over Amberville land.

But she remained deeply troubled.

Dropping the reins, she glided over to a massive oak tree, and just as she sat down upon the snow-covered ground she saw a circle of flames appear above the rushing stream.

"Harmony," she murmured when her sister materialized from within the ring of fire.

Wearing the jewel-studded satin cloak Emil had given her, Harmony neared the chestnut mare and swiftly tied the horse's mane into countless elf knots. "Oh, that felt wonderful," she exclaimed. "I haven't performed a bit of mischief in . . . I cannot even remember!"

She waited for Splendor to scold her, but her sister remained silent. And then Harmony noticed Splendor's tears. The diamonds glittered brilliantly upon the dazzling white of the snow.

"Well?" Splendor said, and sniffled. "Are you nay going to laugh, sing, and dance, sister? 'Tis what you always do when you see me sad."

Harmony felt torn between good and evil. Her very nature demanded that she find happiness in Splendor's sorrow, but another part of her—one she had only just begun to realize existed—drew forth from her a rush of concern.

"Why do you weep?" she asked, forcing herself to sound nonchalant.

A profound need to give voice to her heartache led Splendor to spill her woes. "I have conceived Jourdian's son, and in one short month I must leave him and take the child away from him!"

"You've conceived? But 'tis wonderful, Splendor! The child will bring strength to Pillywiggin! I shall go inform Father immediately!"

"Wait!" Splendor shouted, flying off her spot on the ground and joining Harmony above the rippling stream. "Do not tell him, Harmony. I still have one month in the human world, but if you tell Father about the babe he will force me to return to Faerie at once! You heard what he said the day he told me I was to marry Jourdian. You heard him say that he would nay allow me to stay in the human world for any longer than was necessary!"

Harmony stared at her sister, never having seen Splendor so overwrought. "Are you saying you do not want to return to Pillywiggin?"

"Aye, that is what I am saying."

"But why? 'Tis your home, sister! Where you belong!"

Splendor turned away.

"Splendor?"

"I . . . I love Jourdian, Harmony, and I cannot bear the thought of ever being without him."

At that, Harmony caught on fire again. She burned furiously for a long while before finally smothering her flames. "Will nothing ever change?" she shouted. "Will you *always* be the first, Splendor? The first to do, to have, and to understand everything there is to do, have, and understand?"

Spinning in the air, Splendor faced her sister again. "What are you talking about?"

"*I* wanted to be the first to know what love was!"

Her sister's jealousy and anger stabbed into the last unaffected part of Splendor's heart. A torrent of overwhelming emotions sapped every ounce of strength from her body, and she felt herself shrink and fall from the air into the sucking depths of the icy stream.

"Splendor!" Harmony cried. Cold fear nearly froze her solid, but hot determination sent her diving into the frigid creek. As soon as she felt the cold water engulf her, her magic turned her into a liquid form that enabled her to easily flow with the rushing current.

Beneath the water's surface, she desperately sought Splendor. Down the stream she drifted, over the creek bed, and past piles of pebbles and bunches of water plants.

Endless seconds became endless minutes, and still she found no sign of her sister. Tears filled her eyes, the diamonds instantly seized from her cheeks by the swirling water.

Hope disappeared like a drop of dew attacked by a torrid sunbeam. Splendor was gone, and the profound sense of loss that clutched at Harmony's heart at that moment nearly stopped its beat.

"Splendor," she whispered, her whisper sending bubbles to the surface of the stream. Not knowing what else to do, she started to emerge.

But a school of iridescent fish quickly surrounded her, nipping at her fluid form and then darting away from her. Confused by their strange behavior, Harmony watched them swim toward a mound of pebble-sprinkled sand. There they began pushing at the sand with their mouths and tails.

Harmony realized immediately that the fish were trying to tell her that Splendor was buried in the sodden sand. Her actions quicker than the rapid flow of the stream, she joined the fish and yanked her sister from the slurping silt. Holding Splendor close to her bosom, she sailed out of the splashing water.

After laying her sister on the bank of the creek, Harmony transformed herself into another sphere of fire and allowed her flames to reach out and lick at Splendor's supine form.

The searing heat quickly revived Splendor. Gasping, she sat up and wiped away the wet hair that plastered her face.

"You stupid, balmy, ludicrous, irrational, dumber than a box of dirt *ninny!*" Harmony ranted. "How *dare* you frighten me like that! I nearly drowned trying to save you, Splendor! Had I a hint of sense, I would have left you in your underwater grave!"

Splendor quickly regained awareness and memory. "I—"

"You could have died!" Harmony shook her head in disgust. "And all because of a human! A *human!*"

"Jourdian," Splendor whispered. "I love him, Harmony, and I—I have to *leave* him!"

"You can still see him every now and again, Splendor! You used to watch him all the time before you met him, do you nay remember that?"

" 'Twouldn't be the same. I want to live with him, and I know full well that Father would never allow such a thing."

When Splendor burst into diamond tears again, Harmony drew back her hand and slapped her sister full across the face.

"Stop that sniveling this very instant, Splendor, and listen to me!"

Shocked out of her grief, Splendor ceased to cry and gazed at her sister with an expression of bewilderment and hope.

"You are such a ninny that I am ashamed to call you 'sister,'" Harmony snapped. "If the solution to your problem were a fire-breathing dragon, it would have leapt out and burned you to death!"

"Solution?" Splendor asked.

Calmer now, Harmony lay back upon the sandy shore and watched frosty tree branches sway above. A naughty smile touched her lips as she decided to make Splendor guess the solution herself. "Emil is in love with me," she announced smugly. "'Tis what I came to tell you this morning. Last night when we left Heathcourte we went sailing in the Mediterranean Sea in a lovely ship with billows and billows of sails that caught the night breeze and carried us far over the waves. On the deck, Emil took me into his arms, kissed me, and told me he loved me. You do know what that means, do you not, Splendor?"

Splendor nodded miserably. "It means that you can stay in the human world forever. Emil's love will keep you alive and well, for human love is the most powerful magic . . . The most powerful . . ." She soared off the stream bank and back into the frosty air. "Harmony! Sweet everlasting, how could I have been so silly!"

"It's always come naturally to you."

"Do you know what I am going to do, sister?"

Harmony rolled her eyes. "I cannot begin to guess."

"I am going to win Jourdian's love! Somehow, I will make him fall in love with me, and then I will never have to return to Faerie!"

"A truly wonderful idea," Harmony replied, and yawned. "I'm surprised I didn't think of it myself. But do not forget that although Jourdian's love will make it unnecessary for you to return to Faerie, you will still have to win Father's approval to stay here. And you know how Father is, Splendor."

Splendor refused to give in to the anxiety created by Harmony's warning. Surely somehow, some way she could convince her sire to give her his permission to remain in the human world. "I will take up that problem when I am facing it."

"You have another problem as well, and 'tis that you remain obligated to give the child you carry now to Pillywiggin," Harmony cautioned. "The terms of the betrothal are irreversible. We need the child to survive, Splendor, and nothing you do or say will change that fact. And if your son inherits the powers of Faerie, he will be king of Pillywiggin one day. Father would never allow a future monarch to live anywhere but in his kingdom."

Splendor's smile quickly faded. "But—"

"Once you win Jourdian's love, explain everything to him. Tell him . . . um . . . tell him you'll give him a dozen more children. Surely if he knows you'll give him a whole houseful of other offspring, he won't grieve over the loss of one. And besides, I am sure that if Father finds it in his heart to allow you to stay with Jourdian he will also see fit to permit Jourdian to visit with the boy often, both in Pillywiggin and at Heathcourte. 'Twould be a simple matter to shrink Jourdian so that he could enter our world."

Splendor knew her husband well enough to know that he would never consent to allow his son to be raised in Faerie. The lad would be his heir, the next duke of Heathcourte, and Jourdian would fight the devil himself for custody of the boy.

Splendor could only hope that the power of love would seek, find, and deliver an answer to that problem.

For now, she would concentrate on obtaining Jourdian's love. Quickly, she mounted Autumn Fire, waved farewell to Harmony, and urged the mare into a swift canter back toward the barns.

After leaving her horse in the kind and capable hands of Hopkins, she skimmed down the pebbled path, across the yards, and soon arrived at the manor.

"Jourdian?" she called upon entering. "Jourdian?"

Using her magic to pop into room after room, she searched the house for him, finally locating him in his office. "Jourdian!" she shouted, her face wreathed in smiles as she glided toward his desk. "Something supremely remarkable happened to me last night, and I—"

"Sit down." He looked up from his desk.

"I did not think it could happen to me, but it has. Last night, you see—"

"Sit down."

"I spoke with Mrs. Frawley, Ulmstead, and Hopkins, and last night I felt all the symptoms they described to me. After you went to sleep, I began to feel—"

"For the last time, sit down!"

His shout shocked her into silence. Unwilling to further antagonize him now, when she was just about to ask him to try to love her, she took a seat in the chair across from him. " 'Twould seem I owe you an apology for my strange behavior this morning," she said quietly. " 'Twas not my intention to anger you, husband. If 'tis what I have done, I am sorry."

Jourdian moved his papers aside, folded his hands upon his desk, and leaned forward. "I have something to talk to you about, Splendor, and I want you to listen very carefully. You—"

"I also have something important to talk to you about. I have fallen in—"

"You interrupted me."

"Aye, that is what I did, but what I have to say is so supremely important that I fear I will burst if I cannot tell you what—"

"When I have finished speaking to you, you may have your say. Now, about your coming into my office whenever the fancy strikes you . . . You will no longer—"

"I have fallen in love with you, Jourdian!" Too excited and hopeful to stay seated, Splendor floated off her chair. "I did not think it was possible for a fairy to feel such profound emotion, but I have every sign of being in love."

She flew higher above Jourdian's desk, her hair falling all over his papers, inkwell, and lamp. "I feel a powerful bond to you, as if I am truly attached to you. And when I am not with you, I am bereft. Many times, I am aware of what you will say before you open your mouth to say it, and when you are happy, sad, or worried, I am happy, sad, or worried. Jourdian," she said softly, her eyes filled with shining happiness, "the short time that I have been with you means more to me than all the years I lived without you."

Jourdian swallowed. He'd wanted her to love him. Had wished for it the night they'd made love in the sky.

And now she loved him. The impossible had happened.

"Jourdian?"

He continued to look up at her, still astonished by her declaration. "You love me."

"Aye." Splendor took a deep breath, hoping with all the hope in the world that he would grant the request she was going to make of him. "And because I love you," she said softly, hesitantly, "I wish for your love in return."

He tensed. His eyes the only part of him that moved, Jourdian glanced at the crushed letter he'd received from Percival Brackett. The orchards. Gone because of his damnable weakness for Splendor.

And now she wanted him to love her?

He almost laughed. Instead, he rose from his chair and walked straight to the door.

"Jourdian?" Splendor called, a vague sense of alarm tainting her joy.

He stopped on the threshold and turned around to face her.

"Will you try to love me?" Splendor asked. "Please will you try, husband?"

He felt a muscle in his jaw twitch.

"No," was all he said, and then he quit the room.

# 21

**D**uring the next fortnight, Splendor caught only passing glimpses of her husband. Jourdian had taken to sleeping in another room on another floor of the mansion, and there he took all his meals as well. He spent the better part of the day in his office, an hour or so riding through the countryside, and passed away the evenings in the library with brandy or port for company.

Splendor soon resorted to becoming invisible. Thus, she accompanied him to his office during the day and to the library at night. While with him she noticed how preoccupied he was. He would begin to work or read, but after only a short time he would leave his desk or chair and either pace or stare out of the windows. Once he even broke pencils, one after another until he'd broken several dozen in half.

She longed to comfort him, but dared not disturb him. Her newly discovered love for him helped her to understand that her invasion of his self-imposed solitude would only provoke him further.

And his anger would only thicken the wall he'd built between them.

Deprived of his strength-giving kisses, however, she had not the energy she needed to remain human sized. At night her lack of vigor presented little problem, for no one expected to see her between midnight and dawn. But during the day she had to make herself seen by the staff.

Her only recourse was to lock herself inside various rooms in the mansion and shrink until she'd regained enough vigor to become human sized again.

But the solution to her dilemma created a new quandary involving Pharaoh. The animal continued to escape from Mrs. Frawley's cottage and had returned to the mansion a half dozen times. Splendor lived in persistent terror of the bloodthirsty Siamese, never knowing if or when he would appear.

And the day soon came when her worst fears were realized.

She'd just become Pillywiggin size in the bedroom Jourdian had taken to sleeping in when Mrs. Frawley entered the room, placed a pitcher of water beside the basin that sat upon a small table, and left without shutting the door. The housekeeper had barely exited before Pharaoh appeared.

Panic nearly caused Splendor to fall off her spot on the dresser. Concealed behind a lamp, she didn't make a sound, but thought her heart sounded like the beating of a thousand drums.

She could see Pharaoh clearly. His long tail swishing through the air like a whip, he padded his way into the room, stopping suddenly when he spied an insect crawling along the floorboard beneath one of the windows. He crouched, his glacial blue eyes narrowing as he watched his prey, the hapless insect.

And then he sprang forward, a flying ball of murder. Splendor gasped, petrified by the thought that the poor insect might have been her.

But Pharaoh didn't kill the bug. He turned away from it and looked toward the dresser, his black nose twitching as he caught the scent of a more challenging victim.

Terror such as she'd never known twisted through Splendor. Her tiny frame shaking uncontrollably, she closed her eyes and tried her hardest to become human sized.

But she had not the strength. The only thing she could do was fly.

She soared off the dresser and landed on the top of a drapery cornice, swallowing bitter fear when she saw gruesome delight flare into Pharaoh's wicked eyes.

Pharaoh raced across the floor like an arrow shot from a

bow. Leaping on to the draperies, he scaled them quickly, his long, sharp claws ripping fabric, his jaws opened slightly in preparation to devour his prey.

Splendor promptly fell off the cornice. On the floor beneath the window, she curled into a tight ball, waiting in horrible anticipation for the killer cat to sink his teeth into her tender flesh.

"Pharaoh!" Jourdian's shout reverberated through the room.

The cat jumped off the draperies just as Jourdian spotted the naked and tiny Splendor on the floor. "Splendor!"

Jourdian almost killed himself trying to reach his wife. But before he arrived at the window, he saw Pharaoh snatch something off the floor, chew it, and swallow it.

"Oh, my God! Splendor! Oh, my God!" Throwing himself to his knees, Jourdian slid the rest of the way to the window. There, he grabbed Pharaoh, pried the cat's jaws open, and stared into the tooth-filled mouth. "Splendor!" he shouted, his lips right next to Pharaoh's. "Splendor!"

"I am here, Jourdian," came her small voice from the floor. "Here, behind the curtains."

Jourdian cast the Siamese aside and quickly took Splendor into his hand. "What—"

"An insect. He ate an insect." Still quaking with the fear that Pharaoh might yet catch her, she crawled up inside Jourdian's shirtsleeve.

He pulled at his cuff, looked into his sleeve, and saw Splendor trying to wrap her arms around his wrist. "He almost ate you!"

"Aye, that is what he almost did. Is he gone?"

Jourdian looked around and saw Pharaoh saunter out of the room. Quickly he rose and shut the door.

"I have had to keep shrinking, Jourdian, because I have not had any of your kisses," Splendor explained, still inside his shirtsleeve.

He walked to the bed and shook his arm until Splendor fell out of his sleeve and landed on one of the plump satin pillows.

"You saved my life," Splendor said, gazing up at the giant who was her husband. "Does that mean you love me?"

Her mention of love, given in the face of what had almost happened to her, rendered Jourdian completely mute for a long, long moment. "I saved you so I would not have to tell the authorities that my missing wife had been eaten by a damned Siamese! What do I have to do, Splendor? Keep you in a cage like a blasted canary?"

"No, but you could kiss me. 'Twould give me the vigor I need to perform my shape-shifting."

"My lips are twice as big as your head!"

"Perhaps 'twill not matter. Just kiss me, and we shall see what happens."

He rammed his fingers through his hair and leaned down toward her tiny form.

Splendor grabbed hold of his huge bottom lip and pressed her face into the soft skin.

Startled by the feel of her tiny fingernails pinching his lip, Jourdian gasped and nearly inhaled her.

"Sweet everlasting, Jourdian, if you do that again, I will find myself trapped inside your lungs!"

"Splendor—"

"Don't talk!" she shouted, the movement of his bottom lip causing her to swing and bounce against his chin.

He started to tell her to let go when he realized that if he spoke he would knock her senseless. Carefully, he pulled her off his mouth and cradled her in his palm. "I can't kiss you, Splendor. Isn't there anything else we can try? I don't want you staying small like this."

Splendor looked down at the bed. "We could make love. Making love makes me supremely strong, Jourdian. Even stronger than does kissing."

He stared at her. "Have you lost your mind? If I can't kiss you, how the bloody hell can I make love to you?"

"Oh. Well, perhaps just the feel of you next to me will help me."

Jourdian didn't know what else to do but comply. He lay down on the bed and placed Splendor beside his arm.

"Take off your clothes, Jourdian," she said.

"Why?"

"It could be that the warmth of your skin and the sound of your heartbeat might lend me a bit of vigor."

He couldn't understand why he had to remove all of his clothes, but he was in no mood to argue.

When he was naked, Splendor climbed upon his chest and sat down on his left nipple. "Would you mind very much if I shifted Pharaoh's shape? 'Tis something I have pondered doing, but haven't yet because I felt I should ask your permission first."

"Shift his shape?"

"Aye. Into something less dangerous. A rabbit."

Jourdian didn't need but a half a second to come to his decision. With Pharaoh being a rabbit, he would no longer have to worry about Splendor's safety. "Do it."

"I cannot right now. I am too weak. But I shall turn him into a sweet white bunny with a pink nose when next I see him."

Jourdian nodded.

"I've missed you."

"Would you just lie down above my heart, please?" he barked down at her.

"Very well." She stretched out upon his warm flesh, positioning her head right above his heart. "I can hear your heart. 'Tis loud and strong. You must be very healthy. Have you missed me, too, Jourdian?"

He sighed without profound aggravation.

His breath inflated his chest, causing Splendor to roll down over his belly straight between his thighs.

"Good God!" Jourdian shouted, lifting his head and seeing her hanging on to his sleeping manhood.

"Jourdian, are you trying to kill me?" Splendor asked. She struggled to her feet, placed her hands on her bare hips, and glared at him.

He'd never seen a stranger sight in all his life than Splendor standing on his masculinity. He was the only man in the entire world whose wife could stand on his sex and not turn him into a eunuch.

Irritated though he was, however, he could not ignore the

odd, but pleasurable sensations her tiny feet caused him to feel. "Uh . . . Splendor, I think you should fly off now."

Before she could ask him why, she felt him harden. And looking down, she *saw* him harden. The sight put her into a playful mood, and she grinned impishly. Singing a merry tune, she held her arms out to her sides and performed a little jig.

Profound amusement made Jourdian smile. Here he was, he thought, lying on his bed with his wife doing a Highland fling upon the length of his arousal. "I'm going to laugh," he warned.

She barely had enough time to dive down to the mattress before he exploded into laughter. Turning to his side, he laughed until tears streamed down his face.

His laughter caused the bed to bounce. "Jourdian, stop!" Splendor shouted, thrown every which way by the rolling movement of the mattress.

Gradually, his laughter faded away, and he gently placed Splendor back on his chest. "Do you feel any stronger yet?"

"Nay. Indeed, I am feeling supremely fatigued." She lay down again, directly over his chest, and within moments the steady beat of his heart lulled her to sleep.

With his pinkie finger, Jourdian rubbed her small back. A long while passed, but he finally saw the first silver stars appear around her, indicating that her strength had returned.

Knowing she would awaken within the next few minutes, he gently placed her upon a pillow and dressed.

He left quickly.

Before she could mention the subject of love again.

❦

Splendor urged Autumn Fire into the snowy woods, Harmony perched between the mare's ears. "I have not seen you or Emil as of late, Harmony. 'Tis been nearly a week."

"Aye."

"You are unusually quiet, sister, and yet your eyes glow with joy. Will you not share your happy secret with me? I confess to be in need of glad tidings."

Harmony hesitated before answering. Her news was indeed happy, but she wasn't sure now was the time to relate it. "I do not know if my news will make you happy for me or sadder for yourself."

"I would hear it nonetheless."

Recalling Splendor's innate goodness, Harmony relented. "The same magic that came to you has come to me. I have fallen in love with Emil. I know love is what I feel because 'tis quite the deepest, most intense emotion I have ever known. Emil has become everything to me, Splendor, and I can think of nothing I would nay do for him."

Splendor's face lit up with joy. "Harmony, 'tis wonderful, sister! 'Tis supremely glorious!"

"There is more," Harmony said, rubbing her little hand down Autumn Fire's left ear. "I am married. Emil and I were wed in secret five days ago in a town called Telford. And . . . and I have already conceived. I carry twins, a girl and a boy. I have not yet told Father because Emil and I have been enjoying what humans call a honeymoon. We have been all over the world. I would have been pleased to stay in Emil's house, but all the traveling we have done made him happy. We returned to his home last night, and when I tell Father that I have wed, I shall also inform him that I will not live without my husband. If I must, I shall leave Pillywiggin forever."

Diamonds brimmed in Splendor's eyes and trickled to the ground.

"I suspected 'twould be so," Harmony said. "My news made you sad. I am sorry, sister."

"Nay, your news did not make me sad, Harmony. I weep with deep happiness for you. When will you tell Father?"

Harmony shook her head. "I am not certain. Perhaps I will know when the time is right."

"I wish for you a long lifetime of love with Emil and your children."

"I wish the same for you and Jourdian. You have but a week left with him, and he has still not told you he loves you. Do you cry every night, sister?"

Splendor brushed her hand across the frosty trunk of an oak tree as Autumn Fire continued to amble through the cold woods. "I have nay the time to indulge in sadness or self-pity, Harmony. Instead, I have been concentrating all my efforts in endeavoring to find a way to win Jourdian's love."

"And?"

"I have decided that what I need is a chance to watch human women whose husbands love them."

Harmony grabbed Autumn Fire's forelock and, using the stiff hair as one would use a long, thick vine, she began to swing across the mare's face. "You have that housekeeper at Heathcourte. Her husband loves her."

"Aye, but I want to see how other women act, speak, and think as well. Perhaps if I study their appearances and mannerisms I will better understand what it is that makes them so lovable to their husbands. I wonder where I might find a mass of women? 'Twould take forever to seek them out one by one, but if I could be in the midst of many at once I could accomplish my task quickly."

Her arms held out to her sides for balance, Harmony walked down the length of Autumn Fire's neck and reclined within a fold of Splendor's velvet riding skirt. "I know where over a hundred human women will be present."

Splendor reined Autumn Fire to a halt. "Tell me!"

"At a ball that will be given by a couple by the name of Lord and Lady Chesterton. 'Tis to be held in six days' time. I was with Emil when he received his invitation. But he will not attend. He says he prefers to be alone with me because our honeymoon is not yet over."

"A ball," Splendor murmured, her mind working furiously.

"A celebration. 'Tis the birthday of the Chestertons' daughter. I think I heard Emil say the daughter's name is Marianna."

"Marianna," Splendor repeated, thinking the name sounded familiar. "Jourdian mentioned her once . . . She wrote him a letter . . . Aye, a letter, inviting him to attend her cousin's wedding in London. The letter smelled of roses. Jourdian said she was very pleasing to the eye."

"What else did he say?"

" 'Twas all."

"There was a time when he considered wedding her. Emil said 'twas her fondest dream to become his duchess. When she learned he had wed you, she took to her bed the way you did when that cat scratched you."

*"What?* What do you mean he considered wedding her? He has been betrothed to me since before either of us was born! How dare he—"

"He did not know he was betrothed, and neither did you before Father had the dream."

Harmony's statement quickly calmed Splendor's anger.

"Have you told Jourdian about the betrothal, Splendor?"

"Nay. Jourdian is a man who likes to control his own life," Splendor stated with all the authority of a woman who understood her husband well. "If he knew he'd been destined to become my spouse since before his very conception, he would be supremely angry."

"He is almost always supremely angry. Even now, he sits in his office brooding over the loss of those stupid orchards."

Splendor picked Harmony up and held her in her palm. "He lost the orchards?"

"You did not know? He did not tell you?"

"Nay."

"A man called Percival Brackett bought the orchards, and Emil says that Jourdian is more than likely furious."

Splendor tried to understand why Jourdian still wanted the fruit orchards. She'd warned him not to buy them.

And then she thought of the answer to her own question. Percival Brackett, she recalled from a conversation with Emil, harbored deep resentment toward the Amberville name. Years before, he and his father had been partly responsible for the near devastation of the Amberville name and holdings.

And now Percival had acquired the orchards that Jourdian wanted.

Splendor dearly hoped that Percival had spent a fortune purchasing the orchards, for they would soon be worthless.

"Will you attend the Chesterton party, Splendor?"

"Aye. I shall see this Marianna Chesterton with my own eyes and try to understand what it is about her that almost had Jourdian marry her."

"What if Jourdian does not wish to take you?"

Splendor peered through the trees, seeing Heathcourte Manor in the distance. "What I learn at the ball will give me one last chance to understand how to make Jourdian love me, Harmony. He will take me. He *must*, for although he does not know it, our very future depends on it."

<hr />

"Yes, we received an invitation to the Chesterton ball, but no, we are not going to attend," Jourdian said when Splendor floated into his library and asked him if their presence had been requested at Marianna's birthday ball.

Splendor stubbornly resisted the hurt his gruffness caused her. She loved him, and no other emotion possible to feel was as powerful as that love. "But I have never been to a ball in the human world, Jourdian, and I—"

"In a few weeks we will be holding a small affair here at Heathcourte in honor of Emil and Harmony. It won't be a ball, but it will give you an idea of how tedious such gatherings can be."

"But I—"

"I still cannot believe Emil is married," Jourdian mumbled.

"The ball began an hour ago, husband. We are late."

He slammed his snifter of brandy down on the table that sat beside his chair, uncaring that the amber liquor splashed onto the expensive Oriental carpet. "Have you gone deaf, Splendor? I said we weren't going!"

A burst of silver stars shot out of Splendor's palm and rained down upon her delicate form.

When the magical stardust finally faded, Jourdian saw his wife dressed in a shimmering gold satin ball gown ornamented with clusters of fragrant pink roses. The bodice of the gown dipped shockingly low, revealing more of Splendor's creamy bosom than Jourdian deemed fitting. Why, if she took a deep breath, or sneezed, or coughed, she'd fall right out of the dress!

He could not take his eyes off her pale chest. It was true

that she was not full busted, but her small breasts were perfect, so beautiful that the mere sight of them made him uncomfortably warm.

God, he thought. He could barely remember the last time he'd made love to Splendor. Shifting in his chair in an attempt to relieve the building pressure in his loins, he decided that his celibacy would end tonight. Bedding Splendor would not only satisfy his lust but perhaps it would also bring about the conception of his son.

"Allow me to compliment you on the elegance of your evening attire, wife, but as I said before, we will not be attending the Chesterton affair." He glanced at the clock. "It's nine-thirty, and we are going to retire for the night now."

She realized instantly that he meant to make love to her, and although the prospect caused her to glow with deep desire, she would not dismiss the opportunity to go to the ball and spy on Marianna Chesterton. The rest of hers and Jourdian's life was at stake, and if she succeeded with her plans tonight, they would have countless more nights to fill with passion.

"I do not wish to go to bed, Jourdian," she announced, tilting her chin up. "I wish to go to the ball."

"We are not going to the—"

"Aye, we are."

"No—"

"Aye." Splendor held out her hand, out of which a spray of silver magic sprang forth and sailed toward Jourdian.

Fairy thrall dressed him in an elegant black suit and snow-white shirt. "Damn it all, Splendor! I told you that we are not going to the blasted Chesterton affair!"

His last loud statement thundered through the elegant ballroom of the Chesterton estate, almost overpowering the strains of a waltz. Looking around, Jourdian needed only two seconds to realize where he was and how he'd arrived.

A few nearby dancers stopped and stared.

Jourdian closed his eyes and counted to ten. "Splendor, do you know what I wish right now?"

"What, husband?"

"I wish the earth would open up and swallow me."

Splendor cupped her cheek. "That does not sound like much fun to me, Jourdian, but if 'tis what you wish . . ."

"No!" He took hold of her slender wrist when he saw her star-filled palm. "Take us home this instant."

"Nay."

Rage stiffened every part of him. "I *wish* for you to take us—"

"Lord Amberville!" two women's voices called.

Jourdian looked up and saw Lady Holden and Lady Briggs waddling toward the doorway where he and Splendor stood. Mildred Holden looked like a large powder puff dressed in her frilly pink gown, and Jourdian thought that Regina Briggs looked like a plump avocado in her drab green dress.

Bloody hell. The women were two of society's worst busybodies, and would no doubt make it their night's goal to stir up as much trouble as possible. "Ladies," he muttered.

"How delightful that you decided to come," Lady Holden said. "And this lovely girl must be your bride. I didn't recognize her with her clothes on."

Jourdian felt his features harden as if they'd been turned to stone.

"My name is Splendor."

"Her name is Lady Amberville," Jourdian corrected.

"Your Grace," the ladies greeted the duchess in unison.

"Beautiful gown," Lady Briggs said, her eyes taking in every detail of the duchess's attire.

"Jourdian bought it for me," Splendor said. "I am supremely fond of all the gowns he has given to me, but I do not care to wear the under things. Many of them scratch my skin, and they are all quite heavy. I much prefer to wear as little clothing as—"

"Splendor," Jourdian murmured.

"Do you not care for shoes, either, Your Grace?" Lady Briggs asked, suddenly noticing the duchess's bare feet.

"Shoes?" Splendor wiggled her toes, feeling the cold marble floor beneath them. "I do not care for shoes, either, but 'twas my intention to wear them tonight. However, I was rushed. Jourdian did not want to come, you see, so I was forced to—"

"We have to leave," Jourdian declared.

"Why, you only just arrived!" Lady Briggs exclaimed.

"True, but—"

Lady Holden clucked her tongue. "Come, come now. Everyone will be delighted to see you. I'm afraid you missed dinner, but I'm quite certain that Lady Chesterton will have a plate brought to you should you wish to eat. Or, perhaps you would rather wait for the cake, which will be served shortly. It is Marianna's birthday, you know."

"I don't imagine you could forget the occasion, could you, Lord Amberville?" Lady Briggs asked, anxious to begin a spot of trouble. "You attended Marianna's last birthday party. Yes, I distinctly remember the two of you swirling the night away in each other's arms. Rumor had it that wedding bells would soon—"

"Rumors have caused the downfall of many people," Jourdian flared. "People about whom the rumors are spread, and the people who so enjoy spreading them."

His warning was so thinly veiled that both ladies quieted for a moment.

"Yes, well, come, Your Grace," Lady Briggs said to Splendor.

When Lady Briggs took hold of Splendor's left arm, Jourdian grasped his wife's right elbow. "I am afraid we cannot stay," he stated sternly. "My wife has suddenly taken ill."

"Ill, Jourdian?" Splendor asked. "But I am not—"

"As you can plainly see," Jourdian began, "she's pale and slight. Such fragility is—"

"I should like to meet Marianna Chesterton," Splendor declared, pulling her arm from Jourdian's grasp.

The ladies tossed smug looks at the duke, and quickly led Splendor farther into the ballroom, leaving Jourdian no choice but to follow.

Every head in the sparkling room turned to stare at him and Splendor. Dancing stopped, laughter faded, and all chitchat ceased. Eventually the orchestra music died away as well, the musicians all wondering what had happened to cast a pall over the room.

But it wasn't gloom that had silenced the merrymaking. It

was mostly curiosity, a bit of disapproval and, on Marianna Chesterton's part, it was fury.

"Mother, I cannot believe you invited them," she said angrily.

Lady Chesterton patted her daughter's bejeweled hand. "Marianna, you know perfectly well that one cannot slight the duke of Heathcourte. It simply isn't done."

Noticing that heads had turned toward her, many gazes seeking her reaction to the arrival of Lord and Lady Amberville, Marianna forced herself to smile.

But her smile could have flattened every bubble in her glass of champagne as she watched the flame-haired girl at Jourdian's side. "Look at her, Mother," she whispered, still feigning a smile. "She is a common trollop who now possesses the title that I tried for months and months to obtain. Had she not suddenly appeared out of nowhere, *I* would be Jourdian's duchess."

Lady Chesterton nodded. "Surely you can take some comfort in knowing that you will soon be the duchess of Bramwell. Now that Jourdian has wed, Percival Brackett is the best catch in the country. And don't forget that Percival managed to acquire those orchards in Gloucester before Jourdian could. It was quite a coup. Everyone is talking about it. And it proves that Percival's power is very nearly of the same caliber as Jourdian's."

Marianna sniffed. *Very nearly* meant that Percival was second best. Jourdian remained the most powerful lord in the land.

"Has Percival not arrived yet?" Lady Chesterton asked. "I don't see him."

Marianna continued to watch Jourdian and the new duchess of Heathcourte. "I haven't seen Percival since Christmas Eve." And she didn't care that she hadn't seen her fiancé. The man was a fop, not a real man like Jourdian Amberville. Even Percival's kisses were fastidious. Just quick little pecks because more passionate kisses would muss his hair.

A shudder passed through Marianna's voluptuous body. If not for Percival's wealth and social standing, she wouldn't have allowed him within a hundred miles of her.

"Percival will be along straightaway, I am certain," Lady Chesterton said. "After all, your father plans to announce your engagement tonight. You do know how pleased your father and I were when you finally accepted Percival's proposal, do you not, Marianna? While we had hoped for an alliance with the Ambervilles, the Bracketts are—"

"Will you excuse me, Mother? Since this is my party, I must go greet and welcome Jourdian and his bride."

Before Lady Chesterton could reply, Marianna nodded to the musicians, who quickly began to play again. Another feigned smile glued to her heavily rouged mouth, she then started toward the Ambervilles.

Jourdian saw and heard her coming. Her eyes glittered with anger. And her royal blue silk gown whispered "rage" with each step she took.

He placed a protective arm around Splendor's shoulders.

And when Splendor looked up at him, she didn't see the husband she'd come to know so well. She saw another man.

The powerful and forbidding duke of Heathcourte.

# 22

"We shall see you in a bit, Your Graces," Lady Briggs said when Marianna arrived.

"Yes, that we shall," Lady Holden agreed.

Jourdian watched both women meld into the crowd of guests, their mouths moving so quickly that the motions of their lips were blurred. He knew that in only moments every person in the room would know that Splendor was barefoot and naked beneath her gown.

And now he would have to contend with Marianna, who stood before him now wearing so much rose perfume that the heavy scent forced him to take a step backward. "Marianna."

"Jourdian, darling." Holding out her arm, she waited for him to kiss her hand and couldn't suppress a feeling of profound desire.

Once upon a time she'd felt those sensuous lips of his on her mouth, and his kisses would remain branded in her memory forever.

Dutifully, Jourdian brushed his lips across the top of her cold fingers, then abruptly let her hand go. "Marianna, may I present my wife, Splendor."

"Charmed," Marianna purred. Her brown eyes slanted as she examined Splendor, and her anger heated as hot jealousy flared within her.

The girl Jourdian had married gave new meaning to the

word beautiful. With skin as pale and flawless as a newly opened white rose, thickly lashed violet eyes that could bring a man to his knees, and luxurious auburn hair as mesmerizing as swaying flames, Splendor was undoubtedly the loveliest female at the ball. The girl shimmered with what was almost an unearthly radiance.

Marianna wanted to scream. She knew then that not only had she lost the wealthiest, most powerful man in the country but she had also lost her own title as the most beautiful woman in England.

" 'Tis supremely wonderful to meet you, Marianna Chesterton," Splendor said, trying desperately to understand what it was about the haughty woman that had caught Jourdian's attention in the past.

Was it Marianna's thick dark brown hair? Her sparkling mahogany eyes, her generous ruby lips? Or were Marianna's breasts what Jourdian liked? Splendor had never seen such a large bosom, and she wondered if Jourdian had ever touched those full breasts. If he had ever kissed or suckled them.

She looked up at Marianna's face again, not caring at all for the way the woman was staring at Jourdian. It was painfully obvious that every wish Marianna had ever made concerned him.

Splendor felt a bit of silver magic fill her closed fist, magic that would quickly turn Marianna into a horned frog. But she resisted releasing the magic, choosing instead to continue studying the woman who had once roused Jourdian's interest.

She glanced at Marianna's jewelry. It looked to her as if Marianna had bathed in a tub of rubies and pearls and that all the gems had stuck to her body. Did Jourdian like a woman to wear a lot of jewelry? He'd offered her jewels once, and she'd refused.

Perhaps she shouldn't have.

"What an interesting name you have, Splendor," Marianna commented. "Or perhaps *interesting* is not the word I seek. *Peculiar*, I think, is a better description."

"*Beautiful* is the best way to describe Splendor's name," Jourdian countered. "A beautiful name for the most beautiful woman here."

"Yes, she is quite lovely, Jourdian," Marianna said, feeling her insides begin to boil. "In a simple sort of way, of course. But then, she cannot help her humble beginnings, now can she?"

"No more than I can help mine," Jourdian replied, subtly reminding Marianna that his own mother had been a peasant before marrying Barrington.

"Oh, Jourdian, surely you jest!" Marianna tapped his chest with her fan. "You are the son of a duke! She is the daughter of—"

"In my eyes, she might as well be the daughter of a king," Jourdian snapped. He curled his arm around Splendor's waist.

"How very gallant," Marianna replied silkily.

"Aye," Splendor said, smiling into her husband's eyes. "That is what Jourdian is. Gallant. And I am in love with him."

Marianna wasn't blind. She saw the glow of profound emotion floating within the duchess's infuriatingly gorgeous eyes. "What a romantic you are, Splendor. Tell me, where did you live prior to moving into Heathcourte three days before your wedding?"

"I—"

"You must have been in dire straits," Marianna interrupted. "We heard that when you came to Jourdian, you had not a stitch on. Why, you poor little thing. You—"

"If indeed Splendor was ever a poor little thing, she isn't anymore," Jourdian said curtly. "Now, if you will excuse us, I should like to dance with my duchess."

Quickly and firmly, Jourdian led Splendor to the dance floor. Taking her into his arms, he began to swirl her around and discovered her to be an extraordinarily graceful dancer. But why wouldn't she be, he asked himself.

Her bare feet never touched the ground.

"You are a wonderful dancer, Jourdian. I—I hope that we can attend many balls together," she murmured.

He saw intense worry cloud her lovely eyes, but before he could question her, he noticed a group of women nearby. They were staring at him and Splendor, their mouths moving almost as quickly as Lady Briggs's and Lady Holden's had.

"I wish I could hear what they're saying," he mumbled.

Splendor glanced at the women Jourdian was watching. "Your wish is granted, husband."

Silver dusted the air. The moment the twinkles disappeared, Jourdian found that he was able to hear every word the women were saying.

"He obviously doesn't care enough about her to give her jewels," one lady said. "All she is wearing is her wedding ring."

"And one would think he would provide her with a lady's maid," another woman added. "Look at her hair. Why, she hasn't done a thing with it, but has merely let it hang all down her body. Take her out of that gown and give her a pail, and she would look just like a milkmaid."

"His Grace doesn't appear at all happy, either," yet another lady observed aloud. "That frown of his is quite the most ferocious I have ever seen."

"Well, he *had* to marry her, you know," a fourth woman spat. "Imagine a man of his wealth and standing being saddled with such a bit of riffraff."

Potent fury sluicing through his veins, Jourdian released Splendor and started toward the malicious women.

But they scattered instantly, vanishing into the crowd so quickly that he lost sight of them within seconds.

"Jourdian?" Splendor tapped him on the shoulder.

He looked down into her compelling violet eyes, immensely relieved that she hadn't heard the vicious things the women had said about her. He might not love her, he mused, but he'd be damned if he was going to permit anyone to hurt her tender feelings.

She belonged to him. And he would always protect what was his.

"I'm going to dance you toward the doors, Splendor, and once we've passed through them I want you to take us home."

"I shall have more time with Marianna first."

"I don't understand your sudden and bizarre interest in Marianna, and I demand that you—"

"This is my first human ball, Jourdian. Would you deprive me of—"

"Yes."

"You are acting uncivil."

"And your impulsive and completely infuriating little manner of getting us here to the ball was such a civil thing to do," he replied sarcastically.

"You—"

"Jourdian, old boy," a man said as he approached them. "So sorry to interrupt your waltz, but I confess that I could not wait another second for an introduction to your duchess."

Jourdian glared at Niall Marston, the earl of Moore. He'd never paid much attention to Niall's rakish conduct with other men's wives in the past, but this was the present. And Splendor had obviously caught the rogue's interest. The man's wide blue-eyed gaze might as well have had teeth, for he was devouring Splendor with all the fervor of a starving tiger.

Jourdian felt a sudden and intense hatred for the man.

"I am waiting," Niall said.

Sensing that many ears were straining to hear his reply, Jourdian complied. "Niall, this is Splendor."

Quickly, Niall picked up Splendor's hand and planted his lips upon her slender fingers. Her skin felt like warm silk, and her delicate flower scent quickened his breath. "Enchanted, Lady Amberville," he murmured, his mouth still pressed against her hand.

"Splendor," Jourdian said, pulling her hand out of Niall's grasp, "this is Niall Marston."

"The earl of Moore," Niall added arrogantly. "But please call me Niall."

"And you must call me Splendor."

Niall felt his mouth water as he watched her lips move. A connoisseur of women, he knew instinctively that her kisses would be sweeter than wild honey. "You cannot know how anxiously I and others have been waiting to meet you, Splendor. I always suspected Jourdian would marry an exceptionally beautiful woman, and now I see that my suspicions were absolutely correct."

Jourdian had heard enough. Pulling Splendor into his arms again, he was just about to sweep her into the throng of other dancers when four more noblemen approached, all begging to be introduced to Splendor.

Irritated beyond his limit, Jourdian made all the introductions. "Now, if you gentlemen will excuse us? My wife and I were dancing, and I—"

"Don't be so selfish, Heathcourte," Niall said as he returned to Splendor's side. "You enjoy Splendor's company every day." *And every night,* he added silently, his eyes resting on her small but gorgeous breasts. "The rest of us, on the other hand, have only just met her." He smiled into Splendor's eyes. "Might I have the pleasure of this dance, Lady Amberville?"

Niall gave neither Splendor nor Jourdian a chance to answer. With speed and grace, he spun Splendor clear across the dance floor to the other side of the room, his desire soaring when he remembered hearing that she wore nothing beneath her gown.

"You are Jourdian's friend?" Splendor asked.

"Yes," Niall lied, knowing Jourdian had never considered him a friend.

"And are you Marianna's friend as well?"

"Marianna?" Niall took a moment to ponder Splendor's questions, guessing that the lovely duchess of Heathcourte had heard the rumors concerning Jourdian's past interest in Marianna.

Splendor's curiosity would work in his favor. "I am well acquainted with both. And I think it shocking that the two of them cannot seem to keep their eyes off each other. I'm sure it's painful for you to witness their mutual attraction, and even more painful to know that there is naught you can do about it. Your husband is a man who gets what he wants, often at the expense of others. You do have my deepest commiseration."

Splendor didn't know what to say, what to think. Did Jourdian still harbor feelings for Marianna? If that was so, her chances of winning his love were fairly nonexistent.

"You're remarkably light-footed, Splendor," Niall said, pulling her closer to his body, closer to the fire her beauty had ignited within him. "Dancing with you is like dancing with a summer breeze."

She couldn't help but feel the bulge of his lust press into her belly. Intuitively alarmed and instantly revolted, she tried to pull away from him.

Niall wouldn't let her. "It's obvious you are not familiar with a waltz," he said, his fingers caressing the length of her spine. "A woman is held close to the man."

"So close that she feels repulsed by his attentions?"

He didn't miss the way her lavender eyes flashed. Violets afire, he mused, and the passion of her anger merely whet his appetite. The woman was like an angel from hell or a she devil from heaven. He didn't know which, but he thoroughly enjoyed the unusual blend of innocence and sensuality.

Bending down to her, he pretended to whisper in her ear.

Splendor went rigid, hating the way his wet lips felt on her neck. This man was not Jourdian's friend. No friend would behave in the manner Niall Marston was behaving.

A bit of punishment was in order, castigation that would make him think twice before pawing another man's wife again. She spied two open doors that led to a courtyard illuminated with a multitude of lanterns. "Let us walk outside for a moment, shall we, Niall? I realize 'tis cold, but—"

"Ah, but I've your beauty to keep me warm, haven't I?" Already she'd succumbed to his charisma, he thought. She could barely wait for his sensual attentions. Smiling triumphantly, he led her toward the doors.

" 'Tis a glorious night," Splendor said as he escorted her into the yard, away from the house, away from the lights.

"And you and I both know a way to make it even more glorious." Confidence and lust seeping from his every pore, Niall ushered her into the black shadows of a cluster of tall trees.

The second he stopped, Splendor felt his mouth on her throat and his groping hands all over her body. She wondered how many other women had been victim to his voracious sexual appetite.

"What a feast you are, Splendor," Niall panted, trying to work his fingers into the top of her bodice. "And how I enjoy such a sweet banquet."

"And how I will enjoy showing you how it feels to be very nearly consumed, Niall."

Silver stardust exploded in the air, coating Niall from head to toe.

He vanished.

"Splendor!"

The sound of her husband's voice sent Splendor floating back to the house. "Jourdian—"

"Where have you been? Where's Niall? Damn it all, one second the two of you were dancing, and in the next second you were nowhere to be seen!"

"Niall had to leave."

"Did he touch you?" Jourdian's anger was rising like steam from a kettle.

"Aye, that is what he did. And I did to him what he deserved to have done to him. He is a man who takes great delight in gobbling up women as if they were naught but succulent fruits laid out on platters for his choosing and pleasure. He is now learning what it is like to be the food that feeds such a ravenous hunger."

Jourdian waited in vain for her to continue. "What did you do to him?" he demanded.

"He hangs above a pit of starving crocodiles."

"Crocodiles." Jourdian smiled. He couldn't help it. Just the thought of Niall at the mercy of a mass of snapping reptiles tickled him thoroughly. "How long will you keep him suspended above the crocodiles?"

"A month."

"Splendor," he scolded softly.

"Oh, very well. Another hour or so."

"Fine. Let's go home."

"First tell me in all honesty what it is you feel for Marianna Chesterton."

"What I feel—"

"Do you love her?"

"*Love* her!"

"Niall said—"

"I don't give a damn what that—"

"But I give a million damns about what he said."

"Jourdian. Splendor."

They turned and saw Percival Brackett standing in the doorway that led into the ballroom.

"Is there trouble in paradise?" Percival asked, leaning

against the door frame. "I and several others heard your shouting."

Jourdian stared at the black silk turban on Percival's head. It took him only seconds to understand that beneath the turban, Percival was as bald as Ulmstead had once been.

"The latest fashion in menswear," Percival explained upon seeing Jourdian's reaction. He reached up and patted the headpiece. "I assure you that every man in society will be wearing one soon. You received my letter, I presume."

"I did."

"We should like to buy the fruit orchards from you, Percival," Splendor said.

"What?" Jourdian blurted. "Splendor—"

"If you will sell the orchards to us we would be supremely happy."

"Oh?" Percival smiled a lazy smile. "Of course, Lady Amberville. I'd be happy to. But you should be aware of the fact that their value has tripled since I acquired them."

At that Jourdian smiled, too, a dangerous smile that matched perfectly the ominous expression in his eyes. "I knew the orchards would prove to be lucrative, but I never imagined they would triple in value within only days of being purchased."

Percival shrugged. "What is this world coming to, I ask you? Prices soar with each passing day."

"Be that as it may," Splendor said, "we will buy the orchards from you as soon as you are prepared to sell them. And I warn you now that we shall pay only a fraction of what you paid for them."

"I'll keep that in mind," Percival replied smoothly, casting an amused look at Jourdian.

"If you will excuse us, Bramwell?" Jourdian said. He took Splendor's hand and led her back into the ballroom. "What did you think you were doing, Splendor?" he ranted quietly. "The orchards are none of your concern, damn it all, and I would appreciate it very much if you would leave the Amberville businesses to me."

"Percival will soon be begging you to buy the orchards from him, Jourdian, and when he does, ask no questions about why he wants to sell. But do haggle over the price. You will get those orchards back for much, much less than you originally thought to pay for them."

"I recall you telling me *not* to buy them several months ago. It was the day you had all those apples and berries inside your robe."

"Aye, I remember that day. But I have since thought of an answer to the problem with the orchards."

"What problem?"

"You will see. But Percival will see first. And then, when the orchards are yours, the problem will disappear."

Jourdian stared down at her. "Splendor, what—"

"Jourdian!"

He saw Marianna hurrying toward him. Bloody hell, would this night never end? "My sincerest apologies, Marianna, but I'm afraid we must leave your party and—"

"Leave? Why, I wouldn't hear of it." Giving him her most seductive smile, Marianna decided then that since she could not be his duchess, she would most certainly be his lover. Jourdian had been intensely attracted to her not so very long ago, and she felt sure she could recover his attentions if she set her mind to it. True, his bride was uncommonly beautiful, but the chit barely had a bosom to speak of.

And Marianna knew Jourdian preferred large breasts. She'd caught him staring at *her* well-endowed chest on numerous occasions.

"Don't you remember how you helped me slice my cake last year, Jourdian, darling?" she asked, stepping closer to him so she could press her bosom against the muscle in his arm. "Indulge me and help me again this year. Your assistance will be your birthday gift to me."

"I'll help you, Marianna," Percival offered, arriving by her side and reaching for her hand.

She yanked it away from him. "Splendor, dear, you don't mind if I borrow your husband for a bit, do you?"

"Aye, I do mind, Marianna."

Her words were stern, but Jourdian heard the pain in her voice. She thought him in love with Marianna, and Marianna's blatant advances did little to convince her otherwise.

But *he* could convince her. Convince her and every other person at the ball that he wanted nothing to do with any other woman.

Fully aware that everyone in the ballroom was watching with avid interest, he encircled one arm around Splendor's tiny waist and draped the other around her shoulders. Love was not among the feelings he had for her, he told himself, but whatever emotion he *did* possess for her would now be known to one and all.

He kissed her. Not sweetly, not gently, but with all the blazing passion of a man well and truly enchanted with his wife.

And Splendor returned the kiss with equal fervor, her every suspicion concerning Jourdian and Marianna melting away in the warm knowledge that her husband was hers alone.

Suddenly, she didn't want to be at the ball any longer. She had the information she'd come for, and now she wanted to be alone with her husband. "Let's go home, Jourdian," she whispered upon his lips.

He gave her one last, lingering kiss, then straightened to study the reactions his display of passion had created.

One glance at the sea of faces told him he had succeeded in his endeavors. The men were looking at him with a mixture of understanding and envy. And although the women pretended to be shocked, he could tell by the sparkle in their eyes that they thought the kiss terribly romantic.

As he had years before for Emil, he would now make it known to one and all that Splendor was to be welcomed into society's tight circle.

And deep in his heart, he knew that one day soon she would not only be accepted by the majority of the ton but that she would also be well liked. Very few people would be able to resist her genuine sweetness for long.

"My lady wife is weary," he said loudly enough for all to hear him. "But before we leave this gay affair, I should like to thank each of you for so kindly welcoming Lady Amberville into your midst. I shall not forget the actions I have witnessed here tonight, and I do assure you that my duchess and I anticipate other social assemblies and look forward to receiving all of you at future gatherings at Heathcourte."

Not a soul in the room missed his warning. He would tolerate not another malicious word about his bride. Splendor had his name, and she also had his protection.

The crowd parted as Jourdian led Splendor toward the doors that led out of the ballroom. "Get us home quickly before anyone notices we didn't arrive in a coach," he whispered.

"I cannot. There are people loitering in the foyer, and a myriad of servants outside."

"Bloody hell."

"I shall create a diversion." She curled her arm around her back, spread her fingers, and sent a spray of silver lights toward Percival Brackett.

A moment later, the man's turban fell to the floor. "Oh, dear God!" he shouted.

One collective gasp filled the ballroom as all eyes moved from the Ambervilles to Percival Brackett's hairless head.

"Percival!" Marianna shouted. "You've gone totally *bald*!"

Frantically, he tried to put the turban back on, but the headpiece had unraveled into one long piece of black silk. "Marianna, my love, I—"

"Your love?" Marianna shrieked. "I am not your love, nor am I your betrothed any longer! I wouldn't marry you now if my very life depended upon it!"

Percival reached for her and started to beg her to reconsider, but he stopped abruptly when he saw her face begin to change color. Bright red blotches crept over her cheeks, nose, and chin, the crimson stains a horrible contrast upon her porcelain skin. "Marianna, what has happened to your face? Dear God, I wouldn't marry you either!"

"My face? What's wrong with my face? Why is everyone staring at me? Mother? Mother?" Marianna screamed.

Lady Chesterton took one look at her daughter and swooned straight down to the marble floor.

"Splendor," Jourdian said, "now. Get us home *now*!"

"Aye." She threw a bit of silver into the air, and as she and Jourdian disappeared, she reflected on the fact that Tessie's face would no longer be stained with the red marks that had so embarrassed her.

And there was one vain noblewoman in England who would never show her face again.

23

J ourdian didn't bat an eye when he found himself in his bed, naked. The Chesterton ball, where he'd been only two seconds before, was now but a memory.

He turned to his side, fully expecting to see an equally naked Splendor beside him, but found her place in the bed cold and empty.

The room was almost totally dark, making it impossible to see. Jourdian rose, threw two logs onto the dying flames in the fireplace, and lit three lamps. When light flooded the bed-chamber, he spotted a woman standing in a spill of moonlight near the window.

But it wasn't Splendor. The woman had dark brown hair that fell just beyond her shoulders. A multitude of jewels glittered on her fingers, her wrists, her ears, and throat. Sapphires, emeralds, rubies, diamonds, amethysts . . . every gemstone he could think of.

She was naked, and Jourdian had never seen a woman with a bosom as large as hers. When she walked toward him, those heavy breasts swung from her chest like two large water-filled pouches.

She reached him swiftly and threw herself straight at him. Kissing him, she began to grind her hips into his.

"Bloody hell!" With one quick motion, Jourdian pushed her away. "Who are you?" he shouted.

"I am your wife."

Jourdian frowned. Her voice sounded just like Splendor's, but the hair, the huge breasts, all the hundreds of jewels . . .

How could this woman be Splendor?

How?

Magic, that was how.

"What the blazes have you done to your hair? And what the bloody hell are these?" He flicked a finger across each of her mammoth breasts.

"They are breasts."

"I *know* that, but whose are they?"

"They are mine."

He could not stop frowning. "They are *not* yours, and I want you to get rid of them this very instant!"

"Nay."

"Nay? What do you mean *nay?*" he roared.

"Nay means nay, and 'tis what I mean. Nay, I will not get rid of my new breasts."

"Damn it all, Splendor, I am your husband, and I am ordering you to put your other breasts back on!" God, he thought. Put her other breasts on? That sounded as if she had a whole closetful of breasts to pick and choose from, and it was the most preposterous thing he'd ever heard himself say!

"Jourdian—"

"And get your red hair back, too. Your long red hair, the same hair you've had since I met you. And for your information, you look like an overly decorated Christmas tree with all that glitter hanging all over you!"

Splendor felt a few tears trickle down her cheeks. The tiny diamonds made pinging sounds when they fell over the sapphires of her necklace. "I—I thought you liked brown hair, big breasts, and lots of jewelry."

As soon as her words floated into his ears, he realized why she'd changed her appearance.

"Marianna Chesterton," he whispered.

"You liked her. You courted her. Once upon a time, you considered wedding her. 'Tis why I wanted to attend the ball tonight, Jourdian. To see her. To find out what it was about her that—"

"I kissed you at the ball to show you that I didn't care about any other woman but you."

"Aye, that is what you did, husband, and you succeeded. I truly believe that you no longer have any feelings for Marianna. But the fact remains that you do not love me. I thought that if I could somehow please you more . . . If I could become better . . . When I saw Marianna's dark hair, her enormous breasts, and all her jewelry, I thought those things were what you liked. And I thought that if you were more satisfied with the way I looked, you . . . would be more inclined to love me."

Talking about love was the last thing in the world Jourdian wanted to do. "I was more than satisfied with the way you were, Splendor. Now put yourself right. Back the way you used to be before knowing Marianna."

Her silver stars of magic glittered as brightly as her tears as she changed herself into her original form. "Why can you not love me? What is it about me that keeps you from feeling the emotion for me?"

He hated the misery in her voice, hated her tears, and he hated himself for causing her such sorrow. Turning on his heel, he crossed to a small cabinet across the room and retrieved a full bottle of brandy.

He splashed a generous portion into a glass and drank the entire amount in one swallow. "I have given you everything I am willing to give, Splendor. You have my name, my wealth, my home . . . Isn't it enough that I care about you? That I'll protect you and see that no harm ever comes to you? Why must you have love, the one thing you cannot have?"

She turned toward the fire, watching the blaze twist and leap, and pondering the fact that Jourdian's love was the sole thing that could keep her with him forever. "Your love is far more valuable to me than anything else you have given me or ever could give to me, Jourdian," she murmured, still gazing into the fire. "I care naught about your esteemed title. Indeed, I would love you were you the poorest, most insignificant man in the world. And I do not care for your wealth or the magnificence of your home, nor do I need your protection. And although I am glad that you care about me, 'tis nay enough. I want your love, and can settle for nothing less."

"I think you can, Splendor. It's but a matter of becoming accustomed—"

"Nay!" She whirled away from the fire, her hair a blaze of shimmer as it swirled around her legs. "If I do not win your love, I shall be forced to return to Pillywiggin!"

Fury hotter than the fire flames made him throw his glass across the room. It hit the far wall, shattering.

He stalked to the fireplace and grabbed Splendor's shoulders. "Don't threaten me, Splendor, do you understand? You will not return to Pillywiggin. Not *ever*! You are my wife, the duchess of Heathcourte, and you will remain with me until one of us dies!"

Die, she thought. If she remained with him one second past the stroke of midnight tomorrow, she would die. But what was the use of telling him that her time with him had come to an end? Either he loved her, or he didn't. Telling him that she would be forced to leave him tomorrow night wouldn't change his feelings.

"I have failed," she whispered. "I love you, but I have not succeeded in—" She stopped speaking, a sudden and vital thought widening her eyes. "You do not realize the depth of my love, do you, Jourdian?"

"I—"

"I have never really proved how much I love you, have I? Perhaps you hesitate to allow yourself to love me because you have no reason to believe that my love is true! You have no proof—"

"Will you stop and listen to me?" Jourdian yelled. "You—"

"I shall show you! I shall sacrifice what is precious to me so you will know how much you mean to me!" Wild with the desperation to demonstrate the strength of her feelings for him, she spun around and lunged toward the cluster of iron fire tools that leaned against the wall near the fireplace.

Instantly realizing her intentions, Jourdian threw himself at her, grabbing her by the waist and pulling her away only seconds before her fingers touched the mass of iron. "Are you crazy?" he shouted, giving her no quarter when she tried to squirm free. "What the bloody hell were you thinking, Splendor? If you had touched that iron you would have lost all your powers!"

*Better the loss of my powers than the loss of my husband.*

She went limp in his arms then, a sense of defeat draining her of all strength, all hope, all will.

Quickly, Jourdian kissed her, knowing that if he did not she would dwindle. But while his kiss lent her the energy to remain human size, he saw immediately that her sorrow remained.

He lifted her into his arms and carried her to the bed. "Go to sleep now, Splendor," he whispered, laying her down on the mattress.

"Stay with me," she begged, her heart breaking at the knowledge that this would be her last night with him. "Here in our room. Please don't go to the other room you've been sleeping in, Jourdian. Please stay—"

"I will."

"Promise me."

"I promise."

She moved over to give him room.

He shook his head. "I'll join you in a while."

"But you promised—"

"I'll be right here, Splendor. I won't leave the room. Now go to sleep."

He crossed the room, retrieved the bottle of brandy and another glass, and sat down in a chair near the fire. Before he'd finished his first portion of the liquor, he saw that Splendor had fallen asleep.

He stared into the fire, knowing that if he watched the flames long enough he'd become mesmerized by them. He didn't want to think about Splendor right now, nor did he want to think about love. He simply wanted to sit by the fire in a mindless state.

But the swirling blazes in the hearth failed to entrance him the way they usually did. He could not keep himself from turning to gaze at the beautiful girl sleeping in his bed.

He made himself look out the window. There, in the night sky, he saw millions of glittering stars, and he wondered which ones belonged to him. They all looked the same to him, and he couldn't imagine which ones held his wishes.

But he knew Splendor would know.

Splendor. God, couldn't he cease thinking about her for a moment?

Shoving his fingers through his hair, he watched the fire again and forced himself to think about the work he would do tomorrow. He had to stay abreast of his investments if he was to maintain the power behind the name of Amberville.

Tomorrow he would begin preparations to build a shipyard in East Riding. He would also look over reports concerning a copper mine in Cornwall and an iron factory in Northampton.

*Iron.*

The metal could divest a fairy of her powers.

It was no use. He couldn't stop thinking about Splendor, no matter how hard he tried.

He returned to the bed.

Splendor was naked and uncovered. He had a mind to draw the blankets over her, but paused for a moment to gaze down at the whole of her loveliness.

The mellow firelight and soft candle glow played over her fragile body, making her skin look as though it were made of translucent pearls. Her thick copper curls appeared alive, seeming to move upon her pale flesh and the dark blue satin coverlet. Like flames, like happy, waltzing flames were those fiery red tresses, and Jourdian felt that if he reached out to touch them, their heat would sear his fingertips.

He settled his gaze upon her eyes. They were closed now, her auburn lashes like tiny, upside down fans lying upon the crests of her exquisite cheekbones. But he saw those eyes clearly. In his mind, he did. Violets were what they looked like, and yet violets didn't dance like Splendor's eyes. Nor did they shine.

How Splendor's eyes shone. With her happiness, and with diamonds when she was sad.

She moved her lips then, almost into a dainty smile, and a bit of breath whispered forth, and then another. Jourdian listened to the small sounds.

And he remembered all the nights he'd felt those sleepy

sighs warm his chest and shoulders while she'd slept beside him.

God, she was so graceful—even while doing nothing but lying on the bed. She was fragile perfection, and for a moment he was certain that if he laid his hand upon her, she would splinter into millions of broken stars that could never be put back together again.

But she was made of stronger stuff, he knew. Proof of that was that she'd survived three months of his temper. Of his cold and domineering demeanor.

Guilt and regret weighed heavily upon his shoulders, and he felt suddenly weary. He lay down beside Splendor, gently, carefully, so as not to rouse her from whatever peace she'd found in her dreams, and he gathered her near, close to his chest, wondering if she could hear how hard his heart was beating.

He buried his face in her hair. Her scent of wildflowers, fresh and too sweet to describe, soothed him and wrapped around him like an embrace. He memorized the fragrance, burned it into his memory so deeply that he would never forget it.

Something hard and small pressed into his cheek. Lifting his face slightly, he saw diamonds scattered all over the mattress where he lay and realized she'd wept before falling asleep.

He kissed her neck, her throat, and finally her lips.

*Splendor*, he told her without words.

*Splendor.*

And the beautiful softness of her name lulled him to sleep.

❧

When Jourdian left his chambers the next morning, he spied Mrs. Frawley a short way down the corridor. "Lady Amberville is still asleep," he told the housekeeper, "and I do not want her disturbed."

"Is she ill, Your Grace?"

The genuine expression of worry and concern in Mrs.

Frawley's eyes made Jourdian smile. "No, Mrs. Frawley, she's not ill. She's simply tired."

Downstairs, Jourdian declined breakfast and went straight to work in his office. He might not have been able to concentrate on business last night, but he wasn't willing to allow the same thing to happen today. And without Splendor distracting him, he felt certain he could get much work done.

He drew up plans to build the shipyard in East Riding and another in Northumberland. He also studied the reports concerning the copper mine in Cornwall, mulled over the possibility of acquiring a textile factory in Manchester, and then read the correspondence regarding the businesses and property he already owned.

With the exception of Ulmstead's arrival with a bit of lunch, he worked undisturbed. The afternoon wore on, turned into evening, and he didn't realize how long he'd been laboring over his enterprises until a knock at his office door caused him to look up and glance at the clock on the fireplace mantel.

It was half past nine.

Immediately, he wondered where Splendor was and what she'd done all day. A vague sense of concern began to prick at him.

The knock at the door sounded again.

"Come!"

Ulmstead entered with a beaver in his arms. The creature was gnawing happily upon a button on Ulmstead's coat. "Forgive me for interrupting your work, Your Grace, but Lord Brackett has arrived demanding a meeting with you. He says he has urgent business to discuss and that it cannot wait. It concerns orchards in Gloucester."

"Where is Lady Amberville? I haven't seen her since this morning."

Ulmstead raised an eyebrow and his chin. "You have given all of us strict instructions not to disturb you while you are working, Your Grace. The duchess has complied."

Jourdian detected a bitter note in Ulmstead's voice and understood that his loyal butler was angry at him for ignoring Splendor. "Send Lord Brackett in, and tell Lady Amberville that I will join her for a late dinner as soon as my meeting is over," he snapped.

"At once, your lordship."

A few moments later, Percival walked into the office, his black turban wrapped firmly around his bald head. "Heathcourte, I am prepared to sell you the orchards, and I should like to complete the sale this very night."

"I see." Splendor had been right, Jourdian mused. Just as she'd said, Percival was in a great hurry to sell the fruit fields. Why, Jourdian didn't know, but he was prepared to trust his wife's advice to buy them cheaply. "Let's begin then, shall we, Bramwell?"

Intent on getting as much money as possible for the orchards, Percival argued over the price for what seemed like several eternities to Jourdian.

Jourdian stood firm, however, and Percival finally accepted less than a fourth of what he'd paid for the fruit fields. He signed all the necessary papers swiftly. "My mistake has just become yours, Heathcourte." He folded his copy of the sale and slipped it into his pocket. "The orchards are worthless."

Jourdian was stunned. "What do you mean they're worthless?"

Percival smiled. "Grasshoppers, I'm afraid. A plague of them. Hardy little devils, I must say. They're not at all bothered by the cold. This morning I received word of their arrival, which is why I hurried to complete this bit of business with you."

Jourdian couldn't, *wouldn't* believe that Splendor had led him to make a mistake. She'd told him to buy the orchards, and he had.

The fields weren't worthless. Somehow they would not only survive the ravaging grasshoppers but they would thrive. "The orchards aren't worthless," he said confidently. "You just sold me a fortune for a pittance."

*"What?"*

Another glance at the clock told Jourdian it was almost eleven o'clock. He hadn't seen Splendor all day.

And he missed her.

He crossed to the door. "See yourself out, Bramwell."

⊷⊶⊷⊶⊷⊶

Jourdian cursed himself for not heeding his earlier sense of concern regarding Splendor's whereabouts. After leaving Percival in the office, he'd begun looking for his duchess, to no avail. And his staff had not a clue as to where she'd gone.

Deep foreboding coursed through him. The hour was eleven-thirty. It wasn't like Splendor to be gone so late. His feeling of dread rising, he left the house. Perhaps if he rode around the estate, he would find her rambling about in the snow. Or, since she was a fairy, maybe he'd find her talking to Old Man Winter.

He started for the barns, but before he reached them, a horse galloped up the driveway. "Jourdian!"

Jourdian watched his cousin leap off the horse and race toward him. "Emil, what—"

"Splendor," Emil panted. "She— she—"

"What? What about her?" Jourdian shouted, his dread deepening to real fear.

"Three months," Emil said, his shoulders heaving with exertion. "After that, they die. Love— She didn't get love, and now she—"

"What the bloody hell are you talking about, Emil?" Jourdian demanded. He grabbed his cousin's shoulders and shook him.

"Time," Emil said, trying desperately to catch his breath. "What time is it? Midnight. She leaves at midnight, Jourdian! Is it midnight?"

"Almost! But what in God's name—"

"Fairies!" Emil snatched Jourdian's hands off his shoulders. "Harmony told me the story before she left for Pillywiggin a short while ago— Splendor's going back— The fairies are all assembled to welcome her . . . Fairies can't survive . . . Splendor's time has come to an end! Damn you for a cad, Jourdian! If you had given her your love, she would have been able to stay here with you forever!"

Wild with rage, Emil drew back his fist and delivered a powerful blow to Jourdian's chin.

Unprepared for the assault, Jourdian fell to the snow-covered ground. Pain and deeper confusion exploded through him.

"She loved you, Jourdian!" Emil blasted out. "And she begged you to love her back! Harmony told me everything!"

Jourdian struggled to his feet and wiped at the bloody cut at the corner of his mouth. Yanking out his watch, he saw that it was eleven-forty. He still didn't understand Emil's twisted, tangled story about love, Splendor, and her midnight return to Pillywiggin, but he did know that he had only twenty minutes to find her.

He bolted toward Emil's horse, pulled himself into the saddle, and sent the tired steed back down the driveway.

The woods, he thought. The woods near the meadow where he'd met her. Hadn't Splendor once told him that her father's kingdom lay beneath the floor of that forest?

Yes.

Jourdian sent his mount into a thundering gallop toward the thicket. Snow and sharp pieces of ice bit into his face and neck, but he ignored the sting, the frigid wind, and the very real possibility that he might not find Splendor.

Finally, he caught sight of the woods and saw a bright light moving within the coal-black shadows. "Splendor!"

As the horse raced closer to the forest, the light became more vivid, and after a few more seconds it was so bright that Jourdian could no longer look at it. Shielding his eyes from its blinding severity, he slowed his mount to a halt and leaped to the ground. "Splendor!"

"I am here, Jourdian."

He lowered his hands from his eyes so he could see her, but the dazzling light in the woods was simply too intense to behold. "I can't see you! The light's too bright!"

Instantly, Splendor draped her long, thick hair over the basket she held. "There. 'Tis not as fierce now."

Blinking, Jourdian directed his gaze toward the sound of her voice and saw her. As he looked at her, he realized that the blazing light he'd seen lay within the basket that swayed from her hands.

Snow, ice, and frozen twigs crunching beneath his boots, he ran toward her. "Why are you returning to Pillywiggin?" he shouted, grasping her bare shoulders. "What is this about leaving at midnight?"

"If I do not return, I shall die," she answered quietly, but her voice trembled.

"Die?" His hands fell from her shoulders and dangled at his sides. "What do you mean, you'll die?"

Splendor nodded, then touched her fingers to the cut on his lip. The wound vanished. "A fairy can remain in the human world but three months. My three months are over at midnight. If I stay longer, I shall perish. The one thing that can keep me here . . . keep me alive and well is the magic of human love, for 'tis a magic far greater than any known in Faerie."

Jourdian tried to swallow, but couldn't.

*Die.*

*Die.*

*Die.*

"Why didn't you tell me?" he shouted. "Why, damn it all? Why?"

" 'Twould nay have made you love me, Jourdian. And when I first came to you three months ago, I did not know I would want to stay. I did not imagine I would fall in love with you. 'Twas not my intention to love you, but when I realized that the one thing you lacked in your life was love, that became the one thing I wanted to give you. In my ignorance, I failed to understand that once I loved you I would nay want to leave you."

When he didn't reply, she sought to fill the tense silence. "Look what I have been gathering," she murmured, holding up her basket. "One by one, all your wishing stars were falling from the sky. But I have found them all."

"I don't want to talk about a damn lot of stars! You're not going anywhere tonight, do you hear me? I won't let you!"

" 'Tis almost midnight," she whispered. "Already I feel a pull toward Pillywiggin."

He wrapped his arms around her, thinking to overpower the tug she felt toward her father's kingdom.

"The strength of your body cannot keep me here, Jourdian," Splendor told him softly. "Only the strength in your heart is mightier than the force of Faerie."

The frosty wind whipped around his body, but he began to perspire. "Splendor," he said, his voice but a hoarse whisper, "try to stay. Fight this—"

"I cannot."

"Yes, you can, damn it all! They can't take you away from me, no matter what they—"

"I must go," she breathed into his ear. " 'Tis time."

He saw specks of glittering silver begin to appear around her, circling her. With one hand, he tried to swat them all away, but more appeared.

And Splendor began to fade.

"Do you love me, Jourdian?"

A myriad of emotions twisted through Jourdian's heart, each vying for his full attention. But he could hardly separate them, much less define them.

"Jourdian?"

"Don't leave me, Splendor." He tried to hold her tighter, but her body lost its substance and she became but an image in his arms.

"I love you," she whispered, her tears falling so quickly that Jourdian's entire shoulder was covered with the diamond bits. "Never forget how much I love you."

The silver magic lifted her out of his embrace and carried her closer to the woods.

"Splendor!"

She didn't answer.

He watched her move her hair away from the basket and draw forth his wishes. She held them toward the sky, and their searing brilliance forced him to turn away.

When he looked back again, Splendor was gone.

The only evidence that she had even existed was a pool of diamonds and an empty basket lying upon a drift of moon-silvered snow.

**24**

A shout caused Jourdian to growl with irritation. Shifting, he sought the comfort of sleep again. The shout came closer, became louder. Jourdian finally opened his eyes, only to have them pierced by bright shards of late morning sunshine that stabbed through a solid wall of windows. He head throbbed; his stomach rolled.

What the hell was the matter with him, and where the hell was he?

Glancing around, he realized he was in the conservatory, lying on the floor amidst a veritable jungle of plants and flowers. Two empty bourbon bottles lay beside him, and he understood he'd drunk himself into a stupor.

He took a slow, deep breath, careful not to move his aching head while he tried to remember what terrible thing had driven him to drink. But no memory would come to his liquor-drenched mind.

"Jourdian!"

Recognizing the shout as belonging to Emil, Jourdian staggered to his feet, holding his head and resisting the wave of nausea that flooded his insides. Out of the corner of his eye, he saw Emil storm into the room.

Emil took one look at his cousin and stopped short. Anger made him want to hit his cousin harder than he had the night before. "Have you been here all night?" he yelled. "Your staff and I have been looking for you since dawn!"

"Emil, please," Jourdian entreated, closing his eyes and leaning against the wall. "Cease that shouting. I feel as though I have been run over by an entire herd of elephants. Be a good chap and fetch Splendor, will you? One touch from her, and I'll be right again."

"Splendor's not here, Jourdian. Did you drink so much that you erased last night from your mind?"

Jourdian tried to understand what his cousin was talking about, but no thoughts could get through the pain in his head. "What about last night?" he muttered, rubbing his throbbing temples.

If he had thought it would have done a bit of good, Emil would have thrashed Jourdian within an inch of his life. "She left you. She had to, don't you remember? She could stay here for only three months without your loving her. You chose not to love her, so she returned to Pillywiggin."

A long moment passed before Emil's words permeated Jourdian's foggy brain, but when comprehension finally came to him, it arrived like a sudden clap of thunder.

He jerked himself away from the wall, wide awake now. "Splendor—"

"You're a cad."

Gone, Jourdian thought. Splendor was really and truly gone.

Guilt ate at him, leaving a huge gaping hole of emptiness inside him.

But no one, not even Emil, would know the extent of his torment.

"As thick as a plank cad, Jourdian!"

"She should have told me, damn it all. She knew she could only stay for three months, but she failed to tell—"

"What does that matter now?"

His head reeling, Jourdian started to leave the room.

Emil grabbed his arm. "How could you? All she needed was your love—"

"Love isn't something that can be turned on and off like a machine!"

"Didn't you feel anything at all for her?" Emil demanded.

"I cared about her. But that's not love, and there you have it."

"You *didn't* love her, or you *wouldn't* love her?" Emil returned coldly.

Jourdian straightened to his full height, ignoring the sharp pain in his head, and trying his damnedest to conceal the ache in his heart. "One can make oneself do many things. If I must, I can make myself smile when I don't feel like smiling. I can eat when I'm not hungry, and I can force myself to read and comprehend literature that is a thundering bore. But I cannot make myself love! Either I love or I don't, and that is the end of this—"

"Splendor," Emil said softly. "She granted every wish you've ever had."

"That's tosh. She—"

"It isn't tosh, and you know it."

Jourdian didn't care for the knowing look he saw in Emil's topaz eyes. "When did you hear me wish for a woman who shrinks when deprived of a few blasted kisses? Who must hide from a cat for fear of it eating her for dinner! Who gets swallowed up by a cloud of mist when her feelings are hurt? When did you ever hear me wish for a *fairy* wife!"

Emil could hold back his temper no longer. He shoved Jourdian's shoulder with all his might. "Splendor's being a fairy ceased to bother you weeks ago! You hated being so lonely, and when she got here you weren't lonely anymore! You wanted someone to understand you, to listen to you, and comfort you, and Splendor did all that and more!"

"You—"

"And you wanted a wife who would love you for who you are inside. A wife who would love Jourdian Amberville, *not* the powerful and wealthy duke of Heathcourte. Splendor loved the man. Not the duke."

Again, Jourdian started for the door.

Emil barred the way. "Those wishes of yours all came true, Jourdian, but there remain a few that haven't. What man doesn't wish to be happy until the day he dies? What man doesn't wish for a lifelong partner who will love him forever?

You should have taken heed of those wishes while Splendor was still here, cousin. They'll never be granted now because the woman who tried to grant them for you is gone, and she's never coming back!"

Stiffly, Jourdian walked around Emil and through the doorway.

Emil followed. "You resisted your feelings for her, Jourdian. It was your own bloody pride that kept you from allowing your emotions free rein. Your pride and your fear!"

At that, Jourdian stopped. "Fear?" he shouted.

"Yes, fear! You're afraid the same thing will happen to you as happened to your father! He almost lost everything, and you—"

"I'm warning you now, Emil—"

"Splendor never had a chance to win your love, did she? You couldn't love her because to do so would have meant risking everything you've worked so hard to attain. The strength behind your name. The might behind your wealth. The power behind your title. Those things mean more to you than the beautiful woman who blew into your life and made you smile. Who made you laugh, and who offered you her love with both hands. You aren't a cad, Jourdian. A cad, at least, is a living, breathing person. You're naught but ice. A finely chiseled block of ice."

Emil pulled back his shoulders. "Now, if you will excuse me, I am leaving to go be with my wife. A pity you cannot say and do the same."

With that, Emil disappeared down the hall.

❦

During the weeks that followed Splendor's return to Faerie, Jourdian barely ate. Barely slept.

He worked. He set the business world on fire, and within a month he knew that not only was the Amberville fortune the most impressive in England but that it was also one of the largest in Europe.

He refused to discuss Splendor with anyone, and by working as hard as he was, he succeeded in keeping himself from
thinking about her. If a thought about her did manage to creep
into his mind, he quickly buried it.

He would forget her, he swore. The three months he'd
spent with her were over. And the memories of those months
were dead.

Until a letter from Gloucester arrived and resurrected them.

The orchards were saved from devastation and would make
a strong and speedy recovery, the overseer of the fields had
written. Out of nowhere an enormous flock of birds had arrived, and the thousands of feathered creatures had neatly and
swiftly consumed every last grasshopper on every last fruit tree.

The overseer added that in all his years of experience, he
had never witnessed such a strange occurrence as the sudden
and timely arrival of the birds, which were not of the same
variety, but of dozens of different species. He called it a miracle.

Jourdian called it magic. Only a fairy could have talked a
huge flock of various birds into doing her bidding.

He felt something open inside him. His heart. And out of it
burst all the memories and emotions he'd entombed there.

Damn it all, why did the blasted letter have to come? He'd
been fine before its arrival! Absolutely and totally fine!

And now he wasn't fine. Now he had memories to deal
with. To somehow bury again.

Laying the letter aside, he rose from his desk chair, pushed
his hands into his pockets, and ambled to the window. Rain
splattered against the pane.

*There are some who believe rain has no color . . . Rain is
silver and iridescent. Your eyes are such a silver.*

Jourdian pressed his warm forehead against the cold pane.
Long moments later when he lifted his head, the rain had
stopped, and he saw a rainbow in the March sky.

*I don't suppose you have ever slid down a rainbow, have you,
Jourdian?*

Splendor. Her name shimmered through him like a handful
of glitter. Even after her return to Pillywiggin without his love,

she continued to watch over him. She'd saved his orchards from certain ruination.

Jourdian turned from the window and glanced at the chair that sat across from his desk. How many times had Splendor sat in that chair watching him work?

*I could never grow weary of watching you.*

The chair was empty now.

Stacks and stacks of business reports sat upon the desk, each paper signifying wealth. Wealth. And more wealth.

Well, he'd worked hard to earn that wealth! And he had every right to be proud of his accomplishments!

But money didn't know what he was going to say before he spoke. It didn't rejoice with him when he was happy, didn't shed tears when he was sad, and it was never concerned when he worried.

For the first time in weeks, Jourdian left a pile of unfinished work on his desk. His hands still in his pockets, he walked out his office and down the corridor. Turning, he traveled down another long hall, at the end of which was one of the mansion's drawing rooms.

Splendor had become his wife in that room. He stopped, looked into the room, and remembered all the flowers that had decorated the parlor that day. Ulmstead had caught a rooster beneath one of the tables, and Mrs. Frawley had fainted.

Splendor had worn a silk shirt.

*I take you for my husband, and I shall endeavor to gift you with laughter and joy every day that I am with you.*

His head hung low, Jourdian walked into the foyer and up the grand staircase. Upstairs he headed toward his room. His and Splendor's room.

But before he arrived, he saw Tessie exit another room down the hall. The maid held a few folded sheets in one arm, and from her other arm dangled a basket.

"Your Grace," she murmured in greeting.

As he neared her, he thought about how pretty she was. Her red birthmarks had concealed her beauty, but now, thanks to Splendor, Tessie's loveliness shone forth.

"Is there anything I can do for you, your lordship?" Tessie asked.

Jourdian noticed how difficult it was for her to be civil to him. The rest of the staff forced politeness in the same manner. They all missed Splendor, and all they knew about her was what he'd told them—that she'd had to return to her family.

But they sensed that he'd had *something* to do with her departure.

"Lord Amberville?" Tessie pressed.

"No. I don't need anything." He started to open the door to his bedroom, but stopped when he saw the basket swaying from the crook of her elbow. He hadn't seen it clearly before, but he did now.

It was the same basket Splendor had held the night she'd left him. The basket that had held all the brilliant stars.

"Where did you get that basket, Tessie?"

She looked down at it. "One of the gardeners found it in the conservatory, Your Grace. He was going to throw it away, but I asked him if I could keep it."

Jourdian's fingers ached to touch the basket. "It belonged to the duchess. Would you mind if I kept it instead? I'll see to it that it's replaced by ten more."

Nodding, Tessie gave him the basket, then returned to her duties.

Basket in hand, Jourdian turned the doorknob to his bedchambers. He hadn't been in the room since Splendor left. Hadn't let himself even venture near it.

The door opened. He stepped inside.

Like a powerful gust of wind, more memories blasted into him. Standing on the threshold, he stared at every part of the room, remembering all the plants that had once grown from the furniture and walls; remembering how each thing in the room, even the ceiling and walls, had once been red, blue, or green; remembering finding Lady Macbeth in his bath; remembering . . .

Remembering.

He closed the door and walked to the large closet. There he saw his purple satin dressing robe. Lifting the luxurious garment to his face, he inhaled its scent, hoping desperately to detect Splendor's fragrance.

But the robe had been laundered. It smelled of soap, not wildflowers.

He tossed the robe back into the closet and approached the bed. With a trembling hand, he reached down and touched the midnight blue satin coverlet. "Your body was so beautiful upon this blue," he whispered to her memory. "Your skin on the blue . . . like a cloud in the sky."

He glanced at the mound of pillows on the left side of the bed, Splendor's side. She'd lain upon those pillows with her glorious copper hair spread all over the snow-white satin pillow cases.

How many times had he loved her on this bed? He couldn't recall, couldn't count.

Looking up, he stared at the ceiling, pondering all the occasions when he and Splendor had floated around the room just as a session of lovemaking had ended. With Splendor's music accompanying them.

He would never drift around the room again. Would never hear that joyous music again.

All the magic was gone.

Because Splendor was gone.

*Jourdian, the short time that I have been with you means more to me than all the years I lived without you.*

Jourdian tried to swallow. But he couldn't.

His heart was in his throat.

He set the basket on the bed and lay down beside it. Loneliness crept through him.

*I am being your company because one of the things that I think will make you smile is not being lonely anymore.*

"Make me smile again, Splendor," he whispered.

*You are in dire need of frequent admonishments.*

God, he thought. What he wouldn't do to hear her chide him over his uncivil streak just one more time.

For hours he lay there, recalling everything he could about Splendor.

She'd slept on top of a canopy once. She wouldn't eat animal. She wouldn't wear her wings because cleaning them was a tedious chore. She wouldn't wear jewelry, but she didn't need it. Weren't her lavender eyes the most beautiful jewels in all the world?

She talked to and understood animals and plants, and was worried about the sick chrysanthemums in front of the manor. Once, she'd thought sensual pleasure came from his leg. She knew every plant that grew on his estate, and knew also exactly where they grew. All the wood violets, foxglove, periwinkle, snowdrops . . .

He couldn't remember the rest of the plants she'd mentioned. She'd tried to tell him, but he hadn't listened.

She liked hens and rabbits, but not cats. Kissing made her strong. Sorrow made her disappear. She cried diamonds.

She'd traveled all the way to China to retrieve one of his wishing stars. She'd knitted him a pair of mittens with her own hands.

Jourdian squinted his eyes; he couldn't see the canopy anymore, for the room had grown dark. He looked toward the windows and saw that nighttime had settled over the countryside.

Stars glimmered in the sky.

*Stars.*

Slowly, he pulled the basket closer to his body, and he ran his fingers over its woven handle. A month ago this very same basket had contained stars. His wishing stars.

The night she'd left, Splendor had held a basket of wishes.

Jourdian frowned then, another memory coming to him. Months before he'd been terribly frustrated and angry over not having a duchess. He'd thought that finding the perfect wife should have been as effortless a goal to accomplish as any and all he'd ever undertaken.

And he'd told himself that finding a basket of wishes would have been far easier.

A basket of wishes, he mused miserably. He'd not only found a basket of wishes, he'd found the perfect wife.

And he'd let her go.

"I'm sorry," he whispered brokenly. "Splendor, I'm so sorry."

*Would you like for me to try to make you laugh again, My Grace?*

"Yes," he murmured. "Yes, Splendor, make me laugh."

But he didn't laugh, and he wondered if he would ever again.

For a solid month, he hadn't allowed himself to admit that he'd missed her. Now, his confession spilled forth on a rumbling groan. "God, I miss you, sprite."

*Your love is far more valuable to me than anything else you have given me or ever could give to me, Jourdian. Indeed, I would love you were you the poorest, most insignificant man in the world.*

Jourdian looked across the room and spied the cluster of iron fire tools leaning against the wall.

*You do not realize the depth of my love, do you, Jourdian? I shall show you! I shall sacrifice what is precious to me so you will know how much you mean to me!*

In his mind, he saw her. Saw Splendor lunging toward the iron tools. "No!" he shouted.

God, he thought. Not only did he "hear" her, he "saw" her as well.

Shoving his fingers through his hair, he rose from the bed and trudged across the dark room, the basket dangling from his hand. Moonlight splashed through the window, and the pool of silver light beckoned him. When he arrived at the window, he saw the stars again. Among them were *his* stars. Splendor had placed them back in the sky, and he knew she continued to guard them.

So they would all come true.

"But they haven't," he whispered. "They haven't come true. I want to be happy, and I'm not. Not without you."

He hugged the basket to his chest.

And he wept.

He didn't try to stop. He felt no shame. He only felt sorrow, and he didn't think it an unmanly thing to grieve. After all he'd lost his wife. What man wouldn't mourn such a loss?

He watched his tears slip into the basket, and finally, after all the long years, he began to comprehend his father's torment after Isabel's passing. His sire had loved his wife. And her death had destroyed him.

Jourdian knew the extent of that anguish now. Understood the agony of losing . . .

Of losing . . .

The thought faded away in his mind unfinished.

Jourdian raised his head and looked out the window again, deliberating just as intently as the stars were shining.

Barrington had mourned Isabel's death.

Death.

Splendor wasn't dead. She was alive in Pillywiggin.

And at that moment, Jourdian knew how he could get her back.

The power of Faerie was strong.

But he knew of a magic much stronger.

**B**efore Magnus came to a complete stop at the edge of the forest, Jourdian leaped off the stallion's back. He fled into the black woods ahead, instantly blinded by the darkness. Shivering with apprehension and cold, he eased his pace and forced to mind every notion he'd ever heard about the Wee Folk.

"Fairy ring," he whispered.

Eyes cast to the shadowed forest floor, he searched for evidence of a glowing circle. Long moments passed; his brow began to bead with the sweat of desperation, and a tinge of hopelessness slowed the frantic beat of his heart.

"Splendor," he called, his voice barely louder than the drifting of a cloud.

He saw nothing. Heard nothing.

"Splendor!" He called her name over and over again, his shout eating up the peace of the silent woods.

Finally, after what seemed like hours, he perceived eerie changes occurring all around him. The cool night breeze warmed as if heated by sunbeams of high noon. The rustling of the oak, birch, and elder branches became almost musical, a soft, stirring melody that sounded like hundreds of flutes playing in harmony.

And Jourdian saw lights. Among the mist-dampened leaves, the sparkles swirled in a small, perfect circle.

They were here. They'd come.

The fairies.

"What do you hope to gain by coming here, Trinity?" a small male voice sang out.

Jourdian crouched lower to the ground, straining to see if Splendor was among the fairies. He saw nothing but leaping shimmers of light.

"Speak now, Trinity!" the voice demanded.

The authority Jourdian heard in the small voice assured him that it was Splendor's father, the King of Pillywiggin, who spoke to him. "I've come for your daughter."

"Leave this place!"

"No."

"Do you dare to refuse me?"

Jourdian realized the danger he was in. The power of Faerie was not to be taken lightly.

But neither was his own power, the magic with which he would win Splendor back.

He stood and glared down at the lights on the ground. "Meet me face-to-face, and don't tell me you cannot, for I know full well that you can!"

The ring remained on the ground, the fairies remained too small to see.

"I want to see Splendor, damn it all!"

He saw the sparkles come together on the dark ground to form one large ball of gleam, and he realized the Little People were discussing his demand. Silence ensued, and then the lights separated once more.

"You will see me first, Trinity!" the voice declared.

Jourdian stepped back as a burst of silver stars erupted from the ground. The glitter faded quickly, revealing a host of naked human-size fairies.

But Splendor was not among them.

"Which of you is Splendor's father?" Jourdian asked loudly.

A very round male fairy glided out of the throng of others, his long white beard flowing down the length of his body. "I am King Wisdom."

Jourdian wasted no time with niceties. "Where is Splendor?"

"You cannot have her back. Now leave this place."

Jourdian neared the fairy king, his face set in tight lines of determination. "I *will* have her back, and I won't leave without her."

"Oh?" The king lifted a snowy eyebrow. "And just how do you propose to get her back?"

Jourdian met the king's smug gaze squarely. "With magic."

At that, the king threw back his head and laughed. Many of the other fairies laughed as well, the resulting sound like a cluster of ringing bells.

"Magic?" King Wisdom repeated, still chuckling. "What is this magic you have, human?"

Jourdian smiled. "A magic far greater than yours, Your Majesty. Love."

Intense quiet fell over the assembly of fairies . . . until a voice Jourdian knew and loved broke the silence.

"Jourdian!"

He saw her rise above the crowd of her subjects. "Splendor!"

She flew toward him, straight into his open arms.

He crushed her to him, her delicate scent of wildflowers surrounding him like a profound pleasure unseen. "I had to come for you," he murmured down to her, his hand stroking her copper hair.

Diamonds streaming from her eyes, she waited for his next words, hope filling every corner of her heart.

"Splendor," Jourdian said, "I tried to forget, sprite. Work. I've worked like a madman every day since you left. I haven't slept for fear of dreaming of you. I—"

"Jourdian, cease this chatter," she chided.

He smiled broadly. "I love you, Splendor. My beautiful, happy, magical Splendor, I love you."

He kissed her then, a kiss so full of his love that Splendor began to shine like a star.

"Hold!" King Wisdom thundered.

The kiss ended instantly.

"How can I be certain you love my daughter?" the king demanded. "Your declaration means naught to me, Trinity. You must prove your feelings before I will believe they exist."

Jourdian gave a stiff nod. "Send Splendor back with me,

and after a three-month period of time you will find her alive and well, thriving on the love I have for her."

King Wisdom shook his head. "That I will not do. You have already had three months with my daughter, and I shall nay grant you any more time. Moreover, Splendor is the princess royal of Pillywiggin. Her place is here, in the kingdom she will one day rule."

"Father, please," Splendor murmured.

Jourdian tightened his hold on her. Defeat tried to come to him, but he refused to give in to it. There had to be some way to convince the fairy king of his love for Splendor.

And then it came to him. The answer.

Splendor had been willing to sacrifice her magic for him.

Now he would show what he was willing to sacrifice for *her*.

"I will give up everything I own," he announced, his voice ringing loudly and clearly through the cool, dark woods. "My estate, my fortune . . . I will relinquish my place in the human world for Splendor." He paused for a moment, his next words coming straight from his heart. "Your Majesty, I will give up my own title so that she may retain hers."

Splendor gasped. "Jourdian, you cannot—"

"I can," he cut off her protest. "And I will."

The rustle of the leaves was the only sound that could be heard as every gaze rested on the king, and all waited to hear his response.

The king stared at Jourdian. "You love her," he whispered. "You truly love her."

"I do," came Jourdian's quick reply.

The king rubbed his beard, and meditated for a very long while. His daughter had won the love of a human! he mused. How many fairies had ever accomplished such a feat? "I suppose then," he began, his mouth quirking into a small smile, "that you may come to live in Pillywiggin, Trinity, for I will nay have it written in the history of Faerie that I, King Wisdom, stood in the way of love."

A deafening shout went up as all the fairies cheered.

"Nay!" Splendor yelled, her voice rising above the din. "Nay, Father, I will not accept these terms! I cannot allow

Jourdian to lose what has taken him years to build! I will live with him at Heathcourte with or without your permission!"

The king gawked at his daughter, taken aback by her anger and assertiveness. How could this be? Splendor embodied the very essence of kindness and gentleness! He'd never seen this side of her before, and could only imagine that she'd learned to be bold while in the human world.

He liked her this way.

But even so, he couldn't allow her to live among humans. And what of the child she carried? The babe was vitally needed in Pillywiggin. "You are heiress to the throne of Pillywiggin, daughter, and as such you must embrace your obligations—"

He broke off when a tremendous burst of silver stars descended from the sky and settled over the woods. From within the bright magic Harmony stepped out, her fingers curled around Emil's arm. She and Emil took one look at Jourdian and Splendor, and knew exactly what had happened.

"Harmony?" the king queried. "Is that you?"

"Aye, Father, 'tis I."

"But—but where is your fire, daughter? I have never seen you come or go without your explosion of blazes. And who is this man you have brought?"

"Father," Harmony murmured, looking around at Pillywiggin's peers, "I did not know I would be interrupting an assembly. Please forgive me."

King Wisdom scowled. Was this polite, soft-spoken fairy really Harmony?

"May I speak?" Harmony asked him.

"What? Uh . . . Aye."

"I have married," she announced quietly, her fingers clutching Emil's arm. "The Trinity's cousin is my husband."

"*What?*" King Wisdom roared.

"This is Emil, Father. He is my husband."

"A pleasure to meet you, Your Majesty," Emil said. "Or may I call you Father?"

The king had never known such rage. "You have married without my permission?" he demanded of Harmony.

"I love Emil, and he loves me. Therefore, I am at liberty to stay in the human world."

"You are at liberty to do *naught* without my leave, daughter!"

"I have conceived, Father," Harmony continued calmly, not about to allow him to destroy the joy she'd found with Emil. "I carry not one child but two, a boy and a girl."

At that, the king's fury vanished. "Twins?"

"Aye."

King Wisdom stared at Harmony and Emil, then at Splendor and Jourdian. What was he to do? he asked himself.

Oh, the trials of fatherhood, he lamented. And without his wife to help him, either! Always off on one of her missions, the queen was rarely available when daughter problems arose.

Massaging the back of his neck, he began to pace, but a sweet and feminine voice soon stopped him.

"Wisdom!" the musical voice called.

He looked up and saw a bright silver cloud. "Pleasure," he whispered.

The queen floated gracefully down to earth, her thick ebony hair cloaking her pale, slender body, her heavy necklace shining like pearls.

"Mother!" Splendor and Harmony cried. Quickly they left their husbands, joined their mother, and began talking at once.

"Daughters, please," Queen Pleasure entreated. "I have only just returned from my lengthy mission, and I am weary."

But at the crestfallen looks on Splendor and Harmony's faces, she relented. "Very well," she said, smiling and caressing her daughters' smooth cheeks. "What is this all-important news you have?"

They explained everything that had occurred in the forest that evening, leaving out not a single detail.

"I see," Queen Pleasure murmured thoughtfully when they'd finished. "Wisdom," she snapped, glaring at her husband, "you are not living up to your name. 'Tis a simple problem to solve, and yet you have failed to see the solution that is right beneath your nose!"

"I . . . I have done the best I— Your daughters are—

These are women problems they have presented, Pleasure, and I am . . ." He stopped speaking, frowned, and raised his chin. "Madam, you will nay speak to me thus!" he declared imperiously. "I am *king*, and you are only *queen*!"

"And an arrogant one you are, too, Wisdom." Queen Pleasure dismissed his anger with a smile and a wave of her hand. Her heavy necklace swaying upon her bare chest, she looked at the man Harmony had married. "Would you be willing to live in Pillywiggin?" she asked, reaching up to touch a lock of his tousled sandy hair.

Emil didn't have to think before answering. "I would, Your Majesty. Wherever Harmony is, is where I want to be as well."

Satisfied, the queen moved her gaze to her eldest daughter. "And you, Splendor. Would you be willing to give the title of princess royal to Harmony?"

"Aye!" Splendor squealed. "Aye, Mother, I will gladly give my title to her, for I would rather be the duchess of Heathcourte!"

The queen nodded. "Then you may return to the human world with your husband." She turned to face Harmony and Emil. "And you, Harmony, will remain in Pillywiggin. Your children will be born and raised here amongst us. One day you will be queen, and your husband will be the prince consort."

"Oh, Mother, truly?" Harmony yelled.

"Truly. And Harmony, dear, give your husband his mountain of gold. I know that is one of his fondest dreams, and 'twill not hurt you to grant at least one wish."

"I shall, Mother! Aye, I shall!" Instantly, Harmony conjured up a huge hill of gold.

Emil's mouth fell wide open as he stared at the mound of wealth and thought about the title he would one day receive. A title, he thought. He would finally have a title! Dear God, every wish he'd ever entertained had been granted to him! "Jourdian, I'm going to be the prince consort! And . . . and look at my mountain of gold!"

Jourdian laughed with genuine happiness for his cousin.

"I am Queen Pleasure," the queen introduced herself to her new sons-in-law.

When they bowed before her, King Wisdom grumbled. "I saw neither of you bow to *me*," he flared out at them.

Obediently they turned and bowed to him.

The queen took Emil's hand. "I visited you many times when you were a child, Emil."

"You—you did?"

She smiled and looked at Jourdian. "But I never visited you, Trinity. You did not believe in me."

"I didn't believe in you?" Jourdian repeated. "I . . . Forgive me, Your Majesty, but I don't understand."

Queen Pleasure shook her head. "You threw your baby teeth away. Emil put his under his pillow."

Jourdian's eyes widened. "You . . . Do you mean . . . Are you saying you're the Tooth Fairy?"

"Aye." Reaching up, Queen Pleasure fondled her heavy necklace, a string of hundreds of shiny teeth. "You believe in me now, do you not?"

"I believe in you, Your Majesty," Jourdian answered readily.

"And you will make certain that your son believes in me? I do not think I am mistaken in suspecting that the babe will be born in September."

Jourdian nodded. "I'll make certain my son believes in . . . Believes . . . September? My son?"

"Jourdian," Splendor said softly. Taking his hand, she placed it upon her lower belly. " 'Tis true, husband. I carry your heir. And Mother is right. We shall hold our son in our arms in September."

For a moment, Jourdian couldn't move, couldn't speak. Could barely take a breath.

And then the most profound joy he'd ever known burst within him. "Emil!" he shouted. "I'm going to be a father!" Wild with elation, he hugged and lifted Emil straight off the ground. He then embraced Harmony, Queen Pleasure, and even King Wisdom.

Finally, his chest heaving, he reached for Splendor. Taking her into his arms, he gazed into her glowing lavender eyes. "The day I met you I held not a hope in my heart of ever finding happiness. But you sailed into my life and offered something I never dreamed I would find."

"I did? What did I give you?"

He kissed her tenderly, with every shred of his love. "You gave me a basket of wishes, Splendor. And they all came true."

# Epilogue

Jourdian watched as Splendor nursed their newborn. Completely unable to take his eyes off the miracle who was his heir, he smiled proudly as the babe greedily slurped and swallowed his mother's milk.

The babe had entered the world only two hours before, and Jourdian's heart was already bursting with love. "He's perfect, Splendor."

"Aye, that is what he is, husband. And he is brave. He did not even cry when he was born. Most babies cry, you know. Mother told me so."

Jourdian nodded. "And look at him eat. With an appetite like that, he'll grow strong."

"He knows what is good for him, and we did not even have to teach him. I am certain that other mothers must show their newborns how to nurse."

"Our son was born smart."

Proud father and mother continued to watch their son as if he were the only infant in the entire world who knew how to suckle at a breast.

Minutes later, the babe fell asleep. Splendor took him from her breast and laid him upon the white satin pillow beside her hip.

Delicious, in the form of a baby chimpanzee, stroked the infant's downy head with a long, hairy finger, then showed a mouthful of monkey teeth when he "smiled." And Pharaoh, now a fat white rabbit with long, floppy ears, sniffed the baby with his pink little nose.

"What shall we call our son, Jourdian?" Splendor asked, caressing Delicious and Pharaoh so the animals wouldn't feel jealous over the new arrival.

Carefully, Jourdian sat down on the bed. "His name doesn't concern me yet, sprite."

Splendor looked at her husband. "What concerns you?"

Picking up his baby's tiny hand, Jourdian gazed at his son for another long moment. "Do you think he takes more after me or more after you?"

"Well, he has your eyes and my—"

"That's not what I meant, love."

"Oh, Jourdian," Splendor whispered. "You wonder if he is completely human or if he . . . Sweet everlasting, husband, will it matter very much to you if he has inherited the powers of Faerie?"

Smiling over her needless worry, Jourdian kissed the tip of her nose. "Not at all. I just want to know if I should go buy a pony or go find a dragonfly in one of the gardens."

Laughing softly Splendor gazed down at her son again and saw him squirming on the pillow. "He is waking up."

"It looks as though he's going to cry."

"Cry," Splendor said.

"Cry," Jourdian repeated.

In breathless anticipation, they watched their son.

The baby flailed his arms and legs, and wrinkled his nose and forehead. His face reddening, he opened his mouth and began to wail.

His little tears rolled off his plump cheeks, splashing upon his pillow.

And there, upon the white satin, gleaming like wishing stars in the sky, lay a sprinkle of tiny diamonds.

# Prologue

*Mexico, 1858*

Ten-year-old Zafiro crawled over to her grandfather's bedroll, sharp twigs and rocks bruising her hands and knees. As she tapped his shoulder, trying to rouse him, the feeling of approaching peril deepened inside her. Her heart pounded frantically, her mouth went dry, and as always happened when the dark foreboding was upon her, she found it almost impossible to breathe.

"*Abuelo*," she whimpered, her gaze darting from his face to the cold black woods that surrounded the camp. "Grandfather, we have to leave now. Something is about to happen. Someone is coming."

Instantly, Ciro Quintana awakened, threw off his blanket, and embraced his young granddaughter. The small sounds he made woke up the rest of the gang, Maclovio, Lorenzo, Pedro, Luis, and Zafiro's father, Jaime. And then the two women, Tia and Azucar, also rose from their pallets.

No one questioned Zafiro's warning.

The little girl was never wrong.

In only moments, Zafiro sat on her father's muscular thigh, her small arms wrapped around his waist as he urged his mount alongside Ciro's steed. Maclovio, Lorenzo, Pedro, Tia, and Azucar followed on their own horses.

Luis brought up the rear, watching Jaime shift his young

daughter into a more comfortable position as she drifted back to sleep.

She'd saved them again, Luis mused. In only a short while a bounty hunter or a posse of lawmen would arrive at the campsite they'd just vacated. Whatever gift it was Zafiro had . . . whatever special sense it was that alerted her to impending danger, it never failed her.

She was the most valuable asset the Quintana gang possessed.

The Quintana gang. Luis sneered. Mexican Robin Hoods, all of them, too kindhearted to truly profit from their thieving sprees, too compassionate to call themselves outlaws. Only yesterday Ciro, the leader of the gang, had given a half a bag of gold to some ignorant peasant farmer whose equally ignorant **wife** had served them all a chicken dinner.

A half a bag of gold for a few chickens, Luis seethed. With that much gold, Ciro could have bought every damned chicken in Mexico.

Soon, Luis reminded himself as he dodged a few low-hanging tree branches. Soon he would break away from the benevolent Quintana gang and form a band of his own. One that showed no mercy to anyone.

And when he did, he would take Zafiro with him.

*Twelve years later*

"ou cannot turn three eccentric old men back into the skilled gunmen they used to be, Zafiro." Sister Carmelita dropped the sack of flour she'd brought to Zafiro from the convent and took a seat on a weathered barrel. Folding her arms over her stomach, she slipped her hands into the sleeves of her brown habit, and shook her head. "Such a thing is like trying to turn raisins back into grapes."

"There is no other way, Sister." The words were hard for Zafiro to speak. Her heart pounded frantically, her mouth was dry, and breathing seemed all but impossible. "Something is going to happen, I tell you. Something very bad. I have had the feeling for three days, and it's growing stronger."

"But perhaps it is not Luis, niña," Sister Carmelita cooed, reaching out to smooth Zafiro's long black hair. "Perhaps—"

"Whatever it is that is going to happen, it is something dangerous. I *know* it."

Standing beside the nun, Zafiro gazed at the thick pine and oak forest that surrounded La Escondida, the hideaway home her grandfather, Ciro, had built to safeguard his gang of aging outlaws. To conceal them from the law, for they were all still wanted for their crimes of the past.

But La Escondida also sheltered *her*. From Luis. He was an evil that haunted her dreams at night and her thoughts during the day.

Zafiro bowed her head. If only her beloved grandfather were still here, she thought. He'd know what to do. But Ciro had died two years before. Jaime, her father, was gone too, struck down by Luis's bullets.

Now she was left alone with the remaining members of the Quintana gang, the two elderly women, Tia and Azucar, and Ciro's final whispered instructions: "They have no one but you now, chiquita. You will be strong. Strong and bold as the Sierras themselves."

His words clinging to her thoughts, Zafiro raised her head and looked up. Beyond the woods rose the majestic Sierra Madres, and the sight of the beautiful mountains eased her agitation.

How she loved the Sierras. Their towering snowcapped peaks. The steep slopes of their edges, and the multitude of cool, clean streams that flowed through the deep canyons and rocky valleys.

The Sierras had endured through centuries. They were hard, unyielding. As Ciro had instructed her, she would be like these mountains. Nothing would wear down her resolve.

She turned toward Sister Carmelita. "To teach old men skills they have forgotten, Sister," she began, "it will not be easy. But I am not a soft nut."

"A soft nut," Sister Carmelita repeated. "That is another of the American expressions you like so much?"

"Yes." A soft nut, Zafiro thought. That didn't sound right. "A nut that can be smashed? I am a hard nut? How does it go, sister?"

The sister shrugged.

So did Zafiro. "It does not matter. What I mean is that no one will crack me. Especially now, when we are in such danger."

Sister Carmelita didn't miss the fire of determination that flared into Zafiro's startling sapphire eyes. She was a stubborn one, Zafiro Maria Quintana.

But tenacity would not transform three bumbling grandsirs into proficient, able-bodied men. "You forget one important thing, Zafiro. To teach, one must know how to do what one teaches. You know nothing about guns and shooting. Ciro did not allow you to handle the weapons. Perhaps that was a mistake, but what matters now is that you cannot teach your men something you have never done."

Zafiro realized the nun had a valid point, but refused to admit defeat before she'd even begun. "What I meant to say, Sister," she hedged, "is that I will help them remember their skills. I will not stop until I have succeeded. I will not rest. You know the saying . . . I will burn oil at midnight until they are the men they used to be."

"Look at them, Zafiro," Sister Carmelita demanded, rising from her seat on the barrel. "There. By the fence. Maclovio is weaving this way."

Zafiro turned and saw Maclovio. Her eyes narrowed with exasperation. "Another bottle. I just took one away from him this morning, and now he has another!"

Weaving alongside a broken fence, Maclovio raised his bottle toward Zafiro, smiled, and then drank deeply. At age sixty, he was the youngest of the Quintana gang, and there had been a time in his life when his proficiency with horses had been unmatched. Indeed, he'd put on numerous exhibitions through the years, performing his astonishing equestrian tricks in front of crowds. The shows had brought in hefty sums of money, none of which Maclovio ever kept.

All of which he'd given away to orphanages, missions, or other worthy charities.

Now Maclovio was a drunk. Zafiro had nearly torn the mountains apart searching for the contraptions he fashioned to make his liquor, but she'd never found a one of them.

"He is not looking where he is going," Sister Carmelita said. "The tree—"

"Maclovio, the tree!" Zafiro shouted. "The tree!"

Maclovio walked straight into the thick trunk of the oak. His head fell back over his shoulders; his bottle slipped from his hand. A moment later, he crashed to the ground, flat on his back, rendered completely unconscious.

Zafiro sighed. "It is just as well, Sister. If the crash with the tree had not knocked him out, the liquor would have."

Sister Carmelita nodded. "He spends more than half his

time in a senseless state. And Pedro spends the same amount of time on his net. Look at him there, niña."

Zafiro glanced at Pedro, who sat on his large rock with his knotted rope net spread out in front of him. A string of keys dangling around his thin neck, he was busy adding and tying more rope to the net.

Another sigh escaped Zafiro as she continued to watch him work on the net. He claimed he lost the other one. The first one that had hauled in hundreds of fish.

The one Jesus had told him to throw over the side of the boat.

Pedro believed he was Peter the Apostle. The keys he wore were the keys to heaven. His rock was the same that Jesus had sworn to build His church upon. And if ever Pedro heard a cock crow three times, he dissolved into tears that only hours of prayer could stem.

Sweet Pedro loved to preach. To tell Bible stories. A pity he always got the sacred tales so mixed up.

He was sixty-six now, the oldest of the Quintana gang. Once upon a time, his expertise with weapons had been the stuff of legends. But the hands that had once handled guns with such precision now tied and knotted rope into a net that was already almost too heavy to lift.

"And then there is Lorenzo," Sister Carmelita said, pointing to the third member of the Quintana gang as he exited the cabin and walked across the well-swept yard.

"Yes, and then there is Lorenzo," Zafiro echoed, smiling as he sauntered toward her.

He was sixty-three. In his prime, a lock or safe didn't exist that he couldn't open. Claiming he could hear soundless clicks within catches, bolts, and other sorts of metal fasteners, he could unlock whatever device the gang needed open.

But tiny sounds within locks were not all his sharp ears heard.

The years fell away, and Zafiro remembered all the times she'd bared her soul to Lorenzo while she was growing up. After her father's death, sometimes she'd sat by the campfire with him while the rest of the gang slept. She'd taken long strolls and gone fishing with him. During those times, he hadn't only heard her speak to him, he'd listened with his heart. But he could not listen anymore, couldn't be her confidant ever again.

Lorenzo was deaf.

He slept almost constantly now, drifting into slumber quickly and without caring where he happened to be at the time. And when he awakened, it was as though he'd hadn't slept at all. Indeed, he immediately continued whatever conversation he'd been having before falling asleep.

"You took your nap, Lorenzo?" Zafiro shouted at him when he neared her.

"Lap?" He returned her tender smile with a toothless one of his own. "Yes, you used to sit on my lap, Zafiro, but you are too big to sit there now."

*"Nap!"* Zafiro shouted again, her lips almost touching his hairy ear. "I asked if you had taken your . . ."

She broke off. What was the use? Lorenzo never heard anything correctly, no matter how loudly one shouted.

"I have been napping," Lorenzo said. Wiping the remains of sleep from his eyes, he slowly sat down on the ground and leaned against the barrel. "Tia is making tortillas, and Azucar is mending a rip in one of her dresses."

Tia and Azucar, Zafiro thought, her gaze rising to the window of the room the two women shared in the cabin. Precious Tia had done all the cooking for the gang while they'd still been in the outlaw business and, declining in years though she was, her culinary skills hadn't diminished. She continued to keep everyone at La Escondida well fed.

"I do not know what I would do without you, Tia," Zafiro whispered. "If only—if only . . ."

If only Tia could accept the fact that her son was dead, she finished silently, compassion for the woman sweeping through her. Tia had lost her little boy to cholera several years before she'd joined the Quintana gang, but nothing or no one could convince the grieving woman that he was gone.

Indeed, she "saw" him in every man she met. With the exceptions of Maclovio, Lorenzo, and Pedro, no man was safe from her unfulfilled desire to mother.

And dear, dear Azucar . . . "Oh, Azucar," Zafiro mur-

mured, another wave of tenderness filling her heart as she con-
templated Azucar.

The woman had seen seventy-one years come and go, and
had spent a little over twenty of those years as a highly success-
ful harlot. When Ciro had met her, however, age had already
stolen her beauty and she'd been but a destitute old woman
with a bag full of scanty crimson gowns and an empty belly.
Ciro's big heart had gone out to her, and the gang had taken
care of her ever since.

*Special* care of her, for Azucar had yet to come to terms with
her age. Though her wrinkled skin hung off her limbs in much
the same way scraggly moss drooped off thin, dead tree
branches, a decrepit woman was not the reflection she saw
when she gazed into a mirror.

In Azucar's dark and bleary eyes she was still the young and
desirable seductress she'd once been. She continued to wear
the scarlet satin gowns that had been her strumpet's garb, and
there was nothing she enjoyed more than talking about all the
sensual things she would do to the next man who paid for her
services.

Through the years Zafiro had learned a great deal about
sexual intimacy while listening to Azucar's vivid descriptions
of lovemaking. Ciro had never told her a thing about what
happened in bed between a man and a woman, and she'd
never asked. Who better to learn from than a seasoned lady of
the evening?

Yes, indeed, Zafiro mused, her thoughts wandering. When
she married, she would know exactly what her husband wanted
from her on their wedding night. She would know exactly . . .

Her daydream ended abruptly. *When she married?* Save
Maclovio, Lorenzo, and Pedro, she didn't know a single other
man. And since it was quite likely that she would be forced to
remain hidden away in these mountains for a good many years
to come, the chance that she would ever have a sweetheart,
much less a husband, was nonexistent.

"Zafiro?" Sister Carmelita murmured. "Do I see tears in
your eyes, my child?"

"Tears?" The very word dried the tears that had just begun

to sparkle in Zafiro's eyes. "I do not have time for weeping, Sister." Holding her head so high that her chin nearly pointed to the sky, Zafiro marched away from the edge of the woods and entered the barn, where Ciro had stored all the weapons. When she exited the stable, she held a pistol and a rifle.

Sister Carmelita watched the determined girl place the guns in Pedro's bony lap.

The white-haired man picked up the pistol.

The rusty weapon fell apart in his hands.

"Zafiro, please do not do this to yourself," Sister Carmelita pleaded, unable to bear seeing Zafiro set herself up for such dismal disappointment. "Lorenzo," she said to the man leaning on the barrel, "please help me dissuade her from trying to do the impossible."

In answer, Lorenzo let out a snore so loud that it frightened several birds out of a nearby tree.

"Where is your faith, Sister?" Zafiro asked. "You are too doubting."

"Yes," Pedro, agreed, his gnarled hands caressing his net. "You are too doubting, Sister. Just like my good friend, Matthew."

"Thomas," Sister Carmelita corrected him. "It was Thomas who doubted."

"Thomas is a tax collector," Pedro argued. "He doubts nothing. Do you know I once saw him bring a dead man back to life? Lazarus was the man's name, and he—"

"Pedro, please," Zafiro pleaded. "Enough stories. Now shoot the rifle."

Pedro lifted the rifle from his lap and raised the stock to his shoulder. Sighting along the barrel, he pulled the trigger. The resulting explosion knocked him off his rock, and the bullet he fired ricocheted off a tree trunk, shot a hole through the top of Sister Carmelita's wimple, and finally smashed into the chicken coop. The wooden birdhouse toppled over, its gate swinging wide open. Squawking and flapping their wings, all twenty-two hens raced around the yard.

"Santa Maria, my chickens!" Knowing the barnyard fowl would disappear into the mountain coves if she didn't catch them, Zafiro scurried after them, Pedro doing his best to help her.

With as much dignity as a nun with a bullet hole in her wimple could muster, Sister Carmelita headed toward the hidden exit from La Escondida. "Help her, Lord," she prayed as she slipped through the secret opening within the rocks and thick brush. "You are the only One who can give her what she needs. A miracle."

Leaving her pet cougar, Mariposa, to guard La Escondida, Zafiro made her way down the craggy slopes. The trip to the convent was much easier and faster upon Rayo's back, but the burro suffered a bruised hoof.

If only Coraje would let her mount him, Zafiro mused as she finally left the pebble-strewn ground and walked into the cool shade of an evergreen forest. But the coal-black stallion had never let anyone but Ciro near him. Now, after two years without being ridden, he was wilder than he'd ever been.

"Five elderly people, a hurt burro, the meanest stallion in Mexico, four missing chickens, and Luis searching the country for you, Zafiro," she told herself aloud. "And do not forget that there has been no meat for the past three days. That the fences are falling down, that the roof leaks, or that every rabbit in the mountains thinks you have planted the vegetable garden especially for him!"

The burden of worry she bore became heavier with each step she took, and by the time the old Spanish mission came into her view, she felt as though she carried on her shoulders one of the Sierras themselves.

She stopped at the edge of the woods, her gaze missing nothing as she surveyed the area surrounding the convent. She truly enjoyed being with the good sisters, but each time she visited she took the chance of being seen by someone other than the nuns.

*No one* could know where she was.

Finally convinced she was alone, she made her way to the convent door and rang the bell that hung suspended from a rusty hook in the stone wall. The scent of cut grass caught her attention while she waited for one of the nuns to come to the door. She also recognized the smell of freshly dug soil, and decided the nuns had been toiling in their gardens that morning.

Other things began to capture her attention as well. The huge statue of the Blessed Mother stood upright in the flower bed. Only last week the granite sculpture had been lying on the ground, too heavy for the nuns to lift. The dead tree was gone too. The one that had been struck and killed by lightning several years ago. Only a smoothly cut stump remained.

And the nuns' quaint little pond was prettier than she'd ever seen it. The good sisters loved to sit on the stone benches around the pond, basking in the sun and watching turtles poke their heads out of the shining water. Sometimes they recited the rosary there too.

Zafiro had made a mental note to help them clean the pond, for the winter months had left the water slimy and filled with leaves and sticks. She'd also been going to try to mend the crumbling stones that encircled the pond.

The stones she saw now, however, were new, and there wasn't a leaf or twig to be seen upon the glassy surface of the water.

Baffled, Zafiro turned to ring the bell again.

It swung open abruptly. "Zafiro!" Sister Pilar exclaimed. "How good it is to see you, my child."

The nun's warm welcome drew Zafiro into the foyer and straight into Sister Pilar's arms. Hugging the sister tightly, she closed her eyes and breathed deeply of all the aromas of the convent.

The perfume of lemon oil swirled around her, as did the smell of burning candles and wood smoke. She smelled roses, the soap Sister Pilar used to wash her habit, and apple cake, too, which was Mother Manuela's favorite dessert.

The familiar scents were so comforting. The whole convent was, and Zafiro visited as often as she could. To find a bit of serenity. And to hear whatever news about the outside world that the nuns learned from travelers who stopped at the holy house for food and rest.

"We've been expecting you, Zafiro," Sister Pilar said.

"You have?" Zafiro stepped out of the nun's embrace. "How did you know I was coming?"

Smiling, Sister Pilar closed the door and headed toward the staircase, which shone with the lemon oil rubbed into the wood. "Sister Carmelita told us about your plans to turn your men back into skilled fighters. We knew that it would not be long before you came to seek the peace you claim to find here in the convent with us."

Zafiro was about to argue, but realized the futility of quarreling with the truth. Smiling over how well the nuns knew her, she followed Sister Pilar up the staircase and into a small room on the second floor of the convent.

There she hugged Sister Carmelita, Sister Inez, and Mother Manuela, who immediately offered her a glass of cool water and a slice of warm apple cake.

"Where are all the other sisters?" Zafiro asked, her mouth full of the savory cake.

"Some have gone to the village for supplies, some are starting supper, and others are at prayer," Sister Inez replied. "How are the men? They have practiced their skills?"

"Maclovio threw a knife and hit the exact center of the front door."

"Oh, that is good!" Sister Pilar exclaimed.

Zafiro shook her head. "He was aiming for the weather vane on the roof."

"Oh, that is bad," Sister Pilar answered.

"Your feeling of danger is still with you, my child?" Mother Manuela asked, sitting down in one of the ornately carved chairs grouped around a small table.

"It is, Reverend Mother. I try not to think about it, but it is always there. Like a sore that will not heal."

Sister Carmelita walked across the room, retrieved a small painting of Saint Michael the Archangel from the mantel above the fireplace, and placed it on the table. "Come, Zafiro, and sit with us. Together we will pray for the answer to your troubles."

"I have already prayed, Sister. I have prayed so often and so hard that I am sure God hides when He sees and hears me coming."

Smiling, the nuns began to pray. Zafiro listened to their whispered pleas for a moment before she began to pace around the room, her bootheels thudding upon the gleaming wooden floor.

After a short while of ambling from corner to corner, she stopped by one of the barred windows, gazed out at the beautiful mountains, and saw a huge flock of white birds skimming through the sky. Sunlight kissed their feathers, making them iridescent. Zafiro thought they looked like a silver cloud passing over the mountain peaks.

"A silver cloud," she murmured, her breath fogging the windowpane. What was that American expression about a silver cloud? "Problems are lined with silver clouds," she guessed softly. "For every trouble in a cloud, there is a line of silver."

Well, however the saying went it meant that for every difficulty there was a benefit.

If only she could find the silver cloud to her difficulties, she mused, lowering her gaze and peering down at the garden below. There she saw rows of newly planted vegetables and a mass of well-shaped rosebushes. The marble statues of various saints sparkled in the sunshine as if just washed, and the white pebble walkway that meandered through the garden was clear of all litter. A huge stack of freshly cut firewood lay piled neatly against the stone wall of the stable, and the sisters' tree swing shone with what could only be a new coat of paint.

Just as she'd noticed in the front yard of the convent, everything Zafiro saw in the garden was clean, tidy, and well done.

In the next moment she learned the reason why.

A man walked out from beneath a canopy of oak trees, his arms full of logs. He was shirtless, a black kerchief knotted around his neck, his tight brown breeches hugging every masculine curve he possessed.

Unnerved by his sudden appearance, Zafiro gasped softly and moved away from the window. A man, she thought. How many years had passed since she'd seen a male younger than fifty?

A man, she thought again. A man with muscle and energy. And youth.

Intense curiosity urged her back to the window again. She stood there spellbound, her eyes and her mind memorizing every magnificent part of the man below.

His long, thick hair flowed over his broad shoulders like a river of burnished gold. Hard muscle coiled through his sleek back, bulged in his arms and thighs, and rippled down his flat belly.

He was tall. Taller even than her grandfather had been, and she imagined that if she stood in front of him the top of her head would not even reach his chin.

Unfamiliar yearnings caught her unaware as she watched him throw the logs to the ground, pick up an ax, and begin to split the wood. His tanned skin gleamed with the sweat of his labor; his back and arms swelled with strength. She wanted to feel those hard muscles beneath her palm, to know what his hair felt like slipping between her fingers. She longed to hear the sound of his voice, see his smile, and learn the color of his eyes.

She felt drawn to him in a way she couldn't understand.

"Zafiro?" Sister Carmelita called softly. "Didn't you hear me, niña?"

"What?" Startled, Zafiro spun away from the window and faced the nuns.

Sister Carmelita sent a small, knowing smile to the other sisters. "I asked what it is in the garden that has taken such strong hold of your attention."

"My attention?" Zafiro bent her head and absently toyed with a fold in her threadbare skirt. "I . . . The roses," she blurted, too embarrassed to tell the truth.

"And the stack of firewood?" Sister Pilar asked.

"Yes, and the firewood."

Mother Manuela rose from her chair, crossed to the window, and looked down below. "And the man who shaped the rosebushes and cut the firewood?"

Zafiro didn't miss the sparkle that came into the Reverend Mother's dark eyes. "Man? What man? I do not know what you are talking—"

"Come now, Zafiro," Sister Carmelita scolded. "There is nothing wrong with a lovely young girl admiring a handsome man. Sawyer came to us three days ago, weary and lost. Since then, he has taken it upon himself to make numerous repairs, he has planted vegetables—"

"And he built a new lamp table for my cell," Sister Inez added. "It does not wobble like the old one."

"He has done a great many things for us," the Reverend Mother said. "In return, we have prayed very hard for him."

"Why?" Zafiro asked quickly. "Is he in trouble?"

Mother Manuela looked down at Sawyer again. "When Sister Carmelita said that he came to us lost, she meant that he has lost all his memories. He knows nothing of himself but his name—Sawyer Donovan."

"He arrived on a mule and had only a small trunk with him," Sister Pilar elaborated. "He could not tell us where he was from or what he did for a living. All he said was that he had been traveling for months. Wandering, with no destination in mind, no plans . . . not even a reason as to why he was wandering."

"But there is pain in his eyes," Mother Manuela said softly. "A sorrow he carries in his very soul. And so it is likely that whatever terrible thing caused such torment inside him also erased his memory. He cannot remember because he does not want to remember."

Compassion for the golden-haired stranger swept through Zafiro. What must it be like to have no memories? she wondered. If Sawyer had a family, he could not remember their faces or their love. He could not reminisce about special things that had happened to him, happy things that made him laugh and feel good.

"Stay and have supper with us, Zafiro," Sister Carmelita said. "Then you can meet and talk to Sawyer."

"Meet him," Zafiro repeated, wondering what it would be like to be near the strong, handsome man named Sawyer.

"Would you like that, Zafiro?" Sister Carmelita asked.

Shy once again, Zafiro felt her cheeks warm. "I . . ."

In the next instant, hard, cold reality erased every tender and timid emotion she'd felt. "*Meet him?* Do you forget that I am in hiding? I can meet no one!" Quickly, she left the window, suddenly angry with herself.

What was the matter with her? How could she have forgotten to take care? On the contrary, she'd stood right in front of the window for a full five minutes in plain view.

"What if this Sawyer Donovan is one of Luis's men?" she asked, her voice rising with her fear. "Or what if he—"

"Zafiro," the Reverend Mother said, reaching out for the trembling girl.

"He has lost his memory," Zafiro pointed out. "Before he lost it he might have been a cruel man. Maybe he has only forgotten how to be evil. He could find his memories again at any time! When they come back to him, he could be a man who knows Luis. Or a man who knows my men are still wanted by the law. I will not take any chances with this Sawyer! He . . ."

She stopped speaking as the familiar, frightening feeling of dread came over her, drying her mouth, pounding through her heart, and causing her to struggle for her next breath. "Sisters," she squeaked. "He—Santa Maria, *he* is the danger that I have known would come! He *must* be!"

Before the nuns could say a word, Zafiro jerked out of the Reverend Mother's hold on her, raced out of the room, and sped down the dim hall. She took two steps at a time while descending the staircase and quickly crossed through the foyer. The sound of her heart beating in her ears like a thousand drums, she snatched the door open . . .

And ran straight into a solid mass of muscle.

Gold eyes like a lion's seemed to penetrate her very soul. The man was huge, his form radiating such awesome power that Zafiro felt the insane urge to bow before him.

"Sawyer," she murmured, backing into the foyer.

His eyes registered surprise. He stepped toward her, stopped, his stance wide, his shadow falling over her, making her feel tiny and vulnerable.

Wild with terror, she fled through the yard and disappeared into the darkness of the evergreen glade.

Sawyer followed. She could hear his footsteps crashing through the brittle pine needles.

Imagined she could feel his piercing gaze stab her back.

Deeper fear lent her more strength, quickened her momentum, and she ran faster than she'd ever run before, flying through the forest as if carried by the wind. Finally the edge of the woods came into view, the sunlight a beacon of hope for escape. Lunging forward, she fairly threw herself toward the pebbled ground around the base of the foothills.

But she didn't make it.

Large, powerful hands suddenly circled her waist, pulling her away from the light, back into the shadows.

And at that moment, Zafiro knew in her heart that her captor—whoever he was—would change her life forever.